# PRAISE FOR LISA EDMONDS

"An action-packed debut with a strong, compelling heroine. Heart of Malice is sure to cast a spell on urban fantasy readers and leave them clamoring for more adventures with Alice Worth."

—JENNIFER ESTEP, NEW YORK TIMES BESTSELLING
AUTHOR OF THE ELEMENTAL ASSASSIN URBAN
FANTASY SERIES

"The complex magic system throughout Heart of Malice is a genuine joy to read and there's danger and intrigue through-out. The characters leap off the page and the secrets which Alice Worth carries make her a wonderful character. I can't wait to read more of this thrilling series!"

—HELEN HARPER, AUTHOR OF THE BLOOD DESTINY
AND LAZY GIRL'S GUIDE TO MAGIC URBAN FANTASY
SERIES

"Heart of Malice hits the ground running with the perfect blend of magic action, compelling characters, and sizzling romance. Snarky and cynical Alice Worth is a complex and flawed woman who is not simply kickass but refreshingly intelligent. Lisa Edmonds conducts the twists and turns of the plot like a maestro conductor, spellbinding the reader with her original and innovative worldbuilding, solid magic system, and a compelling backstory that haunts the main story in surprising ways. It's an absolutely delightful, one-sitting, devour it now read."

— DEBORAH WILDE, AUTHOR OF THE UNLIKEABLE<br>DEMON HUNTER AND MAGIC AFTER MIDLIFE URBAN<br>FANTASY SERIES

"Fast-paced and action-packed, the story created by this author is both intriguing and addictive, as is the world she builds. Her prose is lively and entertaining and laced with just the right amount of humor. [ . . . ] This suspenseful urban fantasy pulls the reader into an imaginative world—one that seamlessly marries reality with the supernatural—through the author's outstanding storytelling skills."

— IND'TALE MAGAZINE

"Edmonds has an eye for both detail and entertaining characters, and her story is fun and energetic. Readers will enjoy this installment and look forward to more in the continuing saga of Alice Worth."

— PUBLISHER'S WEEKLY

"It's no secret that this is one of my favorite series and that Alice is my girl. The author shook me with this book. From the story to the action to the characters, it left me with a huge book hangover. [ . . . ] I. Loved. Every. Minute. Of. It."

— THE LITERARY VIXEN

# HEART OF STONE

## ALICE WORTH SERIES
### BOOK FOUR

## LISA EDMONDS

STORYBOOK
*House*

*To Bill— For twenty years of road trips, good music, and bad puns. You make loving fun.*

# ALSO BY LISA EDMONDS

**The Alice Worth Series**

*Heart of Malice*

*Heart of Fire*

*Heart of Ice*

*Heart of Stone*

*Heart of Shadows*

*Heart of Vengeance*

*Heart of Lies*

*Heart of the Pack*

*Heart of the Damned*

**Short Stories and Novellas**

*From the Ashes*

*Just For One Night*

*Blood Money*

*Ghosting 101* (included with *Blood Money*)

*Perfectly Magical*

*Alice Worth and the Elite Death Machine*

**The Alice Worth World Novels**

*Mortal Heart*

# THE PLAYLIST

Jackson Browne, "Running on Empty"
Gregory Abbott, "Shake You Down"
AC/DC, "Dirty Deeds Done Dirt Cheap"
Foreigner, "Cold as Ice"
Phil Collins, "I Wish It Would Rain Down"
U2, "Mysterious Ways"
Mike + the Mechanics, "All I Need is a Miracle"
Pink Floyd, "A Pillow of Winds"
Bill Withers feat. Grover Washington, Jr., "Just the Two of Us"
Amy Winehouse, "You Know I'm No Good"

# CHAPTER I

I RAN THROUGH THE TREES, MOVING AS QUICKLY AND QUIETLY AS I COULD. Small twigs and branches I couldn't see in the dark whipped across my face, leaving scratches that stung mercilessly.

Behind me, sirens blared and bright lights swept across my path, searching for targets. I thought of the snipers on the walls of the compound and my back itched. I expected to hear shots and feel an impact at any second. I ran faster.

I chanted swear words in my head as I ducked under branches and dodged the searchlights. *Where the hell is Arkady?*

I had little time to worry about my partner's fate. Dark figures moved in the trees to my right, heading in my direction. I veered left, hoping to find cover and a chance to regroup while I came up with a strategy for avoiding capture.

I stole a glance at my watch. Only a little over an hour until sunrise. Dawn meant safety and hopefully escape. I'd survived this long—surely I could make it just one more hour.

A twig snapped behind me. I dropped to my stomach in the mud and held perfectly still as stealthy footsteps passed less than ten feet away. I held my breath as they went by, my heart pounding in my ears.

I waited until my pursuer was out of earshot before I belly-crawled through the mud to hide behind a downed tree and catch my breath.

If Arkady was still out here, she'd be headed in the same direction I was going, hoping to either meet up with me or reach a secure position to wait it out until our rescue arrived. I heard shouting back in the direction of the compound, but I couldn't tell what they said. If those shouts meant she'd been captured...well, I'd have to deal with that later. Either way, I couldn't stay where I was. I needed to keep moving.

I listened hard but heard only the usual chorus of nighttime insects, rustling leaves, and branches creaking in the wind. I moved to a crouch and peeked over the top of the tree trunk.

Nothing.

I rose and grimaced at the mud covering the front of my long-sleeved black tee, borrowed BDU pants, and combat boots. I'd actually thought I looked fairly badass and had a little bit of Arkady-style swagger, but that was before we'd tripped some kind of perimeter alarm near the compound, given away our position, and had to split up to avoid capture. And before I'd had to crawl through the mud.

I swung my legs one at a time over the downed tree and continued heading east. As an earth mage, my affinity to the land meant my internal compass was stronger than most. Heavy cloud cover meant lack of moonlight with which to see or navigate, but I knew which way was east. With any luck, I'd make it to the rendezvous, find Arkady waiting there, and get the hell out of Dodge.

Just as I thought that, the earth literally fell out from under me.

One second my boots were on firm if muddy ground, and the next I was falling. It happened so quickly I didn't have a chance to do more than gasp.

My body landed in what felt like rope webbing. That broke my fall, but then the webbing gave way. I fell about four more feet and landed face-down in—of course—more mud. The impact knocked the wind out of me and left me stunned, unsure of what had just happened or where I'd ended up.

I raised my head, spat out a mouthful of mud and leaves, and found myself in a pit about the size of two graves, six feet wide by ten feet long and ten feet deep.

And I was not alone.

Arkady Woodall, my new best friend and the person I wanted to kill most in the world right now, grinned at me and picked leaves out of her hair. She sat with her back against the side of the pit, and she —almost unbelievably—was covered with more mud than I was. "Hey, Alice. Are you having fun?"

"Am I having *fun?*" I hissed, pushing myself up on all fours with a grimace. I spat out something slimy I didn't look at too closely. "I have mud in my boots, mud in my bra, and mud in my...never mind. No, I am *not having fun!*"

She laughed. "Liar."

I flipped her off and pushed muddy hair back from my face. "When I said I'd do a girls' weekend with you, this is definitely *not* what I thought we'd be doing. A two-day intensive survival camp? *Really?*"

She rolled her eyes and pulled a twig out of her hair. "What did you think we'd be doing, champagne brunch, mani/pedis, and seaweed wraps? You know me well enough to know I wasn't taking us for a spa weekend. And hey, look at this." She wiped some of the mud off her face and held up her hand. "People pay hundreds of dollars for mud treatments at spas, and it was included here at no extra cost."

"This mud smells like something died in it, Arkady."

"That probably makes it even better for your skin."

I didn't know whether to laugh or cry, so I made a sound that was a little of both. "I'm so tired. And cold. And thirsty. And I smell like... God, I don't even want to know what I smell like." I looked up at the top of the pit. "How long are they going to leave us in here?"

"They'll come get us at dawn."

I groaned. I was getting perilously close to whining. "That's almost an hour from now! Why not just come get us? We lost. We surrender. We're dead. Why make us suffer more?"

"You signed off on the rules, same as me." She settled in more comfortably. "Just think of it as more time for us to bond."

"I think I've already bonded with you as much as I want to for one weekend. We bunked together last night and we had to use the communal showers in the locker room, remember?"

"Oh, yeah." She grinned again. "That was fun. It's like being at summer camp, right?"

I'd never been to a summer camp. Activities like that weren't an option when you were a prisoner of your grandfather's crime syndicate from ages four through twenty-four. I'd rarely gone beyond the walls of his compound for months at a time, much less spent weeks away at camp, doing whatever it was non-mage kids got to do at such places.

"Yeah, just like summer camp," I said after a moment. "So, how many times have you made it to the extraction point without getting caught?"

"Twice."

"Out of how many attempts?"

She rested her forearms on her knees. "I've lost count. They change it up every time—different traps, different patrol routes, different objectives. It's never the same challenge twice. That's why I like it. If I could beat it, I wouldn't get better. I'm here to improve my skills, not to win."

"I don't see why the two should be mutually exclusive," I grumbled. "Or why we have to stay in this pit until sunrise."

"They'll actually probably come get us sooner than that. The last time, it was only about twenty minutes before they got me out."

"The *last* time? How many times have you fallen into one of these?"

She frowned at me. "That's not the point, Alice."

"So, a couple of times."

"Four times," she muttered.

I laughed.

Arkady made a *pfffft* sound. "Hey, you think this is bad, you should try getting caught in a snare and dangling upside down ten feet off the ground by one ankle. Then you *really* want them to come get you quickly."

"I don't remember that from the orientation."

"Yeah, they discontinued that one. Something about too much risk of head injury and the insurance company was going to cancel their coverage."

"Insurance companies are such killjoys," I said dryly. "Head trauma, spine injuries, blah blah blah."

"No kidding." She looked completely at ease sitting in a mud pit in the deep woods. "So, how are things between you and Sean since you guys got back from the Bahamas?"

"It's been good," I said, smiling despite how cold and gross and miserable I felt. "Really good. This two-day getaway with you is the longest we've gone without seeing each other since we got back." And I missed him more than I'd ever admit to anyone. I'd had a hard time falling asleep last night without him next to me, even as exhausted as I'd been after nearly twenty hours of running around trying to evade capture by the camp's employees.

"You two thinking about maybe moving in together?"

I shook my head. "We haven't talked about it."

Sean had hinted once or twice about the possibility, but I'd ducked the conversation. I saw no way for him to move into my home, which was much smaller than his, and the thought of members of his pack coming and going from my house all the time, invading my space, made me almost break out in hives.

At the same time, I couldn't just move in with him; my basement was a heavily warded fortress that had taken nearly five years to create, and giving that up didn't seem like an option. Particularly not when recent events made it likely I might be found by my grandfather and I'd need all the protection I could get.

Arkady distracted me with another question. "And things with the pack? Better?"

My smile faded. "About the same."

"Is Sean's beta still giving you trouble?"

I shrugged. "I've only seen Jack once since we got back. We crossed paths outside Maclin Security one day when I met Sean for lunch, and he just ignored me. I've heard he pretends I don't exist and doesn't say anything if the subject comes up in conversation with other pack members. It's pretty obvious he and his wife Delia still strongly disapprove of Sean and me being together, but Sean warned him to keep his opinions of me to himself, so that's probably why he hasn't been bad-mouthing me."

"But the rest of the pack likes you, right?"

"Most of them. There are some others who also think Sean should date a shifter, but none of them are as angry about it as Jack and Delia." I made a face. "And Caleb."

"Caleb's the kid who got bitten a couple of months ago and is having a hard time controlling himself?"

"Yeah. He moved in with Jack and Delia so they could keep an eye on him, and they're just three little Alice-hating peas in a pod. I'll be seeing them all later today. There's a birthday party for one of the pack and everyone's getting together to celebrate." I decided to change the subject. "And how are things between you and Matthias?"

She waggled her hand in a so-so gesture. "Okay, I guess. I'm still hurting over Fortune. Matthias is being gentlemanly about it."

Arkady's lover Fortune had been an enforcer for Charles Vaughan of the Vampire Court. He'd been killed about a month ago during an attempt on Charles's life. She'd been instrumental in the death of the man who killed him and that had helped, but it would take her some time to heal.

I was glad to hear that Matthias, who was also a Court enforcer, was patient and supportive. It didn't surprise me, though. The man practically worshiped the ground beneath her combat boots.

"So you two haven't...?" I asked.

She gave me a wry smile. "We've fooled around some, but I'm still not at a point where it feels like the right time. It's not that I feel like I'd be betraying Fortune, but..." She shrugged.

"It's okay. I get it. Matthias can wait until you're ready."

She grinned. "Damn right he can. I'm worth waiting for."

Footsteps crunched on the ground above us. I looked up to see four well-muscled men standing at the edge of the pit. Their haircuts and the way they stood said former Army. Two of them had paintball rifles slung over their shoulders. They were either the snipers or part of the patrols who'd hunted us for the better part of two days. I couldn't help but glare balefully from where I sat at the bottom of the pit.

"Hey, Joe," Arkady said casually, as if we'd just run into some old friends in a bar. She draped her arms over her knees. "How's it hangin'?"

"Still lower than my ex's new husband." The man in the center of the group regarded us with his hands on his hips. "You ready to get out of there?"

"Nah." She settled back against the wall of the pit. "We were right in the middle of some serious girl talk. Could you give us another ten, fifteen minutes?"

"Shut up, Arkady. Yes, we are ready to get out of here." I lurched to my feet on tired legs and almost fell over when my boots sank into the mud. "Do you have a ladder?"

The end of a rope dropped into the pit beside me. I stared at it, a little nonplussed.

Grinning, Arkady got to her feet. "You're getting soft, Joe. A rope? Last time I had to scramble up the dirt wall while you yelled insults."

Joe gripped the other end of the rope with both hands. His biceps strained the fabric of his T-shirt. "Your new friend doesn't look strong enough to get out of there without help." He flicked the rope at me. "Let's go, princess. Grab the rope and I'll haul you up."

My eyes narrowed. "Hey, Arkady? You want to get out of this pit without their help?"

She put her hands on her hips and studied me. "What are you thinking?"

"I'm thinking G.I. Joe Junior up there can kiss my ass." I crouched, stuck my hands into the mud, and started spooling earth magic. "You ready to go for a ride?"

She didn't ask for an explanation, just planted her feet shoulder-width apart and braced herself. "Okay, let's blow this popsicle stand."

"What'cha doing, princess?" Joe called. "Grab the rope. We got stuff to do."

"I'll show you princess," I muttered and pushed earth magic into the ground.

The earth trembled beneath us. The men stumbled back from the edge of the pit, cursing as the rumbling grew in volume.

In a burst of bright green earth magic, the ground heaved us up as though we were surfers riding a wave made of dirt instead of water. Arkady whooped and laughed as we shot upward in a spray of mud, rotten leaves, and twigs. The wave deposited us on the ground next to the pit and dumped a hundred gallons of smelly mud on Joe and the others, covering them from head to toe in muck. They stared at us, dumbfounded, blinking like muddy owls.

"Oops," I said insincerely, as the magic faded and the ground went still.

Arkady brushed leaves off her shoulder and gave Joe her biggest smile. "Guess we didn't need your help after all."

She turned to me and gestured at the lights of the compound. "Matthias is due to pick us up in forty minutes. Let's hit the showers and get the hell out of here."

And so we did.

"WOMAN, how much longer are you going to be in the shower?" Sean asked from the bathroom doorway. "It's been almost thirty minutes. Aren't you clean yet?"

"I may never be clean again," I muttered as I rinsed shampoo out of my hair. I turned and scrubbed my face in the spray. "I'll be out in a minute."

The shower door opened and closed and warm arms wrapped around my middle. I turned and found myself staring at the world's most perfect chest and the world's most perfect...everything else. Yum.

Sean smiled mischievously. "Fancy meeting you here," he said, kissing the tip of my nose. He inhaled and frowned. "How on earth do you still smell like mud after all this scrubbing?"

"I don't know!" I wailed. "I've washed everything at least twice!"

"Everything?" He raised an eyebrow and slid his hands down to my hips. "I'd better double-check. You may have missed a few spots."

I wound my arms around his neck and pulled him down for a kiss. "I missed this," I murmured, resting my forehead against his chest so I could inhale his familiar scent that always reminded me of a forest in spring.

I sensed him smiling. "You missed what? My shower?"

"I *definitely* missed your shower," I said wryly. "The ones at the camp were awful. But no, I meant that I missed being here with you."

"And I definitely missed you." He lowered his head and nuzzled my neck, pressing light kisses along my shoulder. "The bed's been cold and lonely these past two nights."

"You didn't let Rogue sleep on the bed with you?"

He chuckled. "He's a great dog, but he's no substitute for you, Miss Magic. And no, I didn't. You spoil him too much. Rogue has his own bed."

"Poor dog."

He nudged me back against the shower wall. "My Alice," he murmured, his lips against my ear. I shivered despite the spray of hot water. "Are you sure you didn't cast a spell on me to make me this crazy about you?"

"Most mage spells don't work on shifters," I reminded him. My voice sounded breathless because his hands were roaming.

"You didn't answer the question," he teased, giving me that almost-boyish grin that made the corners of his eyes crinkle.

"You're right, I didn't." I winked. "I guess you'll never know for sure whether I did or not."

He did something with his fingers that made my legs turn to rubber. He caught me and lifted me up, pinning me against the wall.

"We don't have time," I protested weakly. "We have to be at Cole and Karen's house by—" I gasped and closed my eyes. "*Oh.*"

"You were saying?" he growled, moving me slightly to get a better angle. "We'll get there when we get there."

I bit his shoulder to stifle a moan and tried to push on his chest. "Sean, wait...they'll know why we're late. They'll smell us."

"Good for them." His eyes glowed softly. "If you want to stop, say stop. Otherwise, let me show you how much I missed you."

Damn it, maybe a stronger woman than I could have resisted those golden eyes and the way the water ran over his arms and chest, still tan from our Bahamas trip, but I just couldn't help myself.

Maybe he'd spelled *me*. I looked into that smoldering gaze and decided that if he had spelled me, I didn't mind at all.

"How much *did* you miss me?" I asked.

He kissed me hard and then he showed me.

⁕ ⁕ ⁕ ⁕ ⁕ ⁕ ⁕ ⁕ ⁕ ⁕ ⁕ ⁕

WE WERE FASHIONABLY LATE ARRIVING at Karen and Cole's house for the birthday brunch, not because of how thoroughly Sean had answered the question of how much he'd missed me, but because I hadn't been able to find the gauzy scarf that went with my dress. I'd turned Sean's closet upside-down looking for it and finally given up, opting to wear the dress anyway without the scarf.

"I hate to be late," I complained as Sean parked his truck in the yard next to a half-dozen other vehicles. "Everyone else is here, even Patrick, and he's late to *everything*."

He chuckled as we got out. "I'm sorry we couldn't find your scarf. I can't figure out where it went."

"I'll probably find it when we get home, in whatever random place I put it." I sighed.

He took my hand as we headed up the sidewalk and kissed me on my neck near my shoulder. "You're beautiful without it. A scarf would just make it harder for me to kiss you whenever I want to."

"You're the worst." I bumped his hip with mine. "I'd have thought you'd gotten enough kisses for today."

He scoffed. "You know me better than that."

The front door opened and the sound of loud voices and laughter drifted out. Nan Lowell smiled as we reached the front porch. "There you two are. We thought we were going to have to send out a search party." The older woman hugged each of us tightly and stepped aside so we could enter the house.

Nan looked to be in her late forties, though werewolves aged more slowly than humans, so she was likely a decade or two older than that. She and her two adult children, Felicia and David, had joined Sean's pack after the alpha of their former pack killed her husband.

This was only the second time I'd been to an event where the whole pack—or most of it, anyway—was present. Sean must have sensed or smelled my trepidation. He squeezed my hand and a trace of golden shifter magic spiraled through my arm. My shoulders relaxed, both from his touch and the calming effect of his magic.

We'd discovered his ability to ease my fears quite by accident, when our flight back from the Bahamas encountered particularly bad turbulence. I didn't enjoy flying at the best of times, and that leg of our trip was rough because of bad weather. The moment Sean took my hand I'd drawn on his strength and calm as if by instinct and it felt like someone took their hand and swept my fear away. We were both so stunned by this new level of our connection that we'd spent the rest of the flight simply holding hands.

I'd recently begun to suspect I had shifter blood, possibly from my biological father, whose existence I'd discovered when a magic mirror showed me a forgotten memory of my parents discussing him. I only knew his name was Daniel and he'd left my grandfather's cabal without knowing my mother was pregnant. My dad had raised and loved me as his own and nothing would ever, *ever* replace him, but the thought that my biological father might be out there some-where was an exciting and terrifying prospect that I'd been thinking about constantly for several weeks.

If I did have some shifter blood, that might explain a number of things, from my connection to Sean to my ability to use shifter magic, at least in a limited way. It was taking me some time to process these new revelations about myself.

When we stepped into the doorway of the living room, conversation ceased and everyone turned to greet Sean. "Hello, everyone," he said. "I'm glad to see you didn't wait for us to start the party."

Karen, our hostess and one of the most submissive wolves in the pack, was the first to approach me for a hug. She had short dark hair, green eyes, and an infectious smile. "Come on in, Alice," she said warmly. "I absolutely love your dress."

"Thank you. I love yours too. You look fantastic in yellow."

"What can I get you two to drink?" Cole, Karen's human husband, asked us.

We both requested coffee. With our cups in hand, we made the rounds, saying hello to everyone.

Our first stop was Ben Cooper, Sean's third and the guest of honor. Sean clapped the younger man on the shoulder. "Happy birthday, Ben. Thirty looks good on you."

Casey, Ben's red-haired human girlfriend, who I adored, tucked her hand in his and grinned. "We have some news," she said and extended her left hand. A diamond ring sparkled on her finger.

I let out an uncharacteristically girly squeal as Sean gave Ben a hug. "You crafty bastard," he said with a smile. "Is that where you two ran off to Friday night instead of joining us for the poker game?"

"Yep," Casey confirmed. "He took me to dinner and then up to the restaurant's roof to propose. There were roses and candles. It was *perfect*."

I hugged her. "I am so happy for you both. Congratulations."

After Ben, we said hi to John and his human husband Brandon, then Nan's daughter Felicia and son David. Karen's brother Patrick was out in the backyard playing soccer with John and Brandon's kids. Eddie and his mate Thea, the only other couple in the pack, were visiting family out of state.

In the backyard, sitting at a table on the deck, we found Sean's beta Jack Hastings, his wife Delia, and Caleb Jennings. Jack was blond and muscular and much taller than his brunette wife. His face bore four faint scars that slashed diagonally from temple to chin, a visible reminder of our conflict.

Jack, Delia, and Caleb rose when we stepped outside. Jack raised his cup of coffee in greeting. "Good morning, Sean." After a beat, he added, "Alice."

"Hi, Jack," I said. "Delia."

She glanced at me. "Alice." Her tone was perfectly polite. Her nostrils flared and her eyes narrowed.

I raised my eyebrow as if to say, *Yep, that's why we were late.* She looked away.

Caleb, as always, wore a black T-shirt, jeans, and sneakers. "Hey, Sean," the young werewolf said. He set his glass of iced tea on the table and shook Sean's hand.

Jack took a swig of coffee. "Just so you know, I assigned someone else to work tonight on that security system installation at the bank. I told Ben to enjoy some more time with Casey. He'd just be distracted anyway."

Sean chuckled. "They're great together. She's perfect for him. I'm happy for them both."

"They certainly got engaged quickly," Delia said, still in that carefully neutral tone. "They've only been dating what, a few months?"

"When you know, you know," Sean said, squeezing my hand. "And you're one to talk, Delia; you and Jack became mates after three weeks of knowing each other. Or was it two?"

"That was different," she argued. "Jack and I are both shifters. Casey's human."

"Humans have good instincts too," Sean pointed out. He grew serious. "Be supportive of them. Unless either one of them gives us a reason to be concerned, this is wonderful news for our entire pack."

"Of course," she murmured, her eyes on the table.

Jack glanced behind us. "I think Karen might have some news for us as well."

Karen and Cole stepped out onto the deck. Her cheeks were a little pink. "We do," she said.

Cole couldn't hold back a grin. "We weren't going to say anything because we didn't want to steal Ben and Casey's thunder, but Ben said they didn't mind."

Sean's smile was even bigger than Cole's. He clearly suspected what the big news might be. "Let's hear it," he said.

"I'm pregnant," Karen said.

A cheer went up from nearly everyone inside and outside the house. There was another round of congratulations, hugs, and toasts. The brunch had turned into quite a party.

The only members of the group who didn't seem quite as excited about all the big news were Jack, Delia, and Caleb. The latter's lack of enthusiasm didn't surprise me; Caleb only seemed to have one expression, and that was a scowl. He'd been bitten while out running and Sean had taken him into the pack, hoping to help him adjust, but he was angry, bitter, and confrontational.

Delia and Jack acted pleased with Karen's news, but I didn't have to be a shifter to sense their hearts weren't in it. I caught them exchanging glances several times when they thought no one was looking. I had a theory as to why.

When Sean and I got a moment to ourselves in the kitchen during brunch, I voiced my thoughts. "I think Jack and Delia don't like all the humans who are joining this pack," I said softly, mindful of werewolf hearing. Everyone else was out in the backyard, but I didn't want to be overheard. "Karen's pregnant, but the baby's father is human, Casey's human, *I'm* human. The shifter-to-human ratio is changing rapidly around here."

Sean sighed and dropped his empty plate into the trash. "I don't disagree with you, but let's wait to talk about it until later."

His head tilted. I realized the voices in the backyard had gone silent. We headed for the open patio door.

A blonde woman stood in the yard in an expensive-looking designer sundress, sunglasses, and high-heeled sandals. Her hair was perfectly arranged in one of those updos that always looked so sophisticated on other women but made me look like I'd just not bothered to brush my hair.

Her face lit up when she spotted Sean. She pushed her sunglasses onto the top of her head and smiled. "Hello, Sean."

Sean's irritation sizzled on my skin and a muscle moved in his jaw. The pack cleared a path for him as he headed for the steps. "What are you doing here, Lily?"

Lily? As in Lily Anderson, the female shifter from another pack Jack had hoped would be Sean's mate?

Unfazed by his cold greeting, her smile remained bright. "I heard you all were having a get-together and thought I'd drop by and see how you were. It's been *ages*." She reached out as if intending to give him a hug.

Sean blocked her hands and pushed them aside. "How did you hear about the party?"

"Oh, you know how these things travel through the shifter grapevine," she said cheerfully. She glanced up to the deck. "Happy birthday, Ben!"

"Thanks," he replied, taking a step closer to me.

Her gaze moved to my face. "Well, this must be Alice. I've heard so much about you."

Sean turned and smiled at me. "Yes, this is Alice, my consort."

Lily's smile vanished. "So I've heard," she said shortly. She turned her attention back to Sean. "Can I have a word with you?"

"We don't have anything to discuss," he stated. "I'm not sure what prompted you to crash the party, but—"

"I think you should hear me out." Her expression was dark. "I'd rather we talk in private, but if you want to do this in front of the entire pack, that's your choice."

Sean's shoulders were rigid with tension. "Two minutes." He glanced back at me. I smiled to show him that I had nothing to worry about. Let her talk; I knew where things stood.

He smiled back, but it disappeared when he turned to Lily. "Let's walk to your car so you can leave when we're done talking."

They headed off across the yard and disappeared around the corner of the house.

About a month ago, Sean had almost died after a cuff that turned out to be an ancient shifter relic attached itself to his arm. It was one of a pair designed to be worn by the alpha and his mate. Without the second cuff, the broken spellwork was killing him. I'd obtained the second cuff in time to save him, but Jack had been searching for it too. His intention was to give it to Lily, who was the daughter of an alpha from a nearby pack, binding them together for life and cutting me out of the picture. He very much wanted Sean's mate to be a werewolf, not a human, and had gone to great lengths to try and keep us apart.

While Sean was trapped by the cuffs and held in a cage in Jack and Delia's basement, I'd unintentionally contacted his wolf through their pack bonds in my sleep. When Jack attacked me, defending against what he saw as an attack on the pack, I'd slashed his face in self-defense, not realizing it was anything more than a dream. Though werewolves' healing ability meant they rarely had scars, wounds created with magic were the hardest to heal.

Ben touched my arm. "You good?"

"I'm fine," I assured him.

I realized the pack had closed ranks around me, with the exception of Jack, Delia, and Caleb, who'd stayed at their table. Ben had taken the spot to my right, as Jack would have stood beside Sean.

Karen joined me at the railing and handed me a glass of iced tea. "I can't believe she came here. The *nerve* of some people. Now I smell her in my yard." She growled quietly and wrinkled her nose.

"So now I've met the famous Lily." I kept my tone light. "I liked her shoes."

"They were pretty great," she admitted. "You sure you're okay?"

"Of course." I winked. "Sean told me long ago that he prefers brunettes anyway."

She laughed.

The others moved away, talking quietly. Some went back into the house while Patrick, David, and Felicia joined the kids in the yard to continue the soccer game that had been interrupted by brunch and Lily's arrival.

Karen and I chatted for a bit about her due date, seven months from now, and her secret hope that she might be having twins, which ran in Cole's family. True to their word, Ben and Casey seemed even happier to share their big day with Karen and Cole, and the atmosphere on the deck was joyful despite Lily's unexpected appearance.

Finally, Sean reappeared around the corner of the house, his eyes bright gold and jaw set. Whatever Lily had said to him, he was angry about it. When he saw me, though, he smiled.

Karen excused herself to go back inside as he met me at the railing.

"What was—" I began.

He picked me up and kissed me hard, causing catcalls and shouts of "Get a room!" from the younger members of the pack.

Finally, he put me back on my feet. "We'll talk about it later," he assured me. "Nothing to worry about." The last seemed directed at everyone, not just me.

I took his hand and squeezed it. "Okay. What do you want to do now? Go inside or stay out here and enjoy the weather?"

Sean lowered his head and brushed my ear with his lips. "I'd like to go home and pick up where we left off."

"Let's not be rude," I admonished him with a smile. "We need to socialize."

He lifted my hand to his lips and kissed it. "Alice, the social butterfly," he teased. His eyes glowed softly. "I love you."

The conversation around us quieted. I realized this was the first time he'd said those words in front of an audience and the first time the pack had heard them. I wondered if it was spontaneous or to make a point in the wake of Lily's unexpected appearance, or maybe a little of both.

He entwined our fingers and tugged me toward the patio door. "Let's go inside and talk to Ben and Casey about possible wedding dates," he said. "A pack wedding is a very big event—almost as big as a birth. It's a great day for the Tomb Mountain Pack." Another round of cheers from those outside.

We headed into the house. Just before we stepped inside, I caught Delia's eye. In the moment before she looked away, I saw raw, unadulterated hatred. Then it disappeared and her expression was impassive once more. Beside her, Jack watched me too, but he looked thoughtful rather than angry.

There were wonderful changes on the horizon for the pack, for sure, but there was trouble too. A month ago, Malcolm had overheard a conversation between Jack and Delia in which Jack had said that if his plan to bind Sean and Lily together failed, they would have to find another way to deal with me. I'd been on guard ever since, but so far they'd both been perfectly polite around me whenever we crossed paths. Delia's expression was a clear indicator that her feelings about me hadn't changed; if anything, she was more resentful than before. For right now, though, I chose to focus on the good and save worrying about the bad for later.

I might have known that decision would bite me right on the ass.

# CHAPTER 2

The party broke up around noon. We helped Karen and Cole clean up and then headed out after a last round of congratulations, hugs, and high fives with the newly engaged couple and the beaming expectant parents.

As we bumped down the gravel drive toward the road, I turned down the radio. "Well?"

Sean sighed. "Lily pleaded her case and I told her I wasn't interested. I reminded her we'd gone on two dates at the behest of her father and Jack, but I hadn't felt any kind of spark between us then and I still don't. She told me that she fell in love with me at first sight. I don't believe a word of it, though. She's spoiled and used to getting anything she wants, and she wants me. The more I refuse, the more determined she gets. It doesn't help that she found out about Jack's plan to give her the second cuff, so now she thinks she's been cheated out of what's 'rightfully' hers."

"How'd she hear about that?" I asked.

"Delia told her, of course. Lily tried arguing that I owe it to my pack to choose a shifter mate and that mages of any sort can't be trusted. There are a lot of members of the Were Ruling Council who agree, but they aren't going to interfere in internal pack issues, or in an alpha's selection of consort or mate." His hands gripped the steering wheel and it creaked. "She seems to think they might in this case, but I think she's over-estimating her father's influence on the Council. Zachary's brother is on the Council and his voice has power, but he's only one of seven. There's no precedent for them to involve themselves. They might not like it, but shifters tend to stay out of each other's business, generally speaking. I told her that I loved you and she should look elsewhere for her mate."

I read his expression. "So what's bothering you?"

"When none of her arguments worked, she extended a formal invitation from her father to meet for a meal. I had to accept the invitation or it would have been perceived as an insult." He squeezed my knee. "Like I said, it's nothing to be worried about. Zachary isn't unreasonable; he's just a doting father who's never said no to his daughter. If I had to guess, I'd suspect he told her I'd be head over heels for her, because what fool wouldn't be, and now he's trying to save face and get his daughter the one thing she wants that she doesn't have."

"This is a love triangle straight out of a soap opera," I complained. "Wait until Malcolm finds out. We'll never hear the end of it."

Sean chuckled. "Your ghost will think it's hilarious, I'm sure." He shook his head. "Lily wouldn't be a bad person if she'd been a little less spoiled. I would like to see her happy, but as long as she keeps chasing someone she can't have and trying to win instead of looking for real love, that won't happen."

I rubbed my eyes. He put his hand on my leg, sending little tingles running along my skin. "You look worn out. How much sleep have you gotten in the last thirty-six hours?"

"What's sleep?" I sighed. I'd had energy when we were at the party, but now I felt every ounce of my exhaustion.

"You need a nap." He winked at me. "Eventually. I have a couple of things I want to do first. I might let you get some sleep later."

I rolled my eyes. "You're insatiable, you know that?"

He grinned. "Anytime you want me to leave you alone, all you have to do is say the word." His hand slid under the hem of my dress and up my bare thigh. His fingertips teased the lacy edge of my undies and I shivered hard. "But I don't think you will." He withdrew his hand from under my dress.

"You don't know how tired I am," I said, but we both knew I wouldn't be saying no—not today or anytime soon.

When he turned into his driveway, I grabbed my messenger bag from the floor by my feet. He pulled into the garage, parked, and turned off the engine. I opened my door to hop out—

—and fell.

I hit the garage floor on my hands and knees with a yelp, startled, confused, and disoriented.

"Alice!" Sean was around the truck and at my side in a blink. He crouched next to me. "What happened?"

I blinked at him. My brain felt sluggish, and it took a moment for his question to compute. "I don't know. I went to get out of the truck and then I got dizzy. I think I fell."

"You did fall." He studied me closely, clearly worried. "You look dazed. Did you hit your head?"

"I don't think so." The only thing that hurt was my knees. "Maybe I slipped or tripped getting out of the truck. I guess I must really be tired."

"Here, let me help you up." He put his hands under my elbows and gently lifted me to my feet. "Can you walk?"

I shrugged out of his grip and took a few hesitant steps. My knees would be bruised but I didn't think anything was broken. "Yes, I'm all right."

Sean shut the passenger door of the truck and picked up my bag. He tried to help me with one hand under my elbow, but I pulled away and walked into the house on my own.

He went to the back door and let my dog in from the backyard. Rogue, a Husky mix who was sixty-five pounds of energy and love, bounded inside and headed straight for me. He skidded to a stop several feet away, his nails scrabbling on the hardwood floor, and whined.

"What's the matter?" I asked him, frowning. I held out my hand. "Do I smell like a bunch of werewolves or something? That's never bothered you before."

He approached me cautiously and licked my hand, then whined again. He backed up and went to his bed by the window, his eyes on me.

"What's gotten into that dog?" I wondered.

"You must smell like something he doesn't like, but I don't know what that would be." Sean followed me upstairs, radiating concern as we went into his bedroom. "I take back what I said about keeping you awake. Why don't you take a nap now? I'll stay with you until you fall asleep." He wrapped his arms around me and nuzzled my hair.

I pushed his hands away. "I'll be okay." My cell phone rang from inside my bag. "Grab that for me, will you?"

"You should just let it go to voice mail and get some rest." Sean got my phone out of my bag. He glanced at the screen and blinked in surprise.

"What?" I asked.

Instead of answering, he handed me the phone. The screen read *Natalie Newton Calling*.

It was my turn to look surprised. Natalie had been my client a few months back. She'd hired me to find out who had stolen some books from her library. The case involved a murderous aunt and a magical weapon of mass destruction called the *Kasten*, containing the bones and vengeful spirit of a long-dead blood mage named Adelbert. I'd gotten stabbed and nearly died, and the case had left some serious emotional scars.

Though Natalie and I had spoken a few times since, I hadn't heard from her in almost two months, which meant this was not likely to be a social call.

I swiped the green button and answered. "This is Alice."

"Alice, it's Natalie Newton." Her familiar voice was strained. "Have I caught you at a bad time?"

"Not at all. What's wrong?"

She took a deep breath. "I need your help. Can you come over to my house right away, please? Just you and Malcolm."

I hurried over to Sean's dresser to grab clothes. "I just got home, so I need to change clothes, and then I'll be over. It'll take me about forty-five minutes to get there."

"Please hurry," she begged.

"Hang on a second." I set the phone down on the dresser while I pulled the dress off over my head. I picked the phone back up and held it between my chin and shoulder as I went to the closet to grab a shirt. "What's going on?"

"I don't want to say over the phone. Just get here as soon as you can."

I reached for a pair of jeans and came back out into the bedroom. "I'm on my way."

"Thanks, Alice." She ended the call.

Sean was standing beside the bed. "What do you think that's about?"

"No idea." I put on the jeans and zipped them up. "Can you make me some coffee to take?"

He crossed his arms. "Sure. You want me to come along?"

"She said just me and Malcolm," I reminded him as I pulled the shirt on over my head.

"It sounds serious." Sean plainly didn't like that I was walking into the situation blind.

"I'm sure Malcolm and I can handle it, whatever's going on." I sat down on the bed to put on my socks and boots. "If I need backup, I'll call you."

Looking unconvinced, he headed down to the kitchen. I finished getting dressed, brushed and braided my hair, and hurried downstairs.

Sean met me at the foot of the stairs with a travel mug of coffee in one hand and my keys in the other. "Be careful," he said, kissing me quickly. "Call me if you need me."

"Will do." I slung my bag over my shoulder, took the coffee, and headed out the door.

ON THE WAY to Natalie's house, when I was stopped at a red light, I found the cool blue-green trace of magic in my mind that was my connection to my bound ghost. I gave it two light tugs, our prearranged signal that I needed him to jump to me. I was tired enough that doing so brought a wave of dizziness and nausea.

I swallowed hard and gripped the steering wheel tightly. "Don't puke, don't puke, don't puke," I muttered until the feeling passed.

Just as the light turned green, one of the crystals on my bracelet buzzed, indicating Malcolm had jumped into it from wherever he was. I touched the crystal with my other hand. "*Release.*"

Malcolm appeared in the passenger area of my car. As usual, he appeared to be wearing wire-rimmed glasses, a button-up shirt, and jeans. "Hey, Alice," he said cheerfully. "Welcome back. How was your weekend with Arkady?"

"Terrible." My tires squealed as I took a corner too fast. "I just got a call from Natalie Newton asking us to come to her house."

"You got a call from Nat?" He looked surprised. "What about?"

"She wouldn't say over the phone. She just said to bring you and get there as fast as I could."

"That does not sound good," he muttered. "You want me to see what's going on?"

I hesitated. I didn't like the idea of Malcolm facing whatever was happening without me, but I was trying not to be overprotective of either of Malcolm or Sean. Both of them understood why I wanted to keep them safe, but they'd made it clear I had to let them make their own decisions about what dangers to face.

"Okay," I said reluctantly. "Do some recon. Be careful."

"Roger that. Meet you there." He vanished.

Due to light traffic, I reached Natalie's house in record time. Her red Mustang was parked in the driveway next to a gray SUV I didn't recognize. I parked on the street and hurried to the front door. Everything seemed quiet.

Natalie's house wards buzzed lightly on my skin. I recognized her familiar magic in the wards. She'd evidently come a long way from the day we'd discovered she had magic. I'd found a mage to teach her how to control and use her magic. Her training must be going well.

The door opened just as I reached the porch. When I'd seen her last, Natalie had been thin and pale and struggling to cope with all of the ways in which her life had been turned upside down. Now, she looked healthy and full of energy, and her bright red hair was long and wavy. She wore a summer dress and her feet were bare. It was a complete transformation from the fragile and uncertain young woman she'd been, and I was glad to see her looking so much better.

At the moment, however, her green eyes were dark with worry and her expression was grim. "Alice, thank you so much for coming over so quickly. Please come in." She ran her fingers along the doorway, granting me permission to pass through her wards.

I stepped into the house and she closed the door behind me. "What's going on? Are you all right?"

"I'm okay. It's my friend who needs your help." She lowered her voice. "Malcolm is here, but he's staying quiet. Come on; we're in the living room."

Relieved that Natalie was all right, I followed her.

The living room had once been filled with cat-themed décor that had belonged to her late grandmother. Natalie had reduced the number of kitschy kitty knickknacks by at least half and hung some art prints on the walls that were more her style. I remembered Natalie had an art history degree and worked at the museum. She was slowly but surely turning the home she'd inherited from her grandmother into her own space.

I sensed Malcolm in the living room, but he'd gone invisible and silent because of Natalie's guest, who rose from her chair as we came into the room. She was about my age, I guessed, and African American, wearing jeans and a T-shirt from a local half-marathon. Her eyes were red from crying. A mug of tea—Natalie's comfort beverage of choice—sat untouched on a table at her right.

"Alice, this is Jana Peters," Natalie said. "Her son Aden is missing."

My stomach lurched. "Have you called the police?"

"I can't." Jana dropped back into the chair and looked at Natalie, clearly at a loss.

"Can I get you something to drink before we sit down?" Natalie asked me. "Tea or water?"

I shook my head. "I'm fine."

We settled on the couch across from Jana. I took a small notebook and a pen out of my bag. "Why can't you call the police about Aden?"

Jana was obviously reluctant to explain. Natalie wouldn't have called me over here unless she believed I'd be better equipped to handle the situation than someone else. I read Jana's expression and thought I recognized the fear, anger, and helplessness in her eyes.

"Do you and Aden have magic?" I asked gently.

She said nothing.

I raised my hand. Bright green earth magic danced on my fingertips, then vanished. "I do too." I drew air magic to me and a breeze blew through the room, making papers flutter and the ceiling fan turn. "I'm good at keeping people's secrets. I'm assuming Natalie told you that."

Jana nodded.

"Are you and Aden unregistered?"

"Yes," she said, her eyes flashing defiantly.

"They're unregistered, just like me," Natalie said. "That's why she can't call the police."

Federal law required all supes and mages to register with the Supernatural and Paranormal Entity Management Agency, or SPEMA. Most followed the law and registered, but many individuals and families, fearing how that information might be used to target them, managed to avoid detection or find other ways to keep their names and abilities out of SPEMA's records. Natalie's late grandmother, afraid her granddaughter would use her magic in public and out their entire family, had bound her magic when she was young and died before she revealed the truth. Others hid their abilities, gambling that they wouldn't be discovered or outed.

Unregistered adults faced federal prison time in one of a handful of high-security supe prisons. Depending on their abilities, minors either went into government facilities or a specialized and rather shady foster care system, and few were ever returned to their parents.

And there were worse fates than that for those caught by law enforcement. Corrupt police had been known to sell unregistered supes or mages, especially children, to human traffickers or cabals. If either Jana or Aden were high-level mages, or had any rare abilities like blood magic, they might disappear.

Jana and Aden and families like theirs were on dangerous ground on their best days, hoping and praying never to encounter police or accidentally reveal their abilities. This situation was a literal nightmare come true for their family.

I had only a fraction of the resources law enforcement did for searching for a missing child, but I couldn't in good conscience advise Jana to report her son missing, knowing there was a very good chance they would both end up in federal custody—or worse. An enormous weight settled on my shoulders.

I sensed Malcolm's light touch. The physical contact made it possible for him to share his thoughts with me.

*This is a bad situation to get involved in*, he said in my head. *I know it's a missing kid, but we're talking federal time for everybody involved if this goes off the rails.*

*I know. Let's see what's going on and then I'll decide what to do.*

*You already know what you're going to do.* Malcolm sounded grim. *Let's just be as smart about it as we can.* He let go of my shoulder and drifted away, back toward the far side of the room.

I realized I'd gone silent while Malcolm and I conversed. Both women watched me quizzically. Natalie glanced past my shoulder, as if wondering if Malcolm was standing beside me.

I addressed Jana. "Tell me what you know and we'll go from there. How old is Aden?"

"He's twelve." She brought me her phone and showed me a picture of a smiling kid with short curly hair, wearing a Pokémon T-shirt.

"He looks like a happy kid," I said as she went back to her chair.

"He is, most of the time, but you know twelve-year-olds. He's happy one minute and shut in his room the next. He's a good kid, though. Never skips school, never worries me, never hangs out with kids who might get him in trouble. This is the first time he's..." Her voice cracked. She took a deep breath. "I just don't know what to do."

"Had you and Aden had an argument recently, something he might be mad about? Would he have gone somewhere to get away, or to make a point?"

She shook her head. "We hadn't argued in several days. Everything was fine, as far as I know."

I'd been hoping the answer would be yes. He still might have run away, though—parents didn't always know what their kids were thinking and twelve was a volatile age. "When did he disappear?"

"About four hours ago, I think." She picked up a piece of paper from the table and I went over to take it. It was a page torn from a spiral notebook. On it was a short note in a kid's handwriting: *Going to the library for some books. Back soon.* He'd drawn a big smiley face with crossed eyes on the paper.

"Does he go to the library by himself very often?"

Jana nodded. "I let him walk to the little branch library near our house sometimes; it's only four blocks. But the library didn't open until noon today and he was gone before nine. I drove around for two hours between our house and there, but there's no sign of him. I've been calling his phone and it goes straight to voice mail. I know something's wrong. Even if his phone died, he would have found a way to call me, or he'd be home."

She took a shaky breath. "I went to the library before I came here. The librarians at the main desk know him by sight, since he's in there all the time, and they assured me he hadn't come in. I searched the library to be sure, but there was no sign of him. I don't know where he went, but it wasn't to the library."

"Have you called his friends to see if he's over at someone's house?"

She made a face. "I called around, but I didn't want anyone to know he's missing because they'd want to know why I hadn't called the police. I made up reasons for calling—questions about snacks and summer reading lists—and asked what their sons and Aden had been up to lately. No one said anything about him."

I'd worked missing persons cases before, but never one where the victim was a child, and never when I had to look for them without tipping people off that the person in question was missing. The entire process would be like walking a tightrope in gale-force winds over a tank full of sharks, and it was more than just my livelihood and possibly my freedom in danger. One misstep could doom Jana and Aden too. Even Malcolm's safety was on the line.

Possibilities ran through my head. Maybe someone along Aden's route to the library had surveillance cameras. He might have started heading that way before he either changed course or was snatched. If Aden had a cell phone, there was a chance the phone could be traced, if I could find someone to do it.

I turned my attention back to Jana. "This is going to be difficult and dangerous for everyone involved, and time is ticking. I want you to think about this decision, about whether or not to call the police.

They have an enormous amount of resources to look for a missing child, from Amber Alerts to local, state, and federal support from a lot of agencies. I'm one person, with limited resources, and I'll have to tread carefully so I don't tip people off that he's missing. I know you want nothing to do with the authorities, but if someone took Aden, you need to consider that getting him back quickly and alive might be more important than the risk you'd be taking by bringing in the cops."

Jana exchanged a long look with Natalie. They'd clearly had this conversation before I arrived. "My son is a null," she told me tonelessly.

"He can null instantly, like I can," Natalie added. "And he can blast someone with the energy he absorbs all at once, in one big bang."

Well, shit.

Most nulls could drain other mages' magic and break wards, but it took time. Natalie could drain a mage and break wards with a touch. That made her valuable, though her natural magic, fire and air, was mid-level at best and unremarkable. Even she couldn't siphon energy, though. A twelve-year-old kid who could null with a touch or use that energy as a weapon would never make it to the police station or a SPEMA field office. He'd be worth his weight in gold to a cabal.

I could sense Malcolm's unease through our link. He knew what the news about Aden's abilities meant as well as anyone. Calling the police or alerting anyone about Aden's disappearance was not an option.

For better or worse—probably worse—it looked like I had a new client, and quite possibly the most dangerous and difficult case I had ever taken on.

Well, good. I'd hate for my life to get boring.

JANA and I talked while Natalie made a fresh pot of tea. She and Natalie had met while running in the nearby park and become friends. On a visit to Natalie's house, Jana sensed her wards and the two women realized they shared a similar predicament: hiding their abilities from others.

Jana was thrilled to find out Natalie was a null. Both she and Aden were low-level earth mages, which meant their abilities had been relatively easy for them to learn to control without needing instruction, but Aden's ability meant he had to be extremely careful at all times. Even something as innocuous as a school trip to an art museum was fraught with danger. Museums tended to use wards to safeguard their treasures, and nulling one would set off every alarm in the building.

We accepted mugs of tea from Natalie. I blew on mine to cool the liquid. "Who besides you and Natalie knows Aden can null?"

Jana shook her head. "Absolutely no one."

"You've never confided in anyone?"

"No," she said emphatically. "There was too much risk to ever tell anyone. I've read articles and heard stories in the news. I know what can happen to unregistered mages who have special talents. I won't let that happen to my son."

"What about Aden's father? Is he in the picture?"

Her expression hardened. "No."

"What's the story there?" When she didn't reply, I added, "The number-one suspect anytime a kid disappears is the estranged parent. We have to eliminate him first. I need his name, address, work info, whatever you've got."

She exhaled. "His name is Preston Allan Garrett. I can give you his cell number. I don't have a current home address, but I can give you a work address."

"That'll do for a start."

"He works at Nyx."

My eyebrows went up. "The vampire club?"

"He didn't work there when we were together, but that's where he's worked for the past couple of years."

"In what capacity?"

"He's a host, or at least that's what they call them. Anywhere else, they'd call him a bouncer. He walks the main floor and takes care of human patrons who get out of hand. The vamps have their own bouncers, but they prefer humans to deal with human troublemakers."

"What did he do when you and he were dating?"

She sighed. "It wasn't really dating, what we were doing. He was a rich white boy and I worked at his daddy's company in the sales department at the time. We met at a company party. They might have forgiven him for sleeping with a black girl, but then I got pregnant and wouldn't get rid of the baby, so his daddy tossed him out. It took me no time at all to realize putting up with Preston was worse than having no man around. I kicked him out, had my baby, and finished my degree so I could have a good job and raise my son."

"So he's never had much interest in Aden?"

"He's been worthless most of Aden's life. Sometimes he would come by with a little present—something he bought for a couple dollars or stole—and ask me for money. I never had much money to spare and he just needed money for drugs anyway. He started hitting the gym a couple of years ago and got work as a bouncer at some strip club near the airport. One of his friends helped get him the job at Nyx. I guess he's doing better, but I don't trust him. He's been calling a lot more lately, telling me he's trying to live right and wanting to see Aden, but I told him to leave us alone. We didn't need him before; we don't need him now."

It sounded like Garrett would be my first stop. The recent increase in attentiveness after years of neglect had my spidey senses tingling. "Let me get that phone number from you."

She gave me the number. "He doesn't know Aden has magic. He doesn't know anything about him. They haven't even talked in over a year. I don't want that man getting his hooks into my son. Aden's doing well in school. He wants to be a veterinarian. I don't need Preston in here ruining his life."

"Is there anyone else who could possibly know about Aden's abilities? His friends, maybe?"

She shook her head again. "No one, I promise you. He knows he can't tell anyone."

"Kids have a really hard time keeping secrets."

Her eyes flashed. "You don't know what it's like, keeping a secret like that," she snapped. "We're talking life and death. He talks, he tells that secret, he disappears. He's known that since he was little."

I *did* know what keeping a deadly secret felt like. It was a terrible burden that chewed you up from the inside. For five years I had kept my real identity a secret and sometimes the weight of it crushed me flat. Aden had been keeping his secret longer than that. Powers like nulling tended to manifest in children between the ages of seven and ten, so for the past several years he'd had that additional burden to bear. I thought about the picture Jana had shown me of a smiling kid and wondered what was going on behind that smile.

I didn't take Jana's anger personally. She was holding up much better than I thought I would in her situation. I wasn't sure if kids would ever be in my future, but I couldn't imagine what it would feel like to have one go missing.

"Does he have a computer?" I asked.

She reached into her bag and handed me a small laptop. "I brought it."

"Are there any passwords I need?"

"He's not allowed to set any passwords."

"What about social media?"

"He's not old enough to do any of that. I told him I would let him try it after his next birthday."

"Is there anything else you can think of that might help?"

"I've wracked my brain and I can't think of anything. If he's not with one of his friends and he's not at the library, I have no idea where he might be, or who might have him." She took a deep breath that sounded like a sob.

I had a place to start—Aden's father—and then if that didn't pan out, I'd see about the possibility of surveillance along Aden's route between his house and the library. I'd gotten Jana's home address, which was only a few minutes away, and the location of the library. Depending on what, if anything, I got from those videos, I'd decide where to go from there.

Jana wiped her eyes and squared her shoulders. "I don't have much money, but I can give you five hundred dollars now and maybe we can work out a payment plan for the rest."

Before I could reply, Natalie spoke up. "Don't worry about that right now. I'll make payment arrangements with Alice and you and I can work out a plan for paying me back."

"I don't want charity," Jana said sharply. "I pay my own bills."

"It's not charity," Natalie told her. "It's a loan. You're going to pay me back. What are friends for, if not to help each other when they can?"

Jana gave her a small smile. "Thank you."

I handed her my card and put my bag on my shoulder. "I'm going to get out there and start searching. If you think of anything at all that might help, no matter how insignificant it seems, call me immediately. If Aden's not with his dad and I don't get anything right away from cameras between your house and the library, I'll want to search Aden's room. Will you be home?"

She nodded. "Yes. I'll head home in a few minutes. I want to be there if—*when* he comes home. Just knock on the door."

"Okay, will do. I'll call you if I need more information, or when I have updates."

"Thank you."

Jana went to the kitchen to pour herself another cup of tea.

Natalie stuck her feet into a pair of sandals. "I'm walking Alice out to her car," she called.

"Okay," Jana replied from the kitchen.

We went outside and stood in the shade near Natalie's car. I sensed Malcolm with us.

"What do you know that you didn't want to say in front of Jana?" I asked.

Natalie sighed. "I don't want her to panic because I don't know if this is in any way related to what's happened to Aden, but just in case, I wanted you to know. You remember Kyra DeWitt, the mage you found to help me learn how to control and use my magic?"

I nodded. "Yes. You seem to be learning quickly, judging by your house wards."

She smiled. "I do seem to have a natural talent for wards, Kyra says. I love using magic to make things. It's like art to me, painting with colors and shapes only I can see." Her smile faded. "Anyway, Jana brought Aden over last week to meet Kyra so she could talk to him about controlling his magic, especially his nulling ability. While they took a break, Kyra and I were in the kitchen talking about Darius Bell."

Bell was the head of a local cabal and the target of ongoing attacks by my grandfather, Moses Murphy, who wanted to kill Bell and take over his territory. Their war had resulted in numerous deaths and a lot of collateral damage, but things had been quiet for several weeks since my aunt Catherine had tried to kill Bell by burning down the condo where he'd been staying. I'd intervened by summoning a thunderstorm to put out the fire and then severely injuring her with a bolt of lightning. I'd been caught on camera controlling the storm but hadn't been identified, causing news agencies to dub me "Storm Girl," a nickname I hated.

Word on the street was Bell and Moses were both searching for Storm Girl, Bell because he wanted her as a weapon against Moses, and Moses so he could get revenge for what happened to Catherine.

"What about Bell?" I asked.

"Kyra said he's looking for nulls," she said quietly. "Some are going to work for him voluntarily. Others...aren't."

Double shit. From somewhere on my left, Malcolm muttered an expletive.

"There's a chance Aden might have overheard us talking," Natalie added. "When we came out of the kitchen, he was in the hallway acting like he was heading toward the bathroom, but he could have been listening."

Well, that opened up a whole new avenue of possibilities and none of them were good. "Let's say he did overhear you. What would a twelve-year-old kid do with that information?"

She shook her head. "I would hope it would make him even more careful not to let anyone know he's a null, but..." She bit her lip. "Aden's a great kid, he really is, but Jana's told me he gets angry when he wants something other kids have and she can't afford it. They're not poor, but single mothers don't have a lot of disposable income. He wants her to not have to worry about money so much, either. I really hope he didn't overhear Kyra say that Bell is offering big money to mages who can null and decide to do something stupid."

"If he did, we'll probably never see him again," Malcolm said.

"How would a twelve-year-old kid even know how to find someone from the cabal?" I wondered. "Bell's compound is gone, and last I heard, no one knows where he's holed up since the fire, so it's not like Aden can go to his house and ring the doorbell."

"It's amazing what you can find out on the internet." Natalie sighed. "I don't want to send you on some wild goose chase with this."

"You did the right thing by telling me. We have to consider all the possibilities. I'm going to talk to Aden's father first, and then I'll go from there. Call me if you think of anything else."

"I will. It's really good to see you. I'm sorry it's under these circumstances." She hesitated. "Can I give you a hug? I promise I won't null you."

I remembered all too well what it felt like to get nulled and how long it took to regenerate my magic afterward, but if she'd learned to control her ability, the danger was minimal.

"Sure," I said after a beat.

She gave me a quick hug. I felt her fire and air magic, but they were muted. I sensed nothing of her nulling ability at all.

"You're looking great, Natalie," I said when she stepped back. "And you've learned so much about controlling and using your magic. I'm really impressed, and I'm proud of you."

"Thanks. That means a lot, coming from you. And wherever my grandmother is, I hope she's proud too."

I didn't have much good to say about Natalie's grandmother for binding her magic instead of teaching her how to use it, but I kept my opinions to myself. "I'm sure she is. I'll be in touch."

Natalie returned to her house. When Malcolm and I were in my car, he went visible again. "Man, I hope this kid didn't run off to work for Bell."

"Me too. I hope he's with his dad. Even if Garrett's as much of a screw-up as Jana says, that's still a million times better than being in the clutches of a cabal." I took out my phone and made a call.

The phone rang twice, and then Bryan Smith, Charles Vaughan's head of security, answered. "Miss Alice," he rumbled, sounding surprised.

I didn't blame him for being startled by my call. I hadn't seen him or his vampire employer in a month. I was still furious with Charles about his scheme to obtain the magic cuff that I'd needed to save Sean's life and trade it for drinking my blood. I'd agreed to the trade and let him bite me in return for the cuff, but my anger had been simmering ever since. And if *I* was mad about Charles's plot, Sean was a pot of boiling rage that I worried might explode if they crossed paths.

"Hello, Bryan," I said. "Do you still have a friend or two who work at Nyx?"

I could almost see Bryan's eyebrows go up. "I do. Are you looking for a part-time job to make some extra cash and need me to put in a good word?"

I snorted. "Hardly. I'm looking for the home address of someone who works there as a host, a guy named Preston Garrett. It's for a case I'm working on."

"Let me see what I can find out. Should I text you?"

"Yes, thank you."

"You're welcome." He disconnected.

While I waited for him to text me Garrett's address, I called Sean and gave him a quick outline of what we knew. I could tell he was concerned about me getting involved in a case involving unregistered mages, but he didn't even hesitate in voicing his support for agreeing to help Jana find her missing kid.

When I mentioned the possibility Aden might have heard Kyra and Natalie talking about Bell, however, the line went silent.

"You're already on Bell's radar," he said finally. "If Aden did do something idiotic like try to go to work for him, what are you going to do?"

"I don't know," I admitted. "This could go a lot of different ways right now. But if Bell's got Aden, no kid deserves that."

I had a feeling I knew what Sean was thinking: that he'd love to tell me that under no circumstances was I to go after Aden and risk capture by Bell. But he wouldn't, because he didn't want that kid in Bell's clutches any more than I did, and because he knew I'd already weighed the risk and decided I'd go after Aden.

"I'm headed over to talk to Aden's father right now," I told him. "For all we know, Aden's mad at his mom and ran away to his place."

"Let's hope so. But if not, we should talk strategy. If Bell has the kid, he's a valuable asset and probably relatively safe for now. We might only have one shot at getting him back, assuming we can figure out where they're holding him."

There was no such thing as *safe* when it came to cabals, but I didn't argue or tell him I knew that from my own experience. My past was still a secret I couldn't share with him. I didn't know if I'd ever be able to tell him I was Moses Murphy's granddaughter.

My phone beeped with an incoming message from Bryan with Garrett's home address and a warning that he had a reputation for being volatile. Fantastic.

I sighed. "Well, Bryan just sent me an address for Aden's dad, so I'm heading that way with Malcolm. I'll let you know if I find him."

"Okay. Be careful."

"I will."

We disconnected. I put Garrett's address into the GPS app on my phone and headed in that direction.

"So, what's your plan for talking to the dad?" Malcolm asked from the passenger seat. "If the kid isn't there, he's going to want to know why you're looking for him. That could get complicated."

"It's going to be tricky," I said, accelerating to get through a yellow light before it turned red. "I've got some ruses in mind that might work. Let's find this kid."

# CHAPTER 3

A QUICK INTERNET SEARCH INFORMED ME THAT PRESTON GARRETT'S FATHER, Preston Garrett Senior, owned a chain of sporting goods stores up and down the west coast. The Garretts were among the wealthiest families in the area, and Preston Junior had enjoyed a life of privilege up until his father disowned him twelve years ago. Now Preston's younger half brother James was the CEO of the company and Preston Senior was semi-retired, spending much of his time traveling the world with his fourth wife.

Aden's father lived in an apartment south of the river. I found a visitor's spot in the little lot next to his apartment building and parked. Garrett lived in apartment 801, according to Bryan. If he'd worked last night, he was probably asleep, so I'd likely be waking him up with my knock.

Bryan's warning about Garrett's temper had me on guard, but I doubted a mundane human posed much of a threat, regardless of how much time he spent in the gym. Besides, I had Malcolm with me, so between the two of us I figured we could manage even a roided-out bouncer.

Malcolm and I took the elevator up to the eighth floor and

followed the hallway to the left. Apartment 801 was on the far end, a corner unit with a balcony containing a couple of chairs, a small table, and a rack of free weights.

I plastered a big smile on my face and knocked loudly.

No answer. I hoped that meant he was asleep and not that he wasn't home. I knocked again, louder.

Heavy footsteps approached the door. Locks clicked and the door opened, revealing an enormous man with dark hair and eyes, wearing an AC/DC T-shirt and basketball shorts. Tattoos covered his muscular arms.

I recognized him from the photos of his younger self, but the former scion of the Garrett Sporting Goods fortune had put on what looked like a hundred pounds of muscle since his days as a fixture on the city's social scene. His body blocked the entire doorway, making it impossible for me to see if Aden was inside the apartment.

I sensed Malcolm moving away and guessed he was going into the apartment to see if the kid was there.

"What?" Garrett rumbled.

"Hi, I'm Alison from Kid Spaces," I chirped. "My company is putting in a bid to construct a playground nearby, and I wondered if you had a few minutes to answer a couple of questions and maybe sign a petition showing your support for the project." I held up a form on a clipboard. A half-dozen signatures were already scrawled on it from the last time I'd used this ruse. "Do you have children who would like a safe place to play, sir?"

"My son is too old to care about playgrounds," he snapped. "Go bother someone else." He started to close the door.

"Even older kids need to get outside and exercise," I said quickly. "A playground isn't just for little kids. There will be a basketball court and an area for other activities, like soccer. Is he here? Maybe he could tell us if he'd like something like that."

His eyes narrowed. "What did you say your name was?"

"Alison with Kid Spaces."

"Bullshit." He was suddenly in my face, two hundred and fifty pounds of fatherly fury. "You're lying. You're not here about any playground. Why are you asking about my son?"

I raised my hands as if signaling that I didn't want any trouble, but I spooled air magic in case he decided to get violent. "I'm just here getting signatures and talking to parents."

"The hell you are. You better tell me what you want with my kid before I decide to shake it out of you." He reached for my arm.

I dropped the clipboard and hit him in the chest with both palms, intending to use air magic to throw him back into the apartment.

Instead, I saw a blinding flash of bright yellow magic and every drop of magic I had in my body was sucked from me in an instant. I dropped like a sack of wet cement and hit the floor of the hallway in a heap, stunned and unable to move.

Well, now I knew where Aden had gotten his nulling ability. Unlike blood magic, which didn't run in families, nulling was a recessive inherited trait that skipped generations and was very rare. It hadn't surprised me that Jana wasn't a null and Aden was; I'd just assumed the ability had skipped her and shown up in her son. Assumptions like that were the quickest way to end up sprawled on a dirty tile floor without any magic or feeling in your extremities. I should have known better, but my long, tiring weekend had apparently taken its toll on my brain as well as my body.

Preston Garrett towered over me, my stolen magic crackling on his clenched fists along with his own. "Tell the ghost to back off or I'll blast him into his next life," he told me.

I'd been nulled so completely that I couldn't even sense where Malcolm was, though Garrett's comment indicated he could feel the ghost nearby and figured out we were a team. The guy wasn't dumb.

Garrett's nulling and his ability to use it meant Malcolm couldn't drop him with a sleep spell. Apparently, like Aden, Garrett could use stolen energy as a weapon. What that much power could do to Malcolm I wasn't sure, but I knew I couldn't risk it.

I didn't want to use Malcolm's name in front of a stranger. I hadn't registered him with SPEMA as the law required, since I was hiding him from Darius Bell, so the fewer people who knew who or what he was, the better.

"Ghost, it's okay." I was getting some feeling back in my hands and feet, but it would be a little while before I'd be able to physically defend myself. "Mr. Garrett and I are going to have a calm conversation about Aden."

Malcolm's cold hand touched my shoulder. *Do you want me to go tell Sean what happened and bring him here?* he asked.

*Not yet. Let's see where this goes.*

Sean's reaction to me getting nulled would be full-on alpha werewolf fury, and I didn't think that would do anything to help me get information about Aden from his father.

I looked up at Garrett. "I'm not a threat to you or your son. I'm trying to help him. Give me a chance to explain."

Garrett crouched next to me. It was strange to feel my own magic sizzling on someone else's skin. "Tell me right now why you're here and then I'll decide whether to talk to you or throw your lying ass out on the sidewalk."

Ruses had gotten me exactly nowhere, so I decided to try honesty. "I just came from talking with Jana. Aden's been missing since this morning. I was hoping he was with you, or that you knew where he was. I'm a private investigator. Jana hired me to find him."

Shock left him speechless for a moment. "Why the hell didn't she call the police?" he demanded finally.

"Because Aden has magic, same as you, and calling the police about him is a dangerous proposition. Do you really want to have the rest of this conversation in the middle of the hallway?"

He looked at me, his expression cold. "Can you walk?"

"Maybe." I gritted my teeth and sat up. Nulling didn't just suck all the magic out of your body; it also left you feeling like you'd been up for three days and then fallen down the side of a mountain.

Malcolm touched my shoulder again. *Do you want to siphon some magic and energy from me?*

I thought about it, then decided against it. *I'll be all right. One of us needs to be at full power in case this goes south.*

*Farther south, you mean,* Malcolm griped.

It took a minute, but I managed to get on my feet. My legs were rubbery and my fingers were still numb. When I was upright and more or less walking, Garrett led the way into his apartment. I shuffled in behind him with Malcolm at my side.

The front room had a large sofa and a recliner. Garrett sat in the recliner. I made it to the couch and fell into the seat.

"Let's hear it," he said.

I told him about Aden's disappearance and the note he'd left saying he was going to the library. Jana's secrets were her own, so I didn't mention that Aden's mother had magic.

"Did you never tell Jana that you have magic?" I asked.

Garrett shook his head. "I've never told anyone. My mother had magic. She died when I was five. My father arranged for me to have lessons so I could learn how to control and hide my magic. He never wanted anyone to know about it. He made sure none of his other wives had it before he married them, and neither of my half brothers have magic as far as I know. I had no idea my son had inherited it from me." He paused. "But if Jana didn't think I had magic, where did she think it came from?"

I didn't reply, but he answered his own question. "She must have magic too. She never told me." The last part sounded like an accusation.

"You never told *her*," I pointed out. "Look, I'm not here to play mediator between you and Jana. I'm looking for your kid. Jana told me you have very little contact with him."

"Up until about a year ago, that was true. I'm sure she told you what a piece of shit I am and that I'm liable to be a bad influence on Aden."

"Pretty much." No sense pretending otherwise.

"Well, I *was* a piece of shit when Aden was born, and for most of his life. I'll admit that. My dad was a piece of shit too, but I'm not going to blame him for me being a deadbeat." He gestured at the apartment. "I've been clean for nineteen months. I've got a nice place and I work forty hours a week. Yeah, at a vamp club, but it's an honest paycheck. I've even got benefits. Jana doesn't want to hear about any of that. She doesn't believe I've changed. She thinks I'm trash and I'll drag Aden down with me. And I'm pissed about it."

"Pissed enough to get Aden to run away?"

"And risk her calling the cops? Hell no. I'm not registered. And I guess neither is Aden, or Jana either, though I didn't know about any of that until now." He swore.

"He doesn't seem to be with any of his friends. I know you haven't had much contact with him, but—"

"We talk or text almost every day," he told me.

I blinked.

He gave me a savage smile. "About a year ago, I got tired of Jana hanging up on me. I gave Aden a prepaid phone so he and I could talk to each other."

"Can you try calling that phone?"

He got his phone from the bedroom and was already calling when he returned. "It went straight to voice mail," he told me. After a moment, he said into the phone, "Aden, this is your father. Call me ASAP to let me know you're safe. If you need help, tell me where you are. I'll come get you. You won't be in any trouble. Your mother and I are worried about you." He paused. "Call me, son." He ended the call.

"Can I get that number from you?" I asked.

He gave me the number and sat back down. "I don't think he's run off," he said heavily. "He's not the type to worry his mom. He knows he's all she's got."

"I'm hearing he's frustrated about money issues and he doesn't have some of the nice things his friends have. Has he expressed anything like that to you?"

He thought about it. "Yeah, but you know kids. They're never happy with what they've got, no matter how much they've got. He knows his mom does the best she can. He might throw a fit sometimes, but it's not going to make him run away. Something's happened to him."

I didn't want Garrett to know there was a possibility Aden might have gotten mixed up with Darius Bell's cabal. The situation called for surgical precision and strategy, and Garrett struck me more as a wrecking ball.

"I'm going to do my best to find him. If you think of anything that might help me, please call me anytime." I held out my business card.

He rose and took it. "How are you feeling?"

"Better." I still had zero magic, but I was able to stand up. "We got off to a bad start, I guess."

"Yeah. I'm not gonna apologize for nulling you since you lied to me and you weren't going to tell me my son is missing."

I shrugged. "Fair enough."

He looked grim. "But now I'm regretting that you're barely able to walk and you're supposed to be out finding my son."

"My ghost companion can draw what's left of my magic from you and then channel it back to me, if you would allow him to do so and not null him. That would help."

"He better not drain me," Garrett warned.

"He won't. You'll still have all your natural magic and nulling power."

"He might as well take my earth magic too; I can't use it for anything anyway. I'm low-level, but it's better than nothing."

Malcolm touched my shoulder. *You sure you want me to do this? If he nulls me, we're both SOL.*

*He wants us to find the kid. It's your call, though.*

*Okay, I'll do it.*

Out loud, I said, "He's going to touch your arm. It'll feel cold. Don't get startled and accidentally null him."

Garrett braced himself. "Do it."

He twitched but held his nulling ability in check as Malcolm siphoned his magical energy.

When Malcolm let go, Garrett rolled his shoulders and addressed me. "I want to come with you to help look for him."

It wasn't unusual for friends or family members to want to accompany me while I searched for their loved one, but for various reasons—some of them legal, some personal—that was a no-go.

I shook my head. "Mr. Garrett—"

"Allan," he rumbled.

He apparently wanted to distance himself from the name Preston Garrett. I couldn't say I blamed him.

"Allan, I can't have anyone with me for liability reasons. It's a legal issue." When his face darkened, I held up my hand. "But here's something you *can* do. Based on where you work and what you told me about your past, I'm assuming you know people who know people."

He eyed me. "Yeah, so?"

"So put your network to use. Make some calls, but be careful. Don't say it's your kid who's missing; tell them it's a friend's kid. Don't mention the kid has magic; just say he went out on an errand for his mom and didn't come back. You probably have a good sense of who you can trust and who you can't to help you out. Even if they don't know anything about Aden in particular, they may know information that might help us. You can't just go all Hulk Smash if you get a tip, though. It's going to take cunning and finesse. Think you can do that?"

"I've worked for vampires for five years," he reminded me. "I can do finesse."

That was a fair point. Vamps didn't suffer fools or big dumb brutes.

"If you get information, you need to tell me before you act," I cautioned him. "Don't go barreling into anything or anywhere without talking to me and working out a plan. I know this is your kid and you want him back safe and sound, but you have to believe me when I say one wrong move could mean we don't get the outcome we want. Do you understand?"

He studied me. "Can I count on you to do whatever needs to be done to get my son back?"

I knew what he saw when he looked at me: a woman of average height and build with no apparent weapons other than her magic, which he'd just nulled. I didn't look all that threatening or imposing, which was very much to my advantage.

Since the day I'd escaped from my grandfather's compound five years ago, I'd been playing a role, pretending to be a fairly normal, well-adjusted human being instead of the killer I was. The façade had become second nature to me, but it was still a façade. Underneath, I was still Moses Murphy's granddaughter. Alice Worth was the disguise I wore. Few people saw the real me behind the mask, and those who did usually ended up dead shortly after. Malcolm and Sean were rare exceptions. They'd glimpsed the killer within and willingly joined Team Alice anyway.

I met Garrett's gaze and let him see Moses Murphy's granddaughter in my eyes. "I'll cut my way through whatever or whoever stands between me and your son," I told him. "You have my word."

Garrett gave me a nod. "I'll make some calls."

I headed for the door, my steps uneven. "Keep trying Aden's phone. If he or anyone else answers, try to keep them on the phone as long as you can in case we're able to trace the call or the phone. Let me know immediately if you hear anything."

"Will do. Find Aden." He shut the door behind me.

I sagged against the wall. "You ready to offload some of that magic?"

Malcolm became visible, hovering at my side. I had to squint to see him, since he glowed brightly with the magic he'd siphoned from Garrett. "I don't know how you're even on your feet," he said, holding out his arm. "Take what you need."

Touching Malcolm felt like touching thick, cold fog. I put my fingers around his arm and lowered my shields, sensing the hum of his power. I drew the magic into myself, slowly at first, then faster as

Malcolm opened our connection wider and pushed his magic over to me.

My instinct was to take as much as I could, but I'd vowed never to treat Malcolm as a power source. The mages who worked for my grandfather sucked bound ghosts dry, draining them over and over. It was perpetual torture for the ghosts, and I'd hated that practice as much as anything else the cabal mages did.

When I sensed I'd taken as much magic as he'd gotten from Garrett and begun to tap into Malcolm's own natural magic, I tried to close the flow of power, but Malcolm kept pushing his energy over to me.

"Stop, stop," I gasped, fighting to close the connection. "That's enough."

"You need more," he argued. "I know you don't like to pull power from me, but you have to have enough to protect yourself until you can get home to Sean and, uh, regenerate the rest."

Sex was a fast and fun way to regenerate magic, but I wasn't about to hit pause on my search for Aden to run home for a booty call. Then again, Sean probably wouldn't mind meeting me somewhere for a quick recharge—

My stomach cramped at the thought and I shuddered involuntarily. What was I thinking? I'd rather get power from Malcolm than Sean. I let Malcolm continue to funnel his energy into me.

Finally, the stream of magic ended. I closed my eyes and breathed deeply. The empty feeling was gone and I felt buoyant.

"Alice, you okay?"

I opened my eyes. Malcolm looked to be at about half his normal power level. I was probably at about seventy percent, but that was a damn sight better than I'd been a few minutes ago. "I'm good, Malcolm. Thank you."

"You're welcome." He floated along beside me as I headed for the elevator. "Where are we headed?"

"To trace Aden's steps from his house to the library." I hit the Down button and waited. "I'm hoping to find some surveillance cameras along his route that might have caught something on video."

"But if he wasn't really going to the library, what are the odds that we'll see him on video?" Malcolm asked as the elevator arrived and I got on.

I shrugged. "It's the best direction I can think of to go right now."

"What about the kid's laptop? Maybe his browser history or e-mails would help us. Sean's off work today. Why not let him see what he can find on the computer?"

"That's not a bad idea." I dug my phone out and called Sean while we exited the apartment building and headed for my car.

He answered on the first ring. "Hey, babe. How's the investigation going?"

"I just finished talking to Aden's dad. Guess who *also* has magic and isn't registered?" I unlocked my car and got in. Malcolm took his usual spot in the passenger seat area.

Sean whistled. "The plot thickens. Can he null too?"

"Yep."

He growled. "Alice, did he null you?"

"Yes, but—"

"Where are you?" I heard rustling and the jingle of keys. "I'm on my way."

"I'm fine, I'm fine," I said hurriedly. "Malcolm shared his magic with me, so I'm recovering. I could use a favor, though. Can you meet me in the parking lot at the branch library near Natalie's house?"

"If you need me so you can regenerate your magic, I'm willing to take one for the team," he quipped. "I've got a Maclin Security SUV. Plenty of room in the back if we get creative."

My stomach cramped again. "No, no, God no," I said vehemently. "Not that. I want to give you Aden's laptop and see if you can find anything on it that might help us figure out where he went."

A pause. "Okay." He sounded surprised. "The branch library near Natalie's house, you said? I can meet you there in about twenty minutes."

"Thanks. I'll see you in a few." I ended the call.

"That was a little harsh," Malcolm said as I backed out of my parking spot and turned onto the street.

"What?"

"The way you shot Sean down. It was kind of harsh. You feeling okay?"

I frowned. "I'm fine. I'm just focused on finding this kid. We don't have time for distractions."

"You're meeting up with him anyway, to give him the laptop. Don't you want to be back at full power?"

"I'll figure something else out, something that doesn't involve sex in the back of an SUV parked behind the library."

"Well, when you put it that way, I guess it does sound kind of tawdry." He looked thoughtful and then grinned. "Although...that would be achievement unlocked, am I right?"

"Malcolm," I warned.

"Fine." He crossed his arms. "Have it your way, you prude. Let's go to the library."

THANKS TO AN ACCIDENT and a traffic jam on the bridge, Sean was already at the library, waiting in his company SUV when I arrived.

He got out as I parked and came around to open my door. "Hi."

"Hey." I retrieved Aden's laptop from under the passenger seat and got out.

He watched me like a hawk, clearly wanting to see for himself that I was recovering from getting nulled. Thanks to Malcolm, I had enough energy to get out of the car without having to use the door for support.

Sean leaned over the door to give me a kiss. I turned my head and his kiss landed on my cheek instead. "Thanks for meeting me," I told him, handing him the laptop.

He took it, his brow furrowed as he looked at me.

"What?" I asked.

He shook his head and glanced at the small laptop. "Nothing. Any passwords?"

"His mom says he wasn't allowed to have passwords, but..." I waggled my hand to indicate my skepticism.

He snorted. "Yeah, I'm sure there are some, but odds are I can get around or through them. I'll call you right away if I find anything interesting. Where are you headed now?"

"I'm going to look for surveillance cameras between here and his house. Even if he wasn't really heading to the library, I'm hoping he at least started walking in this direction before whatever happened, happened. If I'm lucky, someone's got video that might help us."

"Be careful." He caught my hand in his, his eyes searching my face. "Are you all right? You don't seem quite like yourself."

"I'm worried about finding this kid." The way he was squeezing my hand made my stomach hurt. I pulled free and got into the car. "I need to get going. I'll check in later." I reached to pull the door shut.

He held it open. "Alice, if there was a problem between us, you'd tell me, right?"

"There's no problem," I said, exasperated. "The only thing I'm worried about right now is finding Aden."

"Okay." He let go of the door. "Keep me posted."

"I will. Good luck with the laptop." I shut my door. Sean stepped back as I shifted into reverse and backed out of the parking spot.

I waited for an opening and pulled into traffic. When I checked my rearview mirror, he was still standing next to the SUV, watching as I drove away.

# CHAPTER 4

It was a little over four blocks from Jana and Aden's home to the branch library. I parked in front of their little cottage-style house and got out.

Jana's gray SUV was in the driveway. I spotted her at the front window, peering through the curtain. She waved. I waved back, then gestured at myself and pointed down the street to indicate I was going to walk Aden's route to the library.

She nodded and settled back in to wait for her son. At the sight of her keeping a vigil in the window, it felt as if the weight of responsibility on my shoulders doubled.

Malcolm went invisible in case we encountered anyone who was sensitive to the presence of ghosts, but I sensed him nearby as I studied the house and its surroundings. This area was quiet, but at the corner I saw cars zooming past on a busy street. The library was down that street and around a corner.

I adjusted the strap of my messenger bag across my chest and started walking. Retracing a missing person's steps let me see things as they saw them. I tried to put myself in a twelve-year-old kid's shoes as I headed toward the busy cross street, past four houses very like Jana's: small, brightly painted, and cheerful. None of them had visible exterior cameras, unfortunately, but I hadn't expected them to.

When I reached the cross street, I paused to look around. The traffic was heavy, even on a Sunday. This street intersected about ten blocks north with an interstate, so many drivers used it to quickly get to the highway. That told me it was unlikely Aden had gotten snatched or picked up on this street; there was simply too much traffic. So either something happened before he got to this street, he'd taken some other route, or he'd headed off in another direction.

For the first block, one side of the street—the one Aden was likely to have walked down—was the side yards of the houses on the perpendicular streets. The other side of the street was an elementary school, closed for the summer. No cameras or anything else that might be helpful.

The same was true of the next block, though houses lined the opposite side of the street. Small shops filled the third block, however, and a busy convenience store occupied the corner where Aden would have turned left to go toward the library. Unfortunately, only one of the shops on this side of the street had exterior surveillance cameras. The antique shop's windows were filled with clocks of every size, shape, and design imaginable. The sign above the door read *Winchell Bros.*

I tried the doorknob and found it locked, even though the OPEN sign was clearly visible in the window. I noticed a smaller, hand-printed sign on the door: *Ring for Admittance.*

I hit the button next to the sign. Inside the shop, a loud buzzer sounded. When several seconds went by without anything happening, I peered through the window.

Finally, another buzzer sounded and the lock clicked. I turned the knob and stepped inside the shop.

My first impression was of utter chaos. Antiques ranging from washing bowls to kettles and oil lamps took up every square inch of space. On closer inspection, I saw not one speck of dust on any of the items or tables.

The shop would probably have been a collector's dream, but the crowded tables and narrow aisles were something of a minefield for a mage. I sensed magic of all sorts: earth, air, fire, and water. Even blood magic tugged on my senses from somewhere in the shop. I kept my hands to myself and avoided brushing against anything. I knew very well magical objects did unexpected things when they came into contact with supes and mages.

"Hello!" A cheerful male voice called out to me. "Come in, come in!"

"Hi," I called back as I followed the voice to a long glass counter at the back of the shop. Behind it sat a short, elderly man on a tall chair, wearing a white shirt with his sleeves rolled up. "What a beautiful store," I told him sincerely.

"Thank you." He rose to shake my hand. "I'm Benjamin Winchell, the owner. What are you looking for today?"

I produced one of my business cards and handed it over. "My name is Alice. I'm a private investigator."

"Well, my goodness." Winchell reached for a pair of reading glasses hanging around his neck, put them on, and read the card. He looked at me over the top of the glasses. "May I see your license, please?"

I showed him my mage private investigator's license. He studied it and gave me a nod. "It seems you are who you say you are. Tell me," he said, leaning forward. "Have I come into possession of hot merchandise? Evidence crucial to a case?" His voice dropped, though we appeared to be the only people in the shop. "A murder weapon?"

I couldn't help but smile. "I don't know about stolen goods or a murder weapon, but you might have some evidence that could help me. I noticed you have surveillance cameras out front. Do they work?"

"Wouldn't be of much use if they didn't." He took off his glasses. "What do you think you might be able to see?"

"I've been hired by a woman who is concerned that her ex-husband has been following their kid around. She has a restraining order against him, but he has a tendency to turn up wherever the kid is. This morning, her son walked over to the convenience store that's just down the block, and she wanted me to try to find out if her ex-husband followed him over there to talk to him."

"So you're just looking to see if the kid walked past my store this morning alone, or with this fellow?"

"Yes, sir. He would have walked by sometime around nine. Would you mind if I took a quick look at your recording?"

"I suppose not." He got up and lifted a hinged section of the counter. "Come on back to the office and I'll see if I can help you."

I followed him down a short hallway lined with shelves full of more antiques, all labeled with little notes about the repairs they needed. The office was small and very neat, with a laptop on the desk.

The security system was in the corner behind the desk. A flat-screen monitor showed four live views: exterior views of the front and back doors and two inside the shop. The video was black-and-white but very clear.

Winchell gestured at the monitor. "Do you know how to find what you're looking for?"

"I think so." The shop's system was a model I'd used before. I pulled up the recording from this morning, starting at eight forty-five and hit Play.

The video showed a surprising amount of foot traffic on the sidewalk for a Sunday morning. A lot of people walked past the camera empty handed and came back a few minutes later carrying bags from the convenience store. Some appeared to be strolling along, enjoying a cool morning.

I figured there was maybe a fifty-fifty chance Aden had walked past the shop, and a slim chance I might see something on the recording that would help explain his disappearance. I studied the video closely, looking for any sign of Aden or anyone or anything suspicious.

At nine-twelve, Aden walked past the shop. I jumped like I'd been electrified and hit the Pause button.

I recognized him immediately from Jana's photo. He wore a HALO T-shirt, shorts, sneakers, and a backpack. He looked very determined and focused, as if his walk had a definite purpose.

"Is that your client's son?" Winchell asked, leaning closer to the screen. "A very serious-looking young man."

"That's him." I used my cell phone to take a picture of the image on the screen, then hit Play.

Aden walked quickly out of the view of the camera. Wherever he was headed, he was in a hurry to get there. I watched the recording for ten more minutes but didn't see anyone who appeared to be following Aden or who set off alarm bells.

I watched the next hour of footage at high speed, but Aden did not walk back past the camera. Winchell watched with me, apparently enjoying the opportunity to play detective.

Finally, I sighed and switched the monitor back to showing the live feed from the cameras. "Thank you for letting me use your system."

"You look disappointed," Winchell said. "Were you hoping the boy's father followed him?"

I was startled by his question until I remembered the ruse I'd used to get him to show me the footage. "I was, actually. If we had some proof, we could take it to the authorities. I'll just have to keep looking, I guess."

"Well, I wish you the best of luck. I'm sorry I couldn't help you." Winchell led me back to the front of the store and raised the hinged counter section for me to pass through. "Feel free to browse around the store before you leave, if you like. Private investigators get a twenty percent discount."

That made me smile. "Well, that *is* a first. I'm pressed for time today, but I'd love to come back sometime when I'm not on the clock and look around. Do you have a card?"

He took one from a holder on the counter and handed it to me. When our fingers brushed, I felt a little tingle of air magic.

He studied me. "Do stop by again sometime," he said earnestly. "I think I have a few things you might find interesting."

"I think you might." I tucked the card into my bag. "Thank you for your help, Mr. Winchell."

"You are most welcome. Have a lovely rest of your day, Ms. Worth." He settled back into his chair behind the counter.

I wove my way through the tables to the front door. It buzzed and unlocked as I approached. I gave Winchell a wave and left the shop.

When we were out on the street, I headed for the convenience store at a brisk walk.

"That shop is full of low-level magic objects," Malcolm said as he floated along beside me. "And he's got a hidden safe in his office with some heavy-duty wards. Makes me think he's got interesting stuff in there. We should check it out when we get a chance."

"I plan to. I think there might be more to nice Mr. Winchell than meets the eye."

I hurried across the parking area to the doors of the convenience store. Around the corner and down the block, I saw the library Aden had claimed to be visiting, where I'd met Sean to hand over the laptop.

I went into the convenience store and spoke to the clerk, giving her basically the same story I'd used with Winchell. She took me in the back to speak to the assistant manager, Margie, who had a dirtbag ex-husband of her own and was more than happy to help. Before I could even finish my explanation of why I wanted to see their recordings from this morning, she'd queued up the video.

Margie put another chair behind the desk so we could sit side-by-side and look at the recordings. The store had nine exterior cameras. Most were focused on the gas pumps and the front door, but the others covered the entirety of the parking area, the sidewalks and streets on both sides, and the rear doors. The video was full color and crystal clear. Hallelujah for store owners worried about shoplifters, robberies, and gas-and-gos.

I knew Aden had passed the antique shop at nine-twelve, but I asked her to start the video at nine, just in case someone was lying in wait at or near the convenience store.

Most of the store's Sunday morning customers seemed to be on foot—local residents buying milk, snacks, lottery tickets, or breakfast. Fuel customers pulled up to the pumps, filled their tanks, and departed. A few people arrived in vehicles to go into the store, but everyone looked like customers and no one seemed to be loitering.

When the little digital clock in the corner read nine-twelve, I started watching for Aden. At the pace he'd been walking when he passed the antique store, he should have been in range of the convenience store's cameras within a minute or two, but minutes ticked by with still no sign of him.

My stomach sank. What if he'd been grabbed between the two stores, out of range of all the cameras? The slight ray of hope I'd felt after seeing him on the camera at the antique store faded.

"Is that the boy?" Margie asked suddenly, pointing at the screen.

I leaned closer. Sure enough, there was Aden, walking slowly into the camera's range from the direction of the antique store. His head was down, looking at something in his hand. A phone. Was he texting someone he intended to meet?

We watched him cross in front of the convenience store, his attention still on the phone. Suddenly, Aden looked up and across the parking lot, toward the opposite street, and waved. He stuck the phone into his bag and hurried toward a dark-colored, two-door car that had pulled to the curb on the far side of the convenience store.

Margie made a little growly sound that reminded me of an angry werewolf. Humans could be fierce too. "Is that the ex-husband's car?"

"No. It belongs to one of his friends' moms," I said, so she wouldn't realize she might be seeing either a kidnapping or a kid running away and decide to call the police.

I leaned over to get a closer look as Aden approached the car and the passenger-side window went down. I couldn't see the driver at all, and none of the other cameras were at a better angle. There didn't appear to be anyone else in the car other than the driver.

After a brief conversation, Aden opened the passenger door and got into the car. The window rolled up and the car pulled away from the curb. It turned left at the intersection and disappeared in the direction of the interstate.

Well, now I knew how and when Aden disappeared, but not why or with whom. "Just so I can set my client's mind at ease, can you run the video back so I can get a picture of the car?" I asked.

We found the best view of the car and I took a photo with my phone, and another of Aden getting into the car. I couldn't see the license plate, but I was pretty sure I could identify the make and model. That wouldn't do us much good unless we had a suspect we could connect with that type of vehicle, but I had visual confirmation that whoever was driving, they had a prearranged rendezvous and Aden got into the car willingly.

I wondered which phone he'd been using to text: the one provided by his mother or the secret phone Garrett had given him. If it was his mother's phone, she would be able to see who he'd been texting, and maybe even the contents of the messages. If it was Garrett's phone, though, he probably wouldn't be able to find out who Aden had contacted, since prepaid phones usually didn't include access to that information.

I sent Jana a text asking her to check her cell phone account and see if Aden had used his phone to call or text anyone in the past day. She replied that she would check and get back with me. I sent Garrett a similar message, and received a text back confirming the prepaid phone account didn't keep records he could access.

I thanked Margie for letting me see the video and headed back toward Jana's house with Malcolm trailing invisibly along beside me.

"It's a shame we couldn't see the driver's face," Malcolm said when we were alone on the sidewalk.

I sighed. "I know, but I'm hoping Jana will recognize the car. Aden waved at the driver, which makes me think he knew who he was meeting."

"Maybe this doesn't have anything to do with Bell after all. I sincerely hope that car doesn't belong to some pedophile." A pause. "Jeez, compared to that, I almost hope it's Bell."

"I hate to say it, but me too."

There didn't seem to be much else to say after that.

MY LEGS WERE sore from all the running I'd done over the weekend and my knees hurt from falling in Sean's garage, but I jogged the rest of the way to Jana's house. The image of that car disappearing out of the camera range with Aden in the passenger seat was more than enough motivation for me to ignore the discomfort.

Jana opened the front door when I was halfway up her driveway. She read my expression and her eyes lit up with hope. "What did you find out?"

I already had my phone out with the picture of Aden walking in front of the antique store. I held it out so Jana could see. "I've got him on video walking in the direction of the library at nine-twelve this morning."

Jana took the phone and stared at the screen as if she was drinking in the sight of her son. Her eyes filled with tears, and she covered her mouth with her hand to muffle a short sob. "But he didn't go to the library."

"No. He was headed to the convenience store on the corner." I swiped the screen to pull up the next photo, which showed Aden crossing the parking area in front of the store with his phone in hand. "It looks like he's texting someone. Did you find out if he sent any texts or made any calls on the phone you gave him in the last day?"

She frowned. "I looked on the account and there weren't any since Friday. How is it possible he's texting in this picture, if it's not showing up on the account?"

Aden must have been using the phone his father had given him, and now I'd have to tell Jana about it. "I'll explain that in a second. I need you to look at this picture." I swiped again, to the photo showing Aden getting into the mystery car. "He was apparently meeting someone at the store. Do you recognize this car?"

She gasped, her reaction part fury, part grief, and part terror. "He got into someone's *car?* I've told him a million times never to get into anyone's car unless I've said it was okay."

"I'm sure you did," I reassured her. "On the video, he waved at the person in the car, then went over to talk to them before getting in. I'm thinking whoever is driving, it's someone he knows. Do you know this car?"

"It's hard to see what kind of car it is." She zoomed in on the car and scrutinized the image. "It looks like it's kind of an older model, doesn't it? Maybe ten or fifteen years old? There's a big dent on the side."

I waited while she thought about it. Finally, she sighed. "I don't know. I'm thinking about everyone we know, trying to remember if any of them drive a car like this."

"Think about it while I look through Aden's room," I suggested.

"Okay. I can do that." Jana opened her front door and led me into the house, which was cluttered and cheerful. I followed her down a short hallway and into Aden's small bedroom.

The kid loved video games, Star Wars, and Pokémon, judging by his bedding, the posters on the walls, and the collectibles on his shelves. He had a small TV and a game system with a stack of games next to it. There was an empty spot on the desk. I wondered if Sean had found anything on Aden's laptop. He probably would have texted or called if he had, so he must still be working on it.

"Other than his backpack, does anything seem to be missing, like a favorite collectible or something like that?" I asked Jana. "Would you be able to tell if he took a change of clothes or any of his toiletries?"

She was instantly angry again. "My son did not run away."

"I'm not saying he did," I said patiently. "But his backpack looked like it had some stuff in it and he met someone at the convenience store and got into their car willingly. Can you see if you notice anything missing?"

She crossed her arms. "What I want to know is how he was texting whoever the hell took him without it showing up on my bill."

I exhaled. "I think I know how that happened, but I don't want to distract you from what you're doing. Remember the most important thing right now is finding Aden."

Her gaze turned flinty. "I need you to tell me right now what's going on."

I told her about my conversation with Aden's father. Since I wasn't sure whether Jana might try to use the information that Garrett had magic against him, I left that part out, but I revealed he'd given Aden a prepaid phone and had been in regular contact with him for the past year. Then I stayed quiet and let her rant and rave about that for a few minutes.

When she paused for breath, I broke in. "Look, Jana, I'll tell you what I told Allan: I'm not here to play mediator or take a side. My job is to find Aden. But something you might want to take into consideration is that Aden has been talking to his dad pretty much every day for a year, and according to you, he's doing great in school and you haven't had any problems with his behavior."

"Are you telling me I shouldn't be angry about this?"

"Nope. I'd be angry too. And I'm the last person to offer anyone parenting advice, so that's all I'm going to say on the subject. You can yell at Allan later, when this is settled and we have Aden back."

"I can't believe he gave Aden a phone," she fumed. "And then Aden used it to talk to whoever is in that car. How do we know he didn't get snatched by someone Preston—sorry, *Allan*—knows?"

"I'm going back to talk to him after I get done here. I'll show him the car. I'm pretty good about reading people. If he recognizes the car or knows something about what happened to Aden, I'll know."

Faint green earth magic sparked on Jana's fingers, a sign she was having trouble containing her anger. "I could just throttle him for this."

"Save it for later," I reminded her. "In the meantime, back to my original question: does it look like anything is missing?"

Still visibly angry, she looked around the room as I searched Aden's desk, checking all the places I would hide something if I wanted to keep my mom from finding it. I didn't know what I was looking for, exactly, so I skimmed all the scraps of paper I found, looking for anything that seemed odd.

Meanwhile, Jana returned from checking the bathroom. "His toothbrush is still on the counter and I don't see any clothes missing," she reported as she sat down on Aden's bed. "I can't swear he didn't take any of his toys with him, but nothing's jumping out at me."

I hadn't seen any obvious gaps on the shelves either, and if there weren't any clothes missing and he'd left his toothbrush, it seemed likely Aden hadn't planned to be away for any length of time. I continued my search while Jana went back to studying the image of Aden getting into the car.

Just as I was starting on his closet, my phone rang. Jana handed it back to me and I answered. "Hey, Sean."

"Hey, Alice." His tone was businesslike. "I've been going through the kid's laptop. He did a good job of clearing the browser history, but I retrieved the information. Are you where you can talk freely?"

"Hold on." I turned to Jana. "I'm sorry—it's a personal call. I'm going to step outside for a moment."

"Go ahead."

Malcolm and I went outside to my car, far enough from the front door that I didn't think I could be overheard. "Okay, I'm outside. What did you find?"

"In the past week, Aden's been searching for anything he could find on Darius Bell." Sean sounded grim. "He's been reading news stories, blogs, and information on the FBI and SPEMA websites about the cabal. He even read a bunch of news stories about Storm Girl and has the video of you controlling the storm bookmarked on YouTube. I hate to say it, but I think Natalie was right—he heard her talking to her teacher about Bell."

I exhaled. "In a weird way, this is almost good news. Obviously, we don't have confirmation Bell has the kid, but if that's the case, Aden is better off with Bell than in the hands of some pedophile. Aden's abilities make him a valuable asset, one that Bell will want to take care of."

"I don't disagree with you, but I hate to think of anyone in the clutches of someone like Bell, especially a kid."

"I know." We were quiet for a moment.

"Why do you think Bell wants all these nulls?" Sean asked me. "What could he be planning?"

I'd been wondering that myself. "It could be a number of things. If Bell was attacked by mages, he could use the nulls for defense. Most nulls have to touch a mage to drain them, but some can form wards, which would mean that any mage who crossed that ward would be nulled and their energy drained into the ward. Considering how much damage Bell's companies have taken from Murphy's attacks over the past few months, that's a likely scenario. If he can get enough nulls who can make wards, he could protect himself better."

"But someone like Aden, who doesn't have those skills?"

I sighed. "Aden's ability to not only drain a mage's power, but also weaponize that energy and offload it in a single blast, makes him more likely to be used as a weapon than for defense."

"Bell's last attempt to take the fight to Murphy didn't accomplish much," Sean pointed out. "If he wanted to use Aden as a weapon, who or what would the target be?"

"It's hard to say." I considered the possibilities. "Catherine and Moses are at the compound in Baltimore, as far as anyone knows. Darren Walker is still here in the city, but he's not one of Murphy's lieutenants; he's a businessman. That doesn't mean Bell won't go after him, but killing Walker won't do much to Murphy's organization. I'm not sure who Bell would go after at this point if he wanted to go on the offense."

"Did you get anything from your canvassing?"

"As a matter of fact, I've got an image of Aden getting into a car at the convenience store down the street from his house. Jana doesn't recognize the car and I can't see the license plate, but it looks like a dark-colored two-door Mazda that's about ten years old and has a large dent on the passenger side. We're looking for the driver of that car."

"Has Jana mentioned the name Ashley Brown to you?"

I frowned. "No. Who is Ashley Brown?"

"I don't know, but Aden was searching for her on social media and online up until yesterday. I'm not sure if he found her or not, or who she is—there are quite a few Ashley Browns in the city."

"I'll ask Jana. Anything else interesting on the laptop?"

"Looks like he recently got a trial membership to that website you use, Magic and Objects of Power, and has been doing a lot of reading on magic, especially nulling."

"That's not surprising. He wants to know more about his abilities. He needed a teacher, not just to be told that he couldn't tell anyone about having magic." I rubbed my forehead. "Jana did the best she could to protect her son, but magic wants out. It itches when you don't use it."

"I'll keep looking and see if anything else jumps out at me. Most of his other searches are the sort of things you'd expect a twelve-year-old boy to look up. He's really into Pokémon, huh?"

I smiled slightly. "You should see his room. It's all Star Wars and video games."

He chuckled. "Sounds like Aden and I would get along pretty well."

"You probably would." I spotted Jana at her front window. "I'd better get back to the house. Let me know if you find anything else."

"I will." A pause. "Be safe."

"I'll do my best." We said our goodbyes and ended the call.

"You know he'd prefer to be here with us instead of home," Malcolm said.

I pretended to still be talking into the phone, so Jana wouldn't wonder why I seemed to be having a conversation with thin air. "I know he would, but I'm not sure Jana would be comfortable with anyone else knowing about her situation."

"Is that why you're keeping him at arm's length? Or is something else going on?"

I frowned. "I'm not sure what you mean."

"Usually when you guys are together, you touch each other constantly. Little nudges or touching hands, stuff like that. Shifters love physical contact, and you've picked that up from Sean. Today when we saw him at the library, you acted like you didn't like him touching you. It's weird, that's all. You mad at him?"

"Now you sound like him," I said, irritated. "No, I'm not mad at him; I'm just focused on finding Aden. Just because I didn't want to have sex behind the library doesn't mean I'm mad about something."

"I'm not talking about sex, Alice. I'm talking about any kind of physical contact."

"Can we please just focus on the missing kid and save all this nonsense for another time?"

I stuck my phone in my pocket and frowned. For a moment, I wondered if Malcolm and Sean were right about me acting oddly, but the feeling faded quickly. We had a lost kid to find. I was focused, that was all. Now was not the time for twenty questions from nosy ghosts or needy werewolves.

I headed back to the house with Malcolm trailing along behind me.

69

# CHAPTER 5

WHEN I GOT TO THE PORCH, JANA OPENED THE DOOR AND STEPPED ASIDE FOR me to enter. Malcolm followed me in and retreated to the living room.

When the door was closed, I said, "I have a colleague looking at Aden's laptop to see what he's been looking up online lately, and a name came up. Do you know anyone named Ashley Brown?"

She frowned. "Ashley was Aden's babysitter for about two years, from when he was about eight until he was ten. After that I let him stay by himself after school before I got home from work. She was a senior in high school and a freshman at the community college at the time. I haven't seen or talked to her since. She'd be twenty or twenty-one now, I think."

"What kind of car did she drive?"

Her eyes widened. "A little two-door, dark blue car. Could that be her at the convenience store picking Aden up?"

"I'm not sure, but I don't believe in coincidences. Do you still have her phone number, by any chance?"

She headed for her laptop, which was sitting on the dining table. "No, but it'll be in my phone records from back then. We called and texted every school day for nearly two years. I just have to find it."

Jana logged into her cell phone account to get the phone number.

"Try calling her," I said. "If she answers, ask if she's seen or talked to Aden lately and then we'll go from there. If she doesn't answer, just leave a message asking her to call you back."

She called the number. After a moment, she said, "It's going straight to voice mail."

"Is it her on the recording?"

She nodded and listened to Ashley's pre-recorded greeting. When it ended, she said, "Ashley, this is Jana Peters. Please give me a call as soon as you get this message." She left her number.

I sent Sean a quick text: *Ashley Brown was Aden's babysitter. Here's her cell number. Can you get me an address?* I sent the number Jana had called.

The response came back almost immediately. *Wolf: Give me a few minutes.*

Jana went back to watching out the window. "I don't know why Aden would have been trying to get in touch with Ashley, or why he would be getting into her car to go somewhere without telling me," she said, peering out through the curtain. "I want to believe there's an explanation for this, like he wanted to surprise me with something and thought maybe Ashley could help him pick it up, but he's been gone too long." She turned to me. "What if they've been in an accident and he's at the hospital and they don't know who he is or how to call me?"

"Why don't you call the hospitals?" I suggested. "We don't want to tip them off that he's missing, so instead of asking about Aden, ask about Ashley."

"That's a good idea." She took out her phone and started looking up numbers.

I used the bathroom while I waited for Sean to text me back. I washed my hands at the sink, soaping all the way up to my elbows. I rinsed, then repeated the washing, scrubbing my arms until they turned pink. I rinsed again and then dried off, scowling at my reflection in the mirror. I really wanted another shower, but that would have to wait until I got back home.

My phone buzzed on the counter. It was a message from Sean with Ashley's full name and address, as well as confirmation that she drove a dark blue fourteen-year-old two-door Mazda. He gave me the license plate and added a note that she had four arrests for prostitution and two for possession of drug paraphernalia.

He also sent her driver's license photo. In that picture, Ashley was cute and blonde, with a big smile and bright blue eyes. A few moments later, he sent a second picture, a mug shot dated one month ago. It took me a moment to realize it was the same person. The Ashley in the mug shot was thin and defiant looking. Her eyes were deeply shadowed and her shoulders looked bony and hunched. The before-and-after contrast between the photos was startling. It looked like Aden's former babysitter was struggling with substance abuse.

The doorbell rang. I sent Sean a quick thank you and headed for the front room.

As I came around the corner, a blast of air magic hit me square in my chest, throwing me back into the wall hard enough to knock the wind out of me. The powerful stream of magic pinned me to the wall like a butterfly on a collector's board. It hurt, but it gave me a moment to figure out what was going on.

The air mage was a brunette woman in a dark suit. She held me in place, her hand raised, palm out to focus her magic. I didn't know her, but I recognized the cold way she studied me, assessing my threat potential with a glance. Everything about her said professional killer.

The enormous blond man with her was evidently the muscle for the operation. He had the same flat affect as the air mage. His eyes were the color of glacier ice and twice as cold. He stood over Jana, who was sprawled on the floor, unconscious. It looked like she'd tried to run toward the hallway before one of them knocked her out, probably with a sleep spell.

"Get the mother," the air mage ordered.

The big man took one step and dropped in a heap, unconscious. I couldn't see my ghost, but I knew he was here. Malcolm with a sleep spell for the win.

Unfortunately, the air mage couldn't be spelled, since high-level mages could resist basic spells with their natural shields, but now it was two against one and I liked those odds a hell of a lot better—especially since my own magic was depleted after getting nulled.

The air mage's concentration wavered when her partner fell, which was the chance I'd been waiting for. I pulled my own air magic to the center of my chest and fired a blast directly into her stream of magic, breaking it and sending her stumbling. She knocked over a small table. A lamp and several knickknacks shattered on the floor.

I landed on my feet and blasted her again, this time with my hands so my aim was more precise. She moved like lightning and dodged the majority of the attack, which probably meant she drank vampire blood regularly to increase her speed and reflexes, like a vampire's enforcer. A mage with enforcer speed and strength was rare. Someone had sent their heavy artillery after Jana. I had a pretty good idea who was behind this attempted kidnapping.

The air mage rolled to a combat stance that indicated she was former military or had equivalent training. She held a pistol with a suppressor in a two-handed grip.

I raised my hands and formed a shield with my air magic, but I wasn't her intended target. Without hesitating, she fired two quick shots into the blond man's head.

I heard a shocked expletive from my left: Malcolm, stunned by the air mage's ruthless method of disposing of her incapacitated partner. It was a move straight out of the cabal playbook: never let yourself or anyone on your team be taken prisoner.

The air mage looked in Malcolm's direction. Most mages could sense ghosts in their vicinity. I didn't like that she seemed to know exactly where he was, however. Either she also had earth or blood magic—which made her more sensitive to ghosts—or she had extrasensory abilities. Who *was* this woman?

The air mage traced a rune in the air and held her left hand palm out toward Malcolm. "*Detego.*"

"No!" I hit her with a blast of air magic, sending her flying, but the blood magic spell she'd unleashed had already hit Malcolm.

The ghost became visible, shrouded in a red haze. The spell wouldn't last long—a minute or two at most—but until it dissipated, Malcolm was visible to everyone, not just me.

The air mage got to her feet. Her smile was even colder than her eyes, and it made the hair stand up on the back of my neck.

"Well, hello there Malcolm," she purred. "We wondered where you were."

Malcolm froze, his face a mask of terror.

Well, if I'd had any doubt as to who'd sent the air mage after Jana, that dispelled it. Malcolm had once belonged to the Bell cabal, and Darius Bell himself had sent Malcolm to be tortured to death by a blood mage. The air mage was one of Bell's henchmen and she knew Malcolm by sight. This was very, very bad and getting worse by the minute.

My fingers itched to send Malcolm to safety in my heavily warded basement, but I had to trust he would jump there on his own if he felt he needed to.

She turned her attention to me. "And you're the mage he's bound to, the one who managed to keep him when we pulled the ghosts back last month. You must be good. He's the only ghost we didn't get back, and he's the one we wanted the most."

She raised her gun and fired three shots before she finished speaking, but I'd sensed her intention and got my air magic shield up. All three bullets were deflected into the wall.

Malcolm flashed over to her and tried to use a razor-thin stream of air magic to cut her in half. She dropped her gun, raised a shield of her own with one hand to block his magic, and slashed at him with a blood magic blade, narrowly missing him. He flitted back to stay out of range of her blood magic and became invisible again as her spell faded.

With her partner dead, the air mage was our only remaining source of information about where Aden was, who had him, and why he'd been taken. As much as I wanted to eliminate the threat she posed to Malcolm, I needed her alive.

She whirled, apparently sensing Malcolm to her left, but he attacked from her right, opening a deep gash across her face, neck, and torso. She tried to slash him with a blood magic blade, but missed.

I flicked out my right hand like I was tossing a pair of dice and bright green earth magic spiraled out of my palm, forming a long whip. While the air mage was distracted by Malcolm, I lashed the coil of bright green fire around her and pulled it taut, caging her and pinning her arms at her sides.

She fought the whip, but the only person who'd ever been able to break it was a vampire and even enhanced by vamp blood, she wasn't strong enough. Her air magic blew papers and small objects across the room but couldn't displace the coils.

When she stilled, I pulled the whip a little tighter. "Answer my questions and you get to live. Where's the kid?"

She laughed. "Are you going to torture it out of me, sunshine?"

For the second time today, I let someone see the darkness in my eyes. "It wouldn't be the first time I've gotten answers that way."

She was still smiling. "I think I like you. What's your name?"

"Where's Aden?"

"Tell me your name and I'll tell you where he is."

Call me cynical, but I didn't think she would keep her word. "Tell me where he is and I'll let you keep your hands." I looped my whip around her wrists.

"Stop it. You're turning me on." She pulled against the loops, making the whip cut into her flesh. Blood ran down her fingers and dripped onto the floor. "You're an amateur at this, I can tell. You should let Malcolm have a turn. Now there's someone who knows about inflicting pain. Isn't that right, Malcolm?" She grinned.

Malcolm's anger and shame was so intense that it bled over to me and left a bitter taste in my mouth.

It was one thing for her to mock me, but I'd be damned if I'd let her torment Malcolm. The longer she stood there, the more likely she would find a way to escape, and I had no doubt she'd kill me the second she had the chance. She was hard, but I could go harder.

I stretched the bright green coil around her left wrist razor-thin and cut off her hand. My cold fire cauterized the stump so she didn't bleed to death.

The severed hand hit the floor with a wet plop. She screamed. Malcolm made a choking sound.

"You've got three more appendages and I can take them one piece at a time," I said as she clenched her jaw, her chest heaving. "If you get to a hospital soon or you've got access to vamp blood, they can probably reattach the hand. The clock's ticking on that, though. Give me a location for the kid and as soon as I get him, I'll let you go."

"I don't believe you'll let me go," she said hoarsely, her face gray. "I'll find you and kill you, and take Malcolm back to Bell."

"Then maybe I'm letting you choose how you leave this world. I can make it quick or I can take my time about it." I tightened the coil around her right wrist. "Give me an address."

"I was wrong about you. You're not an amateur after all." Her mouth twisted into a smile. "I think I'm the second-coldest bitch in this room, and that's not something I get to say very often. We might have been friends someday. It's a shame to kill you."

Her eyes went white. Her body became a vortex and sucked all of the air toward her as if someone had opened the emergency door on a plane.

I'd thought she wasn't powerful enough to break my earth-magic whip, but in that second between the air sucking into her body and the blast, I realized she hadn't really been trying. That whole struggle to escape was pure fakery to make me think she was less powerful than she was. She'd hidden her true ability behind her shields until now, much as I usually did.

I'd already expended a lot of magic in our earlier fight and used more to block her bullets and create the whip, and I hadn't been at anything close to one hundred percent to begin with. What was left of my air magic would do little to protect me against what was about to happen.

Malcolm's terror seared my skin. I wondered if he thought he was about to watch me get blown to smithereens. I had one chance to survive, and it meant revealing a literal ace up my sleeve I hadn't told anyone about, not even my ghost.

I reached for the magic held in the dragon tattoo on my right arm. "*Draco*," I breathed.

The protection spell ignited, displacing the air with a snapping sound like wings unfurling. Magic flared and formed a cocoon around me at the same moment that the blast hit.

The air mage's bomb-like blast of air magic blew my whip apart and made her stagger. The targeted burst propelled me backward at breathtaking speed. My cocooned body blew a hole through the wall behind me and sailed across the kitchen. I hit a second, much sturdier wall, and the impact sent me spinning off into oblivion.

I DRIFTED in and out of consciousness for what seemed like a long time. I was aware on some level of familiar voices, flashes of magic and pain, and movement, but every time I started to break through the fog, the darkness dragged me back under.

When I finally woke, I seemed to be sitting upright and belted into the passenger seat of a car. My first thought was that I felt very, very sick.

"Going to barf," I mumbled, hoping someone would hear me.

The vehicle immediately swerved sharply to the right and screeched to a halt. I heard the sound of a seatbelt unfastening, a door opening and closing, and footsteps running around to my side of the car. Someone opened my door, released my seatbelt, and scooped me up. I couldn't quite get my eyes open yet, but I recognized the feel of Sean's arms and his unmistakable scent as he carried me a few feet before lowering me to my hands and knees on what felt like grass.

I would rather have walked blindfolded across a field of dog poop and broken glass than vomit in front of anyone, even—or maybe especially—Sean, but the situation left me no choice.

He held me up with an arm around my middle as I threw up what little I had in my stomach and then dry-heaved miserably.

A vicious headache made my eyeballs throb and my brain felt like it was filled with sand, a sure sign that someone, presumably Malcolm, had used a healing spell on my head—hence the nausea.

Finally, I got my eyes open and found myself on the lawn of a closed bank a few miles from Jana's house. We were on a side street and mostly hidden from view of passing vehicles by my car, which was parked at the curb with the engine still running and the passenger-side door hanging open.

Sean handed me a couple of paper napkins he'd somehow had the presence of mind to grab from the center console of my car.

I took them gratefully and wiped my mouth. "Sorry," I rasped.

"Please don't apologize," Sean said firmly as I hung my head and concentrated on just breathing. "Malcolm warned me this might happen. It's my privilege to take care of you when you're sick or injured. Plus, I'm so glad you're alive that I'd do this a hundred times over." He pressed a kiss to my hair. "Other than sick, how do you feel?"

Memory returned in a rush. My stomach lurched violently in a spasm that had nothing to do with healing spell-induced nausea. I pushed his arm away. "Where's Jana? *Where's Malcolm?*"

"Malcolm's fine. He drained himself healing you and jumped

back to your basement to regenerate and stay protected behind your wards. I'm sorry, but Jana's gone. Nora Keegan, the air mage from Bell's cabal, took her."

"Oh, no." I struggled to rise despite my dizziness.

Sean started to lift me up. I pushed him back and lurched to my feet. I took a couple of unsteady steps to put some distance between us. "Why didn't Malcolm stop her?"

"There was a third person with them, the driver of their vehicle." Frowning, Sean stayed where he was, giving me some space as I stumbled around on rubbery legs. "Nora had him carry Jana back to their SUV. She held Malcolm back with her blood magic and threatened to discorporate him if he interfered. Since that might kill you outright, he had to let them go. Then he jumped to me to tell me what happened, jumped back to Jana's house, and nearly burned himself out trying to heal you."

I struggled to clear my head and keep up with what he was saying. "So you came to Jana's house to get me?"

"Yes." He crossed his arms. "When I got there, I found a hole blown through the back wall of the house and you lying unconscious and beat to hell in a crater in the backyard. You were wrapped in some kind of glowing magic cocoon and neither of us could get through it. Finally, you opened your eyes, saw us, and broke whatever spell was protecting you before you passed out again."

I didn't remember doing that at all, but obviously I had because the protection spell was gone. I pushed up my sleeve to examine my right bicep.

Sean leaned forward to get a closer look at my arm. "Whoa. What happened to your dragon tattoo? It used to be dark greenish-black and now it looks gray."

Gingerly, I touched the tender skin and winced. "That tattoo held the protection spell that saved my life today."

Sean didn't seem surprised by that news. "I suspected your tattoos hold magic. Sometimes they shimmer. At first I thought it was just a trick of the light, but after a while I realized they weren't just for decoration. Are all of your tattoos magical, or only the dragon?"

"They're all magical," I admitted. "Different purposes, but all magical. I don't use them unless I have no other choice because they require a ton of power and a visit to a mage tattoo artist to regenerate. The dragon was my strongest protection spell, my last line of defense when it's either that or *adiós* Alice."

"But if that was a protection spell around you, why did you get banged up so badly?"

"Even the strongest protection spells have limits. Its job was to keep me alive, not to keep me unscathed. It did what it was supposed to do and that's what counts."

The dragon spell was a version of the protection spell that kept me alive the night I'd escaped from my grandfather's compound five years ago, courtesy of an explosion that blew me through the exterior wall. While everyone assumed I had died, my only real injury had been a broken arm, thanks to the spell.

He glanced at the car. "I want to hear more about it and tell you the rest of what I know from Malcolm, but we need to get moving. I don't want you out in the open like this."

"Let's go to my house." I headed for the car, still a little unsteady. "I need to check on Malcolm and figure out what my next move will be."

Sean went ahead of me to hold the passenger door open while I got in. "I'd rather take you to my house," he said carefully.

I paused with one foot in the car. "Why? The safest place for me to be is my house, with Malcolm, behind my wards."

A muscle moved in his jaw. "The safest place for you to be is with me. Bell and his people know who you are now. They know you have Malcolm and they want him back. Your connection to me and my pack is one of your best protections against them. If they come after you, they're coming after the whole pack and the Were Ruling Council too. Bell would be a fool to do it."

I took my foot back out of the car. "I am not going to cower behind the pack and the Council."

"No one said anything about you cowering." His eyes turned golden. "That was your word, not mine. We stand beside you, not in front of you."

"If I go to your house, it's like I'm hiding out. You'll call on members of the pack to help guard me. That sounds more like cowering to me."

He growled. "If it were me who was threatened by Bell, my pack would join me wherever I was to face the threat. Would you say I was cowering behind them or that they were there to fight at my side?"

"That's not the same thing. The pack recognizes you as their alpha and so does everyone else. They know you stand front and center. I don't have that status. I'll be there to be protected, not to protect and fight."

"What makes you so sure? You know the pack senses your strength and power. Do you think anyone in my pack believes you're a helpless human who needs protecting? Because I don't think so. In fact, I *know* no one sees you that way, not even Jack or anyone else who would prefer my mate be a shifter. You may not be a werewolf, but you are a force to be reckoned with and they know it."

He moved closer, forcing me to take a step back to avoid touching him. "I know you hate needing backup and you don't want anyone believing you're a coward. I think this is more about your aversion to the idea of anyone putting themselves at risk on your behalf. You know you're a target now and you don't want Bell's people coming at me or my pack."

"Of course I don't want to put you in danger," I said, irrationally irritated at how well he understood how my mind worked.

"We're well beyond that now, Alice. Our relationship is not a secret. You are the lover and potential mate of the alpha of the Tomb Mountain Pack. Anyone who comes for you will come for us as well. That's how being part of a pack works. I know you know that— you've been around shifter packs before. You don't want to put us in danger; I get that and I'm grateful for it. But when our pack accepted you as my consort they accepted responsibility for you as well, just as they did the mates and spouses of other members of the pack. You're my partner, in good times and bad, in peace and in war."

My shoulders sagged. "I'm sure your people didn't think they might be facing a cabal when they made that decision."

"Give them more credit than that," he said gently. "I promise you it was discussed. I won't say no one voiced concerns, but very few pack members even balked at the prospect. Those who did, did so based on their preference that I date a shifter, not because of possible cabal conflicts. We aren't afraid of Bell or his people, Alice."

I'd always known I might bring danger to the pack's doorstep because of my grandfather, but the Storm Girl incident had turned that distant threat into an immediate danger and doubled it by putting me in the crosshairs of not one but *two* cabals. I didn't doubt Sean's word that the pack had taken possible cabal conflicts into consideration when discussing me, but it was difficult for me to accept that they were willing and able to face that kind of danger on my behalf. Since Moses murdered my parents when I was eight, no one had ever been willing to do that until Sean and Malcolm entered my life. Even now, knowing they would and had fought for and with me, I found it hard to accept. Twenty years of cabal captivity left deep scars.

Sean must have sensed the little stab of pain thinking about the cabal caused. His face softened. "I'm going to ask you a question. I want you to really think about your answer and be honest with both of us. Where do you feel safer: at home behind your wards or at my side?"

When it really came down to it, that was the question at the crux of my internal debate over moving in with Sean. The argument in my head wasn't really about the size of our shared space or whether I'd struggle to get used to pack members always coming and going and feeling the alpha's home was also their den. The real question was, if my home was where I felt safest, was that behind the wards I'd spent the last five years building, or with the alpha werewolf who'd made a place for himself in my heart?

Not long ago, my immediate answer would have been behind my wards. I wouldn't have even had to think about it. My home was my fortress—a fortress of solitude, Sean had called it once, half-jokingly, comparing it to Superman's famous lonely lair. My house was the first thing that was ever truly *mine* after I escaped from my grandfather. After being a prisoner in his compound for twenty years, I felt that I had to have my own home if I was to ever have a chance at finding out who I was. I'd lived under his rule for almost my entire life. My home was my own compound in a way, where I made my own rules and took the first cautious steps toward making a new life for myself.

I opened my mouth to say I felt safest in my home, then closed it. I thought about how I felt when I was next to Sean, whether it was cooking dinner at his house, sleeping in his bed, or walking down the street—all activities far from my house and its wards. Didn't I feel safe at his side? Had I ever felt afraid when we were together, unless it was fear for him?

Sean watched me, his frown deepening. "Are you all right? Are you still hurt?"

I realized I'd wrapped my arms around my abdomen and hunched over. I couldn't tell if it was still nausea from the healing spell, my worry about Sean and his pack being pulled into my conflict with Bell's organization, the question Sean had asked me, all three, or something else entirely.

"I'm still sick to my stomach," I admitted. I took a deep, shaky breath. "I feel safe in my home, behind my wards, but I also feel safe when I'm with you. You want me to say where I feel safer and I can't, not right now. If you and your pack are in danger as a result of me or my actions, then my place is with you and them, to fight back."

He smiled. "That's an honest answer I can live with. Let's swing by your house so you can pick up what you need and then we'll figure out what the next step is." He reached for my hand.

My stomach cramped painfully. I winced and avoided him, lowering myself gingerly into the passenger seat. He shut my door and hurried around to the driver's side.

As he pulled away from the curb, I noticed my messenger bag in the back seat and my phone in the cup holder. "Thanks for grabbing my bag and phone. What else did you find in the house when you got there, besides the hole in the wall?"

"A demolished living room and a second Alice-sized hole through the living room wall," he said dryly. "Assorted bullet holes and broken furniture. Also a pile of ash in the shape of a human body, which was all that was left of the man Nora Keegan shot. Malcolm said she torched his body with a burner spell before she left. She shot her own partner?"

"Rather than risk leaving him behind as a prisoner, yeah. Malcolm put him to sleep, so he went from asset to liability."

"And so she disposed of him without a second thought." He sounded grim. "Malcolm told me a little about this Nora Keegan. Apparently, she's one of Bell's top lieutenants."

That news didn't surprise me. Someone with those skills and psychopathic tendencies would move quickly up the ranks in a cabal. "I'm guessing she's who Bell sends out when he needs to make an example of someone, or when he needs something done and doesn't want to worry about whether it gets done right."

He paused. "Malcolm also said she was there when he died."

If I'd had a lick of magic left, it would have flared. I clenched my fists. "Was she the blood mage who killed him?"

He shook his head. "No, but she was an enthusiastic witness."

I had to take several deep breaths to calm myself. "The next time I see her, she's dead."

"Malcolm told me what you did to try and get information about Aden." He glanced at me. "For the record, I didn't find a hand. Apparently, she took it with her."

I made a face. "Damn it. She'll probably get it reattached. Hey, what about your truck? Did you leave it there?"

"I asked Ben to get it and drive it back to my house. I thought it was more important to get your vehicle out of the area."

"Thanks." I wrapped my arms around my stomach and wondered why the nausea and abdominal pain from the healing spell hadn't abated.

Several times during the drive to my house, Sean started to put his hand on my leg or arm, but after I leaned away slightly each time he stopped trying to touch me.

As we turned onto my street, he said, "You don't want me to touch you right now while you're feeling sick and worried, is that it?"

That seemed like as reasonable of an explanation as anything. I nodded and rubbed my stomach.

"You're more anxious than I've ever seen you, I think." He turned into my drive and parked in front of the carport. "I can't tell you not to worry, but try not to let it make you sick or want to push me away. I won't crowd you, but you've been avoiding touching me since we got back from brunch and it's making me uneasy." He turned off the car and faced me. "Just tell me if there's more to it than the case and you not feeling well."

"It's just the case and my tummy acting up." I opened my door and got out. At least my legs were steady and my hands had stopped shaking. Now if my stomach would stop churning, I would be a lot less miserable. "Let me pack a bag or two and grab Malcolm and we'll be ready to go."

Sean followed me to the front door and waited as I unlocked it. We went inside, passing through wards keyed to let us come and go freely but would incapacitate or kill anyone else who tried to cross them.

The familiar sensation of my house wards was like a warm blanket and suddenly I couldn't think of anything I wanted to do more than take a hot shower and curl up in my bed. Rest wasn't on the agenda, however—not even close. I sighed, my shoulders drooping.

Sean shut the door and locked it. "Let me know what I can do to help, okay? Don't overdo it right now. You won't be helping anyone if you act like a hard-ass because of your pride."

I snorted and rubbed my queasy stomach ruefully. "Nice bedside manner."

"You want coddling, find yourself a candy striper," he said with a smile. "I'm a werewolf. We tend to call it like we see it." He gestured toward the stairs that led to the second floor and my bedroom. "Now, Miss Magic, let's get your stuff and your ghost and get gone."

# CHAPTER 6

I STILL FELT DIRTY FROM LAST NIGHT'S WALLOW IN THE MUD AND NOW I WAS covered in drywall dust and dirt, so I showered and scrubbed myself from head to toe before dressing quickly and braiding my wet hair.

I already had some stuff at Sean's house, so I didn't need much. I filled one suitcase with clothes and put a few personal items and toiletries in a duffel bag. Sean carried them out to the car as I made my way slowly down the stairs, using the handrail and the opposite wall for support.

The exertion left me wobbly, but I had to go down to the basement to get my magic supplies and fetch Malcolm. My basement, protected by heavy-duty wards of its own, contained my library and my magic workshop.

I declined Sean's offer to carry me down the basement stairs, since I was clinging to the shreds of dignity I had left after barfing in front of him. He carried a second suitcase and followed me down, his hand outstretched and ready to grab me at the first sign of trouble.

I couldn't understand why him being close by made me itch between my shoulder blades. It was probably part of my new anxiety about Bell and the threat his cabal represented to the pack.

I packed the second suitcase full of magic-related items, including some blood magic implements. I wasn't sure what I might need to find and rescue Jana and Aden, so I took anything I thought might come in handy. Transporting those illegal items was moderately risky, but when did I ever do anything that wasn't at least moderately risky?

As Sean carried my second suitcase upstairs and stowed it in the car, I turned my attention to what to do with Malcolm. I thought about just taking the ghost with me in the crystal he'd jumped into from Jana's house, but it didn't have the kind of heavy-duty protection and containment spells that the one on my bracelet did. Mine would protect him from any attempts to recall him and only I could release him from it, unlike the one he was in, from which he could come and go freely. The safest option was to boot him out of his crystal, let him know what was going on, and then stash him in mine. I needed to get him somewhere where he could safely regenerate his magic.

When I picked up the medium-sized blue crystal from the work table, it buzzed faintly against my palm. That told me Malcolm was inside and still low on energy. *"Release."*

Malcolm appeared next to me. "Hey," I said, relieved to see him.

Instead of responding, he drifted back from me, saying nothing.

Worried, I put the crystal back on the table. "What's wrong?"

"What's *wrong?* How can you ask me that?" he demanded. Despite his diminished energy, his anger buzzed on my skin.

I rubbed my face. "Malcolm, I feel like I've been run over by a fleet of trucks, so you're going to have to explain what you're upset about because I am just not capable of figuring it out right now."

"I just watched you cut someone's hand off and threaten to take her apart *piece by piece.* Believe it or not, I find that pretty damn upsetting." He flitted in place, an indication of how furious he was.

The basement door opened and closed and Sean came downstairs. "Did you get Malcolm relocated?"

The ghost and I stared at each other. "Not yet," I said finally.

Sean frowned. "What's wrong?"

I sighed. "Malcolm doesn't think my actions at Jana's were justified—specifically, what I did to Nora."

Sean's frown deepened. He turned toward where I was looking and addressed Malcolm. "Nora Keegan had knowledge of Aden's whereabouts. She would have killed Alice and taken you to Bell if given the chance. What would you have wanted Alice to do, other than what she did?"

"I wasn't going to let her walk out of there, not after she recognized you," I added. "She was a dead woman already, as far as I was concerned. I figured I might as well do everything in my power to find out where Aden is."

"You told Nora it wouldn't be the first time you'd gotten answers by torturing someone," Malcolm said hotly. "How could you do that after what you've been through?"

I was taken aback by Malcolm's ire until I realized that seeing me hurt Nora had probably triggered some very traumatic memories for him. Even so, I was angry and tired of being berated. "You know *where* I was when I was being tortured? In the hands of a cabal, which is where Aden is *right now*. When I was twelve, they were already cutting me up and burning me to get me to do what they wanted. I wasn't much older than Aden the first time they stripped skin off my back."

Sean reached out to touch my arm, but I didn't want comfort. I sidestepped him and put my hands on my hips. "We don't have the luxury of a moral high ground here, not when we're dealing with monsters like Bell and the people who work for him. If you think Aden's age protects him from the same kind of suffering we went through, think again. Bell is more than capable of doing all of that and more to Aden if he thinks it will make him compliant. They don't look at young mages as kids; they see them as assets. An asset only has value as long as they're of use, as evidenced by Nora's dead partner, Mr. Double-Tap."

Malcolm and I eyed each other.

I rubbed my arms. "Look, I know you're angry, but we have to put a bookmark here for now. I need to put you in my bracelet for the drive over to Sean's house. You'll regenerate faster that way and be safer in case they try to recall you with some kind of magic we don't know about."

He sighed. "I understand, but let me just say this: I don't think the moral high ground is a luxury—it's a necessity. Our morals are what make us different from them. I'm not saying we shouldn't do what's necessary to protect ourselves and the people we care about, because I'm not that idealistic. I'm not sure cutting off her hand was necessary and I think you did it just a little too easily. You're better than that."

"After all the suffering she's inflicted on people and the enjoyment she got from watching them torture you to death, what's your justification for making me the bad guy here?"

"You're not the bad guy, but two wrongs don't make a right. Nora is a monster and maybe she deserves to die. I could accept that as justice. But taking someone apart piece by piece isn't justice. It's sadistic and it's wrong. I know that's not the person you want to be."

"She knew where Aden is," I pointed out.

"Maybe she did, maybe she didn't, but she wasn't going to tell you no matter what you did. Unlike you and I, she doesn't work for her boss under duress; she works for him because she *likes* it. She's one of his best lieutenants and she takes a lot of pleasure in her work. I'm sure you knew people like that in the cabal you belonged to."

I certainly had known a lot of people like Nora. Most of my grandfather's lieutenants were sadistic psychopaths eager to inflict pain and suffering on command. Worst among them was Carter Kade, who'd enjoyed watching torture in general and mine in particular. Next to Moses himself, Kade was the person from the Murphy cabal I most wanted dead, and preferably not in any quick or merciful way.

I took a deep breath and exhaled. "All right, you've said your piece and maybe some of it makes sense, but here's where *I* stand. I'm going to get Aden and Jana back from Bell because I know what happens to mage kids who belong to a cabal. They end up dead like you, or they turn into people like me and Nora. If that means I have to slice-and-dice my way through some bad people, I'm prepared to do that because Aden deserves to have a better life than you and I have had. You don't have to like my methods, but I'm going to need your help to get him and his mother out and I want to know that I can count on you to have my back."

"Of course I have your back," Malcolm said, exasperated. "Let's just try to get him back without severing any more appendages, okay?"

I rubbed my arms, which were itchy, I supposed from the hot shower I'd taken. "I'm not making any promises, but I'll try."

Sean was getting antsy. "We need to go."

"You ready?" I asked the ghost.

He nodded. "Don't go up against anyone without me."

"I won't," I promised. "*Contain*."

Malcolm vanished. The green crystal on my bracelet buzzed.

Sean sighed. "I'm sorry Nora put you in that position, Alice. I don't have any issue with what you did, but I wish to hell you hadn't had to do it. I agree with Malcolm on one point: I know that's not the person you want to be."

"It might not be the person I want to be, but it might just be the kind of person I am," I said quietly.

"I don't believe that for one minute," he stated. "But we'll argue about it another time."

Sean followed me as I slowly climbed the stairs. He turned off all the main floor lights except the one in the foyer.

When we heard vehicles out front, Sean went to the window next to the front door and pulled the curtain aside. "Three SUVs just parked in front of the house," he reported. "No one has gotten out, but I think we both know who they work for."

An icy calm settled over me. "I'm all packed and ready to leave. Let's go."

He didn't argue. I turned the deadbolt and opened the front door. We stepped out on the porch.

The rear doors of the first and third SUVs opened as we walked down the front steps. Four people—three men and a woman—exited the vehicles and took up positions on either side of the back door of the middle SUV. I wondered who was in the center SUV. No doubt Nora was still out of commission getting her hand put back on, so it was probably another of Bell's lieutenants.

I wasn't surprised they'd shown up, but the big show of force was unexpected. Was it just posturing, or did they intend to say to hell with pissing off the pack and the Were Ruling Council and try and capture me?

Sean's eyes glowed bright gold. He radiated alpha power as we crossed the yard and stopped just inside the perimeter wards. They were currently dormant except for the spellwork that alerted Malcolm and me when someone crossed them, but they could be activated instantly.

The rear door of the second SUV opened and Darius Bell stepped out.

I'd never seen him in person, but I recognized him. Judging by the surge of tension I sensed from Sean, he did too. I kept my face carefully neutral, as if the heads of crime syndicates routinely made stops at my house.

His escorts stayed with the SUV as Bell stood on the sidewalk. We studied each other. He was in his late forties and African American. He wore a button-up shirt with the sleeves rolled up and suit pants—no tie or jacket. His watch probably cost more than my car. The overall effect was a businessman relaxing after a long day at the office, or wherever he was holed up now, with his compound and several of his businesses destroyed.

Bell was a high-level air and blood mage, though he rarely used his magic, preferring to leave that to mages who worked for him. He was attractive if tall, muscular, and murderous was your thing. There were fan sites devoted to him. I didn't understand the appeal myself. When I looked at him, all I saw was hard, soulless eyes and expensive clothes and cars bought with people's lives.

I didn't wait for him to speak first. "We were just about to leave."

"I can see that." His voice was very deep. "I don't intend to keep you long. I'm on my way to a dinner meeting."

"What brings you to my door?"

He stuck his hands in his pockets, feigning a casual pose. It was meant as an insult; he wanted to give the impression he considered me perfectly harmless. The number of escorts he'd brought indicated quite the opposite. "Curiosity. Nora speaks so highly of you. I thought I must meet the person who made such an impression on my lieutenant. She sends her regards, by the way, and hopes to see you again soon."

"I'm also hoping our paths cross again." I smiled slightly. "I have to *hand* it to her—she got the best of me today, but things might turn out differently next time."

Bell chuckled. "You might be interested to know she said much the same thing to me." He glanced at Sean. "Mr. Maclin. I trust you're feeling no ill effects from the mishap with the shifter relic a few weeks ago?"

"None whatsoever," Sean said coldly.

I wasn't surprised Bell knew about the cuff that had attached itself to Sean and nearly killed him. Bringing it up was his way of demonstrating he had insider information about the pack. It was a subtle threat. Everyone was being so very polite. I wondered when the gloves would come off.

"We need to leave. Have you satisfied your curiosity?" Sean asked.

I sensed a rise in magic from Bell, an indicator that he was irritated. "For the most part. I also came to present an offer to Ms. Worth."

I shook my head. "I'm sure I'm not interested in any offer you might make."

"Even so, do hear me out." He tilted his head. "Your presence at Jana Peters's home today leads me to believe she hired you to look for her son. Some of my associates think your interference makes you a problem that needs fixing."

Beside me, Sean tensed. Shifter magic rose and crackled along my skin.

Bell kept his gaze on me. "At the moment, I'm inclined to see this as an opportunity for both of us. I feel quite certain you and I are destined to have a mutually beneficial arrangement in which you, Mr. Maclin's pack, and your ghost remain safe, and you profit handsomely in return for performing the occasional magical feat on my behalf."

"I'm just a mid-level earth and air mage, Mr. Bell," I said, raising my hands, palms up. "You have people like Nora working for you who are far more powerful than me. I'm not capable of any feats, magical or otherwise." The masking spells in the stars tattooed on my left side hid my true level of power and made me feel like a mid-level mage to anyone with magic.

"Please don't insult my intelligence by playing dumb." Bell's expression hardened. "You're registered as such, but no mid-level mage would have been able to kill the blood mage tasked with recalling Malcolm. I have a good idea of what you're capable of, yet you work as a mage PI for a pitiful wage when you should be rewarded for your power and skills. Your abilities make you a valuable commodity."

My stomach lurched at his categorization of me as a commodity. That was all I'd been when I belonged to Moses. When I'd escaped his cabal, I'd sworn I would die before I'd let myself be treated that way again.

"I'm not a commodity and I'm not for sale to anyone at any price," I stated. "You think you have an idea of what I'm capable of? You talked to Nora, so you know what she thinks of me. You've had a chance to form your own opinion in the past five minutes." I spooled just enough blood magic for my eyes to glow. Beside me, Sean fixed his own bright stare on Bell. "You have no idea what I'm capable of, Bell. And while you're thinking about that, you might want to look behind you." I gestured at the street.

He glanced to his left. Four black Vampire Court SUVs cruised through the stop sign at the corner and turned onto my street. Several of Bell's security team exchanged glances as the motorcade glided to a stop in front of my house, forming a barricade around Bell's vehicles.

Bell raised an eyebrow. "Did you summon them?"

I smiled. "I didn't have to." Let him chew on that.

The rear door of the lead vehicle opened and Ezekiel Monroe emerged. He was Valas's daytime representative and arguably the most powerful human associated with the Vampire Court. Monroe appeared to be in his mid-forties, but rumor had it his age was closer to twice that. Drinking vampire blood regularly—especially the blood of one of the oldest and most powerful vampires in the nation, if not the world—had effects not dissimilar to the mythical Fountain of Youth. As always, he wore a tailored suit, his blond hair loose around his shoulders.

To my surprise, Bryan Smith, Charles's head enforcer, stepped out of the second SUV. The entire vehicle moved when he got out. Bryan was the size of a small mountain. He joined Monroe as he strode up the sidewalk toward us. A half dozen black-clad enforcers followed them.

Bell held his ground as they approached. "Monroe, you're a long way from Northbourne Manor."

"Bell," Monroe acknowledged him, standing to my right with Bryan behind him. "You're a long way from the sewer."

To my surprise, Bell chuckled with what sounded like genuine amusement. "What brings you to this part of town?" His tone indicated exactly what he thought about my neighborhood. It was a petty insult, which told me he was more thrown by Monroe's arrival than he'd let on. Point to Monroe.

"On behalf of Madame Valas, we came to personally present an invitation to Ms. Worth for an event at the Manor." Monroe took a red envelope from his interior jacket pocket. Bryan took it from him and brought it to me. The front bore my name in shiny gold leaf. Fancy.

Bell glanced at the four SUVs parked strategically around his own and the six enforcers flanking Monroe and Bryan. "This seems like overkill for delivering an invitation. One would think a simple courier would suffice."

"Ms. Worth is a valued associate of the Court and a personal favorite of Madame Valas," Monroe said smoothly, putting a bit of emphasis on *personal favorite*. "It was very important that we deliver the message without delay to ensure there are no misunderstandings."

Bell seemed to be weighing Monroe's words. If my status as Sean's consort wasn't enough to hold Bell off, being named a favorite of the head of the Vampire Court should buy me some time. Even if Bell was willing to take on the pack and the Were Ruling Council, only an idiot—and a suicidal one at that—would cross Valas and the Court.

Bell's eyes went to Sean. Perhaps Monroe had designated *me* as off-limits, but he'd said nothing about Sean, the pack, or Malcolm. Maybe Bell couldn't come straight at me for the time being, but he was clearly thinking that I might have other vulnerabilities.

Sean's thoughts must have mirrored mine. He took a step toward Bell, his eyes shining like golden lanterns. "The Were Ruling Council is aware of the situation," he said, which was news to me. He must have reported today's events either before I woke up or while I was packing my suitcases. "Alice is my consort and a pack associate. The Council and the pack stand with her in all matters, and she with us. No one here is for sale, Bell, least of all Alice."

Silence.

It wasn't exactly a standoff, but it was close enough to remind me of the final tense showdown among the three main characters in *The Good, the Bad, and the Ugly*, which Sean and I had watched together just last week.

I wondered if any of my neighbors had spotted our sidewalk tête-à-tête and if so, what they were thinking. If anyone recognized Bell, they'd probably call the cops. The odds of police coming to confront the city's most powerful crime boss were slim to none. The feds would come, though, if for no other reason than to see what or who had caused Bell to pop his head out after staying in hiding for several weeks.

Bell must have been thinking the same thing. He smiled and checked his watch. "I'd love to stay and continue this conversation, but I'm already late for my dinner engagement. Are we still meeting tomorrow evening for drinks at Luciano's, Ezekiel?"

Monroe gave him a nod. "Eight o'clock."

Bell turned to Sean. "A pleasure meeting you, Mr. Maclin. And an honor to make your acquaintance, Ms. Worth." He smiled. "You certainly make an impression. Do give my offer fair consideration. I'd prefer us to be partners rather than adversaries."

"I don't recall an offer of partnership," I said. "Besides, I've already given you my answer."

"Then I can only hope you reconsider. In either case, you'll be hearing from me again soon."

With that threat hanging in the air, Bell returned to his SUV. He opened the rear passenger door, gave me a last glance, and got in. When everyone was back in their vehicles, the lead Court SUV moved to let Bell's caravan depart.

As they turned the corner at the end of the street and disappeared, I turned to Monroe. "Either you have the world's best timing or you got a tip-off Bell was headed this way."

He smiled. "It was, in fact, a little of both, though it's been said the minions of vampires have the devil's own luck." He grew serious. "You appear quite diminished, if I may say so without insulting you too much. The Court offers its assistance in your recovery." He reached into his jacket pocket and withdrew a small stoppered black vial with runes etched into the glass. He held it out to me. "Madame Valas left instructions that we provide this to you whenever it might be needed."

Beside me, Sean went very still. I hadn't told him that I'd asked Valas for her help to save his life when he'd been trapped in the cuff or that I'd had to make a deal to secure her assistance. Being called her *personal favorite* and now Monroe's offer of her blood, the value of which was beyond reckoning, was likely to lead to some pointed questions later. Damn it.

"Thank you, but that's not necessary," I said. "I already healed myself from what happened earlier. I'm just tired."

He continued to hold the vial out. "My instructions are to ensure your ability to defend yourself is in no way compromised. If I permit you to decline this offer of healing and you're injured or killed as a result, I'll be held accountable."

I had no doubt that was true, but he'd willingly accepted that kind of responsibility when he became Valas's daytime representative and I didn't feel obligated to drink her blood to keep his ass out of the fire. Doing so would allow her to have influence over me, and who knows what other consequences there might be. I had no idea what kind of magic Valas had and she was extremely powerful, so drinking her blood might turn me into her puppet. Hell, for all I knew, she might be able to use me to influence Sean and the rest of the pack through their bonds.

"You can assure Valas when she wakes that I'm fine, or that I will be," I assured him. "Drinking her blood when all I need is coffee and some sleep would be like going to the ER with a paper cut. I appreciate the concern, though."

He returned the vial to his pocket. "Very well. I'll pass along your response."

I waved the red envelope. "Is this a real invitation, or a convenient excuse for showing up at my house?"

Monroe smiled. "It's quite real. Next week, we will welcome Elizabeth, head of the Chicago Court, and her entourage. Madame Valas and the rest of the Court will celebrate her visit with a gala event. Your presence is requested. You may, of course, bring Mr. Maclin as your escort." He gave Sean a nod. "We've opened an account for you at a dress shop to provide attire for both you and your guest. Their card is in the envelope."

My eyebrows shot up. "I didn't know the Chicago Court planned to visit. That's a rare event."

"The plans have been kept confidential for security reasons, as you might expect," he said. "Hence the rather last-minute invitation, for which I apologize."

There was no point asking why Elizabeth was coming for a visit; the vamps wouldn't share that information with outsiders. Instead, I asked about something else that was bugging me. "So, drinks with Bell tomorrow evening, huh?"

Monroe smiled mirthlessly. "Moses Murphy's aggressive attempt to establish a foothold in the city has made for strange bedfellows."

"The Court is backing Bell against Murphy?" Hoo boy. That wasn't surprising, but my brain started spinning in circles thinking about how that might affect things. "Enemy of my enemy, and all that?"

"It doesn't make us friends. We are uneasy allies, what you might call 'frenemies,' at least in the matter of Murphy's attacks on the city." Monroe shook his head. "Perhaps it's an exercise in futility to argue that one cabal leader is better than another, but Bell is the devil we know."

Moses was the devil *I* knew, and I certainly didn't want him anywhere near my city. The sooner Bell and the Court put an end to his campaign to take over Bell's interests here, the better.

He glanced at my house. "You are now a target of Bell's organization. As a valued associate of the Court you will have a protective detail, and you are invited to move into an apartment in Northbourne Manor. Mr. Maclin is welcome to join you, if he desires."

I shook my head. "Thanks for the offer, but I decline the protective detail. Sean and his pack stand with me."

Monroe didn't look surprised by my refusal. "When she wakes, Madame Valas may insist you accept our protection."

"Alice's safety is my primary concern," Sean said. He'd stayed quiet, letting me take the lead in my conversations with Bell and Monroe, but the prospect of Valas "insisting" on anything related to my safety brought an end to his silence. "I appreciate the Court's concern, but Alice is not an employee of the Court. She accepted your protection against Kent Stevens because his escape from custody was a direct result of a botched Court operation, but this is a matter arising from one of Alice's cases. The Court has no authority to force her to accept a protection detail from you. My attorney can confirm that, if you wish."

Like most of the Vamp Court's daytime reps, Monroe was a lawyer. "Legally speaking, you are correct," he said. "But Madame Valas's concern for Ms. Worth's wellbeing is likely to supersede her concern for following the law." In other words, go cite legalities somewhere else.

"As my consort, she has the support of our pack and the Were Ruling Council. More to the point, she is more than capable of defending herself, as you well know," Sean said.

"Besides, you just called me not only a Court associate but also a personal favorite of Valas," I pointed out. "Bell's not stupid or desperate enough to come after me and jeopardize losing the Court's support against Murphy, much less risk pissing Valas off. She'd eat him for breakfast and he knows it."

"I tend to agree with you on that point," Monroe said. "However—"

I sighed. "If I think I need the Court's help with Bell, I'll let you know. Right now, I don't think it's necessary."

He gave me a nod. "I will share your perspective with Madame Valas. In the meantime, do you intend to stay in your own home or with Mr. Maclin in his?"

"With Sean." My stomach cramped and I wrapped an arm around my abdomen. Blasted healing spell. I wondered what Malcolm had done differently this time for it to still be making me sick hours later. "Though I'm in the middle of a case, so I probably won't be at the house all that much."

"I sincerely hope Mr. Bell takes our warnings seriously and opts to avoid causing you trouble, but should he become an immediate threat, do contact us immediately. In the interim, perhaps it would be prudent to avoid crossing paths with his lieutenants."

I didn't comment on that, since I had every intention of crossing paths very soon with one of his lieutenants in particular.

The corners of Monroe's mouth turned up, indicating he knew very well what I was thinking. "We'll let you be on your way." He glanced at Bryan, who'd stood silently at his side since their arrival. "Will you be returning with me to Northbourne or rejoining Mr. Vaughan at his home?"

"I'll go to Mr. Vaughan's residence," Bryan rumbled. "I need a moment with Ms. Worth before I leave."

Monroe returned to his SUV and three of the four Vamp Court vehicles departed.

As they disappeared around the corner, I turned to Bryan. "What's up?"

Bryan's expression was grim. "What do you know about the stone Mr. Vaughan purchased at the auction you attended together?" he asked without preamble.

I blinked. "The Tepes stone? Only what I read on the Magic and Objects of Power database since Charles was so damn cagey about it. The MOP website's records on vampire objects of power aren't very extensive. The one Charles bought at the auction—assuming it's the same one I found described on the website—was once part of Vlad Tepes's collection of vampire objects of power, but it probably dates back at least a couple hundred years prior to Tepes's reign in Romania. Its primary purpose is as a weapon, from what I understand, allowing its bearer to drain the life energy from a victim, whether that be a human, a shifter, or a vampire. The problem is keeping the stone can come at a pretty high cost." I studied him. "Why do you ask?"

The enormous enforcer seemed to be debating what to say. "Mr. Vaughan is...not well," he said finally.

Beside me, Sean growled softly. "Define 'not well,'" I said.

Bryan lowered his voice. "He's dying."

His words hit me like a punch in the stomach. "*What?* Why the hell hasn't anyone done anything to help him?"

"There are few people who are experts in vampire objects of power, and they have been consulted. Several mages who work for the Court have examined him but could do nothing. The stone has become...poisonous. I don't know of a better word to describe what it's doing. It's like he's dying from the inside, and every night it's worse. For the past three days, I haven't been sure when he retires in the morning if he'll rise again at sunset."

In all the years I'd known him, I'd never seen Bryan this worried. "Why did no one call me?"

"He forbade it."

I blinked. "What? Why?"

"He didn't say."

"So you're telling me this against his orders?"

He nodded.

Well, shit. If I hadn't already believed the situation was dire, that clinched it. I glanced at the sky. "Sunset is in what, a little over two hours? I'll be there. Will he see me?"

"I'll see that he does."

"You know that disobeying his orders could be bad for you, even if it's in an attempt to save his undead life?"

"As far as I'm concerned, I have no choice." He studied me. "He hasn't been the same since his walk in the sun. He's changed, become morose. I'd almost go so far as to say he wants to die, or at least he's not fighting it."

I'd gotten Charles involved in my search for a spelled cup that allowed a vampire to walk in daylight for one hour. He'd used the cup—against everyone's advice, including mine. By the end of the walk, the daytime excursion had turned from a miraculous event to a source of torment. He'd rediscovered the pleasure of feeling human, only to have it taken away. Though he'd made the decision to use the cup, I had made it possible, and now I felt at least partly responsible for his mental state.

"I'll see you at sunset," I said.

Bryan gave Sean a nod. "Mr. Maclin. Miss Alice." He started to leave, then paused. "Thank you."

I shook my head. "Don't thank me unless I can figure out a way to save him."

"Thank you for agreeing to try. I know you're still angry about the cuff, so this can't have been an easy decision for you."

"Actually, it *was* easy." I shrugged. "Charles saved my life after I was stabbed by Amelia Wharton and again when Kent Stevens shot me. I'm squaring our account—or at least, I hope to square it."

"I'll be seeing you later, then." He headed to the remaining SUV and got in. The vehicle pulled away from the curb and accelerated down the street.

"You and your ledgers," Sean said as we watched the vehicle turn and disappear around the corner. His tone was light, but tension rolled off him in waves.

"I burned the list of the things I thought I owed you for," I reminded him, heading for my car. "Vamps keep ledgers too, you know, and they're a hell of a lot more aware of who owes whom. Charles has saved me twice. Maybe the Kent Stevens shooting was a direct result of the Vamp Court's decision to change their plans at the last minute, but I still feel like I owe him for saving me after Amelia Wharton stabbed me. Call it irrational and maybe it is after everything he's done, but I want to settle that debt so it doesn't bother me anymore."

"Notice I'm not telling you that I don't want you to go." He got into the driver's side of my car as I lowered myself gingerly into the passenger seat. "Nor did I say your feelings were irrational. I *am* concerned that Bryan ignored Vaughan's orders, which means Vaughan is going to be angry when you show up at his house at the vampire equivalent of the crack of dawn, intending to get involved. Depending on how much his condition has deteriorated, he may not be entirely rational, and that makes him more dangerous than usual."

He turned the key in the ignition. "Not to mention you need sleep, Alice. You look absolutely exhausted. Maybe you can nap at my house before we go."

"Maybe." I *was* tired, but too much had happened for me to be able to sleep anytime soon. I'd cut someone's hand off, been thrown through not one, but *two* walls, lost Jana, puked in front of Sean, argued with Malcolm, been threatened by Darius Bell, been named a personal favorite of Valas, and found out Charles might be dying. Even for me that was a full day, and it wasn't even over yet—not by a long shot.

# CHAPTER 7

I'D EXPECTED MY STOMACH TO FEEL BETTER BY THE TIME WE MADE THE HALF-hour drive to Sean's house in the Heights, but the painful churning sensation only got worse. By the time he turned into his driveway and parked next to his truck, which Ben had apparently already dropped off, I was hunched over in my seat, my arms wrapped around my middle.

When I started to open my door, Sean said, "Alice, I'm worried about you. I've never seen a healing spell have this much of a lingering effect. Why are you still hurting?"

"I don't know." I sighed and pushed my door open. It took more effort than it should have. "I need to put Malcolm into a circle to speed up his regeneration and make a couple of phone calls. Then I'm going to lie down for a while and see if that helps. I'm sure it will get better soon."

Sean got my first suitcase and my duffel bag and escorted me to the front door.

To my surprise, it opened as we approached, revealing Ben. "Hi, Alice." His smile disappeared when he saw how I looked. "Let me get those so you can help her," he said, reaching for the suitcase and bag Sean carried.

Sean handed them over, but I made it inside on my own two feet, sidestepping Sean when he tried to take my elbow. Ben hurried upstairs with the bags and then went out to my car.

"Where's Rogue?" I asked.

"Out in the yard," Ben said as he passed us again, carrying my other suitcase.

I needed privacy to make my calls, but that wouldn't be easy with werewolf ears. Normally the easiest thing would have been for me to go upstairs to one of the guest rooms and shut the door, but at the moment the stairs seemed particularly daunting. I'd have to go up at some point if I intended to lie down, though, so I might as well tackle the steps now.

"Come outside for a moment," Sean said to Ben as I headed for the stairs. "I want to ask you something about the truck."

"Sure." Ben followed Sean out the door.

When it was closed, I began the slow process of hauling myself up the steps. I appreciated that Sean had taken Ben outside so he didn't see me struggling to climb stairs.

By the time I made it to the top I was out of breath. I was still uneasy, but the painful churning in my stomach had eased, thank goodness.

I headed for Sean's room, where Ben had put my suitcases, but paused at the threshold. For some reason, I thought I might rest better in one of the guest rooms. At first that didn't make sense, but the uneasiness and churning sensation faded when I thought about not being in Sean's bed, so I moved my bags to a room down the hall and closed the door.

This bedroom shared a connecting bathroom with the other guest room. I took my chalk into the bathroom, moved the bathmats aside, and spent ten minutes drawing the spellwork for a power circle on the floor. When it was done, I placed Malcolm's crystal in the center, pressed my hand to the runes around it, and closed the circle. In my Second Sight, the runes glowed with energy as they began amplifying the energy in the crystal. I hoped Malcolm would be recovered enough for me to take him with me to Charles's house.

I sat on the bed, took off my boots, and sighed. I had two calls to make, neither of which I looked forward to. I decided to bite the bullet and make the harder one first. I scrolled through my contacts and called Allan Garrett's number.

The phone rang once and then he answered. "Did you find him?"

I rubbed my face. "Not yet. Are you somewhere you can talk?"

"I'm at home," he said shortly. "What's going on?"

"I don't know where Aden is, but I know who took him and why." Briefly, I explained what I knew about Bell's recruitment of nulls and how Aden might have found out about it. And then I told him what happened at Jana's house—leaving out Nora's name.

When I finished, Allan went nuclear. "How the hell did he even know how to find someone from Bell's cabal?" he demanded. "He's twelve, for fuck's sake."

"I'm not exactly sure yet, but I have camera footage of Aden getting into a car at the convenience store near Jana's house this morning at about nine-twenty. The car may belong to his former babysitter."

"So this babysitter might have taken him somewhere to meet Bell's people?"

"It's possible. If I can find her, she might be able to give us some answers."

"You swore to me that you'd get my son back," he said harshly.

"And I will. That hasn't changed."

"You screwed up and now they've got Jana too. How do you propose to get them back from a cabal? They've got an army and you're one cocky bitch whose mouth is writing checks you can't cash."

"Look, you're pissed, I get it. Yeah, I lost one battle today and I'll be sorry about that for the rest of my days. But I'm going to get Aden and Jana back, I promise you." I took a deep breath. "The silver lining is that Aden is probably safer now than he was before. If they have Jana, he'll do as he's told, I'm sure. That means they won't hurt him or Jana. I'm not trying to downplay what happened, but my biggest fear for Aden was that they would hurt him to try to get him to follow orders and that's less likely now."

"Yeah, this is some great fucking news," Allan snapped.

I couldn't blame him for being angry. "I think you need to pack a bag and stay somewhere else and keep your head low. They might come after you too if Jana tells them who Aden's father is."

"Let them try."

I sighed. "Allan, the person who came to Jana's house shot her partner twice in the head when he became a liability and then blasted me through not one, but *two* walls. She has blood magic and is the most powerful air mage I've ever met. Now, imagine they send her plus a couple more mages and a dozen soldiers. Null or not, you can't fight them all off. If they get you, you're not only one more thing they can use against your son, but imagine if they find out you're a null like Aden. You're more powerful than him. They'll go from using Jana to get Aden to do what they want, to using *Aden* to get you to fall in line. Do you want to watch them torture your son?"

"Fuck no," he said automatically.

"Then take my advice and hide out somewhere until I call to tell you that I'm ready to make a move to get Aden and Jana back, and then we'll go in together. Meanwhile, keep trying to find out where Bell might have these nulls hidden, but be smart about who you ask. Use burner phones and leave your own phone at home. Don't take your own car and take a couple of days off from work so they can't get you at Nyx."

"It ain't my first time on the run," he said shortly. "You find my kid and Jana, or you'll have me to answer to." He ended the call.

I put the phone on the bed and took several deep breaths. Then I called Natalie.

That conversation went about as well as I'd expected. Natalie blamed herself for letting Aden overhear her talking with Kyra and then cried. I preferred Allan's cussing to Natalie's tears. Being cursed out just made me more determined to fix the situation. Listening to Natalie cry made me feel like garbage.

When we disconnected, I curled up on the bed. Unlike the bed in the master bedroom, the guest bed didn't smell like Sean. The simple faint aroma of fabric softener eased some of the tension in my shoulders and the uneasiness in my stomach.

My thoughts went to Charles. My feelings about him were far more complicated than I could articulate to Sean or anyone else. I was angry at him for getting the cuff I'd needed to save Sean and trading it for a drink of my blood, not to mention he'd bitten me once before, without my consent or knowledge, while I lay in a coma. While the transaction for the cuff had been difficult, I was more angered by his scheming to get the cuff than his bite. Drinking from me without my consent while I was defenseless was unpardonable, though. I knew I'd never be able to forgive him for that.

And yet, I had to admit we were alike in many ways. I'd realized that after the cuff incident. I'd freed Sean from the cuff by putting on the matching artifact and then having Valas kill me, causing both cuffs to fall off. She'd brought me back, obviously, but I hadn't warned Sean about what I was going to do, and he and his pack thought I had died.

Sean had forgiven me, but in the interim I came to realize I had only slightly more capacity for empathy than the average vampire. I'd plotted and schemed to get the cuff off of Sean, even going so far as to arrange my own death and resurrection, without a thought to how feeling me die would affect Sean and the rest of the pack. I'd thought the end justified the means, and it was only after Sean nearly ended our relationship that I'd realized how wrong I'd been.

And then there was my reaction to Charles's bite. I wished I could say I'd hated the experience, given how painful it was and how I'd ended up having to trade the bite for the cuff I needed, but that would be a lie. The bite had been excruciating because I hadn't allowed him to give me any pleasure to offset the pain, but even then I'd known on some level I liked it too. It wasn't just because of the pain, because pain by itself didn't arouse me, but I'd found myself enjoying Charles's bite and I knew it was because of him.

I should hate him for everything he'd done to me, and I did, but I felt something else for him too, something that might have been fondness for someone only slightly more messed up than me.

Someone rapped quietly on the door. "Alice, are you awake?" Sean called. "I brought some tea that might help your stomach."

My tummy, which had been feeling better since I came upstairs, started churning again. "Okay," I said, curling up a little tighter on top of the covers.

The door opened. Sean came in, carrying a mug. "Did you make your calls?"

"Yes, thanks." I grimaced and forced myself to sit up against the headboard. "And thanks for the tea." I took the mug from him and blew on the hot liquid. It smelled like peppermint. I didn't feel like eating or drinking anything, but hopefully the tea would help, so I forced myself to sip it. "Is Ben still here?"

"Yes. He's hanging around, helping me keep an eye on things. Someone else will take a turn later, whenever we get back." Sean sat on the side of the bed. I drew my knees up to my chest to make more room for him. "I promise not to invite the whole pack over until you're recovered." He smiled, but when I didn't smile back, it faded. "What else can I do to help?"

I drank some tea. "Nothing I can think of."

"What about your magic? You don't have much, do you?"

I shook my head.

"And with Malcolm still recovering, you can't draw more from him." He met my eyes. "Do you want my help to regenerate your magic?"

My stomach cramped. "No," I said, more harshly than I'd intended. "No, no thank you," I amended, softening my tone. "My stomach really hurts."

"I can be as gentle as you need me to be. It's absolutely your decision, but I don't like you being so vulnerable."

For a moment, I was tempted, despite my upset stomach. Maybe if we took it slow and I let him do most of the work—

My stomach cramped again, so painfully this time that I thought I might throw up. I made a sound that was part groan, part sob. "No. Please go away." I said it without thinking.

He looked stunned. "You want me to leave?"

"I'm sorry," I said, rubbing my face. "I don't know why I said that. Losing Jana to Nora Keegan, Malcolm being mad at me, Bell and Ezekiel Monroe showing up at my house, Charles being sick...I'm just not myself."

He flexed his hands, a sign of how tense he was. "I want to help you. You know I can't just sit by idly while you're hurting. Let me at least take some of this pain from you."

As an alpha, Sean could take pain—physical or emotional—from members of his pack who were hurt or grieving. Because we'd shared magic, he had been able to use that ability to help me, taking my discomfort during healing spells and even my cravings for a drug called Black Fire so I didn't become addicted to it. At first I'd thought he was simply able to dispel the pain, but I'd found out he felt it instead. Ever since, I'd been reluctant to let him take my pain, since the idea of someone suffering on my behalf, especially Sean, was as difficult for me to accept as my hurt was for him.

I shook my head. "It's not that bad."

His eyes glowed bright gold. "Don't lie to me. We have an agreement; you don't tell me you're fine when you're not."

"I didn't say I was fine—just that it's not so bad that I need help. This pain from the healing spell can't last much longer. I'm going to regenerate my magic and then try to rest a bit before we go to see Charles."

"How are you going to regenerate your magic without help from either Malcolm or me?"

"By siphoning power from a ley line."

He stared at me. "That's like trying to get a drink from a fire hose. There has got to be a better, safer way."

"I've done it before. Not for a while, granted, but desperate times and all that."

"Alice, it's your body and your choice, but I'm trying to understand why siphoning power from a ley line sounds like a better idea than sex with me." He was getting angry. "I may not know much about your kind of magic, but I *do* know what you're proposing is dangerous."

"It's not that it sounds like a better idea than sex," I told him, though some part of me argued that it did. "I need a *lot* of power, more than sex can give me. I'm at practically zero now, and I need to be at one hundred percent to help Charles, not to mention in case Bell decides to say to hell with Monroe's threats and send people after me. You want me to be as strong as possible, right? The ley lines are the best and fastest way to do that."

A muscle moved in his jaw. He wanted my magic fully restored, but that desire battled with his concern.

"I've been using ley lines for power all my life," I reminded him when he didn't reply. "I'll be fine."

"If you say that's what you have to do, then that's what you have to do. I don't like it, but I understand." He studied me. "I'd also like to understand why you brought your things to the guest room instead of leaving them in our room."

I blinked. "Our room? You mean your room?"

"No, *our* room. Our room, our bed, our space that we share." He crossed his arms. "You've rejected me in every way you could today since the party and I'm starting to think there's something you need to tell me."

"There's nothing I need to tell you that has anything to do with this. I don't feel well and I'm worried about everything that's going on, and that's all it is."

He reached out to touch my leg. I forced myself to sit still as his hand rested on my knee.

"You used to love touching me and being touched," he said quietly. "I don't know what's changed, but I feel like I don't know what's in your heart anymore."

I didn't know what to say to that. I did feel like something had changed between us, but I couldn't say what it was, when it started, or why.

I finished the tea and held out the mug. "Thanks again for the tea. I'm hoping once my magic is back to normal my stomach will stop bothering me. Maybe all this worrying lately gave me an ulcer." I managed a small smile.

He took the mug and rose. "I'll leave you to it, then. If you want to be at Vaughan's house at sunset, we'll need to leave in a little less than an hour. Will that give you enough time to do what you need to do?"

"It should."

He headed for the door. "I'll keep Ben company in the meantime. Let me know if you need me."

"I will. Thank you."

He paused in the doorway, clearly reluctant to leave. I saw hurt in his eyes, and worry, and anger too. For a moment, I felt a twinge and I almost reached out for him, but the impulse faded.

"Be careful, Alice," he said. He left, closing the door quietly behind him.

TAKING a drink from a fire hose was probably the best analogy I'd heard for siphoning power from a ley line.

Thankfully, I'd done it enough times that I felt fairly certain I could manage the process with minimal danger, but I hadn't used a ley line this way since leaving my grandfather's cabal. One of the reasons I'd chosen this city as my destination when I ran away from

Moses was it was located at the intersection of two powerful ley lines. If my grandfather ever found me, I could use those lines to protect myself. As an earth mage, I had a natural affinity to the lines and could do more with their power than non-earth mages.

I lay on the bed, holding a large crystal in each hand I could use to offload energy if I ended up conducting too much. When I used the lines to boost my natural magic, I grabbed them with my earth magic and hung on, becoming a conduit for their power. To siphon energy at a low, steady rate, however, what I needed to do was more like touching the tip of a finger to the line and then controlling the flow of power. Learning how to do that had taken years of painful practice.

"Okay, kids, don't try this at home," I muttered.

I squeezed the crystals in my fists, closed my eyes, and focused on the sizzle of the closer and less powerful of the two lines. Carefully, I reached out and gently touched the line.

The burst of power seared every nerve and I clenched my jaw to keep from screaming. The pain was far more intense than I'd expected, probably because I'd really put my body through the wringer today.

The ley line pushed at me, trying to turn me into a conduit. I kept the valve almost closed and allowed only a trickle of energy through. When I felt like I had control over the flow of power, I opened the valve a bit more and let the ley line's energy fill me up.

Unlike when I drew power from Malcolm, siphoning energy from the line was painful and required all of my focus. Any lapse in concentration would be disastrous and potentially deadly, so I kept my mind blank and focused on the uncomfortable sensation of ley line energy filling my body. My magic swelled and grew, replacing the unpleasant hollow feeling with a prickly fullness.

Just as I reached the point when I was ready to close the valve and release the line, my mind conjured up an image of Sean's expression at the moment I'd inexplicably told him to go away. I'd hurt him and I didn't understand why. My stomach cramped and I lost focus for a moment. That was all it took for the flow of energy to surge.

Fortunately, I shut the valve almost instantly and the crystals in my hands took the majority of the surge, but they filled immediately and the power backed up into my hands. The overflow felt like someone took a blowtorch to both of my palms and I couldn't hold back a short scream as magic flared around my hands.

I had to release some of the extra power somehow before it caused nerve damage. If I'd been at home, I would have simply offloaded it into my house wards, but I hadn't put any wards on Sean's house. All I could think to do was grab the circle helping Malcolm regenerate and dump the energy into it. Then I let go of the crystals and focused on breathing.

When I opened my eyes, I was startled to find Sean standing next to the bed, his eyes glowing bright gold. He must have heard my scream and come running. He knew better than to touch me when I used magic, but I was sure holding himself back was difficult.

"Are you all right?" he asked.

"Yes. I'm sorry about the yell. I got a surge of power, but I contained it."

He gestured at the bed. "Mostly, anyway."

I pushed myself up to sit against the headboard and stared. "Oh, no."

The flare of magic around my hands had turned the bedding to ash where my hands had been. A closer inspection revealed my magic had burned all the way into the mattress. "Oh, no," I said again. "I'm so sorry, Sean. I'll replace everything."

He sat on the bed. "I'm a lot more worried about what the surge did to you."

"I'm fine. Really," I added when he frowned. "I used those crystals to contain the extra power and offloaded what was left over to Malcolm's circle. It hurt, but no damage to me, just your bed." I showed him my hands, which were unscathed except for some redness where I'd been holding the crystals.

"Do you feel better?"

I nodded and rubbed my stomach. "My tummy is still acting up, but that should go away soon now that I have magic again."

He started to brush my hair back from my face, but I tucked the loose strands behind my ear. He touched my arm instead. "Do you want something to eat before we leave?"

I sighed. "Not really, but if I'm going to use magic to help Charles, I need some food. We can pick something up on the way."

"I'm not sure fast food is the way we want to go with your stomach still upset. I can make you a sandwich and a salad."

"Thank you. That sounds...good." Not really, but using magic required fuel. Nausea or not, I had to eat something. "Let me check on Malcolm while you're getting dinner ready and then I'll change and come down." I looked at the burned bed and closed my eyes. "Damn it."

"Don't worry about the bed—I've been meaning to get a new one anyway. I've had this one for a long time." He smiled. "Luckily, my bed has plenty of room for both of us."

My stomach suddenly cramped again. I flinched.

Sean's brows drew together. "Maybe you don't need to go to Vaughan's house tonight."

I shook my head and slid to the edge of the bed. "Bryan said he's not even sure if Charles will rise tonight and he's not given to hyperbole. He should have called me days or weeks ago instead of waiting until it got this serious. Now every minute counts." I rose and went to the bathroom to splash water on my face.

"If this is because of a vampire object of power, what kind of help do you think you can give him?"

I dried my face and studied myself in the mirror. I looked better thanks to the ley line power, but I was pale and my eyes were shadowed. I needed sleep, but that would have to wait. "I have earth and blood magic, which are the closest natural magics to vampire magic. Beyond that..." I hesitated. "I have an affinity for vamp magic."

He moved to stand just outside the bathroom doorway. "As a

result of Vaughan biting you, or from drinking vampire blood for healing?"

"Neither, actually. Some blood mages—no one is really sure why —have an innate affinity for the dark magics, of which vampire magic is one. We can usually sense a vampire's proximity and the bonds between master vampires and their offspring."

He smiled, though it didn't reach his eyes, which were still golden. His concern and frustration prickled on my arms. "You're a never-ending source of surprises. Let me make you some food so you have time to eat before we leave."

"Okay. Thank you."

For a moment, I felt inexplicable sadness as he went downstairs. A little voice in the back of my head insisted I would have preferred him to stay and keep me company. I was puzzled by my reaction. I'd never liked anyone to fuss over me, so why did I feel as if I needed his touch and comfort? I frowned and the urge to call him back vanished.

In any case, I needed to hurry and get ready to leave. I shook my head to clear it and opened my suitcase. I pulled out a pair of slim black pants, an emerald-green top, and a pair of ankle boots.

By the time I'd changed, done my makeup, re-braided my hair, stuck a few blood magic implements into my bag, and made it downstairs, my stomach had settled down. Sean and Ben were talking out in the garage. I found a sandwich and a salad on the dining table. I took the food into the living room and sat on the couch.

Now that my stomach felt better, I was ravenous. I finished the sandwich and salad in record time and went to the kitchen to make coffee and find something else to snack on.

I was eating a snack cake and pouring coffee into a travel tumbler when Ben came in from the garage. "Hey, Alice. Feeling better?"

"Much better, thank you. And thanks for coming over here to help us."

"It's no trouble at all. It's the least I can do. Are you ready to leave?"

I blinked. "Where's Sean?"

"He had to run an errand. He asked me to go with you to Mr. Vaughan's house and he'll meet us there."

I was surprised and relieved, though I wasn't sure why that news made the last of my tummy flutters go away. Odd, but I'd have to deal with that thought later. I had kidnapped mages to find and a vampire to save. "Great. Let me grab my stuff and we'll go. You want to take my car or yours?"

"Sean asked me to take you in a Maclin Security vehicle, if that's okay."

Given the possibility of trouble from Bell's people, I'd expected as much. I'd gotten used to riding in Maclin Security vehicles of late. "Sounds fine with me."

I grabbed my coffee and bag and followed him out to the large black SUV parked at the curb. Sean's truck was gone. It must have been an important errand for him to send Ben with me instead of driving me himself. Probably something to do with a client, if I had to guess. In any case, it was a relief to get away from him for a while, since his constant worry had become a bit smothering.

On the way to Charles's house, I reread everything the MOP database had on the Tepes stone. It wasn't much. The Vampire Court's library probably had more information than the MOP database, but I wasn't sure they'd be willing to share it with me. Might as well try, though.

I texted Kim Dade, the Vamp Court researcher I'd worked with a few times before, and asked her to call me when she had a moment.

To my surprise, my phone rang immediately. "Hey, Alice," she said warmly. "Are you feeling better?"

I wasn't in the least surprised that she'd heard about the day's events. Small southern towns had nothing on the Vamp Court grapevine. "Much better, thanks. Sorry to get right to the point, but

I'm on my way to Charles Vaughan's house and I need some information."

A pause. "I've heard he hasn't been himself lately," she said carefully. "How can I help?"

"I've read what the MOP database has on the Tepes stone, but it isn't much. I was wondering if the Court had more information, something that could give me a clue how to help him."

Her response was pretty much what I'd expected. "Unfortunately, I can't release any information from our archives without clearance from a member of the Court or one of their daytime representatives."

"Damn it." I sighed. "If I can get someone to sign off on this, will you send the info to me?"

"Of course. I'll queue up the file so I can send it as soon as I get the word."

"Thanks, Kim. I'll see what I can do." I ended the call and tapped my phone against my lower lip, debating who to call.

Finally, I scrolled through my contacts and called Juliet LaRoche, Niara's daytime representative. Niara and Charles were both on the Vampire Court and were frequent bedmates. That by itself didn't mean they cared for each other; for vamps, sex usually didn't have the same emotional and psychological component it did for most humans. But I'd seen Niara and Charles around each other often enough to know there were feelings there that went beyond physical attraction.

I'd only spoken to Juliet a few times over the years. She was as stiff and formal as Ezekiel Monroe was friendly and outgoing. Still, I figured she was my best bet for getting info from the Court library.

"Ms. Worth." Juliet's voice was brisk. "How may I help you this evening?"

I told her where I was going and why, and what I needed.

A long silence. "My understanding is Mr. Vaughan does not want you involved in this matter."

Apparently, everyone knew about Charles but me, and it pissed me off. Things had been bumpy between us of late—largely because of his actions—but he'd deliberately excluded me from this situation and I wanted to know why.

"Well, tough, because I'm involved now and I'm going to do my damnedest to save his undead ass," I snapped. "I know Niara cares about him and I doubt the details about that stone are vampire state secrets. Besides, I have an NDA on file with the Court that covers any info you share with me, so you know it's going no farther than my eyes. Help me out on this, Juliet. Or ask Niara after she wakes up if you have to, but from what I understand, we don't have a hell of a lot of time."

Another long silence. "Niara has just woken. I will ask her permission to send you the information."

I glanced at the horizon, where the sun was still visible. The older the vampire, the earlier they were able to wake, though they still had to avoid sunlight. "I'm going in there with or without that information, but it would make it a lot more likely I'll succeed if I knew what you all know about the stone."

"I will speak with Niara and notify you of her decision." Juliet ended our call.

Ben slowed and stopped at a red light. "So, what can you tell me about this stone?"

"I can tell you what I know. The Tepes stone—or at least that's what I call it—is about four inches long and oval-shaped. To my knowledge, no one really knows how old it is, except that it was created at least a couple hundred years before Tepes obtained it. Originally it was undecorated except for some etched runes, the spellwork that shapes its power. Once Tepes got it, someone painted a portrait of him on its face. The database says that many of the vampire objects of power he owned bore his likeness in one way or another."

"Well, that doesn't surprise me. Fifteenth-century Wallachian warlords were a cocky bunch," Ben said. At my raised eyebrows, he smiled. "Vlad the Impaler and Dracula myth are sort of a hobby for me."

"A werewolf who is a Dracula fanboy," I teased. "Now I've seen everything."

He grinned. "So what does it do?"

"The stone sucks the life energy out of victims and transfers it to its host, leaving vamp victims temporarily mortal and other non-immortal people dead."

I'd seen Charles use it the night of the auction when Vincent Barclay, a vampire from Seattle, and his entourage attacked us in an attempt to kidnap me and steal the stone.

"Its host?" Ben asked. "Interesting word choice. Not its user?"

"Yeah, its host. Best case, the stone is basically a symbiont. As long as the host drains people's energy and keeps it fed, the stone makes the host stronger."

"And if the host doesn't keep draining people?"

"Then the stone turns on its host and starts eating them from the inside out."

Silence.

Charles had been glib about the danger when I'd confronted him about it, pointing out that it was better he had possession of the stone than someone like Barclay. And maybe he was right, but even then I'd worried about what might happen if Charles didn't use the stone as intended. It would appear my worries had been well-founded.

"So, basically, Vaughan has been walking around with this stone in his pocket for the last month and now it's eating him alive?" Ben paused. "Er, eating him undead?"

I shook my head. "The stone is *inside* him, Ben. That's why the person using it is called a host. When he bought it, he disappeared for about fifteen minutes, way longer than the rest of the bidders were gone paying for their purchases. Later, when I read up on the stone, I found out where he was during that time: getting his abdomen cut open and the stone put inside. He waited for the incision to heal and then came back out like nothing happened."

Ben muttered something that would have made Juliet LaRoche threaten to wash his mouth out. "I've heard of objects of power like that, but I can't imagine sticking one in my body. The cuff that grabbed onto Sean's arm was bad enough."

I'd hoped for a quick response from Juliet, but as the minutes ticked by my frustration and anger grew. I'd thought Charles would be worth enough to Niara that she would tell Kim to send me the file on the stone, but maybe I was wrong. Damn heartless vamps.

Finally, just as I was sure I was going to have to go in with no more knowledge than I already had, my phone beeped. To my surprise, it was an email from Kim Dade with an attachment. Niara had come through after all.

I opened the file and started reading. Halfway down the first page, my stomach lurched. "Oh, shit," I said involuntarily.

Ben glanced at me. "Is it bad?"

"No, it's worse."

"How could it be *worse?*"

"Just trust me; it is." I swallowed hard. "Drive faster."

# CHAPTER 8

We arrived at Charles's estate at sunset. The gate swung open as we turned into the drive.

Black-clad enforcers patrolled along the walls and more walked the grounds. Charles had become more security-conscious after anti-vamp extremists targeted him. His beloved bar Hawthorne's—the first establishment he'd opened in the city on his arrival decades ago—was bombed, and then one of the bombers escaped capture and attacked his entourage last month, killing Arkady's lover Fortune and nearly killing both Charles and Bryan too. Hawthorne's was nearly rebuilt now, but Charles had relocated his offices to a more secure suite above his much fancier downtown wine-and-cocktail bar, 1792.

Ben parked in front of the mansion, off to the side of the wide main steps next to two Vamp Court SUVs. Sometimes it felt like everyone in my life drove a black SUV but me.

The front door opened as we climbed the steps, revealing Bryan's sister Adri, another of Charles's enforcers. "Alice, thank you for coming."

"Why didn't he want me to know about this?" I asked as we walked past her into the house.

She shut the heavy door and sighed. "You'll have to ask him that. I can only speculate."

"Where's Bryan?"

She smiled humorlessly. "He's Mr. Vaughan's breakfast today."

Ben twitched. I'd long ago stopped feeling squicky about a vampire's eating habits, but not everyone spent as much time around the fangy undead as I did.

As his head enforcer, Bryan drank from Charles regularly, which made him almost as strong and fast as a dhampir. That strength would benefit Charles now, as the effects of possessing the Tepes stone grew worse.

"How long until Charles is ready to see me?" I asked.

"A few minutes, I think."

"Does he know I'm coming?"

She shook her head. "Bryan and I have decided it will be better to ask forgiveness for this than permission."

As far as I knew, neither Adri nor Bryan had ever disobeyed a direct order from Charles. For their sakes, I hoped their boss would be in a forgiving mood when this was over.

Adri led us down a hallway I hadn't taken before. Ben was on high alert, his sharp eyes taking in everything and everyone around us. Having him at my back was reassuring.

Near the end of the hall, Adri stopped and faced us. "I'm taking you down to Mr. Vaughan's private apartment. No one other than his most trusted employees and Niara has ever crossed its threshold. If you use the information about its location or anything you see or hear while there against Mr. Vaughan in any way, you will answer to all of us."

I knew Adri well enough to know her pronouncement was more of a promise than a threat. I took no offense and accepted her warning in the spirit in which it was intended. "I understand."

"I understand," Ben echoed.

She placed her hand on a small black glass panel on the wall. A flash of red light indicated it was a biometric scanner. Several heavy locks disengaged and a section of wall swung inward, revealing another hallway. I wondered what would happen if the estate lost power. No doubt there were other manual methods of opening the door, but they weren't likely to share those with us.

We followed Adri through the door and it shut behind us with a very imposing *thud*. Ben's tension quadrupled at the realization that our escape route was effectively cut off. We passed a half-dozen doors on our way down the hall; probably living quarters for some of Charles's most trusted employees.

At the door at the end of the hall, Adri paused and got a faraway look that indicated she was talking to someone in her head, probably Charles, asking permission to enter.

She opened the door, revealing a landing and a set of wide stairs going down. The passage reminded me of the original Hawthorne's. The decor was unmistakably Charles's style: dark wood, subdued lighting, and brass fixtures.

We started down the stairs with Adri in the lead. If Charles didn't know Adri was bringing visitors, he would likely be hearing our foot-steps now. Given what Adri and Bryan had said and what I'd read in the Vamp Court file on the stone, I had no idea what kind of recep-tion we would receive or what we'd see when we reached Charles's room.

Charles called out to us when we were three-quarters of the way down the stairs. "Alice, come no farther." His voice was slightly hoarse, but stronger than I'd feared it would be. He must have asked Bryan who was with Adri, or maybe he recognized the sound of my boots.

Adri's steps faltered at his command. I nudged her forward. "Go ahead and yell, Charles, but I'm here and I'm not leaving," I said as we reached the bottom of the steps and Charles's private apartment.

The room was part bedroom, part library, and part museum.

Bookcases and display cabinets lined the walls. The ceiling mural featured a breathtaking sunrise painted in an Impressionist style.

I realized I'd seen a glimpse of this room once before: when I'd used a tracking spell to find the cuff that matched the one killing Sean. Somewhere in this room was the wall safe where Charles had kept the cuff. I didn't see a safe, but it was probably hidden behind some books or one of the paintings hanging on the walls.

Charles's bed was much as I'd imagined it: an enormous and imposing four-poster piece of furniture. The dark-haired vampire struggled to rise from the bed but Bryan held him back with a hand on his shoulder. Given Charles's taste for luxurious clothing, I'd expected him to sleep in silk pajamas or something equally decadent —or heaven help me, in the nude—but instead he wore simple cotton pants and a long-sleeved tunic.

Despite having just drunk Bryan's blood, Charles was pale and his skin had a bluish tinge. His eyes were entirely black. Like all vampires, he'd always been slim, but now he was almost skeletal. Most telling of all, Bryan held him back with one hand on his thin shoulder and without straining very much. Charles was dangerously weak.

My stomach contracted painfully at the sight of him. Hard on the heels of my dismay came anger. "Why the hell didn't you ask me for help?"

He ignored my question. "I gave orders," he ground out. "You were not to be called."

"Yeah, I'm pretty ticked off about that, but thankfully someone did call me." I approached the bed. "I told you that you had a tiger by the tail with that stone. Looks like it mauled you."

"You must leave." He still had a bit of the familiar fire in his eyes but I also saw pain. Worst of all, I saw resignation. He'd all but given up and it pissed me off.

"Make me," I said.

He knocked Bryan's hand away, surged to his feet, and came at me.

Ben moved like lightning to meet Charles's attack. Charles got a hand on Ben's arm, but at the same moment I hit the vampire with my hands and unleashed a controlled burst of air magic that sent him flying back to land on the bed.

Bryan and Adri stepped between us, but Charles didn't rise and attempt to attack again. That one burst of energy had left him drained.

I approached the bed with Ben at my side. "I don't know why you didn't call me for help, and I guess I don't care. I'm here to save you whether you want me to or not, so suck it up, buttercup, and let me help."

"You do not know what you risk," he rasped, sitting up with effort. "This magic...it is like a disease. It can spread."

"I know. I read the Vamp Court file on the stone."

His frown was thunderous. "On whose authority?"

"Niara's. There are a lot of people who don't want to watch you die, even if you've gotten to the point where you don't care one way or the other." I sat on the bed, despite Ben's soft growl. He probably didn't like me being so close to a vampire, but if Charles let me try to help him, we'd be getting a hell of a lot closer before the night was out.

Charles's expression darkened further. "There are many who would be glad to see me dead, I think."

"Then you should live just to spite them. That's what I would do."

"Of that, I have no doubt." The corners of his mouth turned up in a ghost of a smile. "From the moment I met you, your defiance has been one of your most defining characteristics. It has been both a source of frustration and amusement for me. More the former than the latter, perhaps, but I find I have missed that fire for the past month."

I reached out slowly and held my palm over his chest. Dark magic crawled and slithered beneath his skin. "When you bought the stone, did you know you'd have to drain people to keep it from killing you?"

He shook his head. "I believed I could take just enough to hold the stone's magic in check, but it would not take only a small amount. The first person I tried to feed from...died." His anger and regret left a sour taste in my mouth. "When I did not feed again, the magic spread so rapidly that I had no time to remove the stone before it took root. And so I find myself on the edge of falling into darkness, whether by dying or succumbing to this evil."

"I'm sorry. How far has it spread?"

He said nothing.

"Charles, answer me."

"I do not know a part of me that does not resonate with this foul darkness," he admitted finally. "The blood mages from the Court tell me there is no chance of removing the stone or extracting the magic. I have received visits from some of the most knowledgeable practitioners of vampire magic and been told the same."

"So you just gave up? Is that why you wouldn't ask me for help?"

Again, he refused to reply.

I pressed him for an answer. "Or was it because you didn't think I could do anything more than what the Court mages and the others could do?"

That got a reaction. "I did not wish to call you because I believe you *can* do far more than the Court mages are able and willing to do," he said quietly.

I stared at him, nonplussed. "You didn't call me because you thought I *could* save you? What the—?"

"This magic is poison," he spat. "I will not trade your life for mine."

Bryan and Adri looked shocked by that pronouncement. Whatever they'd thought Charles's reason was for refusing to ask for my help, that hadn't been it. I was startled myself, actually. Most vampires wouldn't have hesitated to sacrifice a human life to save their own, but then again, I'd come to realize Charles wasn't most vampires.

"I will not allow you to do this." He pushed my hand away from his chest. "I do not wish to live with your death on my conscience. I would rather end my time and take this cursed object with me."

He'd already made peace with his death, but I hadn't. "I believe I can save you and not die from doing it."

He shook his head. "I will not risk it."

Blasted vampire stubbornness. I took his hand and placed it over my heart. "You can sense deception. You know truth. Listen to me." I met his eyes. His cool gray vampire magic was a thin shadow of itself. "I can save you without dying. I know what that stone is, and what it does, and what its magic can do. I'm a stronger blood mage than any you have working for the Court. I will take that stone from you and pull the magic out of your body, and then I will destroy the stone so no one else can use it as a weapon." I held his cold hand in mine. "You've saved me twice, Charles. It's my turn."

Charles seemed to really notice Ben for the first time. "Good evening, Mr. Cooper. Where is your wolf, Alice?"

My stomach lurched for reasons that weren't quite clear. "He had an important errand to take care of. He's coming by later."

"He's upstairs," Ben said, looking up from his phone. "Do you want him to come down?"

"No. I need to be alone with Charles to do this."

Ben shook his head. "I'm not leaving you alone with him."

"I'm not leaving him alone with you," Bryan rumbled.

"You either trust me or you don't," I told him. "If I wanted him dead, I would have simply said I couldn't help him. I wouldn't have fought this hard to save him. Ben can stay because he doesn't have any vamp magic, but you and Adri have to go upstairs so your connection to Charles doesn't become a liability for all of us."

"Sean isn't going to like this," Ben said.

"I know, but I can't afford to be distracted." I took a deep breath.

"You can tell him I'm not throwing myself on a grenade; I'm defusing it."

"I'm not sure about that analogy, but I'll tell him." Ben sent a text message.

Charles, Bryan, and Adri had apparently been conferring telepathically while Ben and I talked. When my attention turned back to them, however, Charles spoke to them out loud. "I will not order you to leave, but I ask you to do so. Alice speaks the truth when she says she means me no harm. She has acted in good faith in coming here and venturing underground. If she cannot heal me without harming herself, she will let me die." He turned to me. "Give me your word, Alice."

"I give you my word." I turned to the enforcers. "You asked me for help, so let me help."

Bryan and Adri exchanged a look, one of those brother-sister moments where they held an entire conversation in a single glance. It had to be beyond difficult for them to leave Charles alone in this condition with a blood mage and a werewolf.

"We'll go upstairs," Bryan said finally.

Charles inclined his head. "Thank you."

"When we're done, he'll need a meal or three—the stronger, the better," I warned them. "So make those arrangements while you're waiting."

Bryan and Adri headed for the stairs. We listened to them climb to the top, open the door, and close it.

I turned to Ben and gestured at the floor. "Can you please roll up that large carpet?"

"Not a problem."

While he was moving the carpet, I addressed Charles. "I know you're feeling pretty bad right now, but I have to ask you to lie on the floor so I can draw a circle around us."

He moved stiffly to the edge of the bed and stood. He shuffled to the center of the stone floor as Ben finished rolling the carpet against the far wall. He sat carefully, as if moving was painful, then lay down with his arms at his sides.

I took a few things from my bag and left it and my phone on the bed. With a thick piece of chalk, I drew a circle around Charles large enough for me to move around him. Then I went to work drawing runes around the perimeter of the circle, forming a ward that would contain any dark magic that got loose. It took quite a while. Ben texted almost continuously while I worked, presumably keeping Sean updated.

When the spellwork was complete, I used the chalk to draw a series of runes inside the circle next to Charles's body. I tucked the chalk into my pocket and knelt beside him with an obsidian dagger.

He studied the dagger with interest, as if calculating its worth. "That is a beautiful artifact."

"Yes, it is." I took a large black crystal from my pocket and placed it next to me. "This is going to get very messy. You're not squeamish, are you, Ben?"

"No." He leaned against the wall. "Am I outside the splash zone?"

"Yes, you should be fine. You might be new to working with mages, so here are the rules. No talking, no sounds, no trying to break the circle and get to me, no matter what you see, hear, or feel. Magic of any kind is dangerous in situations like this and that goes double for dark magic. You'll have to trust that I know what I'm doing or wait upstairs."

Ben muttered something I didn't quite catch, but that caused Charles's eyebrows to raise slightly. "I understand," the werewolf added grimly.

"Okay." I held my hand over Charles's chest. "Where is it?"

He lifted his shirt, baring his abdomen and the scar that ran across his pale stomach just below his waist, where he'd been eviscerated before he was turned. During our daytime walk last month, he'd told me the story of how he'd gotten the scar and how he became a vampire. The story continued to haunt me.

He took my hand and placed it on the left side of his abdomen.

Dark magic pulsed beneath his flesh like some kind of nightmare heart of stone. Most magic was neither good nor evil; it was the practitioner's intent that shaped how the power could be used. This magic within Charles, however, felt evil in a way I hadn't experienced before, and I felt an uncontrollable urge to destroy it.

I rolled my shoulders and looked down at Charles. "Ready?"

He wrapped cold fingers around my wrist. *I am afraid*, he said, his voice in my head very quiet.

We'd once been able to share thoughts with each other regardless of distance, thanks to the bond we'd had as a result of him drinking from me, but our link had been severed by Valas for reasons that weren't clear. Without the link, Charles could still share his thoughts with me when we were in physical contact, as he had before, but I couldn't share thoughts with him. Now it was more a matter of him listening to my replies.

*That's all right*, I told him. *Fear is normal. It would be weird if you weren't afraid.*

*Fear is normal for humans, but I am not human.*

I smiled slightly. *You're still a little human, Charles. Do me a favor and stay that way.*

*If I am, it is because of you.* His eyes searched my face. *You are the single spark of life that remains in my world. If you die attempting to save me, neither your wolf nor his third will have to kill me; I will end my own life.*

I wasn't prepared for that level of candor from Charles. I chalked it up to him being forced to confront his own mortality.

*Nobody's dying here tonight*, I said firmly. *Now, let's do this before things get any worse.*

He released my wrist. I closed the circle around us and the wards flared powerfully, making the loose hairs around my face stick straight out. The wards would contain any magic surges while I worked and keep the dark magic from affecting anyone else.

I picked up the dagger and took several deep breaths, breathing in through my nose and out through my mouth, to center myself. I spooled blood and earth magic as I shut everything else out that might distract me. The room, Ben, and even Charles faded away.

When I was calm and focused, I channeled blood magic into the dagger until the runes etched into its blade glowed with power and it resonated like a bell ringing. The vibration traveled up my arm, a familiar and peaceful feeling. I so rarely used blood magic anymore. When I'd belonged to my grandfather's cabal I'd used it mostly to harm, but contrary to popular belief, blood magic had many other uses. It could save lives, not just take them.

Like most well-trained mages, I was ambidextrous when it came to writing—or carving—runes and spellwork. I took the dagger in my left hand and used the razor-sharp tip to cut four runes into the inside of my right forearm. The cuts weren't deep, but blood ran down my arm and dripped from my fingers to the floor.

Charles's fangs slid out, an involuntary response to the sight and scent of my blood. It was a testament to his age and power that even in his condition he held himself in check, but I could tell his control was not as strong as it should be. I had no time to waste.

I set the dagger down and cupped Charles's cool face with my left hand. "Do you trust me?" I asked.

It was hell of a question, given the circumstances, but his response was immediate. "Yes."

A fast cut would be more merciful. With my hand still resting on his face and my eyes locked on his, I pushed blood magic into my right hand and out through my fingertips to form a blade. I sliced into his gut.

Charles cried out. He cut the sound off quickly and set his jaw. Cool blood poured from the wound.

I invoked the spell I'd carved into my arm and it flared to life, sheathing my arm and hand in black, purple, and red blood magic. My fingers slid inside Charles's abdomen, first up to the knuckles and then almost to my wrist as I searched carefully through cold viscera for the stone.

My fingertips touched something hard. Dark magic flared,

battering my blood magic protection spell. A whisper brushed against my mind and I pushed back with my shields.

My fingers closed around the stone. I pulled but it resisted with a surge of power. Its magic had invaded Charles's body like tentacles and it wasn't giving up its host without a fight.

The Vamp Court file had warned that once these tentacles took root, removing the stone would be next to impossible. If it was forcibly excised without removing the magic as well, its host would die anyway, consumed from the inside.

I ran my thumb over Charles's cool cheek. His eyes were full of pain. I picked up the black crystal and took a deep breath. "Here goes nothing," I said, and dropped my shields.

The dark magic surged into me in a flood that seemed to turn my insides to rot. Fighting nausea and revulsion, I invoked the spellwork in the crystal and it flared in a blast of heat and energy that traveled up my arm and through my body. The dark magic, sensing what seemed like an even stronger source of power, surged more and passed through my body and into the crystal.

My intent was to be a conduit, channeling the stone's dark magic out of Charles and into the crystal, where it could be contained and then destroyed. It was working, though I gagged at the sensation of it passing through my body. I had no idea how Charles had withstood the horrible rotting feeling for so long without going mad.

And then it stopped working. The flow of magic ceased. Dark tentacles spread in my own body as the magic attempted to take control.

Charles sensed it too and tried to pull away, but I held onto the stone and refused to let go. Time for Plan B.

I unleashed the full power of my blood magic on the dark magic in my body. The blood magic began consuming the stone's magic with a sensation like something pulling and pushing at my insides. I retched but managed not to lose my dinner.

The stone's magic retreated into Charles. I pushed my blood magic through my hand into his body. He writhed as my blood magic consumed the tentacles of dark magic, burning its way through his body and destroying the stone's trace. It had to be agonizing, but he didn't cry out.

He coughed wetly and black bile ran from the corner of his mouth. Damn it. I didn't know exactly how much of the dark magic remained inside him, but if I didn't get that stone out now I couldn't be sure he would survive much longer.

I grabbed the stone again and pulled. My hand emerged from his abdomen covered in gore and clutching the triple-damned Tepes stone.

The stone pulsed in my hand, its dark magic fighting to get to me, Charles, or anyone else who could serve as its host. Charles had paid nearly two hundred grand for this cursed thing, believing he could hold its power in check, but the deadly magic could not be opposed for long.

I took a moment to think about the fact I was holding an object once owned by Vlad Tepes the Impaler, Wallachian warlord and inspiration for one of humankind's most fascinating and terrifying supernatural legends. His current whereabouts were a closely guarded secret. Some speculated that he was truly dead. Others believed he was at the top of the vampire world order, amassing untold wealth and power and pulling strings from a secret lair somewhere.

One evening over Scotch, I'd asked Charles if Tepes was the Keyser Söze of vampires. Surprisingly, Charles understood the reference. His response: Yes, in that Tepes was the threat used by older vamps to scare young ones into following the laws of the Vampire Courts. But a thing such as Tepes—and that was the word Charles had used, *a thing*—would never pretend to be weaker than he was to hide his identity. He would have put everyone in that police precinct on pikes out front and strolled past them on his way out.

I put the black crystal down and transferred the stone to my left hand. "One last time," I told Charles softly, sliding my fingers back into the wound I'd made in his side.

There was very little of the dark magic left in his body. Without the stone and diminished by my blood magic, it was like a guttering candle. I pushed blood magic into Charles's body and destroyed the last of the stone's magic.

Charles's skin was gray and the puddle of blood around us had spread until it reached the barrier of the circle.

I took his hand and placed it on the wound to hold it closed while it healed. "The worst is over," I told him.

His eyes went to the stone. "Danger," he rasped. "Do not destroy it."

"I read the Vamp Court file," I reminded him. "Magic this dark and powerful will break any ward eventually. There's nowhere you could keep it where it couldn't be found and taken. I know it was expensive, but—"

"Money is not my concern," he said harshly. "Losses are part of the risk a dealer in antiquities accepts. What I do not accept is that destroying the stone may harm you."

"This won't be the first vampire object of power I've nuked. This circle will contain the flare."

"It is not the flare of power that I fear; it is Tepes's magic that may—"

The crystal cracked with a sound like a gunshot. Dark magic erupted from the broken crystal and hit the barrier of the circle. It sizzled against the wards, trying to break them and consume all life energy it could find. Time was up; the stone had to be destroyed.

Normally I would have used an air magic burner spell, but that wouldn't even scratch the paint on the damn thing. Using my earth magic, I reached into the stone, grabbed the particles that formed the rock itself, and broke them apart. With a sharp crack and a burst of power, the stone turned to a pile of sand in my hand.

I sensed a presence in the circle a fraction of a second before an unseen hand gripped me tightly by the throat, cutting off my air. I clawed at my flesh, trying to pull the hand away, but there was nothing there. My fingernails gouged my own skin.

The cold fingers on my throat tightened. My vision tunneled. Choking, I fell onto my back.

Charles, holding his guts in with one hand, struggled to sit up, though I wasn't sure what he thought he'd be able to do. Ben stood just outside the circle, eyes bright gold as he watched us.

I'd brought Malcolm with me as backup, safely stashed in my bracelet, but this was no ghost crushing my throat. It *was* a spirit, but the living spirit of a being so powerful it could travel through the trace of its own magic and throttle someone. I had no doubt it would simply discorporate Malcolm without even having to try very hard, probably killing me in the process.

A dark voice whispered in my brain in a language I didn't know. It sounded like *tay-may-tay day meenay*. I had no idea what that meant, but threats sounded generally the same in all languages.

I only had a few seconds of consciousness left. It was time to find out just how much affinity for vamp magic I had.

I slapped my bloody hand to the runes I'd drawn on the floor, grabbed the spirit's cold gray trace, and unleashed my blood magic on it. "*Obliterate*," I croaked.

The runes flared in a burst of power. The spell was my ace in the hole, my backup in case my plan for removing and destroying the stone went awry.

My magic impacted the dark magic with the force of two trains colliding and the shockwave shook the building. The floor trembled and the chandelier above us swung madly as artifacts and paintings fell off walls and shelves and broke on the floor.

A roar of fury filled my head. The fingers squeezed and twisted sharply, as if trying to break my neck in that last moment, and then vanished with a pop of displaced magic as the last of the dark magic and gray trace burned away.

I sucked in air and rolled onto my side, coughing uncontrollably but thrilled to get air into my lungs. I was vaguely aware I had just rolled into the puddle of Charles's blood, but I couldn't care about the mess at the moment because breathing was the only thing that mattered.

When my vision cleared, I saw Charles sitting next to me holding his stomach. Bryan and Adri had joined Ben outside the circle. They'd probably come running when the building shook.

I felt like I'd been run over, but I managed to focus enough to break the circle. "Okay, it's safe," I croaked. "Your boss needs food."

Bryan headed for the stairs, presumably to go fetch whoever would be providing Charles's first course. I didn't want to be here to watch him feed because it would make me think of him biting me and the less I thought about that, the better.

Charles looked like undeath warmed over, but he somehow had the strength to help me sit up. His fingers trailed along my arm before he sat back. His shirt covered the wound in his abdomen, so I couldn't tell if it had healed. Probably not, since most of his blood was on the floor around us.

"A thank you would be shamefully inadequate," he said, his voice thin but firm. "I do not know how best to show my gratitude, but I assure you I will compensate you justly for the risk you took to remove and destroy the stone."

"You saved my life twice before," I reminded him, my voice hoarse. My throat ached and I could almost feel those cold fingers still wrapped around my neck.

He shook his head. "You were shot by Kent Stevens because of an error in judgment on my part. I healed your injuries after the construction site murders with no expectation of repayment. Most importantly, I provided care at no risk to myself, whereas you risked your life to save mine. My honor demands I offer just compensation."

I had no energy to argue with him about it tonight. "Then let's say you owe me a boon and leave it at that for now."

He inclined his head. "That is satisfactory."

Several sets of footsteps were coming down the stairs, presumably Charles's much-needed meals. That was my cue to leave. I staggered to my feet and nearly lost my footing in the blood on the floor.

My stomach still roiled from the dark magic and nausea made my skin clammy.

Bryan appeared, accompanied by Matthias and two other enforcers. I gave Matthias a little wave. He responded with a slight nod, which was about as much of a greeting as I was used to getting from the notoriously stoic enforcer. I turned to head for the bed just as a fifth person reached the bottom of the stairs.

Sean.

My stomach lurched. I flinched and wrapped my arms around my middle.

Sean stopped near the bottom of the steps, keeping his distance. His face was hard, almost expressionless. No doubt he was angry about being kept upstairs.

Charles had been walking slowly to his bathroom. Bryan and Matthias were at his sides but he did not lean on them. He paused. "Maclin."

Sean studied him, his eyes golden. The last time they'd seen each other was minutes after my death and resurrection. Charles had broken down the door of Jack and Delia Hastings's house trying to get to me. The air was thick with tension. No one breathed.

"Vaughan," he said finally. "I'm here to see to Alice, nothing more."

Charles inclined his head. He continued to the bathroom, his steps unsteady.

When the door closed behind the vampire and his guards, Sean approached me, his worry prickling on my arms. "Are you all right?"

I nodded. "It's not my blood. It's all from Charles. The stone is destroyed and the magic is gone. Thank you for waiting upstairs like I asked."

A muscle moved in his jaw. "We'll discuss it later. What happened to your neck?"

I hesitated. I had a strong suspicion about whose spirit had tried to throttle me, but it seemed so farfetched that I couldn't bring myself to say the words out loud. I might ask Charles about it later in private, but right now there were a half dozen other people in the room, none of whom I wanted to think I was nuts.

"The magic in the stone did that," I said finally. "I'm fine now."

Adri joined me next to the bed. "Come with me upstairs. You can use my bathroom to clean up."

"Thanks." I put the dagger into its sheath and the broken crystal into a small velvet bag and dropped both into my bag with my phone.

Sean glanced at Ben. Some kind of unspoken command passed between them. The younger werewolf took my messenger bag. "Here, let me get that so you don't get blood all over it," Ben said. "You look like Carrie at the prom."

"I bet I do." I sighed. "I'm very much looking forward to a shower."

Ben and I followed Adri to the stairs. Sean fell into step behind us as we climbed up to the main floor. His concern and anger still scoured my flesh. I sensed him watching me as we walked, but he was silent. Part of me wished he would touch me, and part wanted him as far away from me as possible. I rubbed my temples.

"You okay?" Ben asked.

"Yeah." I forced a tight smile. "Just feeling sick from the vamp magic, I think."

Adri led me to a door halfway down the hall and took my bag from Ben. "You can stay in the hall," she told Sean and Ben. "She's safe in my apartment. There are no other exits."

I expected Sean to argue, but he leaned against the wall opposite the door. "We'll wait out here," he said.

Adri and I went inside. Her apartment was about the size of a hotel suite, with a kitchenette, small living room, bedroom, and bathroom.

She led me into the bathroom, took a black plastic bag from a cabinet, and handed it to me. "Put your clothes in there and I'll get them cleaned and back to you. I'll get you some clothes that fit and leave them here on the counter."

She went into the bedroom to give me privacy. I stripped quickly and stuffed my bloody clothes into the bag, then handed it to Adri. "I'm jumping in the shower."

"Towels and washcloths are in the cabinet. The green soap is really good for washing blood off your skin. Help yourself to whatever else you need." She shut the door.

Before I got in the shower, I used my phone to look up the words of the spirit who'd tried to crush my throat. I wasn't sure how to spell them, so I went to a translation website, used the speech-to-text function, and repeated what I'd heard.

When the search results came up, I stared at my phone.

*Did you mean "Teme-te de mine"?* the website asked.

*Translation: "Fear me."*

The language was Romanian.

Well, shit.

# CHAPTER 9

When I emerged from Adri's apartment thirty minutes later, scrubbed clean and wearing the signature black shirt and pants of a Court enforcer, I was surprised and relieved to find Ben waiting alone in the hallway and no sign of Sean.

"He's back at the house," Ben said in answer to my unspoken question. "There was another incident involving Caleb."

I sighed and put my bag on my shoulder. "What now?"

"He didn't shift in public this time, which is good, but he got into a bar fight and the cops were called. He went out the back and drove home to Jack's house. By the time he got there, Sean had already gotten a call from the bar's owner, so he had Jack bring him over to talk about it."

Adri led us back down the hall toward the main security door. "I thought things were getting better with your young wolf."

"They have, but he's still having trouble controlling his temper," I said as she placed her palm on the scanner to unlock the door. When the locks disengaged and the door opened, I felt some of the tension ease out of Ben's shoulders. Few people liked to feel trapped and that went triple for shifters.

"I guess I shouldn't jump to conclusions until we know the cause of the fight," I added as an afterthought. "It's possible Caleb didn't start the fight, but he should know better than to get mixed up in a bar brawl. He's not even twenty-one, so he shouldn't have been in a bar in the first place."

"I think that's another thing Sean is talking to him about," Ben said wryly.

We followed Adri to the front door of the mansion. She walked with us out to the SUV.

"Thank you for coming here and saving Mr. Vaughan," she said as Ben went around to the driver's side and got in. "All things considered, I thought you might not want to get involved."

"Like I told Bryan, Charles has saved my life twice. Even if he says he didn't expect repayment for it, I still felt like I owed him."

She tilted her head. "And now it's he who owes you."

I shook my head. "I wanted to square our account, not tilt things back the other way."

She took a step forward and pressed her lips to my ear. "Don't refuse the boon," she murmured. "Powerful forces are at play. Mr. Vaughan is an ally you'll need, maybe sooner than you think."

"What do you mean?" I asked, just as quietly.

"That's all the warning I can give." She opened the SUV door. "We'll see you soon. Take care and watch your back."

"Thanks. Good night."

Our drive back to Sean's house was quiet. I was tired, but the spirit's threat and Adri's warning kept rattling around in my head. I had a feeling I would probably have a hard time falling asleep, despite how long I'd been awake and what I'd been through in the past thirty-six hours.

Ben stopped at a red light and turned to me. "You can tell me to mind my own business if you want, but how are things between you and Sean?"

A little sizzle of pain passed through my abdomen. I wrapped my arm around my stomach. "I guess I'd rather not talk about it. No offense."

"None taken." A pause. "Does your stomach hurt?"

"A little. Probably from channeling the vamp magic." I leaned my head back against the seat and closed my eyes.

When we turned onto Sean's street, I saw Jack's truck still parked in front of the house and stifled a sigh. I wished I could just get in my car and drive back to my own home. My stomach was churning again. Was I that worried about facing Jack? Surely not.

"Alice? Are you going to jump out before I even get to the house?" Ben's voice startled me. His tone was teasing, but he was frowning.

I took my hand off the door handle and reached down to pick up my bag. "Sorry. I'm feeling jumpy."

"You really haven't seemed like yourself at all today."

"That's what everyone keeps saying. It's been a really tough day."

Ben turned into Sean's driveway and parked behind my car. My uneasiness grew at the thought I wouldn't be able to leave if I needed to.

"Can you park over there instead?" I asked, gesturing at the third bay of the garage. "I doubt he'll be taking the jet skis out tonight."

Without commenting, Ben re-parked the SUV over to the far side of the driveway and we got out.

Instead of following him toward the door, I hesitated by my car. I had the nagging feeling I was supposed to be somewhere else, but I couldn't think of where.

"Planning on running away?" Ben leaned against my car, watching me. "You look like you'd rather be anywhere else but here. What's wrong?"

"Nothing." Reluctantly, I headed for the front door.

"I'll see if I can get them to wrap up their discussion as quickly as possible so you and Sean can go to bed," Ben said. "You probably just need some sleep and some werewolf TLC."

My stomach cramped painfully. I leaned against the brick wall. "Maybe I should go back to my house."

He looked worried. "You're sick. Let's go inside and get you upstairs to bed. Maybe you've got a stomach virus."

I'd been thinking my tummy trouble was caused by healing spells or the stone's magic, but Ben's theory made a lot more sense. It didn't explain my anxiety, but a bad stomach virus could definitely be making me feel out of sorts.

The door opened. Sean and Jack stood in the doorway. "We're in the middle of something," the taller blond man said brusquely. "What's going on out here?"

"I don't know." Ben moved closer to me, almost protectively. "I think she's sick and not thinking clearly. I'm having trouble getting her to go inside. She wanted to go home instead."

Jack's brow furrowed. "You need to stay here with us for safety," he said, surprising me.

"Come inside, Alice," Sean said, stepping aside. "Ben can help you go upstairs and get settled while I finish talking to Jack and Caleb."

Still confused and a little on guard because of Jack's apparent concern for my wellbeing, I went into the house, followed by Ben. Sean closed the door behind us.

Caleb stood in the living room, wearing his usual black T-shirt and ripped jeans. He strongly disliked me, partly because Jack and Delia didn't like me, and partly because I'd told him to back off when he tried to intimidate me the first time we met.

Still, I greeted him. "Hi, Caleb."

"Hey," he said shortly.

"Patrick will be here in about forty-five minutes so you can head home," Sean told Ben. "In the meantime, can you go up to the guest room and flip the mattress and put some clean sheets on the bed? There's extra bedding in the hall closet."

If Ben wondered why I was staying in the guest room, he didn't comment. He headed up the stairs.

I started to follow, but Jack's voice stopped me. "Alice, just a minute."

I turned back. "Yes?"

He crossed his arms. "Just to make it clear where I stand, I've always believed it would be best for the alpha of a werewolf pack to choose a shifter as a mate and that hasn't changed. However, if there's a threat to you, we stand with you."

"That doesn't make any sense," Caleb objected. "Why stick our necks out for her? Like Delia said, it's Alice's problem; let her deal with it."

"That's not how a pack works." Sean joined Caleb in the living room while Jack and I stayed in the foyer. "An attack on any of us is an attack on all of us. Delia should know better than to say something like that. You're new to being a shifter and in a pack, but this is something you need to understand and feel: kinship with the rest of your pack."

"But Alice *isn't* pack," he argued. "If we were talking about Ben or Jack or Karen, sure, yeah, I'll step up. She's just your girlfriend or whatever. That doesn't make her pack."

Sean's eyes went bright gold in anger and he snarled. "Alice is my consort. It's a shifter title that makes her more than a girlfriend. She's a potential mate. She's human, but she's a powerful mage and she's demonstrated she can use shifter magic as well. In any case, I don't have to explain why she's important to me, but I want you to understand why even Jack, regardless of how he feels about Alice, is standing with her. It's a matter of honor, both his and the pack's. He might not want to admit it, but his instinct is to protect Alice, even if he wants something different for me."

A muscle moved in Jack's jaw. "He's right," he told Caleb. "When you accepted our invitation to join our pack, you took an oath to stand and fight with us. As long as Alice and Sean are together, that means protecting her too."

I pressed my hands to my abdomen and backed toward the kitchen. "I'm going to get some water and then help Ben upstairs. I'll try to catch a couple hours of sleep. Wake me up if anything happens."

"There's some over-the-counter medicine that might help you in our bathroom," Sean said. "Let me know if you need me to go get you anything."

"Thanks." I got a cup of water from the kitchen and headed for the stairs.

Sean met me at the foot of the steps, his expression softening despite the tension in the air. "Do you want me to come up and help you get settled in?"

I shook my head. "Finish your conversation with Jack and Caleb. I'll be fine. I probably picked up a stomach virus somewhere and all I need is fluids and sleep. Good night."

"Good night." He gave me a quick kiss on my forehead.

When I got to the top of the stairs, Ben stuck his head out of the guest room. "I'm about done in here. You need anything else?"

I shook my head and followed him back into the room. "The bed looks great. Thank you."

"Do I even want to know how you set the bed on fire?" His eyes twinkled.

I gave him a wry smile. "Accidental magic flare earlier. Happens to the best of us."

He grew serious. "Get some rest, okay? You look like you're about to collapse. And I know it's asking a lot, but trust us to keep you safe. I know you can protect yourself, but you're one of us now and that means you don't ever face anything alone. At some point you'll start believing that and it will give you more strength than you can imagine."

Sean had said something similar to me after the cuff incident, when he'd told me he loved me. My stomach cramped and I flinched.

"I'm going to take a shower and go to bed," I told Ben, rubbing my stomach.

He frowned. "You just took a shower at Vaughan's house, didn't you?"

"Oh. Right." I set my water cup on the nightstand. "Well, maybe

I'll just wash my face then. Thanks again, Ben. Say hi to Casey for me."

"I will. Good night, Alice."

"Good night." I closed the door behind him.

I took off my boots, cleaned by one of Charles's employees while I'd showered in Adri's apartment, and left a trail of clothes on the floor on the way to the bathroom. I'd intended to put on pajamas, wash my face, and go straight to bed, but I found myself turning on the shower. A hot shower would help me sleep, I reasoned.

I stepped under the spray and adjusted the taps until the water was nearly scalding. I shampooed, scrubbed, and soaped myself several times until my skin was red, but I still didn't feel as if I were clean.

Finally I emerged from the shower, dried myself off, and put on my pajamas. My stomach felt much better and I was suddenly so exhausted I barely made it across the room to turn off the bedroom light. I crawled under the covers and curled up.

I dozed off almost immediately, only to be awakened a few minutes later by a soft knock on the door. "Alice?" It was Sean.

My stomach began to churn again. I rolled over and pulled the covers over my head.

A long pause, then his footsteps went down the hall and into the master bedroom.

Silence.

I put a second pillow on top of my head and closed my eyes. In moments, I was asleep.

A GENTLE HAND shook my shoulder. "Alice."

I pulled the covers back, brushed hair back from my face, and blinked groggily, trying to focus.

Sean stood next to my bed, wearing an undershirt and khakis and holding his phone. It looked like he'd been in the middle of getting dressed when something had interrupted him. "I'm sorry to wake you up, but I wanted to let you know Ashley Brown has been found."

It took my fuzzy brain several seconds to remember who Ashley Brown was. I pushed myself up and rubbed my eyes so I could see the clock on the nightstand. It was a little after seven. I'd gotten about five hours of sleep.

"Where is she?" I asked, sounding half asleep.

"Dead, it looks like," he said grimly.

I tried to wake up. "It doesn't surprise me, really. What happened to her?"

"They found her car burned early this morning, out on a service road on the west side. There's a body in it, or what's left of a body. It's probably her, though I'm sure it's going to take dental records to know for certain."

"How'd you hear about it?"

"We always have someone listening to the police scanner up at the office. I asked them to let me know if a woman's body was found, or if her name was mentioned. The police found her a little after six o'clock this morning."

I threw the covers back and swung my legs over the side of the bed. "I'll go see if I can find anything out."

"It's a crime scene," he reminded me as I headed for the bathroom. "I can call people I know in the department and get some information. I didn't want you to get out of bed. You need more sleep."

"I can take Malcolm and have him snoop around without anyone knowing."

He halted me with a hand on my arm. I pulled free and stepped back.

He studied me. "How are you feeling?"

"A little queasy still, and obviously tired, but okay otherwise."

He gestured between us. "So this isn't because of you being tired or sick. This is something else."

I exhaled. "I don't know. Maybe."

His expression darkened. "What's happened in the last twenty-four hours? In the shower yesterday morning, everything seemed fine. But the moment we got back from the party, just like that—" He snapped his fingers "—everything changed. You pushed me away and couldn't get away from me fast enough. You haven't wanted me to touch you since. You flinch every time I come near you. Ben said you were your usual self when you were with him, but the second my name came up or you saw me, both at Vaughan's house and back here, you acted like you wanted nothing to do with me."

He took a step closer, his eyes locked on mine. "When you look at me, I don't see any of the feelings I'm used to seeing. I'm reeling because this has all happened in less than a day. Or over a weekend at the most, because Thursday night we almost broke the bed and I had to go to work on Friday looking like shit because we made love so many times that you wore *me* out and that has never happened once since I became a shifter. So I am asking you to tell me what's going on, and I want the truth."

I backed toward the bathroom. "The truth is that I need space. We've been together pretty much every day since before we left for the Bahamas and I feel smothered."

"I never once sensed you felt smothered," he argued. "Not while we were on vacation or since we got back. You had Arkady drop you off at my house yesterday morning instead of going back to your place because you wanted to be here with me, right? I even asked you if you wanted to go home first and you said no."

I frowned. I *had* wanted to come to Sean's house. I'd missed him so much over the weekend that the thought of not seeing him as soon as I got back, especially after the terrible night I'd had running through the woods, had been nearly unbearable. I'd wanted the comfort of his arms and his bed more than anything—I remembered that. Had it only been twenty-four hours ago? And yet at this moment the sight of him made my stomach churn like I'd swallowed a bunch of eels.

What the hell *had* happened? And why hadn't it occurred to me to wonder until now?

Sean flexed his hands. "Ben also said you looked relieved when he told you he was going to drive you to Vaughan's house instead of me."

"Is that why you had Ben take me?" I asked slowly. "To see how I'd react to you not going with me?"

He nodded. "The Alice I know would have been angry, or at least confused that I wasn't coming with you and instead went to go run some errand without telling you in person. You definitely wouldn't have been *relieved* that it was Ben driving instead, or glad I'd already left when you got out of the shower in Adri Smith's apartment."

I scowled. I didn't blame Ben for telling Sean all that—it *was* the truth, after all, and Sean was Ben's alpha—but damn it, none of it made sense to me, especially in the context of how I'd longed for Sean's comfort just yesterday morning.

"I need to take Malcolm out to the crime scene," I said finally. "Time is ticking. The longer I wait, the less chance there is of finding anything that might help us figure out how Ashley was involved and who killed her. This, whatever *this* is, will have to wait."

"I have a meeting at work, but I can probably get my partner Ron to sit in for me so I can go with you."

I shook my head. "I'll be fine. Bell won't make a move against me, knowing I'm in Valas's inner circle and I'm your consort." My stomach twisted and I sighed. "I'll call for backup if I need it."

"I do have some questions about how you became Valas's personal favorite."

I opened my mouth to tell him I didn't know, then closed it. Despite everything, I couldn't lie to him. Not volunteering the information was one thing. Lying was something else, something I'd promised myself I wouldn't do, because I cared about him and he loved me.

I *did* care, didn't I? No, I didn't. But didn't I?

I rubbed my temples. None of my thoughts made sense. "Let's put a bookmark there for now, okay? Go to work. I'll go out to the scene if you'll give me the address and we'll see what we can find out."

"And then I'll come home and we'll figure out what's going on with us." He frowned. "What's wrong with your arms?"

I realized I'd been scratching while I slept. Both of my forearms were red and some of the scratches were bloody.

"Oh, no," I groaned. "Did I get poison ivy or something out there in the woods?"

"I don't see any rash," he said. "It just looks like you've been scratching. Do they itch?"

"Yes." I sighed. "I guess I'll stop by a pharmacy on the way. Damn it, I wish I'd never agreed to go out there with Arkady."

"Given what's happened since then, I'm starting to think that too," Sean said grimly.

I went into the bathroom. Just as I was about to shut the door, he spoke. "Be safe, Alice. I love you."

My stomach cramped. I was glad my back was to him so he didn't see the moment I came close to bursting into tears. What the hell was wrong with me?

"Have a good day at work," I said and closed the door.

# CHAPTER 10

On the way to the west side, I stopped at a pharmacy for anti-itch cream and sat in the parking lot to apply it to my arms. I'd been tempted to pick up some antihistamines to help with the itching, but I figured they'd make me sleepy and since I was already running on very little sleep, making myself *more* tired wasn't really an option.

While I was stopped, I tried both of Aden's phone numbers and Ashley's number to confirm they were still all going straight to voice mail, and they were. If those phones were off, it would be difficult or nearly impossible to locate any of them, but if they were just set to go straight to voice mail, there was a good chance one or more would be trackable. Either way, it was worth trying.

My usual resource for such things, black-hat hacker Cyro, had been MIA for almost a month. Before she'd vanished without a trace, she showed up in person during our trip to the Bahamas to warn me that Catherine Murphy Atwood, my aunt, had survived being struck by the bolt of lightning I'd smited her with. Cyro had also revealed, in the form of a note, that she knew my real identity, and then disappeared.

The only number I had for her had been disconnected and she

hadn't made any contact with me since. I was left to wonder how much she knew and what she intended to do with the information she had. Her warning indicated she was at least marginally on my side, but the silence was unnerving.

I'd had many sleepless nights worrying about what might have happened to her, including whether she'd been caught by the feds and what information she might give up to them in exchange for leniency.

I couldn't tell anyone about my fears, since no one else knew my real identity. Sean knew Cyro had gone dark and he was concerned about it, but not in the same way I was, because he didn't know the real reason her disappearance had me on edge.

Cyro wasn't my only hacker acquaintance—just the best and fastest. Before Sean introduced me to Cyro, my go-to guy for this sort of thing was a college kid who called himself Flyboy. I got my burner phone from the glove compartment and turned it on. I sent a text containing Aden and Ashley's cell numbers to a number listed in my Contacts as OB/GYN.

While I waited for a reply, I headed for the southwest side of the city and the address Sean had given me. That part of town had a lot of industrial parks and factories, most of which were closed on the weekend. It would be a good place to get rid of a car and a body without being seen.

I realized I was scratching my arms again and gripped the steering wheel with both hands. If we didn't find anything out from the crime scene and I didn't get any other tips I could follow, maybe I should try to drop into a minor emergency center and see if a nurse could figure out why I was itching so badly.

The crime scene was a dead-end service road behind a factory that made extreme sports protective gear. Despite the maze of streets in the area, I found the scene without any trouble, thanks to the yellow police tape, a dozen emergency vehicles, and uniformed offi-cers and detectives in suits combing the area for evidence.

I didn't want to attract attention, so I turned into a lot about a block away and parked in a visitor spot in front of a different manu-facturer. I couldn't get into the scene to get a look at the car and find out what the cops knew, but luckily I had the perfect invisible spy who could.

I touched Malcolm's crystal on my bracelet. "*Release.*"

"Hey, Alice," Malcolm greeted me from the passenger seat area. He looked around. "Good morning, I guess. Where the heck are we?"

I told him about the burned car and the body. He whistled. "I hope she was dead before they set the car on fire."

"Yeah, me too. I would appreciate it if you'd go over there and see what you can find out."

"I'm on it. Back in a jiff." He went invisible and zipped away.

As I waited for him to get back, my burner phone buzzed with a text response from Flyboy. *Phones are currently not trackable. Number you referenced as AB last tower ping yesterday 1100 hours near Argex Road and Forty-Third West. Try again later?*

My heart sank. That tower was about three blocks away; I could see it from where I was parked. "Not trackable" meant the phone wasn't just off; it was probably toast.

I sent back a text: *Not at this time. Thank you.* I turned the phone off and stuck it back in my glove compartment.

About five minutes later, Malcolm returned. "It's a mess over there," he said heavily.

I blew out a breath. "Yeah, I figured. What do the cops know?"

"There's not much left of the car and whoever torched it took the plates, but they were able to find a VIN they could read and ID the owner. It's registered to Ashley Brown. The body is in the driver's seat, but there's high-velocity blood splatter and skull and brain matter on the pavement. They think she was killed outside the car and then put in the seat before they set it on fire. The ME said it looks like she was shot in the forehead with something big, like a .45, judging by the size of the wound, but he won't know for sure until they do the autopsy."

"Well, shit. Did they find anything else besides the car, the body, and the brains?" I asked.

"Two cell phones in the car. One of them might be Aden's, but they're just blobs of melted metal, glass, and plastic. The cops don't think they'll be of any use."

"The kid had two cell phones," I pointed out. "I wonder if Aden managed to hang onto one, or if they took it thinking they could use it somehow."

I got my burner phone out again and asked Flyboy to try tracking Aden's phones later, just in case someone had one and turned it on.

"Did you hear that?" Malcolm asked suddenly.

I put down my phone and listened intently. "What am I listening for?"

"I heard a scream. At least, I think that's what it was."

My eyebrows rose. "A scream?"

"Yeah. Hang on, I'm going to go check it out." He left the car.

My phone buzzed with an incoming message. *Wolf: What did you find out?*

I texted back a brief summary of what Malcolm had seen and overheard at the scene.

*Wolf: Shot in the forehead sounds like an execution.*

*Me: I know. So much for finding out what she knew about Aden.*

*Wolf: What's your next move?*

*Me: Not sure.*

*Wolf: Keep me posted.*

Malcolm popped back into the car. "Alice, you'll never guess what I just found," he said excitedly.

"I give up. What?"

"Ashley Brown."

I blinked. "I'm not following you."

"That scream I heard? It was her."

"But I thought she was—" I stopped. "You found her ghost."

"Yup."

I went from despair to hope in an instant. "Where is she? Did you ask her what happened?"

"Well, that's the thing...she's kind of a mess. She's over by her car, just kind of hovering and shrieking. I can't get anything coherent from her yet."

Ghosts who'd died suddenly or traumatically often manifested in the way he described, trapped in the moment of their death, reliving the terror and pain in an endless loop.

"Will you stay and see if you can get through to her? I don't know how much she'll be able to remember, but she might be our best source of information right now. Jump to me if and when you have something for us to go on."

"What are you going to do?"

"I'm going to see if I can get a meeting with Ezekiel Monroe. He and Darius Bell are allies these days, apparently."

"*What?*"

I explained how Bell had shown up at my house the previous afternoon only to be met by Monroe and his Vamp Court entourage. "The Court is backing Bell against Moses Murphy because Bell is the devil they know, according to Monroe. Bell has lost quite a few assets trying to keep Moses out of the city, so he needs the Court's support. That being the case, I'm hoping to talk Monroe into asking Bell to let Aden and Jana go."

"He might know why Bell's been collecting nulls, seeing's as how they're friends now." Malcolm's voice was bitter.

"Monroe said they were uneasy allies and frenemies at best." I didn't like seeing him so upset. "I'm sorry Bell found out where you are. I wish I'd protected you better. If I hadn't taken Jana's case, this wouldn't have happened. I'm sorry about that too."

His reply surprised me. "I'm not sorry. We had to help. No kid deserves to be in Bell's hands. We both knew the risks when we said we'd take the case. I'm more worried about you than me. If he doesn't already suspect you're Storm Girl, he will soon. He may decide coming after you is worth risking his alliance with the Court and pissing off the shifters."

"I doubt it, but I'm on guard just in case."

"You need someone watching your back, Alice. If I'm here trying to talk to Ashley the Banshee, I'm not protecting you. You don't want Sean with you for whatever reason, fine, and you don't want a whole Court security team for obvious reasons. Ask Monroe to give you Arkady as a bodyguard. They did that before, when Kent Stevens was after you."

"I'll think about that. It's a better option than a whole team, but Arkady works for the Court so she'll be following their orders. I don't want to put her in a position where our friendship conflicts with whatever those orders might be." I rubbed my face. "I keep trying to keep my personal and professional lives separate, but it never seems to work that way anymore."

"That's an impossible goal for someone like us. There's no division between personal and professional lives when you're a mage. I think you'll have to come to peace with that. You thought there was a difference before because you didn't *have* a personal life. You can't expect life to fit neatly into compartments and stay that way. People's lives are messy and yours is no different."

"Have you been reading philosophy books again?"

He grinned. "Nah, that was pure Malcolm. Being dead gives you perspective, maybe. I'm going back to try to get through to Ashley. Let me know what you find out from Monroe and whether Arkady will be backing you up. If you decide not to go that route, we'll come up with another plan, but I don't want you running around by yourself until things settle down, whenever that will be." He made a face. "Though this may be our new normal for a while. See you later." He left the car.

I scrolled through my contacts list and called Ezekiel Monroe's number. I expected it to be answered by one of his assistants, but Monroe himself greeted me. "Miss Worth, good morning. Do you need assistance?"

"Morning. I know it's asking a lot, but I wondered if you might have a few minutes in your schedule for a face-to-face? I could come to Northbourne anytime this morning."

"I'm actually downtown at the moment, just wrapping up a meeting. I have another engagement soon, but I could spare a few minutes if you could meet me nearby."

"It's the sort of conversation I wouldn't want anyone else to overhear."

"I suspected as much. My limousine is secure and warded against eavesdropping. Is that sufficient?"

"Yes, thank you. Where can I meet you?"

He gave me an address. "The car is in the private garage, sub-level two. You'll be expected."

"I'll be there in about twenty minutes. Thank you."

"You're most welcome, Miss Worth. We'll see you shortly."

WHEN I WAS HALFWAY to my destination, my phone beeped with an incoming message from Sean. *Wolf: My meeting is almost finished. Can I meet you somewhere?*

I responded at the next red light. *Me: Not right now. On my way to a meeting with Ezekiel Monroe.*

*Wolf: Where are you headed after your meeting?*

*Me: Depends on what he says.*

The light turned green just as his reply arrived. Traffic was heavy, so it was several blocks before I had a chance to read it.

*Wolf: I want you to be safe. Keep Malcolm with you.*

Resentment swelled. At the next red light, I responded. *Me: Malcolm is back at the scene trying to talk to Ashley's ghost. I'm fine on my own.*

Instead of a text reply, my phone rang. *Wolf Calling*. Grudgingly, I answered the call using my car's built-in speaker. "Hello."

"So, you found Ashley's ghost?" he asked.

At the sound of Sean's voice, my stomach began to churn. Whether it made me aggravated at him, or his call did, I wasn't sure. "Yes, but she's not very coherent. Malcolm is trying to get through to her. I'm driving downtown, so I really can't talk right now."

"When you're done meeting with Monroe, I want us to talk. Can we meet at your house?"

"It depends on what he tells me," I said, irritated at having to repeat my earlier statement. "I may have more important things I need to do."

Silence.

"Your case is important," he said finally. "I'm not suggesting it isn't, but I'm of the opinion there is nothing more important than us."

"Aden's life is more important."

"Are you going to ask Monroe for help getting Aden and Jana away from Bell?"

"Yes."

He pondered that. "There's a chance it might work, if Monroe will do it. Bell won't want the Court on his bad side."

The car in front of me stopped suddenly and I had to slam on my brakes to avoid rear-ending them. "I seriously need to drive. I'll talk to you later." I ended the call before he could reply.

I was only a few blocks from the address Monroe had given me, so I put Sean out of my mind and focused on finding the entrance to the garage. I found the correct building and the garage. I pulled up to a rolling metal door marked PRIVATE ENTRANCE and waited. After a moment, the door rolled up.

I followed the ramp down to sub-level two. There were several cars parked on that level, but only one limousine. A uniformed driver waited next to the rear passenger door. I parked in the spot next to the limo and got out. The driver gave me a nod and opened the limo's door. I climbed in and he closed the door behind me.

As I slid into the rear-facing seat, Ezekiel Monroe slipped a red file folder into his briefcase. Today he wore a charcoal-gray suit with a dark gray tie and a red pocket square as a subtle nod to his employers. His hair was held back with a gold clasp. He looked grave. "Miss Worth, you look no more rested today than when I saw you yesterday. Madame Valas was most displeased by your refusal to accept her offer of healing, as it was freely given and a gift of great value." He reached into his inside jacket pocket and withdrew the black vial. "Will you reconsider? Perhaps you didn't want to accept in front of Mr. Maclin, but he need not know."

"Whether or not to accept is my decision and no one else's. I don't answer to Sean any more than I answer to anyone else." I realized I sounded defensive and cleared my throat. Damn it, I *really* needed some sleep. "Once again, I appreciate the offer, but it's not necessary. I'm just tired. I didn't get as much sleep last night as I hoped I would."

"Because you were called to Mr. Vaughan's home to save his life." He returned the vial to his pocket. "The Court is deeply grateful to you for the risk you took, though the loss of the stone is regrettable. It's unfortunate you were forced to destroy it. Its value was immeasurable."

"I really had no choice. If that magic had gotten loose, it would have consumed everyone in the building and possibly everyone in Charles's line, and maybe anyone who'd shared his blood too. The stone was a vamp WMD. It never should have been sold on the open market. An object of power like that doesn't need to be floating around."

"And yet it was," Monroe said thoughtfully. "The stone is not the first such item to become available in recent months. One wonders why the sudden influx of such dangerous objects. I should make inquiries." He checked his watch. "Unfortunately, my time is limited, so I must ask why you wished to speak to me in person."

"I'm assuming you've heard about Darius Bell's recent interest in recruiting mages who can null."

He nodded. "We are aware."

"Do you know why?"

"I don't have that information."

My eyes narrowed. "That wasn't exactly an answer to my question."

The corners of his mouth turned up slightly. "I don't personally know the answer to your question. Is that a better response?"

"Yes." Meaning someone else *did* know. Possibly Valas. Hmm. "Well, then you probably also know not all of the nulls who have gone to work for him did so of their own free will."

"Many of the people who work for Bell did not join his organization voluntarily. That is common in cabals, unfortunately."

He wasn't wrong about that. "Well, yesterday he took a kid named Aden Peters." I held up my phone and showed him the picture of Aden in his Pokémon T-shirt. "Aden's mother Jana hired me to find him. Then one of Bell's lieutenants showed up at Jana's house, blasted me through two walls, and took Jana too, probably to use as leverage against Aden to get him to follow orders."

"Also a common practice."

His dispassionate replies grated on my nerves. "It's an evil practice. Here's why I called you. I would like you to ask Bell to let Aden and his mother go. Taking adults is one thing, but Aden is twelve. No child deserves to be in Bell's hands."

Monroe's eyebrows went up. "Did I give the impression I have any authority over Bell?"

"No, but Bell needs the Court's backing against Moses Murphy, so you do have some influence. Aden's a *child*, Ezekiel. I wouldn't ask otherwise."

"The situation is complex. There are a great many factors involved, far more than you realize. This is no simple favor you're requesting."

"I know it's not, but this is a child and his mother. The Court cannot possibly allow Bell to kidnap and torture children. You don't want Murphy taking over the city and Bell is less of a butcher than Murphy; fine, that makes sense. But there has to be a line somewhere, and if this isn't over the line then I don't know what is."

He tapped his fingers on the leather seat. "I would help you if I could."

"You said the Court was grateful to me for saving Charles's life." I leaned forward. "I just pulled your guy back from the edge, Zeke, when no one else could or would even *try*. So compared to that, making a couple of phone calls and using your unrivaled negotiation skills to spring a kid and his mom from your frenemy seems pretty doable."

"Please don't call me Zeke." Monroe sighed. "I will try."

"No, *do*. Or do not. There is no try."

He gave me a look of exasperation. "Are you quite finished quoting *Star Wars?*"

I thought about it. "I have a bad feeling about this."

He chuckled. "I must be on my way. I'll contact you when I have news. Is that satisfactory?"

"Yes. Thank you, Ezekiel."

"You're welcome. Do try to rest, Miss Worth. I would like to be able to tell Madame Valas when she wakes that you are back in fighting form."

"I'd find it easier to sleep if I knew Aden and Jana were back home."

"I'll make every effort to arrange their homecoming so you may rest easier."

"Thanks." I reached for the door handle.

The moment I touched the latch, the door swung open and the driver offered me his hand. With his help, I slid almost gracefully out of the limo as he closed the door.

"Thanks," I said with a smile.

He smiled back. "No problem. I'm Chris." He was a few inches taller than me and very muscular. He was also quite good looking, a detail I hadn't really attended to when I first arrived, since my mind was on Aden, but I was very much noticing now.

"I'm Alice," I said. We shook hands.

"I'm glad to finally meet you," he told me. "I've heard about you, but our paths never seemed to cross." He glanced at the limo. "We have to get going, but I hope to see you again soon."

"I'd like that. See you around, Chris."

He headed around to the driver's side and I got into my car. When I was inside, I felt a strange pang of guilt. Had I just flirted with someone without once thinking about Sean? On some level that felt wrong, but I couldn't figure out why. Sean was nosy and controlling and it made me sick just to be near him. Chris was good-looking and seemed nice. I hoped I'd see him again.

The limo pulled smoothly out of its spot and headed up the ramp. I turned the key in the ignition and followed. When we reached street level, the rolling door opened. The limo turned right. After a hesitation, I turned left and headed toward my house. I'd gotten only five hours of sleep since early Saturday morning and my eyelids were heavy. I wouldn't be of much use to Aden or anyone else if I didn't get at least a little more rest.

I hoped Monroe would be able to negotiate for Aden and Jana's release, but if he couldn't, I'd have to find them and figure out a way to get them out myself.

I CAUGHT myself speeding several times on the way home and had to force myself to slow down. I felt like I needed to get to my house as fast as I could, but I wasn't sure why. I wondered if Malcolm had made any progress talking to Ashley. If he had, he would have probably jumped to me, so he must still be trying to get through to her.

As I drove, I made a mental list of the people I wanted to call to see if they knew anything that might help me. First phone calls, then sleep, then maybe reconnaissance, if anyone had information about where Bell or the nulls might be. I scratched my arm and made a face. No, first a shower, I amended. Then phone calls, *then* nap.

When I turned onto my street, however, I spotted Sean's truck parked in front of my house. So much for a nap. I sighed and parked under my carport.

My front door opened as I trudged up the front steps. Sean wore an emerald green Maclin Security polo shirt and khakis. I wondered if he'd picked the green because it was my favorite color on him, or if it was coincidence. Green always brought out the gold flecks in his dark brown eyes, that little hint of werewolf I used to like so much. I frowned. That I *used* to like, or still liked? Why did my feelings about him seem so jumbled up?

"Hey," he said.

"Hey."

He closed and locked the door behind me. I took my bag to the living room and put it down on the couch. "Sean, I appreciate you coming over to check on me, but I need to make some phone calls and I'm really tired. Can't we do this later?"

He stopped a few feet away and studied me, his arms crossed. "I can't remember the last time you didn't ask me to join you for a nap, or when your eyes didn't light up when you saw me, but just now out front you looked at me like you don't even know me." He reached for my hand.

A sudden wave of fear and revulsion made me step back. "Don't," I said involuntarily.

His expression hardened. "Okay, that's it. What the hell is going on, Alice?"

My stomach churned. "I don't want you here. Go home."

"No. There's something wrong with you, and until I know what it is, I'm not leaving. The last time I did that, you were spiraling into depression and I let you push me away when you needed me. You're pushing me away again. This time I don't even think you know why you're doing it and that's the most worrisome thing of all."

The longer he stood next to me, the more panicky I became. I hadn't had a full-blown panic attack in months, but I felt like I might be on the verge of one now. I backed away from him, my hands pressed to my cramping stomach.

I had the sudden thought that if I could get far enough away, the fear and pain would disappear. I could go to my basement and use the wards to keep him out. I turned and ran.

He intercepted me halfway to the basement door, his hand closing gently on my upper arm. "Alice, wait—"

At his touch, it felt like broken glass ripped through my insides. I screamed.

He let go instantly as the pain drove me to my knees. Nausea surged. I coughed and blood splattered on the floor.

Sean swore and crouched next to me, but I scrambled away, desperate to put as much distance between us as I could. My back hit the wall and I huddled near the doorway to the kitchen. I wiped my mouth, leaving a streak of blood on the back of my hand. My arms and legs itched mercilessly. I coughed again and more blood came up.

Sean's eyes blazed with fury, but he stayed where he was. "This is some kind of magic, isn't it?"

I was shaking so hard that I could barely talk. "I c-can't be spelled," I managed to say. "I have n-n-natural shields."

His expression softened. "Someone's figured out how to spell you anyway, despite your shields," he argued. "There's no other explanation for what's happening to you and how you've been acting. How would they do it? Think, Alice."

I scooted farther back, retreating to the corner. "All I can think about is getting away from you so the pain stops."

He growled. "Then get Malcolm here and we'll figure out what's wrong. Someone did this to you, and when I figure out who, I will tear them apart."

"Malcolm's trying to talk to—"

"I don't care, Alice." His fists clenched as he struggled to hold himself back from coming to me. "You're coughing up blood. Please summon him *now*, before this gets any worse."

Part of me resisted doing what he said, but I needed Malcolm's help. Yesterday when I'd summoned my ghost, it made me light-headed and nauseous. This time, the wave of dizziness caused me to black out for a few seconds.

When I opened my eyes, I found myself lying on the floor. With effort, I touched the buzzing crystal on my bracelet. "*Release.*"

Malcolm appeared, hovering above me. His eyes widened. "What the hell is going on?"

I curled into a ball. "I don't know."

The pain in Sean's eyes made my stomach twinge. "Every time I get near her, she panics and tries to run," he told Malcolm. "I touched her arm and she coughed up blood. This has to be magic of some kind."

"Not our kind of magic," Malcolm said. "She's a high-level mage, so her natural shields mean she can't be spelled like a low-level mage or a mundane human can."

"Then what other kind of magic could do something like this?"

Malcolm floated back, his expression grave. "Come over here and smell her."

Looking puzzled, Sean started in my direction.

My stomach cramped and I whimpered. "No, stay away."

He moved back, his eyes golden, fury radiating off him in waves. "If I get near her, I may cause her more harm than I already have."

Malcolm seemed to be thinking. "Is there someone else from your pack who could come over here and see if they can smell something strange? Someone Alice trusts?"

"Alice, can I ask Nan to come over?" Sean asked me gently.

"Okay." My stomach churned and panic threatened to sweep over me again. I was almost hyperventilating. "Please go into another room."

He took his cell phone and went into the kitchen. After a moment, I heard his voice speaking urgently, but I couldn't tell what he was saying.

Malcolm hovered over me. "I told you something was wrong."

"Nobody likes people who say *I told you so*," I told him through gritted teeth. I wrapped my arms tighter around my knees and closed my eyes. "Did you get anything from Ashley?"

"No, but I'm not giving up. I'll keep trying, once we figure out what the hell is going on here."

"Why did you ask Sean to smell me?"

"Because I think I know why you're scratching your arms and feeling like you're still dirty, even though you've showered a million times since yesterday. You *have* been spelled, but not by a mage."

I opened my eyes and stared at him. "You mean—?"

"Yep," he said grimly. "You've got a witch after you, Dorothy, and not the cute nose-twitching kind. More like the flying monkeys and skywriting kind. I do believe you've been hexed."

# CHAPTER 11

NAN ARRIVED ABOUT A HALF-HOUR AFTER SEAN CALLED HER. BY THEN THE pain in my abdomen had faded to a dull ache, but I had an odd metallic taste in my mouth and my arms and legs itched ferociously.

When she knocked, Sean came out of the kitchen and headed for the door. Even the sight of him made my stomach rebel and I had to close my eyes and try to think of something else so I didn't vomit.

I heard quiet voices and then soft footsteps hurried from the foyer into the living room. "Oh, Alice," Nan said, her voice a combination of worry and anger.

I opened my eyes as she knelt beside me and put her hand on my forehead. My mother used to do the same whenever I was sick. Her warm touch was comforting. I closed my eyes again. Tears pricked my eyelids.

"Sean tells me I'm supposed to see if I can smell anything odd," Nan said, stroking my hair. "Is it all right if I lean close to you?"

I took a shaky breath. "Yes."

She inhaled deeply several times. "Sean, I smell her blood and your house, of course, plus several other people and a lot of incidental odors from the places she's been today. All that seems normal.

The only thing that's strange is a smell that reminds me of mud and rotting plants, but with notes of something like burned hair. It's faint, but I don't think I've ever smelled anything quite like it before."

"She's smelled like mud since yesterday," Sean said from the kitchen. "I assumed it was because of the camp. I thought it was odd, though; if she'd showered, the scent of mud should have been faint or nonexistent, even to me. That plus the way she acted…" He growled. "Damn it, I should have listened to my instincts. They were telling me something was wrong."

Nan's mouth became a grim line. "What's going on here? What's wrong with this poor girl?"

"We think she may have been hexed," he said.

"Hexed, as in by a witch? What in heaven's name for?"

"Since the effects of the spell seem to only kick in when she's around me, I think it's pretty obvious what the hex was supposed to do." His anger prickled on my arms. "Somebody's trying to drive us apart, and they don't care if it kills Alice in the process."

Nan went back to stroking my hair. "You don't think Jack is behind this, do you?"

"Hiring a witch to hex someone isn't his style. If he was trying to undermine our relationship, he wouldn't be underhanded about it. This…" He growled. "This is more like something Delia might do."

"First things first," Nan said briskly. "We have to undo this hex so poor Alice doesn't suffer any more, and then we'll have to figure out who was behind it. You mustn't jump to any conclusions. We'll follow the evidence and see where it leads us, just like a good investigator would do. Isn't that right, Alice?" She squeezed my hand. "Now, how do we get rid of a hex?"

"We need a witch," Sean said.

Nan frowned. "How on earth are we going to find a witch? The internet?"

"The Vampire Court has witches who work for them," I interjected shakily. "I can call Bryan or Adri."

"Not the Court," Sean stated. I could see his shadow in the

kitchen doorway. He stood just around the corner, as close as he could get to me without being in my sight. "I don't trust anyone they'd send to help you. I know a witch. I'll call her now."

As Sean retreated into the kitchen to make a phone call, I closed my eyes and tried to ignore the nausea and my itchy arms and legs.

I had no idea Sean knew any witches. He'd never mentioned it, but then again witches and witch magic had never really come up in conversation between us as far as I could remember. I wondered how he'd met a witch.

"By the pricking of my thumbs," I muttered and scratched my arm.

Nan smoothed the hair back from my face and finished the quote. "Something wicked this way comes."

I INTRODUCED Nan to Malcolm while we waited for Sean's witch acquaintance to arrive. I hadn't wanted members of Sean's pack to know about Malcolm, since he was hiding from Darius Bell, but I believed Nan could be trusted—and besides, I reflected grimly, Bell knew where Malcolm was now, so keeping my ghost secret wasn't as crucial as it had been even yesterday morning.

As I expected, Nan took the news of my ghost sidekick in stride. "Nice to meet you, Mr. Ghost."

"Call me Malcolm," he told her cheerily. "*Mister* Ghost is my father."

Nan smiled. "A spirit with a sense of humor. You and Alice must get along well."

"Generally speaking, we do, yes." He hovered over me, clearly worried. "Despite all the trouble she gets herself into, I stick by her side."

Nan helped me move from the floor to the couch, but that was as far as I could make it without being carried. She sat down next to me, put my head in her lap, and rubbed my back. My guts churned like I'd swallowed a food processor and my arms and legs itched so badly I had to hug myself tightly to keep from scratching myself to death—maybe literally.

"Alice?" Sean called from the kitchen. "Can I talk to you, or does that still make you sick?"

At the sound of his voice, the broken-glass-in-a-blender feeling in my stomach intensified, along with the urge to get somewhere far away from him. I set my jaw and fought to stay calm. Intellectually I knew the sickness and panic were probably the result of a hex, but knowing that didn't make the pain and fear go away. My frustration became anger and the anger displaced my fear.

"Go ahead," I said through gritted teeth.

"You know I want to be holding you right now and it's making me furious that I can't." His anger prickled on my skin.

"I know." My stomach cramped so hard I couldn't stifle a pained sound. Blast it, I couldn't even think about us being together without the triple-damned hex kicking in.

Sean snarled. "I'll find out who's behind this and make them pay."

"*I'll* make them pay," I corrected him. "Since I'm the one coughing up blood, I get first dibs."

He growled. "I'll flip you for it."

I managed a small smile. Nan squeezed my hand.

"If Malcolm's right about this being a hex, how is it possible that a witch can spell you if mages can't?" Sean wanted to know.

"Because our magic is completely different." I took a few deep breaths, trying to settle my stomach so I could at least explain this part of the problem. "There are many kinds of magic, not just one. My magic is natural magic, and my ability to control the power of earth and air is innate. Shifter magic, like vamp and fae magic, is supernatural in origin, which is why mages can't use it. Witch magic is metaphysical and spiritual. Their power comes from working with what they call universal and elemental energies, and from their gods and goddesses. My natural shields have no effect on witch magic, and I can't sense their spells or hexes any more than a mundane human can."

"That makes sense," Sean said. He paused, then added, "You're probably wondering how I know a witch."

"I was, actually." I forced myself to stop scratching my arm.

"There's a bit of my Alice." He sounded relieved. "Her name is Carly Reese. A mutual friend introduced us after you and I split up a few months ago. We went on a few dates." His voice was uncertain, as if he was concerned about how I would react to the news.

I blinked. I hadn't really thought about whether Sean had dated anyone in the month or so we'd been separated after I'd almost died because of Amelia Wharton and the *Kasten*. I'd been afraid of the intimacy we'd shared and wary of letting him get close enough to realize how traumatized I was, so I'd picked a fight with him and pushed him away.

"Alice?" he prodded. "I'm sorry I never mentioned her. We had a little bit of a spark, but it wasn't what either of us were looking for."

"It's all right," I said. "You have nothing to apologize for."

"He was still thinking about you," Nan said with a smile as she rubbed my back. "Even before I met you, I knew you had to be an extraordinary woman because all that time you were on his mind."

"You were all I could think about," Sean admitted. "Carly sensed it. She told me I needed to call you or I'd always regret that I didn't."

My stomach cramped. "It's all right," I said again, my voice strained. "Your friend can just drop what she's doing and come over in the middle of the day?"

"She said it wasn't a problem. She owns a coffee shop and said her employees could take care of things while she was gone. She should be here any minute."

"A witch who owns a coffee shop. I think she and I could be friends." I closed my eyes and curled up a little tighter.

A few minutes later, I felt a tingle as someone crossed the

perimeter wards. "I think she's here," I said, squeezing my eyes shut so I didn't see Sean heading for the front door. He went outside.

Nan gently pulled my hands away from my arms and held them tightly. "You're scratching yourself bloody. When we find this witch who hexed you, I don't know what I'll do to them, but it will be unpleasant!"

"Not half as unpleasant as what I'm going to do," I muttered.

The front door opened. "Now you stay outside until I tell you it's all right to come in," a firm female voice said. "I need her thinking clearly so we can get to the bottom of this."

"All right," Sean said reluctantly.

The door closed and footsteps moved quickly from the foyer into the living room. I heard a thump, as if someone had set a heavy bag on the floor.

"Well, my goodness, you *are* a mess," the newcomer said finally.

I opened my eyes. The petite brunette witch stood with her hands on her hips, her brow furrowed as she looked me over. She wore a blue button-up shirt with the sleeves rolled up to her elbows, a knee-length black skirt, and tall black boots. She appeared to be in her late thirties.

"Thanks," I said dryly. "I like your boots."

"Aren't they great? Clearance sale this spring." She approached the couch. "Hi, I'm Carly Reese."

I managed to sit up. "Alice."

As Nan introduced herself, I got a better look at my guest. She wore simple hoop earrings and several ornate rings, but I couldn't see any overt signs she was a witch until I spotted the amulet neck-lace tucked inside her shirt.

The inside of her right forearm bore a colorful tattoo of flowering vines. When I looked closer, I saw runes disguised in the foliage. My own tattoos contained hidden runes and spellwork. I wondered if Carly's held magic too, and if so, what kind.

"Well, let's see if we can figure out what's going on," Carly said briskly. "I'm told you're itchy and your stomach hurts and you smell like mud, rotting plants, and burned hair. That could be a couple of things, so let me ask you some questions. When did you start feeling like you didn't want Sean to touch you?"

I thought about it. "Yesterday morning, on our way back to his house after the birthday party, I think everything was fine. When we got back to his house, he tried to put his arms around me and I didn't want him to. Then he wanted to lie down with me to take a nap and I remember thinking I wouldn't be able to sleep with him so close to me."

"And the dirty, itchy feeling? Did it start around the same time?"

I made a face. "A few hours later, I think. That one's harder for me to pin down because I spent the weekend at a survival camp with a friend and I came home feeling dirty from that. We crawled around in the mud a lot."

"That sounds like a lot of fun," she said. She'd clearly never been to one of the damn things. "Does the dirty, itchy feeling intensify when you're around Sean?"

"That seems fairly constant. The nausea and stomach pain do get worse, though—much worse."

"Did it start out as mild and get more severe between yesterday and today?"

I nodded. "Yesterday, it was more like discomfort. At the time, I thought the nausea and pain were caused by healing spells and anxiety about the case I'm working on. Now, looking back, I realize it got worse when we were together and better when we were apart." I gestured at the floor. "Today, I panicked and tried to run away from him. When he grabbed my arm, I coughed up blood. That's when we figured out I might have been spelled or hexed."

Her mouth became a grim line. "Yesterday morning, at some point after you left the birthday party, can you remember feeling dizzy or disoriented, or maybe smelling smoke?"

"I don't remember smelling smoke, but something strange did happen right as we got back to his house after the party," I told her. "When I went to get out of his truck, I blacked out for just a moment and fell. I thought I was just tired or I'd tripped on something. I didn't think anything of it at the time. Is that when the spell kicked in?"

"I certainly think so. That's likely the moment the spell was invoked. One more question: have you noticed any items of clothing or jewelry go missing recently?"

I frowned. "Yesterday morning I couldn't find the scarf I'd planned to wear to the party." Anger made magic spark on my fingertips. "A piece of my clothing would be a key ingredient in a spell like this, wouldn't it?"

"If it's the type of hex I think it is, yes it would. And since Miss Nan can smell a hint of burned hair on you, I'd guess they used some of your hair, too."

My thoughts raced. "They couldn't have come in here to get anything. My house is heavily warded."

"I noticed," Carly said wryly. "Being inside it feels like I'm standing next to a high-voltage power line. When this is over and we've gotten you de-hexed, I'd love to talk wards and spellwork with you and compare notes."

"I'd like to do that, really. I've never really gotten to talk magic with a witch." I pressed my hands to my stomach. "I had the scarf at Sean's house, so whoever took it was someone he let in."

Nan spoke up. "Not the witch who cast the spell, but someone else—someone in our pack." She was angrier than I'd ever seen her. Her eyes were bright gold. I had the sudden feeling Sean might not get a chance to deal with the traitor, not if Nan got to him or her first.

"Very possibly," Carly said. "The first order of business is to undo this hex. I'm fairly certain I know what kind of spell this is, and if I'm right, I can break it without too much trouble."

"Great. Did you bring what you'll need to break it?"

"Yes, but it's not that simple."

I sighed. "Of course it isn't."

Carly sat on the loveseat. "Let me explain what I think happened. Based on what you've told me, I believe you've been hexed with a spell called *Push a Lover Away*. Its original purpose was probably to cause you to no longer have feelings for Sean and break up your relationship."

"But why make her feel itchy and dirty?" Nan wanted to know. "And if the spell was just supposed to make Alice push Sean away, why is she in so much pain and coughing up blood?"

"If I had to guess, I'd say the itching and unclean feelings were added at the request of whoever bought the hex, probably to make Alice as miserable as possible. You're probably looking for someone who is spiteful and thinks they were wronged."

I knew quite a few of those people, unfortunately. "And the pain? I thought witches believed in doing no harm—that by causing others pain, they risked bringing it back on themselves threefold."

"Most do believe in the Rede and the Threefold Law. *I* certainly abide by them. Obviously the witch who made the spell doesn't. I can't know for certain just yet, but the pain you're experiencing might not have been intended." Carly waved her hands. "I'm getting ahead of myself, so let me back up. I think someone approached a witch with a request to break up your relationship. The witch created a poppet, or a lifelike doll, and filled it with the necessary ingredients. Then she spoke the spell and gave it to whoever wanted it, along with instructions on how to invoke it by saying your full name three times. But if they said your name more than three times—five or seven times, let's say—it would make the spell stronger, to the point of causing you pain. If they said your name more than that, it could kill you outright."

"I guess I should be glad they only said my name five or six times, then," I said. I knew what a poppet was, but this kind of magic was so very different from my own that I had a difficult time envisioning how the spell worked. "What did the witch put in the poppet, do you think?"

"I hope to find out for sure, but my guess would be a piece of your missing scarf, some of your hair—possibly taken from your brush—grass and dirt for the unclean feeling, poison ivy for the itching, and live or dead ants so you'd feel, well, antsy." Carly's dark eyes blazed with anger. "The hex prevented you from realizing anything was wrong with either your actions or your thoughts. It stole your free will. I'm very sorry a witch did this to you, Alice. It's immoral and unethical."

I was scratching like mad again. Nan took my hands in hers and held them still. "This is diabolical," she said. "What do we need to do to break this hex?"

"First, I need to go tell Sean what we've figured out before he wears through your sidewalk with his pacing," Carly told us. "Then I'll try a tracking spell to see if I can find out who has the poppet. Once we get it, I can break the hex and you'll be yourself again."

"You have tracking spells?" I asked, surprised. "How do yours work?"

"Similar to yours, I think. I get a glimpse of where something is and usually who possesses it."

"How do you see it, though? Through scrying?"

She shook her head. "I don't have that gift, though I know practitioners who do and I can call them for help if I need to. The spell I use grants me brief visions." She stood. "Let me go speak with Sean and then I'll come back and try the tracking spell."

When she was gone, Nan squeezed my hands. "Alice, I'm sorry someone has done this to you. I don't want to think someone from our pack is behind this hex, but if something of yours has been taken from Sean's house, I can't think of any other explanation. If Carly is right and whoever invoked the spell made it stronger by saying your name too many times, they could easily have killed you."

A loud noise from outside startled both of us. Nan sighed. "I do believe that was your trash bin. Sean will have to replace it, I suppose." A second bang, much louder. "And that as well, whatever it was. It might have been the side of his truck, judging by the sound." She squeezed my hands again and stood. "Let me go talk to him. Will you be all right for a few minutes?" She glanced around. "Mr. Ghost—Malcolm—will you watch over her?"

"Always," Malcolm said, his voice coming from the kitchen door-way. He'd gone invisible when Carly arrived and stayed in another room to avoid being noticed by her, but he'd been able to hear what was said.

We heard another loud noise from outside. "You'd better go out there before someone calls the cops about a crazed werewolf destroying his truck with his bare hands," Malcolm said.

Nan hurried out the front door. We listened but didn't hear anything more from out front. Yay, Nan. She'd probably marched out there and scolded Sean like an errant child.

Malcolm became visible and floated over to me. "Witch magic is so weird," he complained. "Scraps of cloth, a handful of dirt, burned hair, and *ants* stuffed into a doll. Rituals and incantations. Stop scratching or I'll zap you."

I didn't want to get zapped, so I sat on my hands. "She'd prob-ably think the same about our magic. Her power is wondrous too. It's just different from ours."

"Well, I just hope she can find out who's got the damn thing so we can get it and break the hex and things can get back to normal." He made a face. "Or what passes for normal around here, anyway."

"Normal is just a setting on the washing machine."

"That's very deep, Tyrannosaurus Hex."

I gave him a look.

"This is why everyone needs comprehensive *hex* education."

"Please stop."

"You better check yourself—"

"Malcolm, I swear—"

"—before you hex yourself," he finished. "Now I'm done. No, wait. What kind of car does Carly drive? I bet it's a—"

"Hexus," I said with a sigh. "Thank you for trying to cheer me up."

"No problem. Is it working?"

I waggled my hand. "Sorta."

"Well, darn it all to hex."

"Malcolm. Language."

The front door opened and Carly and Nan came back inside. Malcolm returned to the kitchen. I caught a glimpse of Sean on the porch, his eyes bright gold and fists clenched, like a volcano about to explode. A flash of pain made me wince. Then Nan closed the door, blocking him from my view.

"What did he do to his truck?" I asked as they returned to the living room.

"He punched it. Twice." Nan sat next to me on the couch as Carly brought her bag to the coffee table and unzipped it. "I told him he could distract himself by calling body shops while we work."

Carly withdrew a small pair of scissors from her bag. "For the tracking spell, I need a little piece from your clothing, some nail clippings, and hairs from your brush. You need to give them to me freely."

I unbuttoned my shirt and took it off, leaving me in a tank top. I held it out. "Take what you need."

"You give this to me freely?"

"Yep. Yes, I give it to you freely," I repeated formally. "Nan, can you go upstairs to my bathroom and bring down my brush?"

As Nan went to get the brush, Carly cut a piece from the shirt about four inches square. With a tiny pair of scissors, she trimmed the ends of my nails and gathered the little slivers in a pile on the coffee table. When Nan came back, Carly plucked some hairs from my brush.

From her bag, she took a black cloth with a pentagram on it and spread it over the coffee table, centering the pentagram carefully on the table.

At each point of the star she placed an item. "A feather for air," she told me, placing it in the upper right and then moving clockwise around the pentagram. "A candle for fire. Stones for earth. A seashell for water." At the top of the star she placed a ceramic figure with wings. "And an angel for Spirit." She took a small cast-iron cauldron about the size of a halved grapefruit and set it in the center of the pentagram.

She withdrew an athame from her bag. "Miss Nan, I know Alice has no issue with the practice of magic done the Old Way, but if this makes you uncomfortable, I understand. I'd just ask for you to step outside so your resistance doesn't interfere with this spell."

"Thank you for asking, but I have no objection to your beliefs or practice." Nan smiled wistfully. "My grandmother practiced the Craft and as a child I spent a lot of happy evenings and nights watching her work. Her kitchen was like heaven to me. So, carry on and don't worry about me."

"Wonderful." Carly smiled. "I need to make a circle around all three of us. Can you sit on the floor?"

Nan helped me stand up from the couch. My knees were wobbly but I felt stronger with Sean outside and out of sight. She lowered me carefully to the floor and sat down next to me.

Carly bent and pointed the tip of the athame at the floor. "I cast this circle three times three to protect those in the circle that no harm may come to them or those outside of the circle." She walked around us three times, clockwise, and then sat cross-legged across the table from us.

She closed her eyes and took several deep breaths, inhaling through her nose and out through her mouth. I did the same whenever I needed to clear my head and center myself before doing complicated spellwork.

Carly took a wooden match from the box and struck it. She picked up the piece of my shirt and focused on it. I sensed a rise of power and caught a trace of a scent I couldn't quite identify, but that smelled like old paper or parchment.

"Universe, hear me," she said, lowering the corner of the fabric to the flame. It caught and began to burn. "Help me find the object that has been hexed to make Alice Worth so sick so I may retrieve it and break the hex." She placed the fabric in the cauldron to burn with the hair and nail clippings and closed her eyes. "As I will it, so mote it be."

We waited. I realized I was holding my breath. A minute ticked by. Two. The piece of shirt turned to ash and the flames died. Nan took my hand and squeezed it.

Carly's eyes opened. "I've seen her in her home, holding the poppet." Her voice sounded a little dreamy. "She is blonde. Very angry. The wolf within her desires Sean. The woman desires power most of all."

Shifter magic sizzled on my skin, but for once it wasn't Sean's.

Nan's eyes went bright gold. For the first time since I'd met her, she growled. "*Lily.*"

⁂

"How do you feel?"

From the front passenger seat, I glanced over at Carly, who was driving. "Angry. Really, really angry." Magic sparked on my fingers.

She smiled. "Other than that. Tummy feeling better?"

"Yes, now that I'm away from…" I hesitated. Saying his name made my stomach hurt, so I just shrugged.

"Miss Nan is a pretty amazing woman." Carly slowed to make a turn as we headed toward Lily's house in her car. "I didn't think there was much chance of us making this trip by ourselves, but she made it happen. I don't know what she said, but he was calm when we left. I think he understood why you wanted to go with me and why he needed to stay at your house until we got back. He didn't like it one bit, but he understood."

Once Carly broke the circle, she and Nan had gone outside together to tell Sean what the tracking spell had revealed. I didn't hear any loud noises, but I could only imagine how furious he was. At first, he'd flatly refused to stay behind while we came to confront Lily and get the poppet, but somehow Nan was able to convince him facing Lily was something I needed to do, and I needed to do it without him being there. Lily had attacked me and this was my battle. Finding out which of his wolves had stolen my scarf and hair from his house was his.

I would have gone by myself but Carly needed to be with me to help find the poppet. Malcolm was with me as well, as backup, but stashed in my bracelet so my witch companion couldn't sense him.

"He's a good man," she added.

I detected a note of something in her voice. Wistfulness, maybe, or regret. "This must be awkward for you," I told her. "I can't imagine what you thought when he called you out of the blue and told you he needed help de-hexing me."

"I'm all right, really," she assured me. "We were introduced through a mutual friend who works at Maclin Security in the installation department. We went on a couple of dates, but I could tell right away he was still so hung up on you that he couldn't bring himself to enjoy my company, like he thought he was somehow cheating on you. Part of it might have been that his wolf thought of you as a potential mate, but the man was already head-over-paws for you too." She smiled at the memory. "I'm an empath, but I didn't need to be to sense how deeply he missed you. The third time we went out to dinner, I swear I felt like you were sitting at the table with us. I flat-out told him that he needed to either give your relationship another try or find a way to let you go. He called about a week later to tell me you'd crossed paths while on a case and were back together."

She gave me a rueful smile. "I won't say I wasn't disappointed because the Goddess knows he's gorgeous and kind, but how could I not wish him all the happiness in the world? And now I've met you, even though you're not at your best, I can see why he couldn't get you out of his mind. Your aura is pure power, Alice. It's unlike anything I've ever felt. He's a fierce man with a good heart and he needs a woman who's like him. He certainly needs nothing to do with this Lily. I know poison when I see it."

We turned into Lily's subdivision. Carly studied the houses and finally spotted our destination, a two-story beige home with a brick mailbox and neatly trimmed hedges out front.

She parked in the driveway and we got out. I'd put on a long-sleeved shirt to hide my arms and redone my makeup to cover the dark shadows under my eyes. I didn't want to give Lily the satisfaction of seeing what the triple-damned hex had done to me.

I marched up the front steps and rang the doorbell.

After a moment, footsteps approached the door. I imagined Lily was peering out through the peephole and getting the shock of her life.

When nothing happened, I raised my voice. "Don't make me huff and puff and blow your little house down, Lily."

The deadbolt turned and the door opened. Lily wore a sleeveless green pantsuit and sandals and her hair was perfectly arranged. I wondered if she was about to go somewhere or had just gotten back, or if she routinely looked so perfect just hanging out at home.

"Alice, hello," she said with a smile so big and fake that it made my skin crawl. "I had no idea you knew where I lived. And who's your friend?"

I glanced at Carly for confirmation that Lily was who she'd seen in her vision. She gave me a nod.

"I want the poppet, Lily," I said.

Her smile froze. "You want what? What's a poppet?"

"A small cloth doll, probably stuffed with dirt, hair, ants, and a piece of a scarf someone stole from Sean's house. Go get it."

"I have no idea what you're talking about," she huffed. "I think you need to get off my property before I call the police."

"You know, at first I was angry, but now I actually feel sorry for you," I told her, ignoring her threat. "You don't want Sean because you love him. You just want to win. You think that's where happiness comes from, but that's the kind of happiness that doesn't last very long. As long as you chase that kind of happiness, you'll never get anything worth having."

Her face reddened. "You don't know anything about me," she spat. "Where's Sean?"

"He's busy. This is between you and me." I glanced around. "Do you want to invite us in or do you want to have this conversation on your front porch in front of your neighbors?"

"Fine." She stepped back and we walked inside. She slammed the front door. "He was *mine*," she snarled.

"He was never yours and you know it. That's one reason your plan was doomed from the start."

"I don't know what plan you're referring to," she snapped.

"The other reason it failed is that you thought it would be a simple matter of turning me against Sean and he'd be yours, but that proves how little you understand him. My strange behavior only made him care *more*, not less. Did you honestly think if I suddenly wanted nothing to do with him, that would cause him to end our relationship? And even if the hex caused us to split up, he still wouldn't be yours because he recognizes you for what you are."

Her eyes turned bright amber. "And what is that, Alice? What exactly am I?"

"Lonely."

She blinked.

"Lonely and spoiled and used to getting your way. And maybe you *do* get your way in most things, but not this time." I spooled magic and let my eyes glow. A cold wind blew through the foyer. "Go get the poppet, Lily. Don't make me ask again, and don't make me look for it myself."

She stared at me, her eyes bright. I held her gaze and didn't blink. Green magic flared on my fingertips.

She spun on her heel and headed upstairs, leaving us in the entryway.

"The green fire was a nice touch," Carly murmured. "I like your style."

"Thanks. We'll see if it worked."

Lily came back down the stairs holding a small wooden box. Carly took it and opened the lid.

Inside was a small cloth figure in the shape of a person, with arms, legs, and a head, but no features except a string tied around its middle like a belt or sash. A plain black button dangled from the end of the string.

"Where's my scarf?" I asked Lily as Carly picked up the poppet and studied it.

"I gave it to the witch."

"Which witch?" I demanded.

Beside me, Carly chuckled.

Lily crossed her arms. "She didn't tell me her name and I didn't ask. I wouldn't tell you even if I knew."

"Who gave you the scarf?"

She narrowed her eyes. "I found it."

She wasn't going to give up her ally in the pack—I could see that. No matter; Sean and I would find out.

Carly looked up at Lily, her expression grim. "When you spoke Alice's name to invoke the spell, how many times did you say it?"

Lily shrugged. "Six or seven. I wanted to be sure it worked."

"Were you not told to say her name only three times?"

"Probably. Who cares?"

"I do." Carly shut the box and stepped toe-to-toe with the much-taller woman. "Magic like this is not to be taken lightly or used carelessly. Speaking an invocation that many times can kill outright. You almost committed murder."

A little of the color drained out of Lily's face. "I didn't know."

"And that's why you need to leave magic alone." Carly rejoined me at the door. "Let's get you de-hexed, Alice."

For a moment, I entertained myself with a brief fantasy of lopping off one of Lily's perfectly manicured hands, but doing so might spark a war between Sean and Zachary's packs. Besides, I'd sort of promised Malcolm I'd try not to cut off any more appendages.

"This isn't over," Lily said bitterly, interrupting my thoughts. "An alpha needs a shifter mate, not some mage. You don't deserve him."

"Maybe I don't, but not because I'm a mage." My stomach cramped at the thought of Sean and I together, but I was angry enough that the pain barely registered. "I promise that if you'd killed me, Sean would have found out eventually what happened to me, and he would have killed you, *slowly*. As it is, you're going to face some serious repercussions from the Were Ruling Council, and you can probably say goodbye to any chance of finding an alpha for a mate after this news gets out. You're going to be the last person any alpha would want." I smiled thinly. "Alphas need partners who lead their pack by example and solve problems, not make them, and they certainly don't want anyone who'd hire a witch to do their dirty work for them. You just screwed yourself for good, and you've got no one to blame but yourself."

I opened her front door. "And this *is* over, Lily. If we have to have this conversation again, I won't be nearly as polite."

Carly and I stepped out onto the porch. The door slammed behind us.

# CHAPTER 12

Carly and I sat on the floor on opposite sides of the coffee table with the poppet on the black cloth between us. She'd invoked the circle around us; now all that remained was to break the hex.

My stomach churned, but not because of Sean. I was nervous about what would happen when the hex broke. Carly assured me that I would simply return to the feelings I'd had for Sean before the spell had been invoked and there shouldn't be any other effects, but this wasn't my kind of magic and I felt powerless with my fate in the hands of someone else's magic.

Malcolm was listening in the kitchen. Sean and Nan waited on the back porch. Apparently, Nan had wandered out back while Carly and I were gone and discovered my garden full of giant carnivorous plants. As with everything else, she'd taken the garden's eating habits in stride. Her comment: "Well, a mage must have a magical garden, after all. Isn't that a rule?"

When we returned, Carly had allowed Sean to see and sniff the poppet, but he couldn't detect any scents other than Lily's and the witch's. He'd wanted to open it to see if the piece of scarf inside had the scent of who'd taken it from his house, but Carly told him the poppet couldn't be opened without risking harm to me. We'd have to find out who took the scarf some other way.

From her bag, Carly took a glass bottle of salt and another of what she identified as rainwater. "Are you ready?" she asked me.

I scratched my arms through the sleeves of my shirt and sighed. "I suppose so."

She paused. "I'm not spelling you, Alice. I'm removing the existing spell. I understand it's a little unsettling since you've barely had time to adjust to the idea you've been under a witch's hex for the past day."

"Can I tell you something stupid?" I blurted out.

She smiled. "Of course."

"I'm afraid you'll break the hex and then I'll be vulnerable again," I confessed.

"Because your feelings for him make you feel vulnerable?"

I nodded.

"Magic can be scary," she said thoughtfully. "Werewolves can be scary. So can vampires and ghosts. All of these you can handle, though. Love is the scariest thing of all because it makes us so vulnerable. It's a leap of faith. There's nothing stupid in fearing that, unless you let the fear paralyze you and steal your happiness. So take a deep breath and jump."

"Break the hex," I said.

"Attagirl. That's more like it." Carly unstoppered the glass bottles and took another match from the box. "Breathe deeply," she said.

Together, we took three deep breaths. I relaxed my shoulders and cleared my mind.

She picked up the bottle of salt. "I cleanse this poppet of all evil intent by Earth." She sprinkled salt on the little cloth figure. "Water." She sprinkled it with the rainwater. "Spirit." She picked up the poppet and held it in the air with both hands. "And burn it until it is ash with Fire and ask Air to take the ash far away that this poppet may never hex Alice again."

She struck the match and ignited both of the poppet's legs. As the flames grew, she placed the poppet in the cauldron. I smelled burning hair and wrinkled my nose.

My heart pounded as the fire consumed the poppet. I braced myself for a wave of dizziness or disorientation like I'd felt when the spell was invoked, but as the last of the cloth figure burned away, nothing happened.

"I don't think it worked," I said with a hint of panic in my voice. "I didn't feel anything."

Carly didn't look worried. "Only one way to know for sure." She raised her voice. "Sean?"

The back door opened instantly, as if he'd been waiting with his hand on the doorknob. Sean stepped inside.

We locked eyes. I flinched, expecting pain, but felt nothing. No cramps, no nausea, no churning sensation...but nothing else, either. I might have been looking at a complete stranger.

Carly stood and walked around the circle counter-clockwise three times. "The circle is open but never broken," she said. "Go in peace and harmony."

She picked up the cauldron and took it out the back door. When she came back, the cauldron was empty and the ashes were gone.

Sean approached cautiously. "Is the hex broken?"

Carly nodded. "Should be."

"Did it work?"

She looked between us. "We're not quite sure yet."

His eyes shone softly golden. "Where do we stand?" he asked me. "Is this our first meeting, our second time starting over, or will I get to sleep with you in our bed tonight?"

Slowly, I rose and crossed the room to meet him. I sensed something building inside me, like a wave about to break. He stayed where he was and let me come to him. I stopped in front of him and looked into his eyes. A shadowy figure passed behind them, as if the wolf was pacing. I reached out and took his hand.

Stars burst in my head and my legs went out from under me. Sean caught me as I fell. Heat raced over my skin at his touch and my nose filled with the scent of forest. I felt like I'd been asleep for a day and had just woken up. My feelings for Sean came flooding back and left me breathless. A fierce protectiveness for this, for *us*, rose in me, and if Lily had been standing in front of me at that moment, I might have said to hell with my promise to Malcolm and cut off something she would miss.

I grabbed a handful of his shirt and pulled him to me. His mouth was hot and hungry and the ferocity of his kiss melted the last of the chill away from my heart.

"I think it worked," Carly said dryly.

"We should probably go," Nan added with a smile. "Come on, Carly. I'll help you pack up."

Sean and I had a million things to talk about—and a lot of making up to do—but first I sent Malcolm back to try to talk to Ashley's ghost, and then we walked Carly and Nan out to their cars.

Nan hugged all three of us tightly and left with Carly's card in her pocket. They'd had a few private conversations over the course of the afternoon and I got the impression they'd made plans for lunch later in the week. I wondered whether Nan had inherited any of her grandmother's gifts and if she wanted to explore them with Carly's guidance.

Carly put her bag in her trunk and turned to us with a smile. "He hasn't let go of your hand since the hex broke."

I raised our entwined hands and smiled ruefully. "I have a feeling we're going to be inseparable for a while."

Sean kissed my knuckles. "Thank you," he told Carly. "My pack and I both owe you a debt of gratitude for your help."

She shook her head. "No debts between friends. I'm thrilled I could help."

"I must ask you for another favor," Sean said, growing serious. "I'm concerned the witch who made the poppet may still have the rest of Alice's scarf or other items that belong to us. I'm going to investigate this on my end, but is there any way to know where Lily got the poppet?"

"Actually, yes." Carly shut her trunk and leaned against the car. "Poppets are often unique to the witch who made them and I know most of the practitioners in the city. That little string with the button is something I've seen before. I think the witch's name is Katrina, and I'm pretty sure I know where to find her. I'll ask her to give me everything of yours she still has."

Sean nodded. "Thank you. I'd like to know how Lily found her and who gave her the scarf and the hair. Any information you could get relating to that would be very much appreciated."

"I'll let you know what I find out." She touched his arm. "Please don't judge all witches by what just happened. Much like your own magic, the Craft suffers from a lot of misinformation, ignorance, and demonization. I know neither of you have much experience with it firsthand, and I'm sorry your first interactions with our practice involved a cruel and dangerous hex. That's not what our practices are about. Our beliefs and practices are for living in harmony with all living things. We help people to cross from this world to the next if they want our help. Most importantly, it's about doing good and positive things to help others and Mother Earth."

"I know," I assured her. "You're right; both of our groups get judged based on what a few of us do. Lots of people think all mages belong to cabals and kill people for our spells. I'm the last person who would blame all witches for what Lily and Katrina did."

"Shifters get their share of bad press," Sean added. "It's easy to demonize a whole group based on a few bad apples. I'm not holding this against you or anyone else except those involved."

Carly startled me by touching our joined hands. Sean and I exchanged puzzled looks.

After several seconds, she took her hand away and smiled at us. "Don't mind me. Sometimes I get these feelings."

Feelings, as in premonitions? Hoo boy. "Anything you need to tell us?"

"Not right this minute." She patted my arm. "Well, I'm needed back at work, so I should go and let you two get on with your day."

I perked up immediately. "Where is your shop?"

Carly took a couple of cards from her purse. "It's called Brew a Cup Tea and Coffee House. We're north of downtown, about twenty minutes from here. We have the best scones in the city."

"I'm not much of a tea drinker, but you had me at coffee and scones." I tucked the cards into my pocket. "I'll definitely be stopping in for coffee very soon."

"Let me brew a cup of tea for you and I might change your mind about tea." She smiled. "Can I hug you?"

A few months ago, I would have declined. Physical contact used to make me sick to my stomach—far worse than the poppet had. When I'd first escaped Moses's compound, even incidental contact, like brushing against someone in the store, could cause a full-blown panic attack. Years of physical captivity and torture left deep emotional scars, not just physical ones.

I'd changed a great deal since then and the past few months with Sean and Malcolm had made me into someone I'd never imagined I could be. I *wanted* to give Carly, someone I'd just met, a hug. That realization made me stand still for a moment.

Her smile was sympathetic. "I understand if not. You're a survivor. I won't insist. Maybe another time."

I let go of Sean's hand and hugged her—not a quick side hug, but a full-blown, rib-crushing, Nan-style hug. "Thank you for giving me my life back," I said before I let go.

She grinned as Sean took my hand again. "It's a good life you've got, and I don't just mean your hot wolf." She got into her car, shut the door, and turned the key in the ignition. The window rolled down. "And if you want to bring your Earth-bound spirit to my coffee shop sometime, I'd love to meet him too," she added with a wink.

My mouth fell open. Before I could formulate a response, the car pulled away from the curb and headed down the street.

"She called me your hot wolf," Sean said, feigning indignation. "I feel objectified."

I scoffed. "You think you feel objectified now, just wait until I get done with you."

He ran his nose along my hairline, drinking in my scent. "You really need to work on your threats," he murmured, his lips on my ear. I shivered hard. "Because if that was supposed to scare me, it had the opposite effect."

"Apparently," I said dryly. "What do you say we go inside so I can apologize properly?"

"I know you're just being playful, but you don't owe me any kind of apology." Sean's anger sizzled on my skin as we headed for the front door. "I called a pack meeting for this evening and we are going to find out who helped Lily by giving her your scarf. I have my suspicions, but Nan is right; jumping to conclusions won't do anybody any good." His hand tightened on mine and I felt a surge of golden shifter magic. "In the meantime, however—"

My phone rang as we went inside the house. I dug it out of my pocket and stared at the screen. "It's Aden's cell number, the one Jana gave him," I said disbelievingly. I swiped the green button. "Aden?"

The response made me stop dead in my tracks. "Alice, this is Jana Peters." Her voice was calm—much *too* calm—and it sent my adrenaline through the roof.

"Where are you?" I asked.

"I just wanted you to know Aden and I are fine. We're safe."

"What? How?"

"I've decided to accept a job with Mr. Bell. Aden is staying here with me. There's no need to worry about either of us."

I sagged against the wall. "Jana…"

"We're perfectly safe unless anyone tries to interfere with my new job." I caught the slightest hint of defeat in her voice. "Do you understand? So just let me work here in peace and my son and I will be fine."

Magic sparked on my fingers. I wasn't sure who I was more angry at: Bell, or myself. "All right," I said, since she—and presumably whoever was listening in—seemed to be waiting for an answer. "I'm sorry."

"Me too. Take care." The call ended.

"Alice—" Sean began, sounding worried.

"Hold that thought." I pulled up my Contacts, tapped one, and hit the green button.

The phone rang three times. "Miss Worth," Ezekiel Monroe said.

I cleared my throat. "I take it you made some calls?"

"I did." A pause. "I take it you received one?"

"Yup." I told him about my call from Jana.

Silence. "I was informed my request was under consideration," he said finally. "I'd thought, in light of recent events, that I might prevail in obtaining freedom for the child and his mother."

My blood went cold. "What recent events?"

He hummed, as if trying to decide how much to tell me. "It will probably not surprise you to hear that we have sources of information within Bell's organization."

"In other news, the sky is blue," I said testily. "The Court has eyes and ears everywhere. What did you find out from your sources?"

"Apparently, late last night or early this morning, Preston Allan Garrett, Aden's father, grew impatient with attempts to rescue his son and Jana Peters and contacted someone with Bell's organization to offer himself in trade for them."

I let out a string of expletives.

"Indeed," Monroe said grimly. "Naturally, Bell's people double-crossed him."

"So now Bell has all three of them: Garrett and Aden for their power and Jana as leverage." I swore again. "I *told* him to stay out of it until we had a plan and then we'd act together."

"From what I understand, that sort of patient approach is not Mr. Garrett's forte. One must sympathize with a man wishing to save his son, but in his desperation he made a poor choice."

I sat on the couch. "I still want Aden, Ezekiel. Let them keep Garrett; he got himself into this mess. They don't need Aden or Jana now. They can let them go in return for Garrett's cooperation."

"I doubt they will consider it. The phone call you received is a clear warning for us to back away from this matter. In their best interest—and ours—I think we should heed their warning."

"You cannot be serious," I raged. "Garrett made his own choices, but Aden is *twelve years old.* Do you know what they do to mage kids in cabals? They torture them until they break them or the kid is dead. They'll make him bleed to get Garrett to do whatever they want."

"Do you think I'm not aware of that?" Monroe snapped, losing his trademark cool. "I can assure you that I receive daily reports about the cabal, many of which are as bad or worse than what you're describing. But in my estimation, Garrett will do as he's told to save his son and Aden will fall in line to spare his mother. As distasteful as I find the situation, Bell is an ally against Moses Murphy. It may sound harsh to you, but there are a great many lives at stake, and we can't jeopardize all of them over one boy."

"No, it doesn't sound harsh. It sounds heartless."

"Let this one go, Miss Worth. You cannot save everyone."

I didn't trust myself to respond, so I ended the call before I said something I'd regret. I got up and headed for the stairs.

Sean came out of the kitchen drying his hands on a towel. "I'm making coffee. Where are you going?"

"Upstairs to punch the heavy bag for about an hour while I think."

He met me at the foot of the stairs. "Would you like a sparring partner?"

"I'm pretty pissed. I might punch you through the wall."

He smiled. "I'll let you try. How about that?"

"I don't want to talk," I warned him. "I just want to punch."

"Fair enough." He took my hand and tugged. "Come on; we've got some time before the pack meeting. Let's punch."

<br>

ORDINARILY, it wasn't uncommon for pack meetings to be held at either Jack and Delia's house or Karen and Cole's home. When shifters gathered, they tended to do so in the country, for a variety of reasons.

This time, however, Sean held the meeting at his house. I understood the impulse to bring the pack together on his turf, given the reason for the gathering.

Everyone arrived and settled in the living room. Even Patrick, who was habitually late, was early. Sean hadn't told anyone why we were meeting, but a same-day mandatory summons never signaled good news and his terse greetings as people arrived ratcheted up the tension considerably.

When all pack members plus their human spouses were present, including Casey, who was attending her first pack meeting as Ben's fiancée, Sean moved to the entryway to the living room so he could see everyone and be seen. He gestured for me to join him, so I did.

Ben and Casey sat on the far left, sharing an oversized chair with her legs over his. Next to them, on the couch, were Nan, Felicia, and David. Jack, Delia, and Caleb sat together in chairs brought in from the dining room. Karen and Cole shared the loveseat. John and Brandon also sat in dining room chairs. Eddie and Thea were on their way back from visiting family and wouldn't arrive until tomorrow.

The low murmur of voices died away. Sean studied his pack, his eyes bright gold. Their eyes stayed focused on the floor; even the humans kept their gazes lowered.

"I'm going to get straight to the point." Sean's voice was quiet, but his fury scoured my skin and everyone in the pack sensed it. "In the past day, there was a near-fatal attack on a member of our pack."

Everyone reacted with shock and anger. "What happened?" Jack demanded, his eyes glowing amber. His reaction confirmed, at least to me, that he'd had nothing to do with the hex. If Sean came to the same conclusion, I couldn't tell.

"As all of you are aware, Lily Anderson was presented to me as a potential mate by Jack and her father, Zachary," Sean continued. "After meeting her, however, I had no interest in her, and more importantly I judged she would not be a good addition to our pack. My decision has met with some resistance, but I stand by it and always will. This incident has proven once and for all that Lily has no place among us." He nodded at me. "In an attempt to sabotage our relationship, Lily paid a witch to hex Alice. The curse's purpose was to drive us apart, but instead it very nearly killed Alice."

The pack sat in stunned silence for a few beats, and then the room erupted in furious voices. Jack, Ben, and Casey sprang to their feet. I wasn't surprised to see as much or more fury in Casey's eyes as the rest of the pack's. She might not be a shifter, but there was no less fight in her than anyone here.

"Have you informed the Were Ruling Council?" Jack asked.

Sean nodded. "I have. They'll speak to Zachary and Lily and decide how best to deal with her. That part is out of my hands. The reason I called you all here tonight is that Lily did not act alone. She was aided by a member of our pack, who stole items belonging to Alice and gave them to Lily. This person may also have given Lily the idea for the hex; we may find out when the Council questions Lily. That they stole from Alice is certain."

"Do you know who stole the items?" Ben demanded.

Sean's eyes went to Delia. "Yes, I do."

Fourteen pairs of eyes focused on Jack's wife. She'd feigned shock and outrage when everyone else reacted to Sean's news, but now she was silent, her eyes on the floor. Her face was expressionless.

A muscle moved in Jack's jaw. "How certain are you?" he asked Sean.

"The witch still had Alice's scarf and she handed it over to us. It smelled like Delia, Jack. And there's no reason for that to be the case unless she was the one who gave it to Lily. You were both over here last Wednesday; she could have taken it then when you and I were talking."

Carly had delivered the scarf to my house, sealed in a plastic bag, just before we left to come to Sean's house for the meeting. Sean had opened the bag, taken one whiff of its contents, and cursed.

Jack crouched next to his wife so he didn't tower over her. "Delia?"

She looked up, her eyes glowing with fury and defiance. "I took the scarf and gave it to Lily. The hex was my idea."

Jack hung his head. "Damn it," he said softly. "What have you done?"

"You weren't doing anything about her, so I had to do something. The cuffs would have been a much better option, but we lost that opportunity." Her eyes snapped fire. "If Lily had followed the witch's instructions instead of saying Alice's name too many times and making her sick, this would have worked."

"Hexes are always dangerous," Sean said coldly. "You had to know there was a chance this could end with Alice's death. If Lily had said Alice's name just a few more times when she invoked the hex, Alice would be dead. At best, this was an assault on my consort, the woman I love. At worst, it was attempted murder. Shifter law calls for punishment either way."

"I don't understand how you can choose *her* over us," Delia protested. "You're letting your human self overrule your wolf. An alpha wolf would choose a shifter mate."

Sean squeezed my hand. "Not that it makes any difference to me, but since it seems to matter to you, you should know my wolf chose Alice even before I did. The night she and I met, my wolf made it clear he wanted her. I followed my wolf's lead, not the other way around."

I managed not to react visibly, but I was sure Sean sensed my surprise. I'd known his wolf considered me a potential mate, but I'd thought that happened later. I didn't know the wolf stated his intention on our first night together. That made me happy, though I wasn't quite sure why.

I saw relief on a few faces, including Patrick and John's, as if they'd shared similar reservations about whether Sean had chosen me over his wolf's objections. I really couldn't blame them and I didn't take offense. Unlike Delia, whose dislike of me seemed personal, they wanted their alpha and their pack to be strong.

The reaction was short-lived, however, as the enormity of what Delia had done sank in. Jack seemed to be having the most trouble processing it. Despite everything he'd done and the way he'd tried to keep Sean and me apart, I couldn't help but feel some sympathy.

Jack and Delia looked at each other for several long moments. Her expression changed from angry defiance to something close to resignation. They stood.

"I admit what I've done," Delia said tonelessly, her eyes on the floor. "And I accept the judgment of the alpha and the Council."

Jack took a deep breath. "On behalf of my wife, I ask for the alpha's mercy."

Sean shook his head. "Jack, if someone had tried to harm or kill your wife, how merciful would you feel?"

"I'd want to tear them apart with my bare hands," Jack said without hesitation. Delia flinched and started to interject. "But I'm asking anyway because I love her."

Delia's mouth snapped shut.

Sean studied them both. "I've warned her repeatedly. She knew what she was doing when she suggested the hex and that it would hurt me and possibly kill Alice. I am out of warnings, patience, and mercy."

Delia gripped Jack's hand.

"Then the alpha's consort grants the mercy," I said.

Silence.

Sean turned to me. "It's in the consort's power to do so," he said, studying my face intently. He had to be wondering how I knew that and why on earth I would do anything to help Delia after what she'd done. "The consort owes us no explanation for her decision," he added as the others exchanged glances. "I do have to ask whether you're sure you want to do this."

"I'm sure." I let go of his hand and crossed the living room to stand toe-to-toe with Delia. Jack moved away, granting me the confrontation I deserved. I spooled magic and let my eyes glow. Delia met my gaze for a moment and then she had to look down.

"My decision comes with a condition and a warning," I said. "The condition is, if you want to make a move against me in the future, you meet me with honor in front of the pack as stipulated by shifter law and custom. The warning is that if you do, or if you ever make another attempt to stab me in the back, Sean won't have to tear you apart because *I* will."

Shifter magic rose. I took a step back as my cold-fire whip spiraled out of my right hand. I nearly bumped into Sean when he crossed the room and reached my side in a blink.

At first I thought Delia was reacting to my threat, but it was Caleb who was growling and on the verge of shifting. The surly young werewolf sat on the edge of his chair, his eyes bright gold and fists clenched.

"You have no right to talk to Delia like that," he snarled at me.

"Caleb, stand down *now*," Sean commanded. The surge of alpha magic nearly knocked me over as the rest of the pack hunkered down where they sat. "If you shift and try to attack anyone, I will kill you."

Jack put a hand on Caleb's shoulder. The contact usually helped calm the pack's youngest and most volatile member, but Caleb knocked his hand away and started to get up.

Jack shoved him back into his chair and this time his grip on the younger man's shoulder was like a vise. "Calm down," he ordered.

"This is between Sean, Alice, and Delia. Alice granted mercy to Delia. You're making the situation worse, and you're going to get yourself killed acting like this."

Caleb stared incredulously up at Jack. "Are you taking *Alice's* side against us?"

"There is no Alice's side versus us." Sean's voice was like steel. "Alice is *one of us.* She just demonstrated that by granting Delia mercy when it wasn't deserved, because she believes it's better for the pack that I not have to kill my beta's mate. Instead of threatening to attack her, you should be grateful."

Caleb started to argue.

"Caleb, shut your mouth," Jack said. "You've been a part of this pack long enough to know better than to do what you're doing. If you need to go out to the pack land and shift and run as a wolf for a while to work off your anger, then we'll do that. I'll run with you. But you have to get control of your temper and your wolf right now."

Since Caleb joined the pack, Jack had tried to help him learn to control his wolf and work through his anger at being bitten and Changed, but Caleb had been angry and volatile even before he became a werewolf. Becoming a shifter had simply made it infinitely worse. I didn't know many details about Caleb's life before he joined the pack six months ago, but he'd come from an abusive household and struggled with substance abuse and self-destructive behavior. He'd discovered that running helped him cope, only to be bitten by a werewolf while on a late-night run in a state park. Jack met Caleb first and brought him to the pack, hoping to provide the family and support he desperately needed.

Jack and Delia didn't have kids, for reasons that weren't any of my business. Jack seemed to think of Caleb as an adopted son. Even as he held Caleb in his chair with an iron grip, I saw worry in Jack's eyes. Despite improvements in his attitude and behavior, Caleb continued to be unstable and that put everyone at risk.

"I'll run with you too," Ben said, surprising me. "I could use some exercise. Gotta fit into that tux." He patted his flat stomach and gave Caleb a good-natured smile.

Felicia spoke up. "I'll run too."

John, David, and Patrick also said they would go for a run in wolf form. Caleb stared at the floor as his pack mates showed their support.

Sean glanced at Jack. The beta took his hand off Caleb's shoulder.

"Caleb, stand up," Sean said.

Caleb got to his feet, his eyes fixed on Sean's shoes. His was still angry, but the shifter magic had faded. My cold-fire whip coiled back into my hand.

"Go run with the others," Sean told him. "It will help. Listen to Jack. Alice and Delia have cleared the air and no one is leaving here as enemies. Draw strength and peace from your pack."

"I'm trying," Caleb said, so quietly that I barely heard him.

"I know you are," Sean said. "You have to try harder. Do you understand?"

I caught a flash of resentment in Caleb's eyes. "Yes."

Sean put his hand on Caleb's shoulder. "Then let's call it a night. Those of you going out running, be safe."

The house cleared pretty quickly. I got hugs from Casey, Nan, Ben, Felicia, and John and little touches on the arm or shoulder from everyone else, even Jack.

The only two people who didn't touch me on their way out were Delia and Caleb, which was fine. Everyone needed time to cool off, including me. I wasn't sure if there would ever be a time when I'd welcome a touch from either of them. For now, it was comforting enough to see them leave.

# CHAPTER 13

WHEN THE DOOR CLOSED BEHIND JACK, WHO WAS LAST TO DEPART, SEAN turned the deadbolt and gave me a long kiss.

When we broke apart, I rested my forehead on his chest. "What was that for?"

"You are a miracle."

Startled, I blinked up at him. "That may be over-stating things just a tad."

He cupped my face with his hands so he could look into my eyes. "I would have dealt with Delia."

"I know. You had every right to do so under shifter law. I can't imagine how angry you are about what she did."

"Angry doesn't even come close." He nuzzled my hair. "I could have lost you. I still haven't fully processed how close Lily came to killing you, and that Delia made it possible. I imagine I'll be angry for a while."

"You and me both. I spared her, but I'll never trust her. I may never forgive her."

"I can't blame you." His face grew serious. "There's another option we should discuss."

"Kicking them out of the pack?" I sighed. "I thought about it, to be honest, but I told Lily today that an alpha's partner leads by example and solves problems rather than causes them. For the good of the pack, I extended an olive branch. If she accepts it, good. If not..." I shrugged. "I'll take care of it."

He kissed my forehead. "Like I said, a miracle." He squeezed my hand. "I take it you've been reading up on shifter laws and what the role of an alpha's consort is?"

I smiled briefly. "It seemed prudent, given the situation, and since that may be all I'll ever be."

"I believe we'll be able to have mate bond if we try someday to do that. The metaphysical link we accidentally opened when we first met, the one that allowed us to sense each other's emotions, is a pretty good indicator that we can be linked. When you put on the shifter cuff, we had a mate bond for a few minutes, until you died."

A pause. My death and resurrection was a bitter memory for both of us.

"If you have some shifter blood, it's even more likely," he continued finally. "Having you at my side is my greatest joy. There's peace in my heart I've never felt before. That tells me everything I need to know about the connection we have now and what we'll have someday."

"That was unexpectedly poetic," I said, blinking rapidly. Must be allergies.

He smiled and kissed the tip of my nose. "I have my moments." He rubbed my shoulders gently. "Still sore from punching the bag?"

"A little, but not as bad as I thought I would be." I smiled up at him. "Not too sore to follow through on my earlier threat."

"The one about objectifying me?" His eyes glowed softly. "I might not mind being objectified by you, now that I think about it."

"There's only one way to find out." I turned and ran for the stairs. "Race you to the—"

Hands caught me around my waist and plucked me out of the air.

I squeaked as he picked me up, tossed me carefully over his shoulder, and bounded up the steps two at a time.

"Put me down!" I protested as we entered his—our—bedroom.

Instead of setting me on my feet, he held me with his hands under my butt so I could wrap my legs around his hips. He kissed me very thoroughly but made no move to carry me to the bed.

Finally, when we paused to take a breath, I wiggled impatiently. "Bed?"

He held me still. "I want nothing more than to take you to bed and see if we can break the record we set on Thursday night—"

"Don't you dare say 'but,'" I warned him.

"*But*," he said firmly, giving me a quick kiss. "By my calculation you've had no more than five hours of sleep since Saturday morning and it is now Monday night. That is sixty hours with virtually no sleep, and during that time you were chased through the woods, dropped into a mud pit, hexed, blown through *two* walls, confronted by Darius Bell, nearly killed trying to save Charles Vaughan, de-hexed, and threatened by a werewolf." He grew serious. "You need a full night's uninterrupted sleep."

"What I need is *you*. We don't need to try and go for a new record tonight because you're right—I'm tired. I'm beyond exhausted. But I'm healing from a rough weekend, all the things you just listed, and a few other things I haven't told you about yet."

He raised his eyebrows. "Such as?"

"Such as a couple of things I will tell you about as soon as I feel like talking about them, which will be after you put me down on the bed and give me some well-deserved and much-overdue werewolf TLC."

"Werewolf TLC?" He grinned. "I like that."

"I stole it from Ben."

"Remind me to say thank you to Ben." He kissed me deeply. "If it will help you heal and rest better, I could be persuaded to offer some werewolf TLC."

I took his face in my hands. "It will," I promised. "Sleep will heal my body, but it's you who heals my heart." I pulled my shirt off over my head and tossed it aside. "Gimme some sugar, baby."

"I knew I made the right choice showing you that movie." He squeezed my butt and headed for the bed.

Just as we reached the bed, I sensed a familiar tingle from the crystal on my bracelet. "Oh, come *on*," I complained.

He set me down. "I'm assuming that wasn't directed at me?"

"Malcolm just jumped to my bracelet. That means he's got news." I sighed and glanced below his belt. "Maybe you should go to the bathroom for a minute so I can find out what's up." I coughed. "Er, what's going on."

"Could have been worse. He might have shown up ten minutes from now." Sean kissed my forehead and headed for the master bathroom, closing the door behind him.

I found my discarded shirt, put it on, and touched the crystal on my bracelet. "*Release.*"

Malcolm appeared next to me. He looked around at the darkened room, the closed bathroom door, and my expression, and sighed. "Oh, God. I interrupted you guys, didn't I?"

"No," I said.

"Yes!" Sean called from the bathroom.

"Thank you for making this even more awkward," I scolded the closed door. I turned to Malcolm. "What have you found out?"

"I got a little bit of information from Ashley. I'm not sure how helpful it will be, but I think I know who shot her and took Aden."

"Ashley's coherent enough to talk?"

He waggled his hand. "Kinda off and on. She still mostly just screams. I'm glad I'm dead or I'd have one hell of a headache."

The bathroom door opened and Sean stepped out. "Sorry," Malcolm said.

Sean crossed his arms. "Let's hear your report. Alice needs her sleep."

"Sleep. Right." Malcolm's tone was dry. "Anyway, I can't get much from her verbally, but sometimes I can catch little glimpses of memories or thoughts when I touch another ghost. I tried to do that for most of the day and didn't get much that would help us. Mostly what she's seeing is a close-up of the barrel of a gun pointed right at her face and then a big boom."

Sean muttered an expletive.

"Yeah, it sucks," Malcolm said shortly. "Imagine watching that on repeat. Anyway, I finally saw a little bit more of the memory and I recognized the guy who pulled the trigger. His name is Tony Larson. Back when I was alive, he was muscle for Bell. I don't know what he does now, but he's who killed Ashley and presumably took Aden."

I wondered if we could tip off the cops about Tony in regard to Ashley's murder. That would be tricky, since our only evidence was a ghost's fragmented memory as seen by another ghost.

I sighed. "Did you see anything else that might help us?"

He shook his head. "Not really. Honestly, I don't know if I ever will. She's basically a wraith at this point. I think she's just hanging on to try and let someone know what happened to her. Have you found out anything from your sources? Did you hear back yet from Monroe?"

"I did hear from Monroe. I also heard from Jana."

His mouth fell open. "*What?*"

I told Malcolm about Jana's call and Monroe's news that Garrett had gotten himself taken prisoner in a botched exchange and that I had been warned to back off trying to get to Aden.

Malcolm flitted around the room in fury. "That stupid ass," he fumed. "And Monroe telling you to let it go, like Aden's life doesn't mean anything."

"Not that it doesn't mean anything—just that it means less than all the lives that will be lost if Murphy wins the takeover. Monroe is being practical." I rubbed my face. "I'm not giving up on Aden."

"I'd like us to send Ashley on," Malcolm said, surprising me.

"She's tormented. We need to convince her somehow that we'll get justice for her and help her cross over. I just wish there was a better and easier way to do that than having you discorporate her. She's been through enough already."

I thought about it. "You know, Carly might be able to help with that. I'm pretty sure she's a medium." I glanced at the clock. "I hate to call her so late, but it might be worth asking. If she says that's not one of her gifts, I can take care of it myself."

Sean's brow furrowed. "You need sleep, Alice."

"I *will* sleep," I promised. "Just as soon as Ashley is no longer suffering."

He closed his eyes and appeared to count to ten.

"I know," Malcolm said sympathetically. "But Alice is our burden to bear."

"Hey, I'm nobody's burden," I protested.

"You are, but that's okay," Malcolm reassured me. "We wouldn't want it any other way."

⁊ ❦ ₰ ⸎ ❧ ⸎ ⸐ ⸎ ⸒ ⸑ ❦ ⸑ ❧ ❦ ⸍ ⸎ ⸏ ⁊⁊

DESPITE THE LATE HOUR, Carly answered her phone with "How can I help?"

I hadn't gotten very far into my description of Ashley's situation before she cut me off and asked where she needed to meet us, and then, to my surprise, asked if Nan would be willing to join us.

Sean called Nan, who immediately agreed and arrived at his house only twenty minutes later. The three of us drove out to the crime scene to meet Carly. She arrived at our rendezvous point a few minutes after we did.

Ashley had been killed on a utility service road that ran behind a manufacturing plant. The plant was closed for the night. The area was deserted and dimly lit, so our activities would go unnoticed. We parked a little way up the road and walked the last hundred yards on foot.

"I thought when I was at your house earlier that you knew an earth-bound spirit who needed my help," Carly said as we walked. "I assumed it was the spirit who was present in your home, but clearly that's not the case as he's quite comfortable being here with you." She shivered. "I can feel and hear her already, poor thing. What can you tell me about her and how she died? You have my word I won't share that information with anyone else—it's only so I know how best to help her find her way."

I gave Carly the short version of what we'd pieced together about Ashley's role in giving Aden a ride and how she'd been shot, probably to eliminate a witness to his kidnapping.

"We don't know all the details of how she got involved or what she thought she was getting into," I added. "My ghost saw a glimpse of her memory of her murder and recognized the person who pulled the trigger, so I'm hopeful we can use that information to bring him to justice."

"That may help." Carly winced. "Poor girl. Now that's a soul in torment if I've ever felt and heard one."

Like most mages, I could usually sense a spirit's presence, though I couldn't always hear or interact with them. I couldn't hear Ashley, which I had to look at as a blessing, but I sensed her nearby. Her misery was a cold and distinctly unpleasant feeling on the edge of my awareness.

There wasn't much left at the scene. The crime scene tape had been removed, along with the burned-out shell of Ashley's car. All that remained was a blackened section of pavement where the car had been and a clean area next to it where someone, probably the fire department, had washed away the blood.

I'd been around death for most of my life, thanks to my grandfather, and then my chosen profession. My grandfather murdered my parents by burning them alive when I was eight, after he discovered they intended to take me and flee. I'd caused deaths with my magic from when I was six years old until I escaped at age twenty-four. As a mage private investigator, I'd investigated murders, interacted with a variety of spirits, and lost my mentor, Mark Dunlap, when he was murdered by a blood mage.

Despite everything I'd been through, I didn't fear death—not as such—but there were aspects of it I *did* fear, like ending up like Ashley, caught in an endless loop of suffering. Maybe that was part of the reason I found her condition so unsettling, or maybe it was because Bell's people had murdered her and I identified all too well with being the victim of a cabal. Maybe it was the tragedy of her short life as she went from college student to addict, and then died horribly on this empty stretch of road. Maybe it was all of the above.

Sean squeezed my hand. He could always tell when things got dark in my head. I drew on his strength and calm as I'd done at the birthday brunch and some of the darkness melted away. Nan brushed my fingers with hers as well, offering support and her own reassurance.

Malcolm, who'd been floating along beside us as we walked, left my side and joined Carly. "Can you hear me?" he asked tentatively.

She smiled. "Of course I can. I wanted to meet you earlier at Alice's house, but I wasn't sure I was supposed to know you were there."

"You weren't, but only because we're cautious about who knows about me. I'm Malcolm."

"Hi, Malcolm." Carly stopped and faced him. "You're a very powerful spirit. Tied to Alice, I think, but the bond goes deeper than that. A true friendship—no, a kinship, like a brother and sister."

"Which one of us is the older sibling in this metaphor?" I asked.

She tilted her head. "You."

I smirked. "Hear that, little bro? You have to do what I say now."

"Yeah, okay, big sis." Malcolm rolled his eyes. "I guess this means I have to steal your underwear and show it to all the kids at school."

"Kids, don't make me separate you," Nan scolded us.

"I'm kidding," Malcolm said. "Nobody wants to see Alice's totally not-sexy Spider-Man underwear."

Carly sighed. "When I said that about being siblings, I was assuming you were both mature enough to take that comment in the serious way in which it was intended."

Malcolm snickered.

"Well, now you know better," Nan said, giving us both a look—or rather, she gave me a look and frowned in the general area where Malcolm was hovering. "What can I do to help, Carly?"

"I'd like your permission to access your power when I try to speak to Ashley. I think it will help me reach her."

Nan looked hesitant. "Other than a few spells and rituals I did with my grandmother, I really don't know how to use any abilities I might have."

"You won't have to do anything but allow me to draw on your power. I'm not just drawing on your energy as a hereditary witch; you also have a calming effect on others in your pack, and Ashley is going to need all the calm she can get if this is going to work."

"Can I help?" Sean asked, surprising me. "I'm not any kind of witch, hereditary or otherwise, but part of an alpha's magic is the ability to provide calm and comfort to others. Could you also draw from me through my bond with Nan?"

Carly smiled at him. "I think I can, and thank you very much for offering. We might be able to help this girl after all. Miss Nan, why don't you put your hand on my right shoulder? Sean, put yours on my left."

They did as she asked. Nan seemed hesitant, perhaps because she wasn't sure she'd be of any help, but Sean was entirely at ease allowing Carly to draw on his power.

Carly closed her eyes and took three deep breaths. I sensed a rise of the same magic and parchment scent I'd noticed when she invoked the tracking spell. Nan and Sean closed their eyes. Shifter magic rose, but not the hot, fiery magic I was used to. This was soft, like morning sunshine.

Even without my Second Sight, I could see the change in Carly's aura. Drawing on the wolves' calm made her energy feel like a warm blanket.

She opened her eyes and turned to Malcolm. "Please introduce me to Ashley, as best you can. Tell her I'm here to help and listen to her."

"Okay, here goes." Malcolm floated over to the clean area, where presumably Ashley had died. "Ashley, stop screaming," he said firmly. "No one is going to hurt you. This is Carly. She's here to listen and help you."

Something cold rushed past me, as if Ashley's spirit had responded to Malcolm's words and flown immediately to Carly's side.

Goosebumps appeared on the witch's arms. Her head tilted, as if she was listening.

Malcolm zipped to my side and touched my arm. *Ashley is talking to Carly, sort of,* he said in my head. *It's kind of jumbled up, but what I'm hearing is that Aden told her he was going to get a job and if she gave him a ride, he'd split his first paycheck with her. She didn't know who she was meeting or she never would have brought him here.* He grimaced. *She blames herself. And now she's screaming again.* He let go of my arm.

"It was not your fault," Carly said firmly. "You couldn't have known. Aden didn't understand what he was doing. This was not your fault. Ashley, *this was not your fault.*"

I couldn't hear Ashley, but the cold feeling intensified. Malcolm winced. "She doesn't believe Carly. She's worried about Aden. She says he's scared and alone."

"Tell her that Aden is with his mom. Jana has him," I said.

Something cold whipped across my face, like the ghost had flown over to me. "Jana has Aden," I repeated for Ashley's benefit. "Aden is with his mom. He's not alone." All true, as far as it went.

The cold feeling faded. Carly sighed. "She's believes you, but she's still seeing her own death on an endless loop and it's making it difficult for me to get through to her. I need help to persuade her to move on."

"Help from whom?" I asked.

She smiled. "A couple of archangels."

I blinked. "Okay."

Carly turned and Nan and Sean took their hands from her shoulders. "Sometimes I can guide a spirit to the veil myself, but when their death was particularly traumatic or there's something powerful holding them here, like unfinished business, it takes someone stronger to persuade them to cross over."

I cleared my throat. "Well, no one's stronger than an archangel."

The situation had become a little surreal. I had no doubt Carly believed what she said, and I certainly didn't *not* believe, but I had a difficult time processing it.

"Actually, there *are* beings stronger than archangels, but that's a conversation for another day." Carly turned to Nan and Sean. "Thank you for your help. Had Ashley's death been less terrible, I'm sure we could have guided her to the veil and through it."

"It was worth a try. Now you can call in the big guns," Nan said. "We'll keep a respectful distance."

"Stand wherever you are comfortable. Only Ashley, Malcolm, and I will be able to see and hear the archangels Suriel and Zlar," Carly told us.

Malcolm flitted nervously. "They don't need to see *me*, though, right?"

Carly smiled. "You have nothing to fear from them, Malcolm."

He avoided my eyes. "Umm, I might."

"You can jump to the house, behind the wards," I told him. "But I'm not sure wards mean a whole lot to archangels if you've somehow managed to get crossways with one."

Carly reached out, and to my surprise, put her hand right on Malcolm's arm. "Whatever you're worried about, put it aside. Suriel doesn't come to pass judgment on anyone, living or deceased."

"Okay," Malcolm said, sounding not at all convinced. He floated back to my side, radiating unease.

Carly turned away from us. She took three deep breaths and then spoke. "I call upon Archangel Suriel for his help and guidance to get Ashley ready to go to the spirit plane."

She'd said the rest of us wouldn't be able to see or hear the archangels, but since I had an affinity for spirits and could see after-life magic I expected to sense Suriel's entrance.

I braced myself for a blast of power or for the earth to tremble, as befitting the arrival of an archangel. Instead I felt a surge of what I could only describe as grace. The air tasted sweet on my tongue.

Carly smiled at someone or something I could sense but not see. "Suriel, thank you for coming to counsel Ashley Brown."

I glanced to my left. Malcolm was transfixed.

No one spoke for a long time—or at least, no one I could hear. Finally, Malcolm roused himself enough to touch my arm. *He's telling Ashley she's not at fault for what happened to Aden and the boy will be saved.* He hesitated, as if he'd started to say something then thought better of it. Finally, he added, *She's followed her path on this plane to its end and it's time for her to be at peace. Ashley said she'll move on.*

*What does he look like?* I couldn't help but ask.

His face was full of wonder. *Like he's made of light. Alice...he has wings. Really, really big wings.*

Carly spoke, startling me. "I call upon Archangel Zlar to guide Ashley to the spirit plane."

The sensation of peace intensified, but only for a few moments. When it faded, Malcolm sighed. *She took the second archangel's hand and they disappeared. She's gone.*

"Thank you, Zlar," Carly murmured. "Thank you for guiding her to peace and rest."

Suddenly, I felt a spike of fear from my ghost. *Malcolm?* I asked.

No response. He was frozen, his eyes wide. He had a faraway look, as if someone was speaking in his head.

I opened the link between us and caught the echo of a voice that sounded as if it was made of many voices all speaking as one. Then it was gone and the feeling of grace faded.

Carly turned around to face us. "Ashley is at peace now." Her gaze went to Malcolm. "And you have some peace as well, I think."

Malcolm blinked several times. The usually glib ghost seemed at a loss for words. Given he'd just been addressed by an archangel, I couldn't say I blamed him.

Carly yawned. "I don't know about the rest of you, but I'm ready to call it a night."

"Was this a typical day for you?" I asked. "Break a hex, counsel spirits, talk to a couple of archangels?"

"Typical day," she agreed, but she was smiling. "It's the life I was born for. Shall we go?"

We headed for our cars. Malcolm floated along beside me, saying nothing. Sean still had my hand in his. Nan looked thoughtful.

When we got to the cars, Carly opened the driver's side door and reached into her purse. "One last thing before we go." She withdrew a small velvet bag. "I have a gift for you."

Generally speaking, I avoided accepting gifts from anyone. Like my aversion to physical contact, it was a result of years trapped in Moses's cabal, where every gift—no matter how seemingly small, well-meaning, or kind—came with many strings attached. Even after I left the cabal, gifts seemed to carry hidden price tags. But I knew better than to refuse a gift from a witch like Carly.

She took out an amulet made of stone. The amulet was carved in the shape of a heart formed by the heads of two wolves with their noses touching in the center. On the back, our names were etched, one on each side. Oddly, it seemed to be deeply scored down the middle and each side had a small hole.

"Does this gift have anything to do with the funny feeling you got this afternoon when you touched our hands?" I asked.

"It has everything to do with that. The funny feeling told me I needed to touch you. The vision I got said I needed to make this for you and you'd call me tonight so I could give it to you."

Well, that was a bit spooky. "What does it do?"

"The charm is called *My Beloved*. It will allow each of you to find or summon the other, no matter how far apart you are. My vision told me you would need it very soon."

A lead weight of worry landed in my stomach and stayed there. "How do we invoke it?"

"Each of you take hold of the amulet on the side with the other person's name. Hold it for one minute to put your own energy into it, and then when I tell you to do so, break it in half."

Sean and I held the amulet between us. His eyes glowed softly as we looked at each other.

"Break it," Carly said finally.

I didn't think I'd be strong enough to break something made of stone, but we each gave our halves a twist and it broke down the middle with a little puff of magic.

Carly handed me a chain. "Put your half of the amulet on this chain and put it around Sean's neck so it hangs at the level of his heart." She winked at Sean. "Don't worry—there's no silver in the chain."

I strung the amulet onto the chain and fastened it. Sean ducked his head so I could put it on over his head. I tucked it inside his shirt. I placed my palm over it and looked up at him, worry in my eyes.

He kissed my forehead gently and put his half of the amulet around my neck. It nestled between my breasts, over my heart. I smelled parchment and sensed the warm feeling I now associated with Carly's magic, along with a trace of golden shifter magic.

"And how do we use it?" Sean asked.

"Just touch it in your time of need and it will lead them to you or you to them." Her expression was grave. "You won't be able to avoid the danger that's coming, but you won't face it alone."

I supposed it said something about the mess that was my life that those ominous words were much more of a comfort than they had any right to be.

WHEN WE GOT BACK to Sean's house, Nan gave each of us a long hug and reminded Malcolm that he'd promised to look after me.

The old Alice would have bristled at the idea that anyone was supposed to look after me, not to mention the hug, but I'd started to understand that being looked after wasn't a sign of weakness or an indication people thought I wasn't capable of protecting myself. It took more than five years of being out of the cabal and a lot of failed friendships and relationships for me to figure that out.

Once Nan headed home, Sean, Malcolm, and I went inside. I was so tired I could barely do more than put one foot in front of the other, but I had some questions that couldn't wait.

"Can you give us a minute?" I asked Sean.

"Sure. I'll go up. Don't be too long or you'll fall asleep on your feet." He gave me a quick kiss and went to the back door to let Rogue in. After the dog greeted me, they both went upstairs. I heard the door to the bedroom close.

Malcolm sighed. "Thanks. I figured you probably wouldn't mind Sean hearing any of this, but I'll let you tell him when you're ready."

"Fair enough." I hesitated. "Can I ask why you were afraid of the archangels?"

He floated back and forth. "Remember when I first showed up in your office in nightmare form?"

I grinned. "With three heads and beetles all over you? You expected me to really freak out."

"Yeah, and you basically just yawned like I wasn't even in the top three weirdest things you'd seen that day." He smiled at the memory. "Anyway, I was originally sent to torment you, which is why I showed up looking like something H. P. Lovecraft cooked up in a fever dream. But then we became friends and I haven't really been doing much tormenting."

"Except for that phase you went through where you kept singing Olivia Newton-John songs, no, you really haven't." Realization dawned. "Did you think you might be in hot water for not tormenting me?"

"Yeah, big time," he confessed. "I honestly thought I might get smited, regardless of what Carly said about Suriel not being there to pass judgment. I thought about jumping back to the house, but then I thought, what would Alice do? She'd stay and face the music, so I did."

I blinked. "Wow. So, what did Suriel say when he talked to you?"

"He told me everything I'd done was exactly what I was supposed to do. He said angels don't send ghosts to torment the living, but sometimes they send spirits to provide care, comfort, and protection. He said you would never have allowed me to stick around if I'd introduced myself as your protector, but you were just odd enough to find a friend in someone who showed up with three heads and threatened to make your life a living hell. I'm paraphrasing," he added.

I frowned. "When you put it like that, I sound like kind of a weirdo." I was irrationally annoyed that Suriel, or whoever had sent Malcolm to me, knew me that well. Part of me felt like I'd been manipulated, but Malcolm had become such an important part of my life that I couldn't stay mad about it for very long. "So he basically said you're doing a good job and that was it?"

"Uh, no. He said he would come back for me when it was time for me to go."

I flinched. He flitted to my side. "It's okay, Alice. He didn't say it like it was a threat. It was more like a promise, like he was reassuring me. He said that wouldn't be for a while yet."

I knew Malcolm couldn't stay with me forever, but I tried not to think too much about the fact that someday he would cross the veil and find the peace he deserved. It was selfish of me to wish he *could* stay with me, and yet I did wish precisely that.

Malcolm interrupted my thoughts. "I asked him if he knew what the condition was that would break our bond."

Recently we'd discovered the spell binding Malcolm and me together had a condition that, once it was met, would sever our bond and release him. What that condition was, neither of us could tell.

"What did he say?" I asked.

"He said revealing it would mean it would never come to pass. Everything would unfold as it was meant to, he said. And then he disappeared."

I raised my hands, palm up. "Archangels. What are you gonna do?"

"I know. Strange guys. Lots of bright light and big feathery wings. He did say one other thing, though, about Aden. I debated telling you, but I can't keep secrets from my big sis." His grin was back.

"What did he say about Aden?"

"He said you would save him."

"Well, that's not exactly breaking news. I'm not sure just yet how I'm going to do it, but I'm going to get him out of there, and Jana too. But why not just tell me that Suriel said I was going to rescue him? You knew I'd never just walk away and leave him in Bell's hands."

"Because he said you would save Aden regardless of the cost. I didn't like the way that sounded."

Neither did I, but I shrugged. "I'm going to save him. I'd like to think I'm smart enough and rational enough to do it in a way that doesn't come with a cost I'm not willing to pay."

"It might be a cost *you're* willing to pay, but that doesn't mean it won't be a cost that's too high for others. Remember when you decided to die to release Sean from the cuff? That was a price you thought was reasonable."

I couldn't think of anything to say to that. I rubbed my face. "I'm about to fall down, Malcolm. Is there anything else you need to tell me that can't wait until tomorrow?"

"No. Go to sleep. I'm going to stick around here and keep an eye on things, just in case someone decides to try and bother us."

"Okay. Good night." I started for the stairs, then turned back. "I never had a brother, Malcolm. Or a sister, for that matter. I like that you're kind of my brother, even if you *are* a ghost and you like Olivia Newton-John."

"And I like that you're kind of my sister, even if you *are* a magnet for trouble and you like Ozzy. Go to bed."

I climbed the steps slowly, as if I had weights around my ankles. I trudged down the hall and opened the bedroom door.

Sean lay in bed with his back against the pillows, doing something on his phone. Rogue was in his bed by the window, on his back with all four feet in the air, snoring. He opened one eye, chuffed softly at me, and went back to sleep.

Sean put the phone on the nightstand as I walked in. "Is there anything I need to hear about tonight? Any of those things you mentioned earlier that you need to tell me about, or anything Malcolm said?"

I thought about it and shook my head. "No. Everything can wait until tomorrow."

"Good." He smiled. "Then get your butt in bed."

I went to the bathroom to wash my face and brush my teeth. I dropped my clothes into the hamper, put on my comfiest pair of pajamas, and turned off the bathroom light.

Sean raised the covers and I climbed into bed next to him. He curled around me and drew me close with his arm around my middle. I felt the hard outline of the amulet he wore against my back and raised my hand to touch the one hanging around my neck.

He kissed the back of my neck. "Whatever's coming, neither of us will face it alone."

"I know. It's a comforting thought." I squeezed his hand.

"I have a confession," he murmured, his lips against my ear. "I love seeing a wolf amulet around your neck."

"I have a confession: I love wearing a wolf amulet around my neck. And I love sharing a bed with a wolf."

I sensed him smiling. "I love sharing a bed with a mage."

My eyelids drifted closed. "So sleepy."

"I know." He kissed my ear. "I will keep you safe. Sleep as long as you like. I took tomorrow off, so I'll be here."

"Okay." I wiggled a little closer and his arm tightened around me.

Just before sleep pulled me under, he whispered, "And for the record, I think your Spider-Man underwear is very, very sexy."

I managed a ghost of a smile. In the next heartbeat, I was sound asleep.

# CHAPTER 14

Late Tuesday morning, I woke up to the smell of fresh-brewed coffee and with Sean curled around me.

"Good morning," he said, his breath warm against my neck. "You slept soundly. There was even a bit of snoring there for a while."

"Sorry." I rolled onto my back and stretched lazily. Rogue's bed by the window was empty; Sean had probably let him into the back-yard to enjoy the sunshine.

"Don't be. You know I think your little snore is adorable." He kissed my forehead. "You needed every bit of that long rest. How do you feel?"

"Good." I stretched again. "I forgot what it feels like to have a full night's sleep. My brain feels so clear!"

He chuckled. "How you manage to function so well on such little sleep is amazing to me, but I suppose you're used to it."

"It's not as easy these days as it used to be to stay up for several days in a row with only a couple hours of sleep," I admitted with a sigh. "By the time we got home last night, I was barely able to hold a coherent conversation."

"Sixty very eventful hours on five hours of sleep, Alice," Sean admonished me. "Most people wouldn't be functional *at all* at that point." He started to get up. "Let me go make you some breakfast."

I rolled on top of him and sat up, straddling his hips. "I *am* starving, but not for food."

His eyes glowed. "I'm pretty hungry myself and you're looking particularly tasty right now."

I rolled my eyes. "Sure, with bedhead and puffy eyes and—"

He flipped us so fast that I yelped. His mouth covered mine as his hand slid under my pajama top and over my ribs to my breast. I gasped and arched up against him.

He raised his head to look into my eyes. "You are never more beautiful than first thing in the morning in my bed." He pulled his T-shirt off over his head, treating me to a view of a perfect chest that never ceased to make me shiver with desire.

I started to pull off my pajama top but he brushed my hands aside and reached for the top button. "I'm taking my time with you this morning," he told me. "Everything that's happened in these last couple of days makes me want to savor every moment."

I groaned. "That's torture."

"The best kind," he agreed.

He worked his way down the buttons with maddening slowness. When the top was open all the way, he pulled the sides away a centimeter at a time, baring my chest and letting the fabric brush over my breasts slowly until I thought I would scream with a combination of arousal and frustration. My hands clutched at the sheets as I fought the urge to move.

When the top was off, he moved the amulet I wore and placed it between my breasts, over my heart. He closed his eyes for a moment. When they opened again, they were bright gold. I saw a shadow moving behind them, as I had when he was waiting to find out if the hex had broken. The wolf was looking out through Sean's eyes. Golden magic rose. The wolf liked what he saw.

So did Sean. He lowered his head and kissed his way along my breastbone. His mouth moved to my right breast.

I cried out and tried to move but he pinned my hands to the bed as he sucked gently and flicked the delicate skin with the tip of his tongue. When his teeth grazed me, I almost came up off the bed. "Oh, God. Sean, *please*."

He smiled wickedly. "I'm only just getting started."

True to his word, he tortured my left breast just as long, keeping me on the edge between pleasure and torment for what seemed like hours. No amount of pleading got me any mercy at all.

When Sean's hands went to the waistband of my pants, I raised my hips to make it easier for him to remove them. He nudged me down and licked across my stomach slowly with the tip of his tongue.

"Your magic sizzles like I'm licking a battery," he told me.

"Why would you lick a battery?" I asked breathlessly.

"Guys do stupid things on a dare."

He resumed his explorations, tugging my pants down a little at a time until finally he slid them off all the way. Despite how long we'd been together, the way he studied my body, his eyes taking in every detail as if memorizing it, made me a little self-conscious.

He moved up the bed to look into my eyes. "You are perfect, Alice."

His hand moved down my stomach and nudged my thighs apart so he could make a first caress between them, as gentle as a feather. I gasped and closed my eyes as he kissed me, his warm fingers moving just right, driving me toward the edge of ecstasy and then over it.

When the starbursts faded and I became aware of my surroundings again, I discovered he'd slid down the bed and replaced his hand with his tongue.

"Sean..." I gasped, my back arching.

He raised his head to meet my gaze with his own golden one. "Again," he said.

I couldn't possibly, not again so soon. I shook my head and tried to pull away, but he held me fast with one hand on my hip. "Oh, you will," he promised, raising me up to get a better angle.

And I did, scant moments later, in a rush no less powerful than the first. I was still shuddering and sobbing out his name when he rose just long enough to take off his pants. He returned to the bed to hold me while the aftershocks faded.

When I could breathe again, I tried to roll him over but he resisted. "This is about you," he told me.

I pushed harder on his chest. "Yes, it is, so let me have my turn."

He gave in and rolled onto his back. I rose onto my hands and knees and gave him the same long, admiring stare he'd given me, letting my eyes devour every inch. I let my hair brush over his chest and against his arousal.

He groaned. "Jesus, Alice, that is not fair."

"Oh, I think it's *very* fair. And I'm only just getting started."

I took my time, kissing and teasing my way down his chest, but I couldn't be as patient as him. I wanted to taste him and I didn't want to wait anymore.

My mouth closed around him. He was fierce and strong, my alpha, and he tasted untamable, like barely caged wildness.

His back arched as he fought to stay in control, his fists twisted in the covers. I didn't want him in control, however. I wanted him uncaged.

I used my hand to form a tight loop around him. I drew him deep into my mouth, then back up, my fingers sliding as I moved. That was all it took.

He came off the bed with a wolf's growl and turned me around to face away from him, his hands gripping my hips hard enough to bruise. I cried out in pleasure at the feel of him as he filled me. He was all power and so impossibly hard and hot. It nearly sent me back over the edge immediately.

"My Alice," he growled, biting my shoulder just hard enough to leave a mark.

"My Sean." It was the first time I'd said it.

His arm moved around my middle to hold me as his movements became more deliberate. Magic rose—mine and his.

I screamed, my head falling back onto his shoulder. My magic poured out in a storm of green and white, with traces of black, purple, and red. There was also blue—the traces of water magic left behind by Malcolm sharing his magic with me—and hot golden shifter magic. It swirled around the room like an indoor hurricane.

Sean shuddered and growled, his arm tightening around my middle as he pulsed inside me. We fell over onto the bed as our magic rolled back through us in a wave of pleasure and power.

A few minutes later, once we'd had a chance to catch our breath, he nuzzled my hair. "When I look back now, all of my memories from before I met you are almost in black and white. I used to ask myself if I was making a mistake, waiting for some mythical perfect woman who would be my equal in nearly everything and better than me in the rest. You weren't mythical after all."

I craned my neck and kissed his jaw. "You don't have to pile on the compliments, you know. I'm already in your bed—and happily so, I might add. No further flattery is required."

"I'm serious, Alice." He kissed the mark his teeth had left on my shoulder. "Sometimes I think that's why I like to bite you so much— I'm making sure you're real."

I laughed. "I thought you just had an oral fixation."

"That too." He smiled, his eyes twinkling. "I don't know if I'm fixated on it, but I very much enjoy it."

"Mmm, me too." I wiggled against him. "Other than catching each other up on some stuff and talking about what I'm going to do about Aden, what plans do we have for the day?"

"I know I said I took the day off, but I need to go inspect a house for a client. Come with me? It's a new home, so there won't be anyone else there. We can chat on the way."

"Sounds good."

He sighed. "And then tonight I'm having dinner with Lily's father, Zachary. The dinner is at his brother's house."

"The brother who's on the Were Ruling Council?"

He nodded.

"Should I be worried about this at all?"

"Absolutely not," he said firmly. "Zachary and I will talk and I'll make my position clear. I'm expecting an apology for what Lily did and for the evening to end amicably."

My stomach growled. "Is that offer still open for making us breakfast?"

He chuckled. "It's lunch now, but yes. Hop in the shower and I'll have something ready by the time you're done."

I leaned over and bit his arm.

"Hey," he protested. "What was that for?"

"Just making sure you're real." I rolled to my feet and headed for the bathroom.

I SHOWERED and dressed and hurried downstairs for lunch. Even though we weren't expecting to see anyone, since our errand was work related, I went with business casual: a sleeveless emerald green blouse, slim slacks, and ankle boots, with my hair in a French braid. My amulet nestled reassuringly between my breasts.

Sean went upstairs to shower and dress while I ate. He came down just as I finished loading the dishwasher, wearing a blue Maclin Security polo shirt and khakis. I noticed the outline of his amulet under his shirt.

"A delivery van just pulled up out front," he said, heading for the door. "Are we expecting something?"

I dried my hands on a towel and joined him in the foyer. "I'm not —not to this address, anyway."

Sean opened the door as the driver emerged from the van and slid the door open to grab a small rectangular box from a bin. He shut the door and hurried up the sidewalk with the box.

We stepped onto the porch to meet the driver. "Delivery for Alice Worth," he said briskly, holding out the box.

I didn't take it from him. "I wasn't expecting anything," I said with a frown. "Who is it from?"

He glanced at the box. "It's not printed on the label, but it says there's a card inside." He offered me the box again and frowned when I hesitated. "I've got a lot more deliveries to do this morning, ma'am. I'm sure if you don't want it, you can find someone else who'll drink it."

I blinked and took the box. It was surprisingly heavy. "Drink it?"

He held out a little electronic device. "Sign, please. Yeah, drink it. I'm from MacDougal's."

Sean whistled. Despite my love of Scotch whisky, I'd never even stepped foot in MacDougal's. Customers shopped by appointment or had to be buzzed in by the staff. It was the sort of place where Charles would feel quite at home, however. If he'd sent this gift as a thank-you for saving his undead life, I would have a very difficult time refusing it.

I signed for the delivery and the driver half-jogged back to his van to continue his appointed rounds. "He's like a young, skinny, blond Santa," I said, cradling the box as we went back inside.

Sean chuckled. "If you were a delivery driver, working for MacDougal's and bringing joy to everyone you meet wouldn't be a bad gig to have."

I set the box on the dining table. The label revealed nothing about its contents, reading only *A Gift For Miss Alice Worth* and Sean's address.

"Do you think Vaughan sent it?" Sean asked, handing me his pocketknife to cut through the thick embossed seal.

"Who else would send me a bottle of expensive Scotch?" I opened the lid and carefully took out the wooden box inside. When I saw the label, my mouth fell open. "I..." I coughed. "Wow."

Sean was already searching for the whisky online. He held up his phone so I could see the results. There were way too many numbers after the dollar sign.

I shook my head. "I can't accept this, not even for saving Charles's life. He should know better by now."

"Where's the card?"

I spotted the card at the bottom of the outer box. I tipped it out onto the table and Sean picked it up. He opened the little envelope and read the card. His expression went flat.

"What?" I asked.

He handed me the card and envelope. The card was handwritten. *Miss Worth, please accept this gift as recognition of your immeasurable value. May our partnership be a long and profitable one. I will see you soon. Darius Bell.*

I stared at the wooden box as if it was a venomous snake. "How did he even know I love Scotch?" My voice vibrated with fury. "That *bastard*."

"What do you want to do with it?" Sean slid the wooden box back into the outer box, put the card and envelope on top, and closed it.

"I don't know. I'm sure as hell not going to drink it. I don't even want him to think I accepted it, but I have no way of giving it back to him since no one knows where he's staying these days." I took the box to the pantry and stuck it on the top shelf, where I didn't have to look at it. "I'll figure it out later. Let's go look at that house."

We left Rogue inside and headed out in Sean's Mercedes, since the truck was still sporting two large dents. He'd made an appointment to take it to a body shop tomorrow.

On the way to inspect the house, I told Sean what Suriel had said to Malcolm about why he'd been bound to me and that I would save Aden. When I related Suriel's promise about returning for Malcolm when the time came, Sean took my hand and squeezed. "He means a lot to me too, and not just because the kid knows his way around a joke." He smiled. "Where is our spirit, anyway?"

"At the moment, back at my house keeping an eye on things and working on some spellwork in the basement." I'd summoned him briefly while Sean was showering, just to check in. "He says there's a Vamp Court SUV parked in front of the house, presumably guarding it against Bell's people."

He sighed. "I'm glad to hear that. I'd like to think Bell isn't dumb enough to mess with you or your home, but sometimes desperate men do dumb things."

"That's why I'm going to let the Court keep an eye on it, just in case."

"You said last night there were some other things you needed to tell me. We've got at least twenty more minutes of driving. What else is going on that I need to know about?"

Telling people things—even Sean—continued to be difficult for me. My instinct was always to keep things secret, especially when they might reveal a vulnerability. When it came to Sean, I had to fight another, more complicated feeling: a reluctance to give him more reason to worry. I'd promised not to tell him I was okay when I wasn't, and he'd recently clarified that telling him there was nothing to worry about, or *not* telling him when there was a problem, fell into that same category. As such, I had a couple of things I needed to disclose.

"First item," I said.

He raised his eyebrows. "There's a list? Do you have a PowerPoint?"

"Hush. Sunday night, when I went to help Charles, everything went pretty smoothly up until I destroyed the Tepes stone." I told him about the unseen force that had attempted to strangle me and the voice I'd heard. "When I looked up the words on a translation website, they turned out to be Romanian for 'Fear me.'"

"Romanian, huh?"

"Yup."

He pondered that. "So, you destroyed an item once belonging to, and then were threatened by, none other than Vlad Tepes?"

"It's possible," I admitted.

To my astonishment, Sean chuckled. "Our resident Dracula fanboy, Ben, would lose his mind if he knew."

My mouth fell open. "Are you not freaked out by this?"

He grew serious. "Of course I'm concerned, but I don't think we're in danger of a visit from Tepes. A vampire that old and powerful must have much bigger fish to fry, I would think. I'm going to focus on more immediate threats unless we have any reason to believe Dracula is headed this way."

He had a fair point. Tepes might be angry that I'd destroyed one of his objects of power, but vampires of his vintage had a long view of things, and Sean was right: no doubt he had more important issues to deal with. No sense fretting about a problem until it became one.

"Second item. As I said when Bryan told us about Charles's condition, I was looking forward to settling our account so I no longer felt indebted to Charles for saving my life at the construction site. However, he insisted on granting me a boon and I was too tired to argue about it. On the way out, Adri advised me not to decline the boon and gave me a very cryptic warning that I might need it soon because 'powerful forces' are at play."

"Now that *does* worry me." He turned onto the on-ramp and accelerated to get on the highway. "That's all she said? Powerful forces?"

"She said she couldn't tell me anything more than that. She was probably risking violating her oath to the Court as it was."

He drove for a few minutes. This much silence usually ended with a hard question. I had a feeling I knew what it would be about: Valas.

I knew I needed to find a way to tell him about Moses. I'd almost told him a half-dozen times since our trip to the Bahamas, but something always silenced me before the words came out. Now, with Darius Bell an immediate threat, I felt even more pressure to share my biggest secret of all—but once again, the words got no farther than my head.

Finally, he spoke. "Alice, you know I make it a policy not to pry. I let you keep your secrets, generally speaking, until either you're ready to tell me, or I feel like I have to push for an explanation because I think there's a danger. This is going to be one of those times. I need to know the truth about why you've become one of Valas's personal favorites."

I'd known that question was coming since Monroe used the phrase in front of Sean and Darius Bell. Bell had to be wondering the same thing, since the reclusive, ancient, and very powerful head of the Vampire Court wasn't known for taking much of an interest in any human, except those in her inner circle like Monroe.

Now the moment was here, however, I found the idea of telling Sean the truth about Valas's involvement in saving his life wasn't as terrible as I'd thought it would be. A month ago, I'd promised myself I'd do everything I could to keep Sean from finding out about the deal I'd made. Now, I felt very differently.

"What do you remember about me putting on the cuff in Jack's basement and what happened afterward?" I asked.

He frowned. "I was in wolf form at the time, and in pretty bad shape. Most of what I remember is feelings and pieces of memory. It's all very fuzzy except for when you activated the cuff and our mate bond formed." His eyes glowed. "It was the most powerful and wonderful feeling I'd ever experienced. I felt...complete, even though I'd never felt incomplete before that moment. None of the descriptions I've ever heard about what a bond feels like even came close to doing it justice."

I drank some coffee from my travel mug to hide my reaction to his words. The bond had felt wonderful to me as well, but hearing Sean describe it in such terms was enough to make me regret, just a little, that I hadn't left the cuffs on instead of freeing us both. I reminded myself the cuffs were a prison and over time they might have changed us, making us crave power—not to mention I'd had no right to bind Sean to me for life without his consent, any more than Jack would have had the right to bind him to Lily.

"Then you died." His voice went flat. "I remember going berserk in the cage, trying to get to something and kill it, but I don't know what it was. There was a shadow there—maybe it was Death. Everything was a blur of rage and grief until the moment the damn cuffs fell off and I shifted back to human and found you in the cage with me, going cold."

I decided to just rip the Band-Aid off. "The shadow you saw was Valas."

Sean swerved to the shoulder and hit the brakes. I braced myself with one hand on the dash.

He pulled farther off the road until the vehicle was partly in the grass, hit the button for the hazard lights, and faced me. "You came to Jack's house with Valas?"

"Valas came to Jack's house with me." It seemed like an important distinction.

A muscle moved in his jaw. "Why?"

"Because I couldn't get to you any other way. Jack had decreed I wasn't allowed to see you. I had two choices, as far as I could tell: fight my way through the pack to get to you, which I didn't want to do, or find another way."

"It was Valas who put them all to sleep, then, not you."

"Yes."

"Valas killed you and brought you back."

"Yes. In a way, it *was* Death you saw—Death in the form of a fifteen-hundred-year-old vampire. She made it painless and faster than I knew what hit me. I never felt a thing."

"I'd ask how she got in and out of the house without leaving a single trace of scent or magic my wolves or I could sense, but I suppose that doesn't matter. Vampires that old have powers you and I can't even begin to comprehend." His expression was grim. "That clears up a couple of mysteries, but now I have an even more important question: why did she help you?"

"She helped *us*. The stability of your pack is important to the Court and Valas knows as well as you and I do that Jack would not be a good alpha. Your pack's troubles would become the Court's troubles sooner or later."

"Alice," he said quietly. "Why did Valas help us?"

I swallowed hard, suddenly afraid of how he would react. "Because we made a deal."

His face lost all expression. The anger I'd sensed earlier seemed to vanish, as if he'd locked down his emotions by sheer force of will. He'd never done that with me before, which told me he was both furious and afraid but trying to hide it, as an alpha would from his pack in a time of crisis. "What did she get in return?" he asked.

"That I can't tell you. The terms of the deal were confidential."

He rubbed his face. "Does anyone else know about your deal?"

"Charles does, but not the details. He figured out Valas had helped me and I couldn't deny it because he'd sense I was lying. That's it." He'd also offered to give me valuable information I could use against Valas if she tried to turn our deal against me, but I kept that to myself for now.

He didn't reply for a long time. I could only imagine what was going on in his head. Even with his emotions hidden, I knew he had to be angry and worried, and probably feeling guilty as well since I'd had to make the deal to save his life.

I touched his arm. "I will tell you this: I did not trade my life or agree to become a vampire in order to save you, if that's what you're worried about. I am not enslaved to Valas *or* the Court in any way. I made an offer and she accepted it, with a bit of haggling. Once the terms of our agreement are fulfilled, I can tell you everything, but for now, that's all I can say."

"If you don't hold up your end of the bargain, what happens?"

I said nothing, but he probably read the answer in my eyes.

Golden magic rose and he growled. "I won't let her turn you, Alice. I'll stop her or I'll die trying."

I cupped his face with my hand. "You'll do no such thing because I will meet my obligations. Valas finds me interesting because the first time we met I wasn't as intimidated by her as she expected me to be."

"Now there's a surprise," Sean said dryly. "You probably defied her openly in front of the whole Court."

I huffed. "I was polite about it."

His laugh was sudden and loud. He kissed me, then rested his forehead on mine. "Thank you for telling me this. I can understand why you wanted to wait. I wouldn't have taken the news quite as well a few weeks ago, given how Vaughan manipulated you."

"I had to be in a different place too," I admitted. "It's not easy for me to reveal secrets, but I'm getting a little better at it."

"Yes, you are. Is there anything else I need to know?"

*You have no idea*, I thought. Out loud, I said, "Yes, but not that I think I can share today. Maybe tomorrow. I need to pace myself with these revelations and not hit you with everything at once."

He turned off the flashers, signaled, and eased back onto the highway. "I do need a little time to process your run-in with Dracula, Adri Smith's cryptic warning, and your deal with Valas. We're not too far from the house now, maybe another five minutes."

"Okay." I turned the radio up and smiled. "Hey, it's our song."

He blinked. "We have a song?"

My cheeks warmed. "Never mind. Forget I said that."

"No, you don't get to say that and then say never mind." He glanced at me as he took an exit. "Why is this our song?"

I picked at a loose thread on the seam of my pants. "It's dumb."

"Alice, I don't think it's dumb." He thought about it while he turned onto a country road and headed away from the highway. "It's the song that was playing when you walked into Hawthorne's the night we met," he said in surprise. "I'm surprised you remember. I saw you walk in, but you didn't see me—not until I walked over and introduced myself."

"I didn't see you until then, but for some reason I always think of this song when I remember that night."

He grinned. "Maybe because you *did* ask me to take you home that night. And I've never stopped being thankful you did."

"Me neither." I smiled and put my hand on his leg.

OUR DESTINATION TURNED out to be a lovely farmhouse on several acres of land. A FOR SALE sign hung on a post in the yard. We parked out front and got out.

We weren't far from the highway, but as I followed Sean up the walk to the door, I couldn't hear anything but wind and birds. It reminded me of Cole and Karen's house, which I loved. I liked living in the city, but there was something to be said about country life.

Sean punched in a code on the lock box and it opened, revealing a key. He unlocked the door and ushered me inside.

"Wow, look at this space!" My voice echoed through the empty rooms. "Is your client looking to buy the house and put in a good security system?"

He nodded. "Why don't you take a look around while I make some notes?"

I explored while he inspected doors, windows, and the outside of the house. The upstairs featured a lovely renovated master suite and two other bedrooms, plus a fourth room that could be used as an office or workout room.

Downstairs, the living room was huge, with tall windows on two sides. Off the living room was a study with floor-to-ceiling built-in bookcases. My favorite part of the house was the enormous kitchen, which had also recently been remodeled. Beside the kitchen, I found the laundry room and a door leading to a small basement. Basements were unusual in the area, but maybe this one had once been used for storage.

There was a deck out back and a two-car detached garage with a large storage building next to it. I opened the patio door and stepped out onto the deck, where Sean stood.

"What do you think?" he asked, tucking his phone in his pocket.

"It's a great house. Lots of sunshine and space, neighbors far enough away that you won't see or hear them very much. Remodeled kitchen, master suite, and bathrooms. Plenty of room for hosting get-togethers if you wanted to have friends over...or an entire were-wolf pack." I turned to look at the trees and grassy field. "I think you should tell me why you really brought me out here."

He took my hand. "Am I busted?"

"Totally busted. What were you doing on your phone while I was looking around? Not taking notes about a security system, that's for sure."

"Online word game. Ben is beating me like a drum." He tugged on my hand until I turned to face him. "I want to go to bed with you every night and wake up next to you every morning."

"We pretty much do that already," I pointed out.

"I'd like to wake up with you in our home. My house is just a house. I've owned it for fifteen years and it's been fine, but it's never been my home, not really. I thought it was feeling more like home recently, but then I realized it doesn't feel that way when you aren't there. Home is not a place for me anymore; it's with you."

When I didn't say anything, he went on. "Your home is *your* home, your space. You share it with me and I love being there with you, but I don't think you'd ever be able to think of it as *ours*, not really. When I'm there, I'm staying over at your house. When you're at my house, even if I think of it as our room and our bed, it still feels like you're staying over with me."

I wanted to argue with him on that point, but he was right.

"What I want is a home for *us*—a place that's ours, not yours or mine. I also want a new home for our pack, instead of a house where we meet. Karen and Cole's place is that for us now, but their family is growing and it's not Karen's responsibility to provide us with that anyway—it's mine. No one has ever said anything, but they know my house hasn't ever been a den for the pack like Henry's home was. But that's not my primary consideration; you are." He squeezed my hands. "Let's live here, Alice."

"Even after everything I told you in the car, you still want to live together?"

"I didn't turn around and drive back home, did I?"

"How long have you been thinking about this?"

"Off and on, quite a while. Seriously since we got back from the Bahamas. I had to find a house that met our needs and budget and wait until I thought it was the right time to bring it up. Every time I hinted at the idea, you shut down, so I knew it was going to be a tough sell. This house came on the market a few days ago. If I've learned anything from everything we've been through, it's that nothing is guaranteed, and if you want happiness, you need to grab onto it when you can."

I let go of Sean's hand and headed off across the yard. He stayed on the deck and let me walk.

I looked around. The house was beautiful. The location was fantastic. That kitchen was to die for. There was a garden tub and a large custom shower in the master suite. The basement was small, but still large enough for Malcolm and me to work on spellwork. I couldn't find one fault with the house, except that it didn't have five years' worth of wards protecting it.

What did my wards protect, exactly? The house? It was just a house, truly, though I was proud of it because it was the first thing I'd ever had that was mine. I'd always thought of my wards as protecting me, but the truth was they didn't, not unless I hid behind them. Except for the wards, there wasn't much keeping me tied to that house. Everything else could be relocated, even my man-eating garden.

Once I admitted my wards didn't really protect me, I had to grapple with the real reason I was reluctant to move in with Sean: fear. Fear he would find out who I was and end our relationship; fear I would bring harm to him and his pack if Moses found me; fear I'd lose my courage if Moses did come looking for me and I'd have to break Sean's heart by disappearing. And now the fear that Valas would find a way to turn our deal against me and I'd end up fighting her for my life and my freedom, a cause Sean had just said he would die for. All of those fears were lead weights in my gut.

But none of them would worsen if we bought this house. I'd have all the same fears, but I'd have them in a home I shared with someone I cared deeply about, and who loved me with all his wolfy heart. Malcolm and I could build new wards fairly quickly to protect the house and those inside it.

When Jack had prevented me from seeing Sean and tried to find the cuff before I did, I'd done what I had to in order to hang on to the one chance at happiness I'd ever had. I'd made deals, died, and risked everything, and I'd done it without a second thought. If I'd been willing to do that, I could put on my big-girl Spider-Man panties and do this. Home-buying could be a long, tedious, expensive, and soul-sucking process, but it couldn't be worse than dying, right? Not even in this sellers' market.

I turned around and marched back to the deck, where Sean waited. I didn't even get to say anything. He picked me up and spun me around. I laughed and kissed him thoroughly as he held me with his hands under my butt.

"I didn't know if you were going to say yes," he said. "I thought I maybe had a fifty-fifty chance at best. Judging by what I was sensing from you, your deliberations were going the other way for a while."

"They were." I took his face in my hands. "But what you said there at the end clinched it for me. If we want happiness, we have to grab it and hang on with everything we've got."

"I've got happiness right here in my hands, quite literally," he said, his eyes twinkling as he gave my butt a squeeze. "I'll call the realtor right now." He lowered me to the ground.

"Hang on one minute," I protested. "Have we seen the inspection paperwork? What's the fair market value for this property? How old is the plumbing? When—"

He kissed me hard. "I have everything in the briefcase in the car," he promised me. "Alice, if there's a happier werewolf around, I don't know who it would be."

"Maybe Ben or Karen," I suggested.

"Maybe, but I bet I could give either one of them a run for their money right now." He slid the patio door open for me to enter and gestured gallantly. "After you, my lady."

"Thank you, my kind sir." I stepped inside. "Get your briefcase and let's get to work."

"First time I've ever been excited to go through that much paperwork." He kissed my forehead and headed out the front door, humming as he walked. It sounded like a slightly off-key rendition of "Take Me Home Tonight."

I smiled and leaned against the kitchen counter. *Definitely our song*, I mused.

# CHAPTER 15

"So you may have pissed off Dracula, got a mysterious warning about powerful forces being at work, granted mercy to the woman who got you hexed, finally told Sean about your deal with Valas, and decided to buy a house? Does that about cover it?" Malcolm asked dryly.

I thought about it. "More or less."

We were in the living room at Sean's home. He'd left early for his dinner with Lily's father since he'd needed to swing by work on the way. I'd summoned Malcolm after he left to catch him up on recent events.

He sighed. "I leave you alone for five minutes and you turn everything upside down. How did he take the news?"

"Which part?"

"All of the above."

"Better than I'd expected. Better than I'd hoped, actually."

"I know the Valas thing has been weighing really heavily on you. It's got to feel better to get that off your chest."

"It does," I confessed. "Though now he's carrying some of the weight too and I feel bad about that."

"That's the point of being together, though, right? Sharing the load? *Lean on me, when you're not strong,*" he sang, not especially tunefully. "You might consider unburdening yourself of some more of those secrets. If telling him about Valas felt good, imagine how amazing you'll feel when you tell him the rest."

"The rest of what?"

He rolled his eyes. "Seriously, Alice. The rest of *everything*. Who you are, where you come from, why you came here, who you're hiding from, why your blood magic has purple in it when no one else's does, why you prefer Boo Berry over Count Chocula like some kind of psycho."

"Boo Berry is much better than Count Chocula," I said huffily.

"I rest my case, you loon." He grew serious. "I mean it. Whatever's in your past, he can handle it. So can I, for that matter. We're on Team Alice."

"Thanks, Malcolm. I appreciate that."

His mouth turned down. "But you're not going to spill the beans."

"It's a lot of beans. A lot of really dangerous and awful beans."

"Now I'm picturing a bunch of shark-toothed beans running around with pitchforks." He waved his hands. "Look, I know it's bad. *He* knows it's bad. We know you used to belong to a cabal and it doesn't get any worse than that. You did a lot of things you're ashamed of and you feel guilty about. Join the club. You know I've done just as bad. You think Sean doesn't have those same kinds of memories?"

"I know he does. He's told me about some of them."

"Well, let me ask you this: If you told him everything tonight when he got back from dinner with Lily's father, what do you think he would do? Be honest."

I said nothing.

He floated over to where I sat on the couch. "You know as well as I do that he'd accept it. He might struggle to process it, he might need some time to come to terms with it, but there is no way that man would love you any less. Look me in the eye and tell me you don't believe that."

"I don't believe it," I said tonelessly.

He flitted back. "You can't be serious. After everything you've gone through and as well as you know him, you still think he'd be so horrified by your past that he'd end your relationship? How could you think so little of him? I know you're struggling with whether you love him, but surely you don't think he's some kind of a monster."

"No, but what if he thinks *I* am?"

He threw up his hands in disgust. "You know what I hear? *Poor me, I'm such a monster. Nobody can love a monster.* I knew you heaped guilt and blame and anger on yourself every chance you got, but I didn't realize you wallowed in self-pity too."

"I don't," I snapped. "I'm not feeling sorry for myself. I'm realistic. You don't know everything I've done, all the lives I destroyed."

"No, I don't, because you won't tell me!" he said, exasperated. "And even if you did, you didn't do it because you *wanted* to—you did it because you had no choice. If you can't see the difference, then maybe that's why you don't think we could either. But I know the difference because I lived it, and Sean knows because *he's* lived it."

He pointed at me, the tip of his finger an inch from the end of my nose. "I got news for you, Alice. Sean knows damn well what you've done and he loves your sorry ass anyway. All you have to do is let him. For the life of me—or the death of me, whichever—I don't know why that's so hard."

I couldn't think of a response that wouldn't irritate him more, so I headed to the kitchen. "I'm making more coffee."

"I thought you were going to get some cheese to go with your whine." His tone was dry. "How long will Sean be gone?"

"Probably quite a while, he said. He was expecting to be there several hours at least. He said he'd text when he was on his way home."

"You want me to stick around?"

"No. I'm fine here." I picked out some fancy coffee beans and poured some into the grinder. "How's the spellwork coming along?"

He sighed. "Very slowly. I've been at it most of the day and haven't gotten anywhere. But I guess if it was easy, someone else would have figured out how to do what we're trying to do already."

I fired up the grinder. When the racket subsided, I said, "Let me know if you have any breakthroughs or anything weird happens at the house."

"Anything weird, or anything weirder than just normal weird?"

I smiled. "Anything weird. We have to be on guard, despite the Court and the Council backing us up. If you feel anything at all that you think feels remotely like an attack on you or an attempt to recall you back to Bell, jump to my bracelet."

"I will."

"And hey, Malcolm?"

"Yeah?"

"Thanks for the tough love. I'll think it over."

"You know I'm right. Just save us both some time and admit it."

I flicked a dish towel at him. He flitted back. "Let me know what goes down at Sean's meeting and if you want me to go haunt Lily. I've been working on some new nightmare forms and they'd be *perfect*."

"Thank you. Maybe some other time," I told him.

He vanished with a tingle of magic.

When the coffee was ready, I poured a cup, added cream and sugar, and took it back to the living room.

I glanced at the clock. Sean and Lily's father were having dinner now. I hoped their discussion would go as smoothly as Sean said it would.

My thoughts drifted back to Malcolm's assertion that Sean knew what I had done. He certainly wouldn't know the particulars, but if he knew I'd run from a cabal, he could probably guess and hit pretty close to the truth.

I sighed and drank my coffee. "I hate it when Malcolm's right," I told Rogue, who was sleeping on his bed by the window. "That seems to happen a lot. Do you think people get wiser after they die, or is all of this just painfully obvious to everyone but me?"

The dog chuffed and got up to stretch.

"Is that a yes that it's obvious? It is, isn't it?"

Rogue sneezed and moseyed into the kitchen. I heard him drinking noisily from his bowl. When he came back, he went to the door. I let him out into the yard and watched him as he peed, chased a couple of insects, and barked at the neighbor's cat, who hissed at him from her perch on a fence post. When he went back to chasing insects, I closed the door and headed for the stairs, intending to take a bubble bath and try to relax.

My phone beeped with an incoming message just as my foot touched the bottom step. I was surprised to see it was from Sean. Dinner must have ended early. I wondered if that was good or bad.

When I opened the message, however, I got a surprise.

*Wolf: Pack emergency. Meet me at the pack land ASAP. West gate on Duncan Road. Will explain when you get here.*

*Me: On my way.*

I put my coffee cup on the dining table and grabbed my keys and bag on the way out the door.

THE PACK OWNED a large piece of land outside the city. They used it on the full moon, when all werewolves were in wolf form from sunset to dawn, and anytime they wanted to run or hunt as wolves, as Caleb, Ben, and the others had done after the pack meeting. I'd only been out there once, but I remembered how to get there. It was about a twenty-minute drive from Sean's house if I ignored speed limits, which I did.

As I drove, I wondered what might have happened. Sean was probably dealing with the problem, but someone else might know what was going on. I called Ben. The call went straight to voice mail. That made me put the phone down and drive even faster. I just needed to get there and find out what was going on.

When I got to the gate, it was open. I drove through and followed the track to the little gravel parking area about an eighth of a mile past the gate.

I expected to find several cars and at least several members of the pack there, but instead the only other vehicle was an unfamiliar black Toyota.

Frowning, I parked and got out. "Sean? Ben?" I called.

My phone beeped with an incoming text message. *Wolf: We're in the woods.*

I spotted movement in the trees to my left. I stuck my phone in my back pocket and jogged in that direction. "Sean, where are you? What's going on?"

My phone rang. *Wolf Calling.* I answered and put it to my ear. "Where are you? Whose car—"

"Where are you?" he interrupted. "I'm in a bad coverage area and your text just came through. You said you were on your way. On your way where?"

I skidded to a stop just inside the tree line. "To meet you at the pack land."

"Alice, I didn't tell you to meet me," he said urgently. "I'm still at Zachary's brother's house. Get out of there *now*."

Something hit me from behind with enough force to knock the phone from my hand. I screamed as razor-sharp teeth shredded my right shoulder and a huge black wolf took me to the ground. I landed on my stomach and my forehead smashed into an exposed tree root, leaving me dazed.

The wolf's jaws closed on my shoulder again and shook me viciously. The bones in my shoulder and upper arm broke with an audible *crunch*. My scream turned into a shriek of pure agony. I got a glimpse of torn flesh and muscle and white bone as my arm flopped on the ground, blessedly numb. I felt dizzy but clung to consciousness. If I passed out, I was dead.

I started to summon Malcolm before I realized my bracelet was gone, ripped off either in the wolf's initial attack or when I fell. If I summoned Malcolm and he jumped to the bracelet, I wouldn't be able to release him and he'd be trapped in the crystal.

Somewhere nearby, I heard Sean's voice on the phone, shouting that he was fifteen minutes away. If I didn't do something *now*, that was going to be about fourteen minutes too late.

I pushed blood magic out through my fingertips to form claws, but my right arm was broken and useless. I was lying on my left arm, which was trapped underneath me by my weight and that of the wolf, who was mauling my back and trying to get his teeth into my neck.

I blocked out the pain and focused my air magic just to the right of the center of my chest. With one burst I flipped us over and sent the wolf flying back. He landed on all four feet, gathered himself, and leaped on top of me.

The wolf snarled and opened his mouth to show me all of his teeth. Hot breath blasted my face. The wolf's eyes were golden brown. Somehow I knew who he was, even though I'd never seen him in wolf form before.

Caleb.

I hoped I wasn't imagining the trace of humanity I thought I saw in his eyes. I fixed my gaze on his neck so the wolf didn't interpret my stare as a challenge.

"Caleb, stop," I said urgently, hoping he'd recognize his own name. "I know you can hear me, Caleb. Think about what you're doing. Jack wouldn't want you to do this and neither would Delia. Think about *Delia*, Caleb. Think about Jack."

For a moment, I thought I might have gotten through to him. The wolf hesitated and raised his head. In the stillness, I heard Sean shouting my name on the phone. He sounded frantic.

The wolf lowered his head, put his ears back, and growled. The sound was low, powerful, and pure animal. *Oh, shit.*

I raised my left arm to shield my face as the wolf's jaws opened wide and he struck. His teeth closed on my forearm, slicing through my flesh like knives. Blood splattered across my face and I screamed.

When he let go, I punched him in the muzzle as hard as I could, but it did little to faze him. He went for my throat.

As the wolf's teeth closed on my neck, I forced my left hand through his fur and pushed my blood magic out through my fingertips. I raked my hand down his side and the blood magic sliced through his flesh like razors. Hot blood gushed down my arm and the wolf released my throat with a howl of agony.

Instead of backing off as I'd hoped he would, he attacked in a frenzy of teeth and claws. I slashed him again and again, but it seemed to have little effect other than angering him more. He was berserk with rage.

The wolf sank his teeth deeply into my throat again. He shook me like a rag doll and something crunched in my neck. My screams became gurgles and I struggled to breathe. My vision darkened. I had no more options.

I thrust my left hand wrist deep into one of the wounds I'd made in the wolf's side and pushed my blood magic deep inside his body, to his heart. With a choked sob, I killed him.

The wolf fell, twitched, and lay still, half on top of me, his teeth buried in my throat. I pushed his head away, but I wasn't strong enough to move his body off my chest.

Sean shouted at me from the phone. I couldn't hear him clearly, but it sounded like he didn't know where to look for me. The pack usually used the gate on the east side. If he went there, it would be a long time until he was able to find me. I tried to call out to him, but all that came out was a bloody gurgle.

Almost of its own accord, my hand went to the amulet around my neck. The chain had survived the wolf's teeth. I wrapped my bloody fist around it and drank in the warmth of Carly's magic and Sean's hot golden shifter trace. "Sean," I whispered.

The stone amulet began to pulse like a heart. I hoped Carly's spell was working and bringing Sean to me. I wasn't getting enough air; something was terribly wrong with my neck. I reached up with my left arm and closed my hand around my shredded throat. I felt blood pumping out of the right side of my neck and tried to put pressure on it with my hand, but my fingers weren't working right. It wasn't enough to be arterial, but something was punctured. I was covered in blood and most of it was mine.

As I lay there, trying to stay conscious, I realized I had another, perhaps even more serious problem.

It began as a nagging feeling somewhere deep in my belly. At first, I thought the discomfort was just another wound, but it spread quickly. I squirmed and moaned weakly as a wave of heat rolled through my body. My arms and legs spasmed, then went limp. A dozen heartbeats later, I felt another wave of heat, stronger than the first, followed by another full-body convulsion. Deep inside me, something lifted its head and began to rise.

In spite of the pain and fog in my head, understanding dawned. I'd been bitten repeatedly by a werewolf. I was infected. The spasms were the first signs of the change.

Not every werewolf bite carried the virus; many werewolves were carriers but couldn't infect others. Others carried an especially virulent strain that infected and spread rapidly. Caleb must have been one of the latter—or perhaps the speed of infection had something to do with my shifter father, or it was a combination of both. I felt the virus moving through my blood. An ordinary human might not have perceived it as clearly as I could, but my blood magic sensed the spread of the infection.

The amulet pulsed faster on my chest. I hoped that meant Sean was getting close.

Another convulsion hit and my back arched. I screamed. The

pain of my wounds faded, replaced by a strong compulsion. From a dark place inside my mind, a pair of golden eyes stared back at me. My wolf was rising and she wanted me to shift. My arms and legs jerked and the bones felt like they were grinding together. I fought against the urge with everything I had.

In the distance, tires crunched on gravel and a car door slammed. Footsteps ran impossibly fast in my direction. I heard an enraged howl and recognized Sean's voice in the sound.

Sean flung Caleb's body away. He pulled me against his chest and rocked me, making a heartbreaking keening sound.

"Not...dead..." I managed to whisper. My voice sounded strangely loud. I opened my eyes. The moonlight was somehow blinding and it hurt.

Sean's face was stark white with horror. "Alice—your eyes." I flinched. Why was he shouting?

I convulsed again and cried out. Despite the pain of fighting the change, it was getting easier to breathe. I reached up to my throat with my left hand. I was still bleeding, but not as badly as before. I had to be imagining it, but my left arm seemed to be working better too. "What's...happening...to me?"

"You've been infected." His tone sounded like he was whispering, but his voice was loud, which made no sense. "Your hearing and eyesight are improving, and you're already healing like a werewolf."

"No," I moaned. "No, please." I struggled to get away, though there was no way to run from what was happening inside me.

Sean held me so tightly that my spasms shook us both. "Where is Malcolm?"

I coughed up blood. "I couldn't summon him. I lost my bracelet."

Suddenly, in my mind, I saw my wolf. She was black, with a lighter band of fur across her shoulders and a streak of white in her tail. Her eyes were bright gold. She opened her mouth and showed me her teeth.

The wolf moved restlessly and my body shuddered, joints

popping as my arms and legs stiffened and tried to bend in ways no human body could. I screamed and screamed, fighting back, fighting the change.

Sean pulled me tighter against his chest. "I'm sorry I couldn't save you from this."

"Not...your...fault," I ground out between clenched teeth.

Gold rolled through his eyes and I wondered if mine were doing the same. "I'm going to call your wolf," he told me. "It will make your first change easier."

"No," I told him emphatically.

"Alice, let me help you. You will not go through this alone." Sean looked like his heart was being ripped out. "I'll take as much of your pain as I can. It's part of what I do for new wolves. The more you fight the change, the more it will hurt. You could die if you don't shift now."

His eyes turned pure, bright gold. As an alpha, he would command my wolf and she would take over. Once I shifted, there would be no going back.

I closed my eyes so Sean couldn't release her. Even as my body convulsed and the wolf moved under my skin, I remembered something. I'd heard of strong blood mages being able to burn the werewolf virus from their bodies. It was rare, but there were a handful of documented cases. I had no idea how they did it—the accounts had all been very vague—but I could feel the infection moving in my bloodstream. If I could feel it, maybe I could use my magic to burn it out, as I'd burned the Black Fire drug from my system when Spencer Addison tried to kill me with an overdose.

"Don't call my wolf," I said, keeping my eyes closed. "I'm going to try something."

Sean gripped my chin. "What are you doing? Talk to me."

I reached up blindly with my left hand and he grabbed it and squeezed. "I'm going to use my magic to burn the virus out of my blood."

He jerked like I'd shot him. "No, you can't—you'll die. Let me help you shift. I know this isn't what you want, but I swear I will take care of you."

"I have to try. It's been done before."

"Do you know how?" It was a challenge.

I paused. "In theory," I said, not quite lying. The wolf within swiped at me again, angrier this time, and I shrieked.

He made a broken sound. "I'm begging you—please don't do this. I can help you change. I can't bear to watch you die."

"Then go, because I'm going to do this, whether you're with me or not."

A long silence. I knew I'd hurt him, but I couldn't worry about that right now. The wolf prowled, looking for a way out.

"You'd rather be dead than be a werewolf?" Sean asked finally. I was glad I couldn't see his face at that moment.

I shook my head. "I don't think I have much time before I no longer have a choice. I want to have a choice."

He pulled me into his arms again and buried his face in my hair. "Most of us never got a choice," he said roughly. "I'll be damned if I'll take yours away. Look at me."

I opened my eyes.

"I love you," he told me simply. "I will always love you, no matter what. If you heal yourself, I will take care of you. If you shift, I'll never leave your side. If I lose you...Alice, I don't know what I'll do."

I kissed him. My bloody hand left streaks on his face.

I looked down at myself. I'd healed a little because of the werewolf virus, but I was still a mess. My right arm and shoulder were badly broken. I was covered in bites and gashes. My neck didn't feel right and I wondered if the wolf had broken something there.

"If I make it, please take me to Charles and ask him to heal me," I told Sean. "He owes me a boon."

He held me tightly. "I'll take you. Just live through this and I'll take you anywhere you want to go, even to him."

My eyes went to the bloody body of the wolf. "I'm sorry. I had no choice."

"I know." He kissed my forehead. "I made the wrong decision bringing him into our pack and letting him stay."

"You believe in people. Don't ever stop believing in people."

"Don't ever stop reminding me of that." He looked into my eyes and brushed bloody hair back from my face.

My wolf stirred. Suddenly, I felt displaced, like I'd been pushed out of the way inside my own head. My wolf looked at Sean through my eyes.

"Oh, my God," Sean breathed. He sounded far away. "I can see your wolf. She's beautiful."

I felt my wolf's desire. She saw a powerful alpha male and she wanted him. She was gathering her strength, as if she intended to leap out of me. I knew I wouldn't be able to hold her back much longer.

I wrenched control away from the wolf and she slashed across my mind with her claws. I screamed and shook with the effort it took to hold her in check. I couldn't let her take over control of my body. I'd fought too hard and given up too much for freedom to lose my autonomy to this wolf within me or to any other foe.

"Move back," I told Sean breathlessly. "I don't know what this might do to you."

Reluctantly, Sean moved away, leaving me alone on the blood-soaked ground. He sat with his back against a tree, his eyes shining like golden lanterns in the darkness.

I closed my eyes and spooled my blood magic as quickly as I could.

As if sensing danger, the wolf threw back her head and howled. My back arched. I opened my mouth and howled with her. I couldn't believe the wolf sound came from me.

From somewhere to my left, Sean howled too. His cry was angry and mournful.

As our howls echoed in the trees and my wolf moved under my skin, I drew my blood magic up and in as if I was taking a huge breath. I concentrated all of my senses inside myself. Everything else faded away.

I sensed the motes of fire that were the werewolf virus in my blood. Carefully, I focused on a single particle of the virus and used a tiny amount of my blood magic to attack it. The mote flared with a spike of pain and heat that made me twitch. Then it disintegrated, leaving behind a blackened, dead cell.

My wolf snarled, enraged. She ran full speed toward the front of my brain.

I convulsed violently. My bones ground against each other and bones broke in my legs. My scream turned into a howl of rage and pain as my jaw popped and dislocated. My body was shifting.

No time to do this carefully or slowly. I focused on the virus in my bloodstream and opened the floodgates on my spooled blood magic.

The surge of power was enormous. My back bowed so violently that something snapped and I went numb from my chest down. I couldn't tell if I was screaming out loud or only in my head. Fire raged through me as my blood magic burned in my veins, incinerating the virus as it went.

The wolf howled in fury, but her run was stopped by a wall of red and black flames. Angry and frustrated, she paced.

The firestorm raged inside me for what felt like an eternity. I had no idea what my body was doing on the ground in the woods; my entire existence focused on the sensation of the virus burning out of my cells.

In the midst of the inferno, the wolf stood, unafraid. She stared back at me, head held high, utterly fearless.

In a moment of clarity, I saw the wolf wasn't some other creature trying to take me over. She *was* me—or some core part of me. I recognized in her eyes the young woman who'd defied her grandfather, who'd refused to be broken no matter what he or anyone else did to her. I feared that without her I'd be weaker and afraid. I had no desire to become a werewolf, but I didn't want to lose this essential part of myself either.

*Stay with me*, I said to her as the flames flickered and died. The virus was gone.

The wolf inclined her head. She changed shape, her limbs stretching out, sliding through me under my skin. Slowly, she settled into my bones.

Finally, everything faded away. The last thing I saw before I lost consciousness were two golden eyes shining through the dark.

# CHAPTER 16

Consciousness returned in stages. I sensed motion and heard a voice, though I couldn't understand what it was saying. As the fog lifted, I realized I was lying in the back seat of a car that was moving very fast, and it was Sean's voice I heard.

"—minutes away. That door had better be open when I get there."

A pause.

"She's alive," he said tersely. "I'll be damned if I know how. There's not enough blood left in her to fill a coffee cup."

I couldn't hear the response. He must be on a cell phone.

I struggled to open my eyes, but my eyelids seemed to be taped shut. I couldn't feel anything below my chest or move my legs at all. My jaw still felt like it was dislocated. I moaned.

"Hold on—we're almost there." Sean sounded strained. "She's awake," he told the person on the phone. "Stay with me, Alice. Stay with me."

The car whipped around a corner and I slid helplessly across the back seat. Somehow, I didn't end up on the floor. Vaguely, I felt pressure around my middle. Maybe a seatbelt.

Sean said, "I'm pulling into the garage. Be waiting."

The car turned sharply again. He drove over a bump, down a steep ramp, and around another corner. We screeched to a stop and Sean flung his door open with such force that the hinges broke.

At the same time, someone yanked open the door by my head. For a moment, there was stunned silence.

"Jesus," I heard a deep voice say finally. Bryan.

A seatbelt clicked. Sean scooped me up and then we were moving. My body was still numb, but I felt air on my face as they ran from the car and across a concrete floor. Their footsteps echoed like we were in an underground parking garage.

"Down the hall. Third door." It was Adri's voice.

Sean ran past her and the sound of the echoes changed. We were in a long hallway. The door to the garage slammed closed and two sets of footsteps—one light, one heavy—pounded down the hall behind us.

Sean turned and went through an open door. Bright white light seared my closed eyelids and a strong antiseptic smell burned the inside of my nose.

"Where?" he snapped.

"This gurney." Charles's voice was tight. "Is she conscious?"

"She's in and out." Sean lowered me carefully onto a hard bed. I whimpered when he let go of me. I heard the snapping sounds of latex medical gloves and metal clinking.

"What is all this?" Sean demanded.

Charles's voice sounded as if he was walking around me. "Human and vampire blood transfusions. I cannot replace all of her lost blood with my own or she will become a dhampir, or rise as a vampire if she dies."

Sean growled. I wasn't sure if it was at the thought of my death or me rising as a vampire, or both. I tried to tell him not to let Charles turn me, but all that came out was a groan.

Charles's cool fingers brushed across my cheek. "Alice, open your eyes and look at me."

Someone ripped off what was left of my shirt. The movement hurt something, somewhere—maybe everything. I couldn't tell anymore where one pain ended and another began.

I moaned and my eyes fluttered open. I was so cold and the light was blinding. Charles's face swam in and out of focus as shadowy forms moved around me. I coughed thickly and blood bubbled up, spilling down my chin.

Sean snarled. "This is taking too long. Don't you have healing spells to use?"

"A healing spell would kill her now," Bryan rumbled from my left. "She's lost too much blood. Her heart wouldn't be able to take the strain."

Charles cupped my face in his hand as I fought to keep my eyes open. "Stay awake, Alice," he ordered. "Get the IV in," he told Bryan.

I blinked slowly and saw Bryan working quickly above me, his face grim. He pulled the cap off a needle with his teeth, poked at my skin with his gloved fingertips, and slid the needle into my vein. I turned my head away.

I lay on a hospital gurney in a small white room filled with medical equipment. A bag of what I assumed was human blood waited to drain into my left arm. On the other side, a bag labeled with a large red V hung from another pole. I wondered how they planned to get any blood to stay in my right arm, which looked like it had gone through a meat grinder. My legs were misshapen, bent in unnatural directions. I was covered in bloody gaping wounds, some so deep that I saw muscles, tendons, and exposed bone. The white sheets on the gurney were already turning red.

I drew on Sean's comfort and wrapped it around myself like a warm blanket. Exhaustion tugged at me and the urge to sleep became irresistible. I closed my eyes and started to drift away.

"No." Dimly, I felt Charles slap my face.

Behind me, Sean growled in warning.

"Peace, wolf. She must stay conscious," the vampire said. He slapped me again, harder.

I forced my eyes open. Charles's face was right above mine, his eyes fiery. "Look at me, Alice. You will not sleep. I will not let you die tonight."

Heat rushed into my left arm. "The IV is in," Bryan said.

Charles's fangs ripped savagely into his wrist and he moved to press the wound to my mouth. My stomach rebelled at the sight of more blood and I turned away with a sob.

Sean swore. Charles held my head still with his other hand while Sean gripped my shoulders. I suddenly couldn't stand to be pinned down. Terror mixed with fury forced me to reach up with broken arms to fight the vampire and the werewolf restraining me. The IV pulled at my skin and pain flared through the numbness.

"Hold her still!" Charles ordered. His torn wrist dripped blood.

"No, don't try to hold her down. That just makes it worse." Sean's face appeared above mine as everyone else let go of me. "Alice, I'm here. No one's holding you down. We need you to drink from Vaughan so you don't die. You're losing blood faster than we can put more in."

"I'm halfway through the second unit of blood already," Bryan rumbled. "I don't know how much longer we have before she goes into shock and her body shuts down. It's a miracle she's even alive."

Sean cupped my face with his hands. "Trust me to take care of you. Drink. You don't have much longer if you don't."

My eyes went to Charles. "I'll drink," I rasped.

Charles bit into his wrist again and pressed it to my mouth. I closed my eyes and drank.

The power and pleasure of vampire blood coursed through me in waves. I moaned. Charles didn't move away and I kept drinking.

Things began to move and heal inside my body. My back and neck spasmed, went stiff, and then loosened. Sensation flooded back to my extremities and I cried out at the sudden wave of agony in my arms and legs.

I felt the other needle going into my right arm and vamp blood rushed through my veins like a tidal wave.

My jaw popped and reset. My broken ribs—injuries I didn't even know I had—rearranged and healed. My arms and legs moved, jerked, and trembled as the various fractures knitted back together. Bryan and Adri carefully held my arms steady to keep the IVs from being pulled out as I convulsed.

Finally, Charles gently pulled his arm away from my mouth. I licked the last of his blood from my lips. As my body continued to repair its wounds, I twitched and shuddered.

When the bites and gashes in my flesh began to heal, it felt like hordes of ants on my skin. I cried out and tried to move, but Sean held me. He lowered his face to my neck and nuzzled my throat. His touch comforted me. The strange sensations faded as I drifted in the pleasure of Charles's blood and Sean's soothing forest scent.

When I opened my eyes, I found Charles sitting on the bed next to mine. He'd probably given me every drop of blood he could without risking his own life. He'd been on death's door himself just two nights ago.

"I'm sorry," I whispered.

"Please do not apologize." His face was pale, but his voice was strong.

My heartbeat felt much too slow. "Will I live?"

"Yes," Bryan said. "But we need to continue with the transfusions and minimize the strain on your heart. Your injuries are healed, but your blood pressure is dangerously low."

I was afraid to sleep, afraid I'd never wake up again if I let go, but I couldn't keep my eyes open. "Sean?"

His gripped my hand and squeezed. "Rest now. I'm here and I'm not going anywhere."

Comforted by his touch, I slipped away into darkness.

I slept for a very long time. Terrifying nightmares alternated with more pleasant interludes of dreamless sleep and dreams of Sean.

A few times I felt as though I might be waking up—I heard voices and sensed movement that seemed real instead of part of a dream—but the darkness always pulled me back under. The scent of forest never left me, however, and whenever I drew on the warmth and comfort of Sean's magic, it filled me and eased my fear. Somehow I knew he'd never let me go in all the time I'd been asleep.

Finally, the darkness receded like a tide going out and I began to surface—not quite awake, but not fully asleep either, as if I were dozing instead of unconscious. Voices rose and fell on the edge of my awareness, voices that sounded like Sean, Ben, and Jack.

The first words I heard clearly were from Ben. "Caleb cloned your phone. That's how he tricked her into going out there. He was able to send texts that appeared to come from you. When she replied, the texts went to both phones."

"And I didn't receive hers until twenty minutes later because I was at that damned dinner with Zachary." Sean's voice was quiet, but it sounded like he was next to me, holding me against his body with an arm around my middle. "He told her it was a pack emergency so she'd be more worried about that than whether it was a trap." He snarled. "I should have seen it coming. I knew he was dangerous." His anger sizzled on my skin.

"I take the blame," Jack said heavily. "I thought he'd find his way if he had a pack's support, but I was wrong. He was just too angry. I don't know what the hell he was thinking. He had to know he'd never get away with it. We'd know it was him, even if he'd succeeded in killing her."

"You and Delia share responsibility for this attack." Sean's voice hardened. "He listened to everything you said about Alice and became fixated on solving what he saw as a problem. He saw her as a problem because *you* see her as a problem—something that needed to be *dealt with*, one way or another."

"I never intended—" Jack began.

"I don't give a shit what you intended. Delia helped Lily hex Alice and then Caleb tried to kill her. A lot of Delia's resentment comes from her insecurity about having a dominant female in the pack, but that doesn't excuse what she's said and done. Your prejudice against Alice was the biggest factor in both of these attacks. That hex nearly killed her. Caleb tore her to pieces and she's been unconscious for almost twenty-four hours."

His arm tightened around me. "I had to ask a *vampire* to save her life, Jack—a vampire I hate because he victimizes her every chance he gets. Every time I see him I want to tear him apart. Instead I had to make Alice drink his blood because it was either that or watch her die. Do you have any idea what that was like? She *smells* like him, even now. There's more of his blood in her than her own."

"I take responsibility for all of it," Jack said. "For the hex, for Caleb's attack, for forcing you to ask your enemy to save your consort."

"Caleb's blood is on your hands. Alice's too," Sean told him.

A long silence. "For the record, my feelings about Alice changed after you came back from your trip," Jack said finally. "The pack has become stronger since then—I sensed it and so have others. I didn't want to believe it was because of her. I was born a shifter and the idea that a human might be a pack's strength instead of a weakness goes against everything I've ever believed. But even I could deny the truth only for so long before I had to admit you were right when you told us she would make us stronger, because she has." A pause. "If I'd communicated that openly to Delia and Caleb, probably there would have been no hex and no attack. If you plan to challenge me, I under-stand." He sounded resigned.

"I plan to discuss the matter with my consort when she wakes up," Sean said. "In the meantime, is the scene cleaned up?"

"Yes." It was Ben who answered. "I went out there before I came here and I can't smell any trace of Caleb or Alice."

"Sean, you need to eat something and take a break." I was surprised to hear Nan's firm voice. "You've barely moved from that bed all day. I'll hold her while you heat up some of the food I brought."

"I want to be here when she wakes up." Sean's voice had that mulish tone I knew all too well.

"You'll be moments away in the kitchen downstairs," Nan pointed out. "We'll come get you if she opens her eyes. She wouldn't want you to go without eating."

"Come on, man," Ben said. "Nan's right. You haven't eaten all day and you barely slept last night. Take a little break. We'll take care of her. She's pack."

Ben's words broke through the last of the fog in my brain and I made a tiny noise. "Alice?" Sean asked.

I moved my hand. He grabbed it and squeezed. "She's awake," he said, his relief and happiness a warm feeling on my skin. "Can you open your eyes?"

I got my eyes open about halfway and found myself in Sean's bed under several blankets. Since Sean was behind me, the first person I saw was Nan, who'd crouched at the side of the bed. "Hello there, sleepyhead," she said, smiling.

Ben and Jack stood behind her. Ben was grinning, as usual. Jack looked haggard. He must be taking Caleb's death hard.

Sean moved so he could see my face. His eyes were deeply shadowed and he had several days' worth of beard that did nothing to hide how strained he looked.

"You look terrible," I whispered.

He smiled and the corners of his eyes crinkled. "My Alice," he murmured and rested his forehead on mine.

Nan patted my arm and got to her feet. "This man hasn't left your side since last night."

"And he looks like it." I managed a smile. "What's this I hear about you not sleeping or eating? You're supposed to mind Nan when I'm not around."

"Who is the alpha of this pack?" Sean asked, frowning in mock outrage.

"You are." I touched his face. "But Nan is the voice of reason, and sometimes even the alpha knows he isn't being reasonable."

"I'm all kinds of unreasonable when it comes to you." He took my hand and pressed a kiss into my palm.

Nan stepped back and gestured at the door. "Let's give Alice and Sean a few minutes to talk, gentlemen. Sean, I expect you to shower and then come downstairs to eat presently."

"Yes, ma'am." Sean smiled. "Thank you, Nan."

She shooed the others out and closed the door.

Once their footsteps had gone downstairs, Sean closed his eyes and hung his head. "Damn it," he said softly. "Alice, it's been almost an entire day."

"Not as bad as the seven-day snooze I took a couple of months back." I brushed hair back from his face, letting my fingertips run lightly over his lips. "This wasn't even a coma, just a really long nap."

The pain in his eyes made my heart hurt. "I thought I'd seen horrors before, but nothing I've seen was as bad as what you went through to keep from becoming a werewolf," he said, his voice rough. "Your legs broke and your ribs broke and your jaw broke and still you wouldn't shift, wouldn't give in. And then the agony of burning the virus away..." He swallowed hard. "I will hear the sound of your back breaking for the rest of my life."

I recalled what for me had been the worst moment of last night: when he'd asked if I would rather be dead than be a werewolf. My own suffering seemed inconsequential next to the hurt I'd unintentionally inflicted on him.

"I didn't choose to burn the virus out because I would rather be dead than be a werewolf." I looked into his eyes so he could see and feel my truthfulness. "The only reason I did what I did was I believed I would survive. What mattered to me was having the choice. I went a very long time without the ability to make any decisions whatsoever about what I did and what happened to my body, and after I got away from all that, I swore I'd never give up that control again."

"I understand." He ran his nose along my hairline. "I realized that when I could think more clearly. I know damn well you don't think there's anything wrong with being a werewolf." His smile made the hurt in my heart go away. "You would have been a magnificent wolf, Alice. I saw her, you know, right before you burned the virus away. Part of me wishes you and I could have run together as wolves, though I know it's a selfish wish."

"It's not selfish," I assured him. "I wish that too. It would have been wonderful, I'm sure." I took his hand and squeezed it. "Speaking of wolves, how'd your dinner with Lily's father go?"

"Not as smoothly as I'd hoped."

"What happened?"

"When I got there, instead of just Zachary and his brother Matt, there were two other members of the Were Ruling Council—one a wolf and the other a panther shifter. Like Matt and Zachary, both of them are of the opinion that alphas should have shifter mates. Our discussion got a bit heated, as you might imagine. There's no law against an alpha having a human mate and each pack has sovereignty over relationships. We'd been arguing for about forty-five minutes when I got your text and left."

"So where do we stand?"

"As far as I'm concerned, there's nothing more to discuss. They expressed their opinions. I told them I respect their views, but I disagree. Zachary admitted there was no agreement between us in regard to Lily and apologized formally for her hexing you. Their pack has been sanctioned by the Council for her actions."

I could tell he was holding something back. "What else?"

His anger sizzled on my skin. "I had to inform the Council last night about Caleb's attack and that you'd killed him in self-defense. Zachary contacted me earlier today to express his condolences. He used the opportunity to say this wouldn't have happened if I'd chosen a shifter as a mate."

"What did you say to that?"

He growled. "I was holding you at the time and you were uncon-scious. I may have told him, rather undiplomatically, to fuck off."

"Sounds like he deserved to be told that."

He rubbed his face. "Alice, I'm sorry I ever let Caleb join our pack. I'm sorry I gave Jack a second chance after he tried to find the other cuff to give to Lily and blocked you from seeing me. Before you woke up, I told Jack that he's largely responsible for both the hex and Caleb's attack, but the fact is *I'm* to blame. That's what I've been thinking about while I've been waiting for you to wake up. I made two poor decisions and that's what led us to this moment. I'm ques-tioning the previous alpha's wisdom in suggesting I would be a good alpha." He growled. "I can't even keep my consort safe from members of my own pack."

I'd never seen Sean with his confidence shaken. I squeezed his hand. "Stop. What was your mistake, exactly? That you believe people can change and be better? I already told you that's not a failure on your part. If you weren't that sort of person, we wouldn't be together now because you wouldn't have believed in *me*. Look at the person I was when we first met—the things I did and said, and the horrible way I treated you. Most people wouldn't have been able to get away from me fast enough, but you stuck it out because you believed I could change. I wouldn't want you to change that about yourself for anything, even if it meant I'd end up hexed and a little chewed up."

He shook his head. "You weren't a *little* chewed up, Alice. You were chewed to pieces."

"Potato, potahto." I waved my hand dismissively. "So you were wrong about Caleb. You weren't about Jack. You heard him; he started to see things more clearly in the past few weeks."

"You heard all that?"

I nodded. "I was waking up while you were talking. He should have told the others what he thought, but look at how he stepped up to help after Bell threatened me and the way he reacted to what

Delia did. He isn't the man he was when he tried to give that cuff to Lily. He *did* change. You were right."

He rubbed his bristly chin. "I don't want to make another mistake, Alice."

"Me neither. None of us do, but we will *both* make mistakes. I have faith that we will get through it. I'll be here to give counsel. You've got Ben, and Nan, and Jack too." I smiled up at him. "Keep calm and carry on, alpha. You heard Jack—the pack is strong and growing stronger."

"I don't deserve you." He took my face in his hands and kissed my forehead. "I must have done something really damn good in a previous life to have been rewarded like this in this one. How do you feel? Strong enough for a shower?"

I moved my arms and legs tentatively. "I think so, as long as I don't have to take one by myself."

He scooped me up and headed for the bathroom. "If I had things my way, Alice, you'd never take another shower alone ever again."

WHILE WE WERE SHOWERING, Sean told me Charles had healed me in a medical facility under 1792. Once my injuries were healed, they'd moved me upstairs to one of the furnished apartments, where they'd continued with blood transfusions until I was stabilized. Sean had wanted to take me back to his house immediately, but Bryan had advised him to wait twelve hours before moving me, just to be safe.

In the meantime, Sean had asked Nan to go to my house to knock on the door and tell Malcolm what had happened. He sent Ben and Jack to the scene to collect Caleb's remains and tasked them with figuring out how he'd been able to lure me out to be ambushed. Ben found my broken charm bracelet in the blood-soaked, torn up earth and brought it to Sean, meticulously cleaned and repaired.

My last memory before I'd lost consciousness was of being covered with blood—mine and Caleb's—but I was clean and wearing my favorite sheep pajamas when I woke. Sean told me he'd washed me with Nan's help at the apartment after they'd finished with blood transfusions. Picturing him carefully bathing me to wash away all that blood, while still unsure when or if I would wake, brought tears to my eyes.

As soon as it was safe to do so, Sean had brought me back to his house, carrying me to Ben's SUV and holding me in the back seat during the drive. Then he'd stayed in bed with me while my body slowly recovered and the pack grappled with what Caleb had done and the young werewolf's death.

The pack had held a meeting at Sean's house while I slept. He'd gone down for a few minutes, leaving me in Nan's care, to tell them what was known and update them on my condition. Everyone was deeply shaken by Caleb's attack.

One question on everyone's mind was how I'd escaped being infected with the werewolf virus. Since telling the pack I'd burned it away would reveal I had blood magic—information that could be used against me—Sean had implied Caleb must have been incapable of transmitting the virus.

Eventually we stopped talking and just held each other under the spray with my forehead against his chest and his chin on top of my head. I was surprised to discover our wolf amulets now hummed ever so slightly when close to each other.

I didn't know what Sean was thinking about, but my own thoughts were all over the place, from Caleb and Jack to Malcolm and even Darius Bell, Aden, Jana, and Allan Garrett. There had been no word of anything brewing in the cabal in the past day, so whatever Bell's plans were, he hadn't made his move yet.

"I have to figure out a way to get Aden and Jana away from Bell," I said finally, my voice muffled by his chest. "Garrett too, if I can, though that's probably asking too much."

"Is it worth asking Monroe again?"

"Not to get them out. He was pretty clear that the Court is reluctant to upset the applecart over one kid. But it might be worth it to try and find out what Bell is planning to do with the nulls. The last time I asked, Monroe said he didn't have that information, but maybe Valas knows." I hesitated. "Maybe Charles knows."

A low growl rumbled in Sean's chest. I raised my head. "I know you hate him and I don't blame you." I pushed his wolf amulet aside and kissed the hot flesh under it, eliciting a more pleasant sound from my werewolf. "Part of me does too and always will for the things he's done. If I had a quarter for every time I've wanted to stake him, I'd have at least enough to buy a large cup of good coffee and a scone." I put my hand on his chest. "I've known monsters, Sean. Charles isn't a monster, though sometimes he does monstrous things."

A long silence. "I understand the difference, though I'm not convinced it applies to Vaughan," he said finally.

"We may have to agree to disagree on that point, at least for the time being. In any case, he might be able to tell me what Bell's planning to do with the nulls."

"He'll charge you for the information." Sean kissed the top of my head. "What do you have to give him in trade?"

"I'll have to think about that. In the meantime, we should go downstairs and get some food before Nan comes up here looking for us."

He shut the water off. "Let's eat with the others and then we'll talk some more about how we're going to find out about the nulls and get Aden and Jana away from Bell."

I paused with my hand on the shower door. "I don't know that *we* need to do that. I think *I* can do that."

"We're officially a *we*," he said, pushing the door open. He stepped out, grabbed a towel, and handed it to me. "It's you and me, baby."

I growled. "I've told you before—don't call me baby."

He grinned. "I'll call you baby all day long if you'll growl at me, *baby*."

Aggravated, I lunged at him. He swung me around with a laugh, then dipped me over backward to kiss me very thoroughly.

I might just be willing to let him call me baby every once in a while, I thought, as long as he paid for the privilege with a kiss like that.

# CHAPTER 17

According to Sean, Malcolm had checked in periodically while I was asleep, but he'd spent most of his time protected behind my house wards. I knew he had to be worried, so I hurried to get dressed. I sent Sean downstairs to get a head-start on dinner and summoned my ghost.

About ten seconds later, I felt the familiar tingle of magic coming from my bracelet. I touched his crystal. *"Release."*

Malcolm appeared. Unexpectedly, my eyes filled with tears. "Hey," I said.

"Hey yourself." He put his hands on his hips. "Are you *crying?*"

I sniffled. "No."

"You are such a liar." He studied me, frowning. "Your magic looks different."

"Different how?"

"There's more of the weird purple-y magic and more of the golden shifter magic too. Uh, did you and Sean just...?"

I shook my head. "No, but I'm sure Sean told you that Caleb infected me with the werewolf virus and I had to burn it out of my blood."

"I like how you say that as if it's no big deal," he said, rolling his eyes. "You realize there have only been a handful of cases *ever* where someone was able to do that. By all rights, you should be a full-fledged member of Sean's pack right now."

I frowned. At my expression, Malcolm floated closer. "What?"

I shook my head. "Nothing. I just had a weird thought. In any case, the changes are probably a result of the infection and the way I got rid of it."

He touched my arm lightly. "I'm sorry I was so angry about what you did to Nora. You were right—I treated you like you were the bad guy and you aren't, not even close. I was worried I'd never get a chance to tell you that."

I squared my shoulders. "You were right about a lot of things too, including what you told me last night, about trusting in Sean."

He grinned. "I told you that you should just admit I was right."

"Hush, you. Remember what I said about people who say *I told you so*. It's dickish."

"So's not listening to your friends," he shot back.

"Touché. One thing I know is you and I need to figure out a spell that brings you to me in a different way. I couldn't summon you to my bracelet because the wolf tore it off when he attacked and yanking you to me would have probably have left me too dazed to defend myself after I was injured. Let's add that to your spellwork to-do list."

"I'm putting it at the top of that list. The other stuff I'm working on can wait."

When I started to argue, he shook his head. "Alice, if you had any idea how I felt when Nan told me what happened and I found out why you hadn't been able to call on me for help, you wouldn't even fuss. I'm not asking you; I'm *telling* you that I am going to prioritize coming up with a way for you to call for help that doesn't depend on the bracelet, or risk knocking you out. I never want to feel that helpless ever again." Malcolm's anger sizzled on my skin.

I understood how terrible it was to feel helpless and how much that emotion could eat you up from the inside. "Okay. We still need those other spells, but you're right; this is more important for both of us. Bump it to top priority."

"I'm on it." He tilted his head. "I'm thinking we may need to anchor the spell in a tattoo, like the protection spell in your dragon. Would you be up for that?"

"Absolutely. I have an appointment Friday morning with the mage tattoo artist who did my dragon tattoo so she can redo the spellwork. Think we could have something by then?"

"Maybe. I'll sure as hell try. In the meantime, you'll have to think of what you want the tattoo to look like."

I smiled. "I have something in mind already. You figure out the spellwork; Jane and I will come up with a design."

"Team effort. I like it." He smiled, but it was fleeting. "Damn it, that was *too* close, Alice."

"I know. Much too close, even by my standards. Stay safe and let me know when you've got something on the spellwork."

"Will do." He vanished.

Before I went downstairs, I sent a quick text message to Adri letting her know I was awake and I would like to speak to Charles at the vampire's earliest convenience. I also thanked both her and Bryan for their help in treating me after the attack.

She texted back that Charles was in a meeting but would call in about an hour. She added that both she and Bryan were very relieved to hear I was back on my feet.

Sean met me at the bottom of the stairs. "Everything good?"

"Yep. Have you guys not eaten yet?"

"We waited for you."

I spotted a huge bouquet of flowers in a crystal vase on the little table in the foyer. "Wow. Who are those from?"

Sean's mouth turned down. He picked up the vase and handed me the little card hidden under it. I recognized the handwriting immediately.

*Dear Miss Worth—Best wishes for a speedy recovery. Darius Bell.*

Magic sparked on my fingers. Mindful of the werewolves in the kitchen, I motioned for Sean to lean down so I could murmur into his ear. "Son of a bitch. Who does he have feeding him information?"

He kissed my jaw and pressed his lips to my ear. "Someone who works for Vaughan, no doubt. The vamps have people in Bell's organization, so you can bet he has informants too."

I crumpled the card and tried to pick up the vase, but it was insanely heavy and I wasn't strong enough yet. I scowled.

Sean picked it up and took the card from me. "Trash bin?"

"Yes, please."

While he carried the vase to the garage, I went into the dining room. I found five places set at the table. In the kitchen, Jack took the second of two enormous casserole dishes out of the oven and carried it to the table.

I blinked in surprise. "You're werewolves and you're having casserole?"

"Werewolves enjoy casseroles," Ben informed me as Sean returned from the garage. If any of the wolves wondered why Sean threw away the flowers, they didn't comment.

Nan finished pouring us all glasses of iced tea. "Protein and lots of carbs. It's the perfect werewolf food."

"Good to know." There were only two dishes, though. I wondered how that would be enough to feed five people when four of us were shifters.

The answer, as it turned out, was the others except for Sean had already eaten dinner, so this was a second evening meal for them. Even so, as I watched them fill their plates, I doubted there would be a crumb of leftovers.

After a full day asleep, I was as hungry as any werewolf and attacked my food with the same single-minded efficiency as the others. As a result, it was several minutes before I realized Jack had done nothing more than take a few bites. He looked like he'd barely slept, and while the others talked, he said nothing.

When there was a lull in the table conversation, I spoke. "How's Delia?"

Jack glanced at me, then studied his glass of iced tea like he wished it held something a lot stronger. "She's taking it hard. We'd both hoped Caleb would find a place with our pack and learn how to control his wolf and his temper. The kid never caught a break ever in his life except the day Sean brought him into the pack. I'm not making excuses for anything he did because a man makes his own choices about how he handles what comes his way, but we just couldn't get through to him after all that. Delia and I tried to give him a home. We all did. It wasn't enough."

"Sometimes it isn't." Sean set his fork down and looked around the table. "Sometimes we do everything we can and we fall short. It's a bitter pill to have to swallow, for all of us."

"And she's angry," Jack added, meeting my eyes with his own tired-looking blue ones. "She's angry because Caleb's dead and her plans for Sean and the pack failed."

"Is she angry because Caleb is dead, or is she angry at me for killing him?" I asked.

A pause. "The latter."

Sean growled. I held up my hand. "That's a natural reaction," I said. "She loved Caleb and I ended his life. The fact I did so only when I had no choice doesn't ease that pain. If there had been any other way for me to survive, I would have taken that option because I didn't want to kill him."

"We know you didn't," Ben assured me. "Delia will have to come to terms with what Caleb did and how he died. I don't imagine it will be easy for her, but it won't be easy for any of us."

My appetite was gone, so I folded my napkin and set it on the table beside my plate. "I can't apologize for doing what I had to do, but I am sorry things turned out this way. Sean's right: it's a bitter pill when your best isn't good enough." I had plenty of experience swallowing that unpleasant medicine, most recently because of my failure to save Aden and protect Jana.

Nan put her hand on mine. "Time and our bonds will heal us. I hope this doesn't shake our faith in each other, or make us question our desire to help and protect those who need our strength."

She had to be thinking about how she and her children had come to join the pack, after the alpha of her former pack killed her mate. Sean and the others had taken them in without hesitation and protected them when the alpha tried to force them to return. Karen and her brother Patrick had joined the pack under similar circumstances, after their former alpha killed their mother. Most werewolf packs wouldn't have done what the Tomb Mountain Pack had done in either case. Packs tended to be insular and preferred to stay out of each other's business. Sean's pack, however, had never been one to turn its back on someone in need. Sean's predecessor, Henry, had set that precedent. He'd welcomed Sean into the pack after he was bitten and turned.

I wondered if Nan had sensed Sean's shaken confidence and spoken up to show her support in front of Ben and Jack. I didn't have a clear understanding of how much the werewolves could sense from each other through the pack bonds, but if anyone would be able to tell Sean felt unsettled by recent events and betrayals, it would be her.

Sean smiled and touched Nan's other hand. "We are strong and getting stronger every day. The pack's heart is growing, along with the pack."

He met my eyes. I read a question in them and gave him a smile.

With my permission granted to reveal our secret, Sean addressed the others at the table. "Yesterday afternoon, Alice and I decided to take an important step for each other and the pack. We've decided to buy a house, and we put in an offer on a home a couple of miles from Cole and Karen's place."

Nan jumped up to give me her most bone-crushing hug yet while Ben gave Sean a manly thump on the back. "Congrats, man."

Jack rose as well and shook Sean's hand. I thought I saw something like relief and pleasant surprise in the beta's weary eyes.

"I'm so happy for you both," Nan told me, kissing my cheek. "This is wonderful, wonderful news!"

Ben hugged me. "And congratulations to you too, Alice. After Casey saying yes and Karen and Cole's big news, this is the best damn thing I've heard in a long time."

I didn't mind coming in third behind an engagement and a baby announcement. "Nothing's final yet, obviously. It's a fantastic house in a great location, so there will be other buyers in the mix, I'm sure."

"It's past time for our pack to have a true heart and home," Sean said quietly. The others grew serious at his tone. "Karen and Cole have been kind in allowing us to gather at theirs over the years, as have Jack and Delia, but it's my responsibility and privilege to provide that place. With Alice at my side, I believe we'll find new strength and continue to grow."

Nan squeezed my hand. "Tell us about the house," she urged.

We described the house while we cleared the table. With five of us helping, it didn't take long. Nan scolded me for insisting on transferring the leftover casserole into plastic containers to store in the fridge. She wanted me to rest, but I felt awkward sitting idly while the others worked.

With the dining table cleaned off and the dishes in the dishwasher, our group moved to the living room to finish the conversation.

Ten minutes later, as I was gushing about the kitchen in the new house, my phone rang. I glanced at the screen and excused myself to go upstairs. I closed myself in the bedroom.

When the door was shut, I answered just before the call went to voice mail. "Hello, Charles."

"Good evening, Alice."

At the sound of his voice, a shudder ran through my entire body and my knees gave out. I went down in a heap. Blasted vampire blood aftereffects.

Charles's sharp ears heard the telltale sound of my body hitting the carpet. "Alice, are you well?"

"I'm okay. Hang on." I muted the call and set the phone down so I could use the bed to stand up.

Two sets of footsteps rushed up the stairs and down the hall. The bedroom door flew open before I could get to my feet. Sean came in, followed by Nan. They'd apparently heard the thud from downstairs and come running.

"Alice," Sean said worriedly, crouching next to me. "What happened?"

I sighed. "I'm all right. I had no idea just hearing him speak on the phone would have such a powerful effect."

Sean's expression darkened. "Here—let's get you up." He lifted me to my feet.

I sat on the bed and shook my head to clear it. "I drank I don't even know how much of his blood and they put more into my veins through the IV. When he spoke, I just dropped."

Sean muttered a curse. "If we'd had *any* other choice—"

"—But we didn't," I reminded him. "I'm good. Thanks for running up here, you guys."

Nan's frown hadn't budged. "You need to be resting and not hosting guests. Take care of your phone call and we'll get going." She hugged me, much more gently this time. "I'm thrilled about your decision to buy a house. We'll talk about it again soon." She headed back downstairs.

Sean lingered, watching me with his brow furrowed.

"I'm okay," I assured him. "Go on so I can talk to Charles."

He kissed my forehead. "Let me know when you're done." He left, closing the door behind him.

I steeled myself, strengthened my shields as much as I could, and unmuted the call. "Sorry about that, Charles. I tripped and fell."

He chuckled. "I do not believe you tripped, but I am willing to pretend that is what occurred."

I shivered hard at his voice, but my shields held. Yay, me.

His tone grew serious. "I was quite relieved to hear you woke. I must confess I was not at all certain you would survive such severe injuries. Your association with the wolves very nearly cost you your life."

"Don't start," I warned him. "My association with the Vampire Court nearly got me killed the night Hawthorne's was bombed, and again when Kent Stevens shot me. That's not what I wanted to talk to you about, though. Before I get to that, thank you for saving me. I guess I had to cash in that boon a hell of a lot sooner than I expected to."

"I do not consider the boon fulfilled," he said, surprising me. "Or perhaps I shall say, I do not consider it entirely fulfilled. I believe myself to still be in your debt."

I frowned. "I saved you, you saved me. How does that not make us square?"

"Because I have said we are not." His voice was crisp. "It is to your advantage that I believe it to be so. Perhaps you should accept this, rather than once again arguing against your own best interest."

I harrumphed. "I don't understand, but fine. I'm calling because I would like to purchase some information."

"Indeed?" I could almost see his ears perk up. "You are employing my services?"

"Possibly. It would depend on whether you're able to get the information I want and how much that information would cost."

"We must discuss terms, then," he said briskly, going into business mode. "Let us treat this transaction as separate from all other business between us."

That would make negotiations much easier. "Agreed."

"What information do you seek?"

"I would like to know what Darius Bell plans to do with all the nulls he's collected."

"A difficult proposition," he said thoughtfully. "None of my usual sources will be privy to that knowledge. Discovering it will likely prove costly and somewhat dangerous."

"Your specialty, in other words."

He chuckled. "The challenge appeals to me. What do you offer me in return?"

"I have a dagger. A very rare one."

"Have I been privileged to see this object?"

"You have. I used it on Sunday as part of the ritual that saved you." I'd noticed him admiring it then and remembered his reaction when Sean asked me what I had to offer Charles in return for the information I wanted. "It's valuable."

"Of that I have no doubt. I have rarely seen its equal. But there are many ritual daggers, and while yours is quite lovely, I do not believe it is quite enough compensation given the amount of risk involved in this endeavor."

"Maybe in itself that might be true, but you're forgetting one thing: whose dagger it is."

A pause. "Ah, yes, a fair point. The dagger is resonant with magic."

"Magic powerful enough to allow someone to cut spellwork or wards without having magic themselves. That makes it *very* valuable."

A long silence. Charles was thinking. I waited.

At last, he spoke. "I find myself wondering why this information about Bell's plans has such value for you."

"He's kidnapping mages left and right and holding them prisoner. He took my client's kid, and then he took my client, and then he took my client's ex." Charles already knew that, so there was no point pretending my motives weren't personal. "He's planning something—something big—and I want to know what."

"What do you intend to do with this information?"

"That depends entirely on what you find out."

"If the dagger is capable of the magic you describe, its value is immense. Perhaps we can reach an agreement if you are willing to add one small item to the purchase price."

I'd expected at least a little haggling. "And that would be—?"

"I wish to dance with you at the upcoming Court gala."

My eyebrows went up. "You want to *dance?*"

"Yes. We have never danced, Alice, and I find myself desiring to do so."

Given my reaction to hearing his voice, I almost flatly refused, but the gala was nearly a week away. Much of the effects of drinking his blood should have faded by then. "It's just a dance," I warned him. "Nothing more. No blood, no bites, no nookie, no nothing."

"I shall refrain from molesting you in any way." His tone had a note of humor, which I was glad to hear given the condition he'd been in on Sunday.

"Very well, agreed. The dagger and a dance for the information."

"I am pleased with our terms. I will begin inquiries."

"Please let me know as soon as you know something, regardless of the time."

"Very well. In the meantime, please do rest."

"I'm going back to bed momentarily," I assured him. "Thank you, Charles."

"You are most welcome, Alice. I shall see you soon."

"Good night."

We disconnected. With a sigh of relief, I flopped back on the bed and stared up at the ceiling. Out front, I heard engines starting. The others must be leaving.

Sean came upstairs and tapped on the door. "Come in," I said.

He opened the door and smiled at the sight of me sprawled on the bed. "You look exhausted."

"I am," I admitted. "How I can feel so tired after sleeping for almost a full day, I have no idea. You'd think I'd be well-rested."

"There's a difference between being unconscious and actual restful sleep," he said dryly. "You should know that by now, as many times as you've experienced it."

"Some would say I'm a slow learner." I rolled off the bed and headed for the bathroom. "Charles is going to find out about the nulls."

Sean joined me in the bathroom. "What was the sale price?"

"That fancy dagger I used on Sunday to save him from the Tepes stone and a dance at the Court gala."

He frowned. "A dance?"

"Yep. Just a dance." I smiled wryly. "He'll regret asking me when he discovers I can't dance, but it seemed like a harmless request."

"It had better be." He pulled his shirt off and dropped it into the hamper. *Mmm.* He shook his head. "Don't look at me like that, Alice. We're going straight to sleep."

"Are you sure?" I sidled over to him and started undoing his belt. "I'm fairly certain I have just enough energy for some fun before bedtime."

He let me undo the belt and the button on his jeans, but when I reached for the zipper, he caught my hand and pressed a kiss to my knuckles. "As much as I'd like to let you keep going, I think I have to insist that we sleep."

I pulled my top off over my head and tossed it on top of the hamper. "Still insisting on sleep?"

He folded his arms and frowned. "Yes."

If that pose was supposed to look intimidating, it had the opposite effect. I hadn't thought it would be possible for him to look any better to me than he already did, but the wolf amulet was like an aphrodisiac, and the way that pose accentuated his shoulders and chest nearly made me weak in the knees.

I slid my hand under the amulet to feel the warmth of the magic it contained and the heat of his skin. His chest rumbled and his eyes went golden. Better.

I unhooked my bra, slid the straps down over my shoulders, and set it on top of the hamper. I kissed him gently, teasing his lip with my teeth as my breasts brushed his chest. His hands rested on my hips and drew me closer. The kiss grew hungrier, but I sensed he was still holding back. Stubborn werewolf. This called for extreme measures.

I turned away from him and slid my jeans off slowly. I stepped out of them on my way to the bathroom door. In the doorway, I turned to glance over my shoulder. His jeans looked uncomfortably tight.

"I'll just be in the bedroom, in case you change your mind," I said with a wink. I headed for the bed, putting a little extra sway in my hips as I walked. I heard a rustle of clothes behind me and smiled.

He was on me before I got halfway to the bed.

We did get to sleep eventually, though I got a bit of rug burn first. It was a small price to pay for some very excellent werewolf TLC.

EVEN AFTER A FULL night's sleep, I was far from recovered from burning the werewolf virus from my body. I spent most of Thursday sleeping, waking only to eat and then going right back to bed. Sean stayed with me, working from home and holding me when nightmares plagued my sleep. Most of the pack checked in on me during the day, either by text message or by coming by Sean's house in person. Sean reassured them I was on the mend, but I needed rest to recover.

By Thursday night, I started to feel more like myself. I showered, ate dinner, and went to bed around eleven, feeling like I'd be back on my feet in the morning with one more night's uninterrupted rest, and then I could focus on finding Aden and Jana and freeing them from Bell. Their situation gnawed on me incessantly during my involuntary day of rest.

The sound of my phone ringing dragged me from a sound sleep long before dawn, however. Sean grumbled as I untangled myself and fumbled around on the nightstand until I found the phone. I rubbed my bleary eyes until I could read the screen.

I took a deep breath, braced myself, and answered. "Charles?"

"Alice, I apologize for disturbing your rest." His voice made me shiver hard. "You did wish for me to call if I had the information you requested."

That cleared the cobwebs from my brain. "That didn't take long," I said, surprised.

"Every man has his price," Charles said. "My profession requires that I know what those prices are. As such, sometimes I am able to expedite matters for my clients."

"So what did you find out?"

"Bell now has approximately a dozen strong nulls in his employment. Most did not come to work for him voluntarily, but their cooperation has been assured via a combination of promises and threats. They are held in small groups at three locations in the city. Who is kept where is information I do not have at the moment."

More than a dozen strong nulls was nearly an army. "What's his plan for them? Defense against another attack from Moses Murphy?"

"I believe they were originally intended as defense, but it would appear Mr. Bell now intends to go on the offense."

I didn't like the sound of that—not for Aden and Garrett's sake, anyway. "What do you know?"

"I do not have all the details as of yet, as my source is not privy to them, but my understanding is that Moses Murphy himself is coming to our city to purchase a weapon he intends to use against Bell."

Moses was coming *here?* For a moment, I couldn't breathe. Shock took my breath away.

Beside me, Sean growled quietly, his eyes going gold as he sensed my reaction. I tried to push the fear away and shake off the paralysis caused by Charles's news, but I couldn't. This was my worst fear coming true.

Oblivious to my reaction to his words, Charles continued, "Bell learned of the transaction a few days ago and plans to use the nulls to gain entrance to the location where Murphy will purchase the item in question."

I rose from the bed and paced. "Murphy will have the weapon

brought to a building he owns to make the purchase. He would never risk a transaction like that anywhere but on his own turf. The building will have the same kind of wards Murphy uses to protect his compound."

"Bell apparently believes a dozen nulls will be capable of breaking the wards on a building that is not Murphy's primary residence."

I closed my eyes. Moses's wards wouldn't break. The landmines they contained would kill every last one of the nulls, including Aden and his father. I knew that because I'd helped make the wards on Moses's compound and on a dozen other buildings he owned. Moses never skimped on the deadliness of his wards.

"Alice?" Charles prompted. "Is this information sufficient?"

I opened my eyes and found Sean standing in front of me, his shoulders rigid with tension and worry.

"Can you find out where Bell's holding Aden and Jana Peters?" I asked.

A long pause. "It is my understanding the Court has advised you not to pursue this line of inquiry."

"That's not what I asked." My hand gripped the phone so tightly that it hurt. "Can you find out or not?"

"It is possible. However—"

"Then please find out. I'll enhance the wards on your private quarters under 1792 in exchange for the information."

"I am reluctant to do so if it means you will risk making an enemy of both Bell *and* Valas."

My hands shook. "If you don't find out for me, I'll find someone who will."

"I will make inquiries," he said finally. "But I strongly encourage you to discuss your strategy with me before you act. It is possible that we may contrive a way to extract your client and her son without making it necessary for you to take matters into your own hands."

"Just get the information and we'll go from there. Thank you for calling." I disconnected and set the phone on the nightstand.

Sean took my hand and led me back to the bed. He sat down and pulled me into his lap so he could nuzzle my hair. "What do you know that you didn't want to tell Vaughan?"

Once again, I thought about telling him I was Moses's granddaughter, and once again the words died in my throat. *He'll think you're a monster*, I thought. No amount of assurances from Malcolm could silence that terrible inner voice.

I couldn't let on that I had personal knowledge of Moses's wards, but I could still tell him what I feared. "No building belonging to the Murphy cabal will have wards that can simply be broken by nulls. If Bell tries to break the wards, all he'll do is kill the nulls, including Aden and his father. Look what happened when Moses broke the wards at Bell's compound last month. Almost every mage died." My magic flared on my fingertips. "They use us as cannon fodder. I won't let him kill Aden like that, Sean. I *won't*."

"What are our options?"

"Even if I find out where Aden and Jana are being held and get them out, that leaves Garrett and the other nulls. I don't want them killed either." I rubbed my face.

"If we go after Aden and Jana, that may put us at odds with Valas and the Court." He rested his chin on my shoulder. "As much as I hate to say it, Vaughan may have a point asking you to talk strategy with him. If there's a way to get Aden and his mom out, he'll know what it is."

I stilled.

His arms tightened around me. "Alice, tell me what you're thinking."

"Every man has his price, even Bell." I moved so I could see his face. "It would be a very steep price, but he has one, and I think I know what it might be."

His expression darkened. "You are not for sale," he said flatly.

"Not at *any* price. Not to Vaughan, not to Bell, not to the Court, not to anyone."

"Sean, I need you to hear me out on this."

"No. Damn it, *no*. You already had to escape a cabal once and you've been in hiding ever since. I will not let another cabal get its hands on you, not even for this kid."

"I don't intend to let a cabal get its hands on me. In fact, I intend to take great pains to make sure that *doesn't* happen." I squeezed his hand. "But I am not going to do anything unless you agree it's the right course of action."

He didn't say anything for a long time. Finally, he kissed my temple. "I realize saying that represents a huge step for you. Not so long ago, you'd have gone ahead with your plan regardless of what I thought. The least I can do is hear you out, but you should know the odds of me agreeing to this are slim to none."

My mouth quirked. "Would it help if I told you Charles plays a pretty significant role in my plan?"

He looked even more grim. "No, it would not, but let's hear it."

THE PHONE RANG THREE TIMES. I glanced at the clock. It had taken me damn near forty-five minutes to talk Sean into agreeing to my plan, and now dawn was only minutes away. *Pick up, pick up, pick up*, I thought.

Just as I thought I would have to leave a message, Charles's voice came on the line. "Alice, this is an eleventh-hour call." To my relief, he sounded fully awake.

"I know, and I'll keep it short." I spoke quickly. "I would like to employ your services as a broker. I have something to sell, I know the buyer who will want it, and you stand to make a truckload of money."

"I am intrigued. We must table this discussion until tonight, as I will be asleep for the day momentarily, but please spare me from spending my last moments of wakefulness in suspense. What is it you wish to sell, and to whom?"

I took a deep breath and took the biggest gamble I'd made in recent memory. "I wish to sell the services of Storm Girl to Darius Bell in exchange for him releasing all of the nulls he's holding prisoner."

A long silence.

"Please come to my home tonight at ten o'clock," he said finally. "We will discuss the matter in person then. Do nothing further until we meet."

I exhaled. "Agreed. Pleasant dreams, Charles."

"Good night, Alice." The call ended.

I sagged as the enormity of what I'd put in motion settled on my shoulders. Sean kissed my temple and put my phone on the nightstand.

"Am I insane to do this?" I asked him as he wrapped his arms around me and we lay back against the pillows.

"Possibly," he admitted. "But if Vaughan can broker your deal with Bell with the Court's backing, we might just pull off the impossible by saving the nulls *and* getting rid of Moses Murphy."

I had nothing to say to that. If my gamble paid off, I could finally be free of Moses forever. If it failed, today might be my last day of freedom.

I wanted to tell Sean the truth. I *needed* to tell him. But damn it, and damn *me*, I just couldn't say the words.

I pulled his arms tighter around me. We stayed like that until long after the sun rose.

# CHAPTER 18

THE BELL OVER THE DOOR JINGLED AS I ENTERED JANE SILVEY'S TATTOO
shop.

"Alice, darlin', come on in," Jane called from the back room. She
emerged, drying her hands on a paper towel. "Hello, gorgeous."

I smiled. "Hi, beautiful." It was our traditional greeting.

Jane was a mage tattoo artist, a burlesque dancer, a pinup model,
and my favorite ex-girlfriend—the one I still fantasized about from
time to time, though our relationship had ended amicably years ago.

Today she wore a fifties-style red and black polka-dot dress with
matching red pumps and lipstick and her black hair was a halo of
curls. If I dressed like that I'd look like a clown, but she was drop-
dead gorgeous. Her tattoos covered her arms, most of her chest and
back, and legs.

She tossed the paper towel into a trash can and studied me with
narrowed eyes. "You look like you've had a rough couple of days."

I wasn't sure if she was reading that in my posture, my expression, or my aura, or some combination of the three. "It's been a
rough week, to tell you the truth."

"It must have been if you had to use the dragon." She inspected my upper right arm. I'd worn a tank top so she'd have easy access to work on re-spelling the tattoo. When she touched my arm, her air magic danced on my skin. I shivered.

"Let's get this beauty redone first and then we'll do the other tattoo in the back room so we have privacy." She patted the chair. "Other than this week, how have you been?"

"Pretty great, actually." I put my bag on the hook on the wall and settled into the chair, tucking my phone into my pocket.

She smiled and put my arm on the plastic-wrapped armrest, adjusting it so it was under my armpit and at the best height and angle for her to work. "I am so happy to hear that," she said as she double-checked to make sure she had all of the ink and equipment she needed on her little cart. "The last time you were in here, getting the Bastet tattoo, you were a mess and your blood smelled like it was about one hundred proof. You and the werewolf back together?"

"Yep. As a matter of fact, we got back together not long after you did the Bastet tattoo. A couple of weeks ago, we vacationed in the Bahamas."

"I thought you looked like you had a bit of a tan. That sounds like a wonderful trip." She sat on a rolling padded stool and pulled over the little cart. "You got a picture of him?"

I dutifully took out my phone and found a picture I'd taken on the little porch of our cabana in the Bahamas.

Jane studied it as she put on black latex gloves. She grinned. "Damn, girl, you could wash your laundry on those abs. If he were mine, I'd forbid him to ever wear a shirt just because he's so pretty, and I don't even *like* boys." She winked. "Maybe I need to explore my wild side a bit more. You know any werewolf gals who like gals?"

"Not off the top of my head," I said regretfully. "I'll try to set you up if I meet one who's available." I paused, then added, "Sean and I are buying a house." It still felt really weird to say it out loud.

She got up to give me a hug and a kiss on my cheek. "That is fantastic. Congratulations! You've come a long, long way since I first met you and you were all sharp edges and sarcasm. Credit to your hunky wolf for some of it, maybe, but I just think you're amazing. Now you really *are* the phoenix." She checked the tattoo on my upper back. "This one still looks great, by the way. I sure as hell hope you never have to use *that* one."

"Me neither," I agreed fervently.

She settled back onto her stool and smoothed her dress across her knees. "I might have guessed you were back with Sean after you sent me the idea for the new tattoo you want."

I hesitated. "It doesn't actually represent Sean."

She arched an elegantly shaped eyebrow. "Well, well. Your inner wolf, then." At my expression, she laughed. "You've been fierce since the moment I met you, Alice. I wouldn't have been surprised to find out you were a shifter, but you're just one of those wild women whose strength seems limitless. No human man or woman would probably have been able to keep up with you, not long term. We had good times, though." She winked. "You ready? Once we start, we can't stop until the spellwork is complete. You need to pee first?"

I shook my head. "I already went."

"Great. Deep breaths, then."

Together, we inhaled and exhaled a half-dozen times. Magic rose.

Jane turned the tattoo gun on and began re-inking the spellwork hidden in the dragon. The pain was familiar and intense. I closed my eyes and focused on breathing.

Jane's magic was in the ink already, but she pushed more in as she worked. The sensation of a spell forming in my flesh, made of Jane's magic instead of my own, was equal parts disconcerting and beautiful.

The process took about an hour. Since the spellwork required all of Jane's concentration, we couldn't chat, so I distracted myself thinking about tonight's meeting with Charles and the offer I was making. It was a dangerous proposition in many ways, but if anyone could negotiate an iron-clad agreement between me, Bell, and the Court, I believed Charles could.

Always distrustful of Charles and his motives, Sean had suggested I ask Ezekiel Monroe to broker the deal and write the agreement, since he was an attorney. When I asked Sean who he thought was more likely to protect my interests, however—Charles or Monroe—he had to admit Monroe's priority would be representing the Court, cautiously backing Bell, defeating Moses, and protecting me, in that order, and neither of us felt anything close to certain that he'd protect me if push came to shove.

Charles had been a broker for nearly two hundred years and had vastly more experience crafting agreements between scheming and devious parties. I believed he would close all the loopholes, anticipate all the schemes, and thwart Bell's inevitable attempts to either use the agreement against me in a way I hadn't anticipated or find an oversight he could exploit. Even Sean couldn't argue there was a better agent for the deal than Charles—a fact that irritated him to no end.

Despite my confidence in Charles, I did fear the consequences of revealing I was Storm Girl. I might have reconsidered the decision if it hadn't been for Sean's confidence. He was concerned, naturally, but not afraid. His support had made the difference and given me the courage to make that call to Charles to set the wheels in motion.

I remembered the night I'd summoned a powerful thunderstorm to help put out the fires caused by my aunt Catherine. Sean had stood behind me, bracing me against the wind and rain. His strength combined with my power and we'd saved hundreds of lives, including Darius Bell's. He was bracing me again, this time against Bell and Moses. The old Alice would never have allowed him to do so because she thought needing help made her weak. The old Alice would have been so totally wrong.

"There's nothing wrong with needing help," I said out loud as Jane finished the spellwork on the dragon.

She tilted her head. "That's true. You want that inked under the dragon?"

I smiled. "No, thanks." I turned my arm and craned my neck so I could look at the tattoo. The colors were vibrant again and the ink shimmered with magic. "It's beautiful, Jane. Thank you."

She wet a napkin with cold water and very carefully wiped the tattoo to remove the blood and extra ink. The cold water felt fantastic, but despite how gently she cleaned me, the sizzle of pain made me set my jaw.

"The longer you wait before you use it, the stronger it will be as your energy charges it," she reminded me as she patted the tattoo dry and wrapped my upper arm with plastic wrap. "It's at about half of maximum strength now. Full power in maybe a month unless you've got a way of speeding that up. I'm concerned there might be some cell damage from this use."

"We thought there might be. It's common in spelled tattoos." I studied the dragon. "So if I use it again, it might be for the last time?"

"It might, and it's likely to leave a mighty big scar too, one that even healing spells would have a difficult time repairing."

"Scars caused by magic are the most difficult to heal." I made a face and rubbed my stomach.

"Nauseous?" Jane asked sympathetically. "You can take the pain like a champ, but your tummy has never liked it. Don't worry—I've got what you need." She filled a small paper cup with water from the cooler and tore open a packet of medicine. "Plop, plop, fizz, fizz. Here you go. Drink up."

I knocked it back and grimaced. "Yuck."

She helped me stand up. "Let's go in the back and talk about your new tattoo. We'll take a break before we start that one."

I grabbed my bag and we went into the private room, where I took off my tank top and bra.

Jane studied my torso critically. "You want it here?" she asked, indicating the area below my left breast.

"Unless that's too close to the stars." I had a wavy line of stars that ran from my upper left thigh to my ribs. "Do you think the spells would interfere with each other?"

She shook her head. "No, I don't think so. Do you have a copy of the spellwork we're doing?"

I got the paper from my bag where I'd drawn the spellwork Malcolm had come up with that would allow me to summon him without needing my bracelet or risking leaving me lightheaded or unconscious.

"Interesting," she said thoughtfully. "A summoning spell for a ghost, of all things. I didn't know you had a ghost. Is that a recent acquisition?"

"Fairly recent."

"I'm kind of surprised you're letting him stick around." She took out a pen and started sketching. "Not so long ago you didn't want a lot of company, but now you've got a ghost sidekick and a werewolf pack. Happiness looks good on you." She tapped the pen against her red lips. "The runes will flow beautifully, I think, and they'll blend nicely with the rest of the design. Give me a few minutes to work it out."

While she drew, I put my tank top back on, used the bathroom, and texted Sean. *Dragon is good to go. Starting the new tattoo soon.*

A few seconds later, my phone beeped. *Wolf: In my fourth meeting of the day so far and missing you. I look forward to seeing your new ink. Should be home by five.*

I hadn't told Sean what new tattoo I was getting, only what the spellwork it contained would do. He was relieved to know I would have a better way of summoning Malcolm. I wondered what he would think of the new tattoo.

"This one's going to hurt a lot more than the dragon because of where it's going." Jane looked up from her sketch. "And we're going to be at it for a while since it's all brand new work."

"I have nothing else scheduled until this evening, so we have plenty of time. And hell, if I can survive getting the phoenix tattoo, I can survive anything."

She laughed. "That is a true story. The phoenix was one of the biggest and most detailed projects I've ever done. You threw up at one point, as I recall."

I made a face. "I barfed *twice.*"

"It was a lot of pain and a lot of magic. I wasn't surprised." She held up the paper. "What do you think?"

I smiled. "I love it. I think I'm ready to get started whenever you are."

SEAN and I arrived at Charles's house just before ten o'clock. Bryan met us at the door and ushered us to the office to await the vampire's arrival.

Charles's office was two stories tall and divided into three areas: a sitting area with couches and chairs grouped in front of the magnificent fireplace, a well-stocked bar with six tall chairs and a black granite counter, and the office, with its large desk and leather chairs. Bookcases lined two walls and a dozen pieces of framed art took up the third wall. Spiral staircases led up to a second-level walkway. Floor-to-ceiling windows overlooked the estate's sweeping backyard. At the moment, the massive curtains were closed.

"Please have a seat." Bryan indicated the chairs in front of Charles's desk. "What can I offer you to drink?"

"Water, please," I said as we sat.

"Same," Sean added. He scooted his chair just a little closer to mine, positioning us side-by-side to face the desk. I smiled at him. We were a united front.

Bryan brought us bottles of water from the small refrigerator in the bar area and took his customary spot beside Charles's chair.

Charles entered. He was still thin and pale, though I was sure he'd fed when he woke, and he seemed to walk slower than I was used to seeing. I remembered Bryan's comment about Charles's change in behavior after his walk in the sun. Was he simply still recovering from the Tepes stone, or was there something more going on?

Recalling my reaction to the sound of Charles's voice the night before, I'd strengthened my shields the moment he walked in. Though it had been almost a full day since then, and three days since he'd saved me, when our eyes met, something passed between us and ran down my spine, making me shiver. I leaned forward. My hands gripped the armrests so tightly that my nails left little half-moons in the leather upholstery as I fought against the pull of his gaze.

He'd shared his blood with me several times before, but I'd never felt such a powerful desire afterward without him even touching me, as if I were drawn to him by a strong magnet. I wondered if he did it on purpose or it was simply the natural consequence of how much of his blood was in me. I fought the surge of arousal and attraction. Part of me was angry that my body was betraying me so intensely. The other part of me—several parts of me, in fact—didn't mind the heat kindled by his nearness and softly glowing eyes.

Sean's warm, comforting magic enveloped me and pushed back against Charles's influence. I hadn't drawn on his power, but he'd strengthened me without needing to be asked. Not so long ago, I would have been angry at him for doing it, but I wasn't that stubborn and insecure woman anymore. I exhaled, let go of the armrests, and sat back.

Bryan took his customary position on Charles's right as the vampire settled into the oversized leather chair behind the desk. "I am glad to see you are recovering well," Charles said.

"I am, thanks," I told him. "How are you feeling?"

"Much improved." He studied me, his head tilted. "I detect the scent of fresh ink and blood. You have added to your collection of tattoos?"

"Yep." I wore a button-up shirt with elbow-length sleeves to cover my redone dragon tattoo. I'd used low-level healing spells on both, but they were still oozing a little. I hoped within a day or two they'd be healed and well on their way to full power.

I wasn't here to talk about my new ink, however. "Let's talk about my proposal."

"Yes, we have much to discuss." Charles took two thick red folders from a drawer and set them on the top of the desk next to a legal pad filled with his neat handwriting. Despite his familiarity with computers, he tended to resort to paper and pen when drafting documents and putting down ideas.

"I suppose it rather goes without saying at this point, but I'm the so-called Storm Girl," I said.

He smiled. "But of course you are, Alice. Who else could have commanded a thunderstorm and conjured lightning? Who else would have risked so much to save others?" He glanced at Sean. "And who but your wolf would stand by your side as you did so?"

"Does Bell know?" Sean asked.

Charles's smile faded. "After Alice's altercation with his lieutenant on Sunday, he strongly suspects. My information indicates he is quite displeased the Court, and the Were Ruling Council have stated in no uncertain terms that you are off limits to him. If it were only the Council, or if he had not taken such heavy losses and did not count upon the Court's backing against Murphy, it is likely he would be far more aggressive in his attempts to add you to his arsenal."

"I thought as much," I said. "If Ezekiel Monroe hadn't shown up at my house the other day when Bell was there, that meeting might have gone a very different direction."

Charles nodded gravely. "Bell would like to find leverage to use against you, but your status as a personal favorite of Valas makes that proposition very dangerous for him. He believes you have some sway with her. As such, he is reluctant to jeopardize making an enemy of her, and rightfully so. Your alliances have proven an effective deterrent, as has your reputation for defending your own interests."

I was gratified to hear my reputation was a factor, not just my associations with the Court and Sean. I might be more enlightened these days about the value of allies, but I still had my pride.

My good feelings were short-lived, however. Charles tapped his fingers on his desk, a sign he was unsettled. "It has come to my attention that Bell has at least one turncoat in his organization who may be leaking information to the Murphy cabal. What information that individual has been privy to, I am not entirely certain, but there is a chance they have communicated Bell's suspicion about the identity of Storm Girl. If so, I am of the belief that your status as a pack consort and a favorite of the Court may not be enough to shield you from Murphy. He desires retribution for the injuries you inflicted on his daughter, and he will be quite motivated to prevent you from allying yourself with Bell." He sounded grim.

I'd known there was a good chance that information would find its way to my grandfather's ears from the moment I decided to stop Catherine from burning down four square blocks in order to take out Darius Bell. I didn't regret my decision then and I didn't now, but it was impossible to quash the spike of fear caused by the realization that my quiet life as Alice Worth might be coming to an end. If Bell had a traitor who was working for Murphy, it was only a matter of time before my name would be mentioned and I would become a target—not because I was Moses's granddaughter, but because I'd hit Catherine with lightning and foiled her attempt to kill Bell.

Sean understood that danger as well as I did, but when I glanced at him, he was calm and unfazed by the possibility of Moses coming after us for the lightning strike. Our eyes met. *I'm with you*, his expression said. My worry faded.

"Do you have any intelligence that would indicate whether Murphy's people know who I am yet?" I asked.

Charles shook his head. "Nothing definite. My sources of information on Murphy and his organization are far less dependable than my informants within Bell's cabal, as you might imagine. I will continue to monitor the situation and will pass on any pertinent information I receive."

"Thank you."

He inclined his head. "For now, let us focus on your proposal. If I understand you correctly, you wish to offer to aid Bell in his planned attack on Murphy when he comes to the city in three days' time to collect his weapon. In return, you require that Bell releases the nulls he is holding against their will."

"That's my proposal, yes."

He leaned back in his chair and steepled his fingers. "If I may speak as your...friend...for a moment, rather than as a broker, you are taking an enormous risk. May I ask what prompted you to make this offer?"

"I'm betting Murphy's property is protected with the same kinds of wards as his compound. If I'm right, that means trying to break the wards will probably just kill all the nulls and the wards won't have more than a scratch. Even if he has enough strong nulls to break the wards, the mages will probably still all die. One of those nulls is a twelve-year-old kid. I don't want all those people to die for nothing."

Charles tapped his fingers together. "I advise against this," he said finally. "The risk is substantial. I understand your motivation to save these people and I commend you for it. You have ever been entirely selfless and have suffered greatly as a result."

He looked pointedly at Sean, probably recalling how I'd died in order to free Sean from the cuff that was killing him, and that Sean had reacted angrily to how cavalier I'd seemed about my death and resurrection. Charles had been unable to understand Sean's reaction and apparently he was still displeased.

Sean met the vampire's gaze, his face expressionless. "Everyone here knows how selfless Alice is. Two of us might not be sitting here right now if it weren't for her penchant for saving others' lives at the risk of her own."

"Alice, I must ask you to reconsider," Charles said. "Perhaps I can arrange the release of the child and his mother without this drastic measure."

I shook my head. "Even if you were able to free Aden and Jana, that still leaves a dozen nulls who will die if Bell uses them to break Murphy's wards. I don't want those people dead any more than I want Aden to die. And you said it yourself, Charles: Moses Murphy is going to come looking for me sooner or later now that Bell thinks I'm Storm Girl. This isn't just about saving the nulls, though that's my primary motivation. If Bell and I can take Murphy out, he's no longer a threat to me or the people I care about. As far as I'm concerned, I *have* to make the first move to save my own hide. So I'm not as entirely selfless as you think."

His brow furrowed. "You present a compelling argument."

"So here's what I want." I squared my shoulders. "I want a joint Bell-Court-Storm Girl mission targeting Murphy at the buy. One big strike. Before we attack, however, Bell releases all of the nulls he's keeping against their will and their families, including Aden, Jana, and Allan. In return, I will break the wards. We kill Murphy and whoever's with him. This is a one-time deal. Bell can never ask or manipulate me for my help again."

"How do you propose to break the wards?"

I shook my head. "That's my business. If the Court is serious about backing Bell against Murphy, it's time to put your money where your mouth is and commit to taking him out. Bell provides foot soldiers and mages who are there voluntarily. The Court provides whatever forces it deems appropriate. Amira and a couple of Hunters would be nice."

Charles addressed Sean. "What role do you intend to play in this attack?"

"I am Alice's partner and protector," Sean told him. "I fight with her, wherever that fight may be."

The vampire made a few notes. "As with any brokered agreement, there will be negotiations. I know what your ideal result is.

What compromises are you willing to make in order to reach an accord?"

"None."

His brows rose. "Alice—"

"No compromises," I said firmly. "All the nulls and their families go free, period. In return, I give Bell his best and only chance to take Murphy out. He doesn't have the power in this negotiation, Charles —*I* do. I have no doubt he'll try to haggle and threaten and negotiate, but without me he doesn't get into that building and Murphy eventually destroys what's left of his empire and kills him. What I need from *you* is an iron-clad agreement with no loopholes or omissions he can use against me because he'll turn on me the moment he figures out a way to do it. You're earning your commission by keeping me alive and out of his hands."

"And just to be clear," Sean interjected, "It had better be the best and most ironclad damn contract you've ever written in your entire undead existence because Alice's life—and therefore *yours*—depends on it."

To my surprise, Charles chuckled. For the first time in a very long time—since before our walk in the sun—his eyes gleamed. "Very well. Challenge accepted, as they say." He picked up his pen again. "Shall we discuss the particulars, then?"

It was nearly three in the morning when Sean and I got home from Charles's house.

We let Rogue in from the backyard and went upstairs. As the dog settled into his bed by the window, I changed into pajamas, washed my face, and brushed my teeth. I put moisturizer on my redone dragon tattoo and the new one, covered each with plastic wrap so they didn't leak onto the bedding, and taped the wrap down before putting on my pajama top.

When I came out of the bathroom, Sean waited by the bed. He'd changed into lounge pants and a T-shirt. His wolf amulet hung around his neck. "I know you're tired, but I'd like to see it again," he said.

I smiled and raised my top to bare my abdomen.

To my surprise, he knelt in front of me. Carefully, he pulled the plastic away from the new tattoo and kissed my still-tender skin so gently that I barely felt it. He put the plastic back in place and looked up at me, his eyes golden. The alpha was on his knees before his consort.

I took his face in my hands and kissed him, gently at first and then more hungrily as golden shifter magic rose. It might have been his, or mine, or both.

He broke our kiss and stood. He led me to the bed and pulled me to him so I straddled his lap. "My Alice," he said, his voice half growl. "When I look in your eyes, I still see her. You burned away the virus, but she's still there, isn't she?"

"She always was," I told him, pressing light kisses along his jaw. How I loved the feeling of his bristly skin against my lips. "That's what I realized the other night in the woods, when I burned the virus away. She's me and always has been, because I believe my biological father was a shifter. Though I'm human, I'm a little bit wolfy too."

He kissed me deeply, his hands on my hips. I moved against him automatically, my exhaustion forgotten. I pulled his shirt off over his head.

We both needed this intimacy tonight, after spending hours thinking about all the ways in which my plan to save the nulls and take out Moses might go sideways. As confident as I was in Charles, I was afraid of what I might face, and so was Sean. We needed comfort and strength.

Afterward, we curled up together. He nuzzled the back of my

neck, drinking in my scent. "So the dragon is a protection spell and the wolf summons Malcolm. What's the spell in your Bastet tattoo?"

I smiled. "An obfuscation spell."

"As in—?"

"It makes me invisible for about three minutes. As with all the other tattoos, it's one-time use only."

"The stars on your side?"

"Masking spells that make me feel like a mid-level mage to anyone with magic, and protect me so I can't be tracked via blood magic."

"The runes on your stomach?"

I hesitated. He kissed my jaw and waited.

"It's…" I swallowed hard. "There was a time when I had reason to worry that I might be used for breeding against my will."

Sean's surge of fury was so powerful I thought it would scour my skin from my bones. I flinched. "Alice," he said, his voice an octave lower than normal, an indication his wolf was beyond angry. "I knew things were bad for you, but…Jesus." His arm tightened around me.

Moses had talked about the possibility of breeding me often in the last two or three years I was his prisoner. It was never a question of who I'd choose as a romantic partner, but rather who he'd select as the sires of any offspring I would have. My consent was not a factor in the decision.

Luckily for me, selecting someone to father children with me was an extremely thorny problem, since that person and his family or cabal would be inextricably tied to Moses, and every candidate he considered had too many potential conflicts. I'd lived in terror that he'd find someone he *could* approve, and it was that dread more than anything that drove me to escape before my worst fear was realized.

"That spell is there in case that ever happens." My voice was toneless. "I won't be bred like cattle. I meant what I said when I told you I spent a very long time with no control over my own body or choices and I would never give that up again."

"Using you for *breeding* against your will. Well, that clinches it," he muttered.

I frowned. "Clinches what?"

He growled. "The night we met, I saw your scars and I swore I would find the people who hurt you and kill them."

Startled, I turned to look at him. "You what?"

A muscle moved in his jaw. "After you fell asleep, I lay awake in your bed for a long time thinking about those scars. I could tell they weren't from an accident. I promised myself and my wolf I would find whoever did it and kill them. I intend to keep that promise, and now, given what you just told me, I'm going to take my time about it."

"You didn't even know me at that point," I protested. "I was a one-night stand."

"No, you weren't, not to me. Maybe that's how the evening started, but before too long I knew one night with you would never be enough." He kissed my hair. "The next day didn't go anything like I'd planned, but here you are with me still, and I haven't forgotten my promise."

I'd had no idea about any of that and his revelation left me stunned. The night we met, I'd invited Sean to my bed for the purpose of recharging my magic and for a few hours of pleasurable fun, thinking we were both on the same page about our hookup being a one-night deal. The next morning, he'd thrown me for a loop by asking me out on a date. I'd certainly never imagined he'd already begun to have feelings for me, or that he'd realized the scars on my back were the result of torture, not an accident. I'd given him so little credit back then. The thought made me sad.

He went back to nuzzling my hair. "And the magic in the phoenix?" he asked finally.

"The symbolism is obvious: a phoenix rising from the ashes of her old self." I took a deep breath. "The spellwork in the phoenix is there in case the people I escaped from find me and I ever have to run."

He stilled. "You told me you weren't going to run. You said if anyone came looking for you, you'd be here waiting."

"And that's what I intend to do, but nothing in this life is certain. There might be a circumstance in which I'd have no choice but to run."

He growled. "Don't run, Alice. I told you before: out there you're alone and vulnerable. Here you have allies. Friends. People who love you and will fight with you."

"Allies change. Friends and lovers…they can die." I closed my eyes. "I don't plan to run, Sean, but I'm prepared in case I have to."

"Then I'll make sure you never have to," he promised. He kissed my shoulder. "And someday when we find the people who hurt you, I'll make damn sure they regret it."

*Not if I find them first*, I thought, snuggling back into the warmth of Sean's arms. If I had my way, those people would never get anywhere near him, the pack, or Malcolm.

In two days, if Charles was successful in brokering my deal with Bell, I might have the chance to take my own revenge and finally, *finally* be free.

# CHAPTER 19

Brew a Cup Tea & Coffee House was a charming little shop in one of the few areas north of downtown that hadn't yet lost their soul to the gentrification that systematically turned formerly eclectic neighborhoods into block after block of generic retail lofts.

Carly had suggested I come mid-morning when the shop was less busy, so I arrived just after nine-thirty and parked out front. I spotted a few people inside at the tables, working on their laptops with mugs of coffee or tea close at hand.

"Looks like a nice place," Malcolm commented as we approached the door. He was invisible but I sensed him on my right.

I paused just outside the front door. "Hey, you feel that?"

"Yup, witchy wards. Very different from our kind of wards. I'm not sure what these do exactly, but it kinda feels like they're either supposed to keep something out or keep something in. Dang it, Alice, why don't I know more about witch magic?" Malcolm sounded disgruntled.

"Well, maybe now we have a chance to learn. Carly did say she'd talk magic with us anytime we wanted," I reminded him.

"What kind of witch do you think she is?"

"Maybe a hedge witch, since her magic smells like parchment. But then again, she owns a coffee and tea shop, so maybe a kitchen witch? Or she could just be an eclectic witch." I shrugged. "Let's find out."

I opened the door and we went inside. The shop smelled the way I imagined heaven might smell: fresh roasted coffee, fresh-baked scones and cookies, and spices. I paused to enjoy the aromas.

I spotted Carly behind the counter, wearing an apron over a black blouse and long purple skirt. She was moving the remaining baked goods onto three trays in the display case while an employee, a young woman with pink hair, focused on making drinks for the customers.

Carly looked up as I approached the counter. "Alice, hello!" she said with a smile. "Come on in. I'm so glad to see you. What can we make for you?"

I eyed the display. "That blueberry scone looks particularly good. How about one of those and a large cup of coffee with room for cream?"

"You got it, dear."

She rang me up while the pink-haired employee, whose name tag identified her as Katy, filled a cup with the nectar of the gods. She set it on the counter in front of me, avoiding eye contact, and disappeared into the back room. I signed the receipt, dropped a five in the tip jar, and picked up my cup of coffee.

"How about you have a seat in that back corner booth, the one with the Reserved sign on it, and I'll join you in a few minutes with your warm scone?" Carly said.

"Sounds good." I added half-and-half and raw sugar to my coffee, stirred it, and headed to the booth Carly had indicated.

As I slid into the seat, I felt an odd tingle of magic. "Do you sense anything weird over here?" I asked Malcolm under my breath.

"Oh, yeah, definitely," he said. "More witchy wards. The spell-work is actually kind of familiar, though. I think it might be designed to prevent eavesdropping. Hang on—let me look under the table."

While he investigated, I sipped my coffee and sighed content-edly. It tasted even better than it smelled. This might just be my new place for good coffee.

Malcolm spoke again from my right. "Yup...there are symbols and runes carved on the underside of the table and both benches. Carly has her own little Cone of Silence area over here. That's nifty. I bet it comes in handy."

Carly headed our way with my scone on a plate and a large mug full of hot tea that smelled wonderful. "What kind of tea is that?" I asked as she sat down across from me.

"It's a blend of my own: dried lemon balm, lavender blossoms, and chamomile. Very pleasant after a hectic Saturday morning. I'll send some home with you."

"Thanks. I'd love to try it." I broke a piece off my warm scone and popped it in my mouth. My eyes widened. "Oh my goodness," I said reverently.

"Don't talk with your mouth full," Malcolm scolded. "I'm sorry, Carly. She was apparently born in a barn."

Carly laughed. "My scones tend to have that effect on people. It's a family recipe and we're very proud of it." She sipped her tea and studied me. "Your heart seems light, despite everything that's come your way this week. What good news do you have to share?"

I told her about our decision to put in an offer on a house. She got up to give me a hug. "That's wonderful news," she told me, reseating herself. "I'm so happy for you both. You complement each other so well. I'm very glad you called this morning. I've been worrying about you all week."

"That danger you saw Sean and me facing...we encountered it Tuesday night." I touched the amulet around my neck. "Thank you for this. It probably saved my life."

"It has saved yours. Soon it will have to save his."

My stomach dropped. "Save Sean? From what?"

She shook her head. "I've seen trees and broken earth and a gray man made of fire, but I can't see the danger Sean will face. There are too many forces at play and the way is not clear."

I had a feeling who the gray man made of fire was in Carly's visions: Moses. "Then I'm doubly glad for the amulets," I told her.

In the five years since I'd escaped the cabal, I'd always imagined that if I ever faced my grandfather, I would do it alone. I hadn't ever wanted anyone to endanger themselves on my behalf, not even—or perhaps especially—against Moses. I thought of him as *my* responsibility, my problem that needed fixing. But now I was part of a *we* and Moses wasn't just my problem anymore.

Ben had told me being part of a pack meant I would never face anything alone, and once I believed that it would give me more strength than I could imagine. And yet, thinking about the risk Sean and Malcolm were taking made me sick to my stomach instead of giving me reason to hope.

Last night, before we went to Charles's house, I'd tried to talk Sean out of coming with me in the attack, but he'd simply reminded me that when and where to fight was his choice to make and I'd promised to remember that.

When I'd suggested to Malcolm that he stay behind, safe behind my house wards, he gave me the finger and that was the end of that discussion.

Carly tilted her head. "Your magic feels different, more fierce. This danger you faced on Tuesday revealed something new and important."

"Yes." I glanced at the people sitting near us. "They can't hear us, right?"

"Not at all." She turned to face the room. "Hey!" she called. No one reacted. She turned back to me and winked. "My *Hush* and *Look Away* spells. This booth is warded against eavesdropping. The other spell encourages onlookers to ignore us."

Between sips of coffee and bites of scone, I told Carly about Caleb's attack and my encounter with my wolf.

When I finished the story, the witch was quiet. Finally, she folded her hands on the table. "I told you I'm an empath, though I'm not sure I'd have to be to sense all of the conflict, guilt, and anger you carry."

"You can say that again," Malcolm said. "She's like one of those boiling sulphur pots in Yellowstone."

"Hey," I protested.

"That's not a bad analogy for how your emotions feel to us," Carly said as I scowled. "Even now, with your happiness about your decision to make a home with Sean, the darkness is still there—it's just buried a little deeper than before. You will have to face that darkness, and soon. I believe your anger, guilt, and pain will be the cause of Sean's impending brush with death. Worse, if you don't find a way to reconcile your three selves—the woman you pretend to be, the woman you were, and the woman you truly are—you will bring great suffering on everyone who loves you."

I sat back in the booth, too stunned to speak.

Malcolm's anger sizzled on my skin. "Did you see all that in your crystal ball?" he asked.

"Not in a crystal ball, but I *have* seen it." She turned back to me. "I don't think I'm telling you anything you don't already know. All those forces I mentioned are converging on you as we speak, but you're fragmented, not whole. If you come face-to-face with the gray man now, you'll fight him and lose."

This was not the prediction I wanted to hear, not when I might be helping lead a coordinated attack on him. "How do I go about reconciling with myself? Er, my selves?"

"Well, that's a very complicated question." She settled back in her seat and crossed her legs. "Many books have been written on the topic. Most suggest a combination of therapy, meditation, and self-reflection."

I frowned. "That sounds like it would take a long time. What have you got that I can do in about forty-eight hours?"

She laughed. "You're used to magic. There's no spell for healing yourself when it comes to your psyche. I don't have any magic words for that and neither does anybody else. It takes a lot of time and work."

I didn't have a hell of a lot of time, but I wasn't afraid of hard work. "Tell me what I need to do, then."

"I counsel people to begin by setting their intention. Create a vision of the life you want and the person you want to be. Fix that image in your mind and let it guide you."

"That sounds doable." Magic worked in a similar way: an intention combined with spellwork and power.

"You've already created a support system and surrounded yourself with people who accept you and believe in you. Listen to them and lean on them when you need to."

Malcolm cleared his throat loudly. I rolled my eyes.

Carly smiled. "She's not very good about that, I know," she told the ghost.

"She's getting better at it," he admitted. "She's still stubborn and a total control freak, but she's had a lot of personal growth this past month or so."

"Still sitting right here," I interjected, somewhat irritably.

"You also already do good things for others, though it's often at great risk to yourself," Carly continued. "Nurture yourself, celebrate everything that's good about yourself, be kind to yourself when you make errors, and quiet the voice within that insists you are unworthy of having friends and loving someone who loves you unconditionally."

Malcolm didn't say anything to that, though I sensed his disquiet. Our conversation the night of Caleb's attack had centered on my belief that I was unworthy of Sean's love and acceptance. Of everything Carly had said so far, silencing that voice was going to be hardest.

Carly leaned forward and folded her hands on the table, her expression grave. "Most important and most difficult of all, you must forgive yourself. You are not a monster. No one who cares about you sees you as one, but your image of yourself is what keeps you from healing and becoming whole. If you want a place to start, start there."

I knew better than to ask Malcolm if he'd told her about our conversation and how I'd referred to myself as a monster. Until this moment, I'd had no idea my image of myself was so obvious to others. Malcolm and Sean had been around me for months, but Carly had only spent a few hours with me and she already saw it.

Several small groups came into the coffee shop at once and a line formed at the counter. Carly slid from the booth. "My other morning shift employee called in sick. Let me help Katy for a few minutes and then I'll be back. I'll refill your coffee while I'm there." She took my cup and hurried to the counter.

"Hey, you okay?" Malcolm asked. "That was rough. She didn't pull any punches."

I rubbed my face. "Yeah, but it's all true, and I've heard most of it from you and Sean already."

"It's easy to help others. The hardest person to help is yourself." I felt a little surge of comfort from Malcolm. "And the hardest person to forgive is yourself. That's true of everyone, I think, though maybe it goes double for people like us."

"Have you forgiven yourself?" I asked. When he didn't answer right away, I regretted asking. "I'm sorry. That's a really personal question and it's none of my business."

"No, it's okay for you to ask. I actually think it *is* your business, since we're friends, or siblings, or whatever." His voice had a hint of humor. "I'm working on it. Intellectually I know I didn't do those things by choice, but that's not much comfort sometimes. I will say I'm closer to making peace with my past and myself today than I was a month ago, or a month before that. It's getting better, thanks to you and Sean. I think we're all three healing together. You've got the farthest to go, but I meant what I said to Carly—you've come a long way since the day I met you."

"So everyone tells me. I think I'm a long, long way from being able to forgive myself, though, or from being able to hush that voice in my head."

"You're a work in progress, just like the rest of us. The important thing is not to give up or let setbacks derail you. You'll get there; I have faith in you."

"At least one of us does," I muttered.

Something thumped me lightly on the back of my head. "Hey," I protested. "How much energy did you use just to smack me?"

"Didn't Carly just tell you to listen to your support system?"

"Damn it. Yes."

"So listen. Oh, and when were you going to tell me about the whole meeting-your-wolf thing?"

"I'm sorry, I didn't think to tell you." I pinched the bridge of my nose. "I'm still trying to make sense of it myself."

"Well, you thought you might have shifter blood, so this more or less clinches it, right? You're part wolf. That is *so cool*."

"Aroo," I said wryly.

"I wonder if Sean's wolf sensed it and that's one of the reasons he was drawn to you," Malcolm mused. "Or maybe it was your general badass-ness and the wolf thing is just a bonus."

Up at the counter, the line was gone. Carly refilled my coffee, topped it off with half-and-half and some raw sugar, and put the lid back on. She headed our way again with a teapot in one hand and my coffee in the other.

She set the teapot on the table and handed over my coffee as she sat. "I hope I made it how you like it."

"It looked like you did. Thank you."

She poured more tea into her mug and set the pot down. "Now, you can take my advice and do with it what you will. Earlier on the phone you said you would like my help with something."

I set my coffee on the table and studied her. "Before I get to that, I need to ask you a question about your assistant—the girl with the pink hair, pentacle necklace, and Triple Goddess tattoo on her right forearm."

Carly's face fell. "What about her?"

"Her nametag says *Katy*. That wouldn't be short for Katrina, by any chance, would it?"

She took a deep breath and exhaled. "Yes, it is."

I watched Katy as she handed a customer a cup of coffee with a smile and then turned to make another order. "So not only did you know her—you sign her paychecks. Is she in your coven?"

She nodded. "I apologize for not telling you the whole truth on Monday after I broke the hex. When I saw the poppet, I knew who made it."

Angry words burned on my tongue. With effort, I held them back. "Why not tell us?" I asked instead, my voice tight.

"Two reasons. I wanted to know why she'd done it first. I came directly here from your house and confronted her. She told me Lily said an evil mage named Alice had stolen her fiancé with magic and she needed help to break up your relationship and get him back." Carly rubbed her temples. "Lily was a very convincing actress. She even cried. Katy thought she was doing the right thing. As her High Priestess, I made it very, very clear that *nothing* about what she did was the right thing. Witches in my coven don't do spells that steal someone's free will. She broke both our Rede to harm none and the Threefold Law, and she knows there are consequences for both— from me *and* the universe."

When I didn't respond, Malcolm asked, "And the second reason you didn't tell us the truth?" He sounded a little angry too.

Carly winced at the question. "When I told Katy what really happened—including that you almost died because Lily said your name too any times—and that Sean is the alpha of a werewolf pack, she begged me not to tell either of you who she was. She's scared someone from the pack might want revenge. Not Sean, but someone more...hotheaded." She leaned forward, her arms on the table. "Alice, I'm sorry I didn't feel like I could tell you. She made a grave error in judgment and I'll make sure she learns from it. I made what I thought was the best choice, given the circumstances. I hope you can understand and keep this between us. If you choose to tell Sean, please make sure he understands why Katy is afraid."

I tried to set aside my anger about the hex that had nearly killed me—no small task—and look at the situation from Katy's point of view. She looked to be seventeen or eighteen at the most, and despite the pink hair and tattoos, she seemed shy and introverted. I could see how she'd fallen for Lily's lies. I was eighteen once, and I'd made mistakes too.

"I'm not likely to forgive her, not anytime soon," I said finally. "Or forget that you held important information back from us. I can understand why you both did what you did, though. I *am* going to tell Sean, but I'll make sure it stays between us."

"Understanding is all I can ask for. Maybe forgiveness will come down the road." She topped off her tea. "Now, what is it you need my help with?"

I explained my proposed plan to participate in an attack with others on a mutual enemy. I left out Moses's and Bell's names, of course, and didn't reveal I had a personal stake in the operation. She listened quietly and drank her tea.

"So here's why I called and asked to meet," I said finally. "I can break the building's wards, but it will take most of my power to do it and I'll be vulnerable afterward. Despite a contract—assuming we can come to an agreement on the particulars—my so-called allies are just as likely to stab me in the back as they are to fight with me. The only people I know I can trust in this situation are Sean and Malcolm." I took a deep breath and spoke three words that didn't often pass my lips. "I need help."

"Protection?"

I nodded.

"Defense?"

I nodded again.

She tapped her finger on her cup. "There are a lot of possibilities. What are your goals in this attack?"

I ticked them off on my fingers. "Keep Sean and Malcolm safe.

Break the wards. Take out the primary target and those with him. Then come back, reconcile my three selves, and buy a house in the country where my dog—and my wolf—can chase rabbits to their hearts' content."

She studied me. "Do you intend to take out the primary target and the others yourself?"

There were few things in the world I wanted *more* than to do that, but the bitter truth was that breaking the wards—the price of securing the nulls' release by Bell—would take most of my magic. Facing Moses with only a fraction of my normal power would be suicidal. I would have to settle for making it possible for someone else to take him out. The important thing was to kill him, not for me to do it myself, as much as I wanted to.

Since divulging any of that would reveal my personal connection to our operation, I simply shook my head. "No, that will be someone else's job. I can't predict what will happen once we break the wards, though, or who or what I might face before it's all over. Even if I don't go looking for the big guns, one of them might find me."

"Hang on a second." Carly went to the counter and came back with a notepad. "Tell me what you know about where you're going and who will be there."

"I don't know the exact location yet, but it will be a fairly sizable building with very stout wards full of landmines, cascades, and other surprises. As for who will be there, let's assume some high-level mages of various sorts, including fire, air, and blood, and plenty of mundane firepower." I exhaled. "Lots of wards in the building and people capable of throwing big magic around. It's going to be a hell of a firefight." And I'd have to spend a lot of it on the sidelines, just trying to stay alive and keep Malcolm and Sean safe.

She finished writing. "Let's start with you. You said you can break the wards and doing so will leave you drained. What if I could help you break the wards?"

I blinked at her. "You're kidding."

She smiled. "I'm not saying I can do it all myself, but I think I can help, and maybe you won't have to use all your power in the first minute." She leaned forward and her voice dropped, despite the *Hush* spell hiding our conversation. "You remember when I gave you and Sean your amulets? Did you wonder how you were able to break a stone so easily?"

"I felt a little bit of magic," I recalled. "Was the stone spelled to break?"

"Yes." She tapped the notepad with her pen. "A similar spell with a lot more power behind it could really pack a punch. The challenge is that these wards are not *my* kind of magic. However, there are spells that disrupt your kind of magic. The problem is, I won't know exactly what those wards are made of. I'll have to guess, which means the result will be unpredictable. Best case, I can break them or at least disrupt them enough to make it easier for you to break them. Worst case, my spells fizzle and you end up doing all the heavy lifting yourself."

"I can probably give you some insight into what the wards are made of," I said. "The kinds of mage wards used to protect buildings are fairly consistent. We can make an educated guess."

"Excellent." She pondered her page of notes. "I need to think about this. You said the attack will occur tomorrow night?"

"That's the current plan, as I understand it. I know that doesn't give us much time. I'll know more after tonight, once we reach an agreement and work out the details." Or at least that was what I was hoping. "We need to work out payment for this. I have a good idea of what things like this would cost if you were a mage or a group of mages. I'm assuming it's similar for witches."

"We'll figure it out once I come up with a plan for how to help you. I'll get back to you as soon as I can." She squeezed my hand as we got up from the booth and headed to the counter.

Katy saw us and scurried into the back room. I sighed and pinched the bridge of my nose. Damn Lily. Katy had made a poor and dangerous choice and I still resented that Carly hadn't been completely honest with us, but Lily was the reason for this whole mess. If there really *was* a Threefold Law, it would be nice if Lily got some payback, I thought.

"Would you like a scone to take with you?" Carly asked.

"I'll take a couple, actually. I'm sure Sean would like to try them. He had to work until three."

"On a Saturday?" She made a disapproving sound.

"He missed quite a bit of work this week thanks to the hex and Caleb attacking me, and had to catch up."

She put the four remaining blueberry scones in a bag and then put a small paper sack on the counter next to it. "Here's some of that tea. Instructions for making it are on the bag. Be careful not to use boiling water or let it steep too long."

I handed over a twenty. "Put the change in the tip jar."

"Thanks, hon." She dropped the bills and a handful of coins in the jar. "You be safe."

"You too." I lowered my voice. "I forgot to ask: what are the witchy wards around the shop designed to keep out?"

Carly winked at me. "It's not so much what they're designed to keep out as what they keep *in*, and that's a secret I'll share another day. Blessed be."

"Blessed be," I echoed. I grabbed my coffee, the bag of scones, and the little sack of tea and we left.

"Well, now I'm *super* curious about these wards," Malcolm said as I got in the car.

I turned the key in the ignition. "Me too. I wonder—"

My phone rang. I dug it out of my bag and checked the screen. Oh boy. I sighed and answered. "Hello, Ezekiel."

"You have an interesting interpretation of the phrase 'back away from this matter.'" His tone was perfectly neutral, which meant he was hopping mad. "Given our last conversation and the risks involved, imagine my surprise when Charles Vaughan contacted me before dawn with a forty-nine-page contract outlining a proposed agreement between the Court, Darius Bell, and an individual referred to as 'Storm Girl.' And before you claim you don't know who or what I'm talking about, you should know Valas and I have been aware you are Storm Girl since the night of the fires."

It didn't surprise me to hear Valas knew I was Storm Girl—I would have been far more surprised if she hadn't known. "Only forty-nine pages? Frankly, given the situation and the parties involved, that sounds too short."

"Forty-nine pages not counting the addenda, of which there are seven." He sighed. "Miss Worth, your motivations are noble, but I'm not sure you fully comprehend what you're risking and what you're asking the Court to do."

"I fully comprehend both," I stated. "Is there anything about me that would lead you to think I rushed into this without thinking it through and analyzing all the alternatives?"

He harrumphed. "No. In fact, as I remarked to Charles, you would have made a fine lawyer and woe to anyone who opposed you in court. Though he drafted this contract, I recognize your single-minded thought process in its conditions and structure."

"You know, we really shouldn't be discussing this informally without my legal representative present," I said. "You've confirmed I know what I'm getting into and no one is strong-arming me to do this. Any other questions should be directed to Charles or whoever he has working on this during the day."

"Very well. The agreement is under review."

"Thanks, Ezekiel."

We said our goodbyes and hung up. I backed out of my parking spot and headed toward my house.

"Why are we headed home?" Malcolm asked.

"I want to work on some spellwork in the basement while Sean's at work. I don't know what all Carly's going to come up with, but we need some whammies of our own." I sighed. "It's been a while since I cooked up spells for weapons."

"Same here, but I'm sure we'll remember how they work." A long pause. "Alice, you know I've got your back. You can count on me to make sure none of Bell's people put a knife in it."

"I know I can, but you and I both know these people don't play nice or fair. They're going to play dirty. That means you and I will have to get dirty too just to save our own hides. You okay with that?"

"Yeah." A pause. "Yeah, I am okay with that."

We drove the rest of the way to my house in silence, each lost in our own thoughts. When I turned onto my street, I spotted not one, but *two* black Vamp Court SUVs parked in front of the house.

"What's this?" Malcolm asked.

"Not sure." I pulled into my driveway and parked in front of the carport. As I got out of the car, the passenger door of one of the SUVs opened and Arkady stepped out with a black briefcase.

I grinned and waved. "Hey, you. What's up?"

She crossed the yard and met me by the front steps. "You look pretty good for someone who got used as a werewolf chew toy." She gave me a hug.

We went inside. Malcolm followed us and hovered silently nearby. I hadn't introduced them to each other, though he knew who she was.

"You're here on official Vamp Court business, I take it," I said as I headed to the kitchen.

"Yep." She closed the door and locked it. "I'm a courier and a minder. Ezekiel Monroe had me bring you a copy of the agreement Vaughan sent to the Court and Bell's lawyers, and I'm supposed to hang out with you until we hear whether they've agreed to the terms of the agreement. Monroe also doubled your guard outside, just in case Bell gets any funny ideas."

I'd figured he would. "You want anything to drink?"

"Nah, I'm good." She set her briefcase on the counter, unzipped it, and took out two thick red folders. "Here's the agreement. I hope you speak legalese."

"I'm conversant in it." I took the folder from her and we headed to the living room. I sat cross-legged on the couch with the folder in my lap. "Who's out in the other SUV?"

Arkady settled into the loveseat. "Matthias and one of Valas's personal guards, a guy named Hanson."

"Oh, I know him." I'd met him the night I went to Valas to ask for help to save Sean. "He's named after a band."

"Yeah, I think he said something about that." She grew serious. "Request for me and Matthias to join the op."

"Why?"

She frowned. "Because we want to have your back. You're going to need all the backup you can get."

When I didn't reply right away, her expression darkened. "Why the hesitation, Alice?"

"I don't doubt your abilities or your motives," I told her. "Please don't take offense, but if the Court sends you with us, it will be to work for them. I don't want to put you in a spot where you'd be forced to choose whether to follow their orders or do something to help me."

"You're assuming those two things are going to be mutually exclusive?"

"I am. I have to be realistic. The Court will always have one prior-ity: protecting the Court and its interests. At the moment, that makes them uneasy allies with Darius Bell and we have a common goal: making sure Moses Murphy doesn't take over this city. I might have some value to Valas, but I have no illusions about where I stand in the hierarchy of the Court's priorities. You and I are friends, but you work for the Court. You know as well as I do there's all kinds of potential for conflicts of interest. The Court will give you your orders and unless you want to lose your job—or worse—you'll have to follow them."

She nailed me with a look. "So, rather than let me make that decision for myself if the time came, you don't want me to even get the chance to decide?"

I felt a little chill that meant Malcolm was beside me. "Alice, you're doing the thing again," he muttered.

Damn it. I sighed. "I'm sorry, Arkady. You're right; it's not my decision to make."

"Wow," Malcolm said, sounding impressed. "More personal growth."

"Shut up," I muttered under my breath. I addressed Arkady. "Okay, if Bell and the Court agree to the deal, I'll request that you and Matthias be included in the Court's contingent."

"Cut that out," she said sharply.

I blinked. "Cut what out?"

"That whole 'Now I have two more people to protect' shit." She stood and put her hands on her hips. "That's the real reason you didn't want us to go, isn't it? Maybe it was the other thing too, but you don't want us in danger."

"I didn't say—"

"It was all over your face." She stared me down. "Alice, I was in the Army. I was a PsyOps specialist out of Fort Bragg. Matthias is a Court enforcer. You are not responsible for keeping us safe. We're well-trained badasses, just like you. I know you know that. So why is this situation different from when we teamed up to take out Kent Stevens? You had no trouble with us being in the line of fire then."

I wanted to say because Moses Murphy was my grandfather and everything about this mission felt personal, but I couldn't tell her that. "I'm sorry. You're right—you don't need my protection. I can't help but worry about all of us facing the kind of firepower Murphy has at his disposal. I don't want any of my friends hurt."

"This is the line of work we're in," she pointed out. "We chose to work for the Court. You chose to be a mage PI. We all know the risks and we like them. And maybe we hate Moses Murphy because he's a killer and a scumbag and we'd like to be part of the team that takes him out. For us, that's worth the risk. Hell, if we kill him, we'll never have to pay for a drink in this town again."

I couldn't help but laugh. "In a number of bars and with certain groups of people, no, you won't."

"I like her," Malcolm interjected. "You gonna introduce us or what?"

I wondered belatedly if Malcolm was secretly glad his secret was out, because now he didn't have to be hidden from everyone anymore. Prior to this week, among the living, he'd only been able to talk with me, Sean, and Natalie. He'd never complained once about feeling isolated or lonely, but it must have been difficult to have so few living people to interact with. Now he'd met Nan and Carly and we had the option of letting others know of his existence. Something told me he and Arkady would get along very well.

Arkady frowned at me. "Earth to Alice."

"Sorry." I set the folder of papers aside. "Not to change the subject, but do you remember how I had a ghost keeping an eye on Sean while he was in the cage at Jack Hastings's house?"

"Yeah, I remember." She looked around. "Is the ghost here now?"

"Yep. I'd like you to meet him, actually, if you're up for that."

She grinned. "Awesome. I've never actually met a ghost. What do I need to do?"

"He'll touch your arm to draw a little energy from you and that will allow you to hear him. It'll be cold," I warned her.

She held her arm out. "Come on over, ghost."

Malcolm went visible and floated over to touch her outstretched arm. She jumped and laughed. "Brr! You weren't kidding. That tickled too."

He let go of her. "Hey, Arkady. I'm Malcolm."

"Hey, Malcolm. Nice to meet you." She looked around. "I can't see him?"

I shook my head. "He's only visible to me, but you should be able to sense him when he's nearby now. Can you feel a little chill next to you?"

She concentrated. "Yes, on my right. Hey, I know a ghost!"

My phone beeped with an incoming message from Sean. *Wolf: I might be done early. Our two o'clock meeting canceled and Ben helped me with paperwork. Heard anything from Bell or the Court?*

*Me: Still waiting on news. Arkady delivered the agreement Charles wrote. I'm about to read through it. We're at my house.*

*Wolf: I'll probably head that way in an hour.*

*Me: Ok.*

I dropped the phone on the couch next to the folder. "I guess I need to read through this. Malcolm, you want to get started downstairs without me and I'll join you in a bit?"

"Yeah, no problem. Take your time," he said. "Nice to meet you finally, Arkady."

"You too, Malcolm."

He disappeared through the floor into the basement.

I headed back to the kitchen. "If I'm going to read a contract, I need coffee. Want some?"

Arkady followed me. "Desperately. Hey, are those scones on the counter for sharing?"

I grumbled. "You can have *one*."

Charles wrote one hell of a contract.

"It's almost as if he's been doing this for nearly two hundred years," Sean said, looking up from the stack of pages on his lap. We sat at opposite ends of the couch, each with a copy of the proposed agreement. My feet rested on his thigh and he rubbed the arch of my foot with his thumb while he read.

"Don't sound so disappointed," I teased. "Were you hoping he'd forgotten something?"

"No," he said, not quite convincingly.

"He totally was," Arkady said from the loveseat. Sean frowned at her. She raised her eyebrows, unfazed, and turned her attention back to her phone.

I stuck the agreement back into the red folder and closed it. "I can't find anything I object to or think of anything he's forgotten. Everything's in here that I wanted and he seems to have covered all the bases. You see any loopholes or omissions Bell or the Court could exploit?"

He shook his head. "It seems iron-clad to me. Your role in the operation is clearly defined. Bell and the Court provide the manpower. Bell releases the nulls he's holding involuntarily and their families before we leave for the op. He agrees to refrain from any further communication with you and you are not obligated to work for him again in the future. Both he and the Court must agree not to cause you any harm, either by action or inaction, during the operation or after." He tapped the stack of pages into a neat pile and slid them into a red folder. "If there's anything he's missed, I'm not seeing it."

"He's good at his job." I got up and stretched.

My phone beeped. I picked it up and saw a text message from Adri. *Bell has indicated he's willing to sign and has requested a meeting for tonight. Ezekiel Monroe has agreed to meet. Luciano's at 11 p.m. Parley rules. Do you confirm?*

I exhaled. "It looks like we're in business."

# CHAPTER 20

As soon as we confirmed we'd meet the others at Luciano's, Sean called Jack and Ben to come over. Arkady went back outside to sit in the SUV with Matthias and Hanson to watch the house and give us privacy for a meeting.

Sean and I told Jack and Ben what we were doing and why—and that I was the mystery mage the press had dubbed "Storm Girl." Both men took the news in stride, admitting they had suspected as much. We discussed the matter up until the point that it was time to leave for the club, continuing the conversation during dinner. I only picked at my food, but the werewolves ate everything in sight, fueling themselves for what might be an eventful evening.

After dinner, I introduced Ben and Jack to Malcolm. Malcolm and Ben hit it off immediately, unsurprisingly, but Malcolm was less than friendly toward Jack. He remained highly suspicious of Sean's beta, despite Jack's apparent change of heart about my relationship with Sean.

Since Sean's truck was still at the body shop and his Mercedes was at the dealership to get the door fixed and the interior cleaned, we took a Maclin Security SUV to the meeting at Luciano's. Sean drove and I rode shotgun. Jack and Ben sat behind us, on high alert for any hint of trouble.

Despite heavy rain and traffic near downtown, we arrived at the club fifteen minutes early. Per instructions, we went around to the private side entrance rather than entering through the club's main doors. A doorman waited under the awning, umbrella in hand.

The doorman hurried from the awning to open my door and hold the umbrella over my head. "Good evening, Ms. Worth," he said solemnly as I got out, briefcase in hand.

He closed my door and escorted me to the awning, then went around to the driver's side to provide cover for Sean as Jack and Ben got out and took cover under the awning. A valet dashed from his kiosk and took Sean's place behind the wheel to move the vehicle to the parking garage.

I smoothed some imaginary wrinkles from Sean's suit, straightened his tie, and smiled up at him. "I need to make you dress up more often," I told him as the rain poured off the awning around us as if we were standing under a waterfall.

He kissed my forehead. He didn't have to lean down very far, since I was wearing four-inch heels. "Anytime you want me in a suit, all you have to do is say the word, as long as I get to pick what you wear," he murmured.

I had a feeling I knew what he'd request for me to wear: my tattoos, the wolf amulet, and maybe the Louboutins. "It's a deal."

"Jeez, you guys," Malcolm complained. He was invisible, but I sensed him on my right. "Can't you go five minutes without thinking about sex?"

"I could, but I'd rather not," Sean said. He took my hand and squeezed it.

I hadn't wanted Malcolm to join us for the meeting, but he'd insisted that he had to face Bell, despite the danger. I understood that need more than I could admit or explain. I needed to confront Moses—not just to get revenge for twenty years of torment, or to bring an end to his reign of terror, but because it was the only way for me to find any kind of peace or closure. That being the case, I could hardly refuse to give Malcolm the chance to find his own peace, though I'd made him promise to jump to safety if Bell or anyone else tried to harm him.

The doorman cleared his throat. "Honored guests, welcome to Luciano's." He opened the door and ushered us inside.

The private entrance led to an intimate lounge, with a bar and a dozen chairs arranged in small groups. Another employee, wearing a tuxedo, waited for us in the lounge. "Welcome, Miss Worth, Mr. Maclin," he said with a small bow. "I am Thomas. If you'll follow me down the hall and upstairs?"

With Jack and Ben—and Malcolm—at our six, Sean and I fell into step behind Thomas as he led us down a long hallway. I had to admit three large werewolves made for an imposing entourage.

I'd only been to Luciano's once before: several years ago with lawyer Aaron Riddell to meet a client. We'd met the client in one of the club's lounges, however, not in one of its private meeting rooms.

The upstairs meeting rooms were a favorite meeting place for people like Bell and Ezekiel Monroe. At nearly one hundred years old and having no affiliation with the Court, any cabals, or the Were Ruling Council, Luciano's was neutral ground. For a hefty price and pledges of committing no violence on the premises, rivals could meet under a flag of truce to discuss delicate matters.

When we reached the stairs, Sean offered me his arm. I slid my hand into the crook of his elbow and we climbed the long flight of stairs to the club's second floor.

At the top of the stairs, we followed Thomas down another, shorter hall to a set of double doors. He opened the doors with a flourish, revealing an elegant boardroom with a square wooden table ringed with twelve leather chairs, four on each side. To the left, I saw a large lounge area with chairs and sofas and doors that probably led to private restrooms.

"Ms. Worth, Mr. Maclin," Thomas announced, then withdrew.

Three people rose from the table as Thomas closed the doors:

Charles, Ezekiel Monroe, and another attorney who worked for the Court, Christine Foreman.

Unlike Ezekiel, Christine was a vampire. I'd met her under highly unpleasant circumstances on my first night working for the Court five years ago. Charles and I found her newly turned and starved almost to madness by her brother Alexander Foreman. He was now serving fifteen years in federal prison for that and several other crimes.

Christine had been turned by a rogue vampire, but Amira of the Court was able to bring her into her line. Christine had retained her sanity and had told me she liked being a vampire very much, despite the terrible way she'd been turned. Now she was one of the few vampire attorneys in the state.

"Ms. Worth, Mr. Maclin, welcome." Charles came around the table to greet us. He shook my hand and gave Sean a nod.

Bryan stood beside Charles's chair. He nodded at me in greeting.

Monroe came around to shake our hands as well. "Ms. Worth, Mr. Maclin," he said brusquely. He was evidently still displeased, whether by the terms of the agreement, my interference in the situation, or both. He was as inscrutable as any vampire when he chose to be. His hair was held back with a gold clasp, which I'd always interpreted as the equivalent of rolling up his sleeves. Monroe was here to do business.

The custom at Luciano's was to wait to serve liquor until business was concluded and an agreement reached. The tradition dated back to the club's first years in business. As such, the trays on the table held crystal carafes of what appeared to be water.

The table was square, so three or four parties could sit around it without anyone necessarily being at the head of the table. I wondered who had sat in these chairs before us and what deals had been struck in this room—and how many lives ended as a result of those agreements. I could almost feel my blood magic tingle, as if the blood of the dead had been spilled here. I wondered how the owners and management slept well at night, considering the kind of people who used their club for those purposes. I supposed they slept well enough; after all, they didn't kill anyone themselves.

Warmth and comfort wrapped around me like a blanket. Sean had sensed my thoughts turn dark and offered support. I glanced up and thanked him with my eyes.

Charles returned to his seat facing the door and Monroe went back to his side of the table. I moved across from Monroe, placed my briefcase on the floor next to the chair, and greeted Monroe's fellow counsel. "Hello, Christine."

"Ms. Worth, it's good to see you again." She smiled warmly. Other than her pale skin, Christine still seemed very human.

Sean stood to my right. "Would you like some water?" he asked me.

"Yes, thank you."

He poured us each a glass of water and sipped mine before setting it on a leather coaster beside his own. Despite the parley rules, Sean wasn't prepared to take anything on faith.

Monroe glanced at his very expensive watch. "Mr. Bell appears to want to make a point by arriving last." His tone indicated what he thought about such transparent power plays.

I doubted anyone in the room would be impressed by Bell's tactic. If Bell thought he was flexing his muscles by arriving after the rest of us, the strategy was having the opposite effect.

When Sean looked at the door, his eyes glowing softly, I figured he heard footsteps approaching out in the hallway. My phone said it was precisely eleven o'clock.

The doors opened, revealing Thomas. "Mr. Bell, Mr. Harlow, and Ms. Keegan," he announced, then stepped aside.

Darius Bell strode in, wearing a tailored suit cut to emphasize his physique. He surveyed us like a lion surveying his pride—or his prey. Moses often entered a room in much the same way. Bell was probably used to seeing people cower at the sight of him. I saw no such reaction from anyone in the room, however. No one here feared Bell. Acknowledged his power and influence, perhaps, but not feared.

The person whose reaction I was most concerned about was Malcolm. How would he feel, coming face-to-face with the man who'd had him tortured to death?

The answer, it turned out, was angry—very, very angry. The heat of Malcolm's fury seared my senses. I'd expected that reaction. What I *didn't* anticipate was that after a moment, the anger faded, replaced by something like acceptance and cold resolve. Seeing Bell had done something important for Malcolm. Bell was no longer the boogeyman; he was just flesh and blood.

Nora Keegan walked in with Harlow, who carried a briefcase and appeared to be Bell's attorney—or one of them, anyway. Behind them were two nearly Bryan-sized security escorts.

Nora scanned the room, cataloguing and assessing those present, before her eyes met mine. I was disappointed, but not surprised, to see her left hand had been reattached. I wished I'd had a chance to turn it to ash. I'd have to do better next time.

Her eyes sparkled, as if she guessed what I was thinking. She appeared to be looking forward to a rematch every bit as much as I was. She gave me a tiny wave with her left hand.

I let the corners of my mouth turn up just a bit. *Anytime, Nora.*

Thomas stood in the doorway, his hands folded behind his back. "The management and owners of Luciano's welcome you to our club. We thank you for your patronage. As a reminder, once I depart, no employee of Luciano's will enter this room until one of you opens the door, thus signaling a conclusion to the proceedings. Should you require additional beverages, food, or other services, please use the house phone to call for a delivery via the dumbwaiter. To prevent eavesdropping by any means, I will raise wards on this room. You have all agreed to meet under standard parley rules. No violence of any sort, magical or mundane, is permitted on the premises. Violations of any club rules will result in a lifetime ban from our club for you and your associates."

Thomas closed the doors to the hall. I sensed air magic as *sub rosa* wards flared around us.

Bell came around the side of the table. "Ms. Worth, I'm pleased to see you've fully recovered from the terrible injuries you received on Tuesday. I hope you enjoyed the flowers." He extended his hand.

There were few people I wanted to shake hands with less than the man who'd had Malcolm tortured to death, Aden and Jana kidnapped, and Ashley Brown executed. To refuse to shake would seem petty, however, and though I was perfectly capable of being petty, I also knew this was not the time.

I shook his hand with a firm, business-like grip. "Mr. Bell."

He held on just a beat too long before releasing my hand. "The operations manager of my fabrication company received a call today from a local non-profit organization called Hands of Hope. They wanted to thank me for donating a very rare bottle of Scotch to their fundraising campaign. They plan to auction the bottle, with the proceeds going to support their efforts."

Donating the bottle of Scotch whisky Bell had sent me earlier in the week to a local nonprofit had been Sean's idea. I thought it was a perfect solution to the problem of what to do with an unwanted gift. I'd delivered the bottle to the nonprofit myself, along with the contact information for who to thank so Bell found out what I'd done with his gift.

I smiled. "I'm familiar with that organization. They do a lot of very good and important work to help survivors of human trafficking."

The corners of his mouth turned up. "I couldn't agree more. I was very pleased to direct my company to pledge to match the amount raised by the auction, doubling the money raised for the organization, and to continue to support them with yearly gifts in the same amount. Anonymously, of course."

Son of a bitch. "How very generous."

Charles spoke. "Shall we begin?"

Bell rejoined his group and sat. Harlow sat to his right. Instead of taking a seat, Nora stood just behind Bell and to his left. The two security guards stood back from the table, near the doors.

Sean held my chair and sat to my right once I was settled in. Jack and Ben stood behind us. I sensed Malcolm close by, on my left. Monroe and Christine Foreman sat directly across from us. Charles sat on the fourth side, with Bryan behind him.

Once everyone was seated, Charles folded his hands on the table and looked around the table at each of us. "Our purpose is to reach an agreement accepted by all parties in the matter of a proposed coordinated effort among Ms. Worth, Mr. Bell, and the Vampire Court to bring an end to Moses Murphy's attacks on our city and Mr. Bell's organization. My function is twofold: to serve as Ms. Worth's representative and to broker this agreement. As such, Ms. Worth has designated me to speak for her in this meeting. Our terms and the exact nature of what Ms. Worth is proposing, along with the conditions for each of the other parties, are clearly outlined in the proposal. Are these terms acceptable to the other parties?"

Harlow spoke first. "No."

Charles raised his eyebrows. "You wish to make a counteroffer or propose a different course of action?"

"We do." Harlow cleared his throat and folded his hands on top of his copy of the proposal. He gave me a condescending look over the rims of his reading glasses. "Ms. Worth's terms are unreasonable. She demands the release of all null mages currently employed by my client's organization."

"All nulls who are unwilling employees of your organization *and* their families," Charles corrected him.

Harlow's smile was downright chilly. "And their families, yes." The smile vanished. "These mages represent a significant resource and investment. You're asking Mr. Bell to trade more than a dozen employees for a single individual based on the questionable claim that one person will be able to accomplish what a dozen cannot."

Bell studied me, his dark eyes coldly assessing. "I find it difficult to believe a dozen nulls will fail in their goal. I also doubt a single person, regardless of her talents for summoning storms or controlling lightning, will be able to do what no person or group has been able to do for more than two decades: break wards protecting a building belonging to Moses Murphy."

"And yet, that is the offer on the table," Charles said. "Ms. Worth has indicated both her willingness and ability to do precisely that. She is, in our assessment, your best and only chance to accomplish the seemingly impossible. Without Ms. Worth, you will not break the wards. You will continue to fight a war of attrition, wherein your holdings are destroyed and your people killed by Murphy and his organization, until Murphy succeeds in eliminating you. Ms. Worth offers you the chance not only to survive, but to prevail. As such, the question becomes: is not your life worth the release of these mages?"

I kept my face neutral and my emotions tightly controlled, but I was impressed as hell with that counterargument. Charles was earning his money with speeches like that.

Bell seemed to be considering Charles's words. He took a moment to confer with Harlow, then turned his attention back to Charles. "I am willing to release Aden Peters and his mother Jana in return for Ms. Worth's efforts."

Charles shook his head. "Our terms are only for the release of all of the nulls and their families. Offering to release two people instead is a ludicrous counteroffer."

Bell's expression hardened. "That's my only offer. I don't believe Ms. Worth's claim that a dozen nulls won't be able to break those wards. I *do*, however, believe Ms. Worth wants to secure the release of Aden and Jana Peters. Perhaps it's a matter of professional pride for her, or sentimentality or tenderness for a child." His expression made it clear what he thought of the latter. "I'm offering the lives of the child and his mother. It's far more than I should offer, but perhaps Ms. Worth's sentimentality is rubbing off on me."

I almost snorted. If Bell was even *capable* of sentimentality, I'd eat my best pair of boots and wash them down with room-temperature instant decaf.

"You need Ms. Worth to gain entry to the building," Charles said.

"I don't believe I do," Bell countered. "Even if that were true, I have no guarantee that once I release the nulls and their families that Ms. Worth will fulfill her obligations."

"Surely Ms. Worth has given you no reason to believe she will renege on this agreement," Charles said, sounding both incredulous and disdainful.

"You'll forgive me if I'm skeptical." Bell raised his hand to forestall Charles's objection. "Many an agreement such as this has proven to be worth less than the paper it's printed on. If I release the nulls, I will have no collateral with which to persuade Ms. Worth to follow through on her role in the operation. Only a fool would agree to the terms you are proposing."

Charles tapped his fingers on the table. "Then we are at an impasse."

Bell sat back in his chair. "It would appear so."

Monroe and Christine Foreman had been conferring during the exchange between Charles and Bell. Monroe cleared his throat. "We propose an arrangement."

Charles inclined his head. "We will hear your proposal."

"Like Mr. Bell, the Court wishes to bring an end to Murphy's violent attempts to establish control of the city. In return for Ms. Worth's and the Court's participation in a joint operation against Murphy, we propose Mr. Bell release one half of the mages and their families outright. The other half, he will release to the custody of the Court as collateral to ensure that Ms. Worth fulfills the terms of our agreement. Once she does so, we will release them. If she fails, we will return the nulls to Mr. Bell."

Charles glanced at me.

I had every intention of following through with my part of the bargain, so the idea of the Court essentially holding half of the nulls as collateral didn't seem unreasonable. I did *not*, however, like Monroe's use of the word "fail." If I failed to break the wards for any reason—many of which were out of my control—the nulls would end up back with Bell. It was one thing to hold them hostage against me reneging on the deal; it was entirely another to turn them over if I did everything in my power to uphold my part but failed through no fault of my own.

Charles's thoughts must have mirrored mine. "If Ms. Worth fails to uphold her part of the agreement, which is clearly defined in the proposal, the remaining nulls would be returned to Mr. Bell. But, as the proposal indicates, there are factors which none of us can know or foresee that may impact the outcome of our operation. As for those elements that are out of Ms. Worth's control, she cannot be held liable if she has done everything in her power to break the wards."

"The success of the operation is contingent upon breaking the wards," Monroe said. "Ms. Worth's proposal claims she will succeed where others have failed. Does she, or does she not, stand by that claim?"

"She believes she will succeed," Charles said, unruffled. "However, as the agreement states, that is contingent upon many unknown factors—most especially the specific location of the meeting between Murphy and the weapons dealer. Certainly the more information she has prior to arrival, the more likely she will be successful, which is why Section Three of the proposal calls on both Mr. Bell and the Court to share all intelligence they have on the personnel expected to be on the premises at the time of the attack. If you wish to increase the likelihood of success, I urge you both to not delay in providing all information in your possession."

Bell tapped his fingers on the table. "If I agree to release half of the nulls and their families and turn the other half over to the Court to hold as collateral, pending Ms. Worth's fulfillment of her obligations, Aden and Jana Peters will be among those held."

Charles glanced at me. He read my eyes and shook his head. "Ms. Worth requires Aden and his mother to be released."

Bell looked thoughtful. "If I release my most powerful bargaining chips, I require something in return—something of commensurate value to Ms. Worth. Therefore, I propose that if Ms. Worth does not hold up her end of the bargain, half of the nulls are returned to me and the Court withdraws its designation of her as a favorite of the Court."

Beside me, Sean went very still. That would mean I would no longer have the protection of an association with the Court. I would still have my status as associate of the Tomb Mountain Pack and as Sean's consort, but Bell—or anyone else—could come after me without fear of reprisal from the vamps. Considering my arrangement with Valas and the value of the work I did for the Court, I doubted Monroe would agree to that stipulation.

I was stunned when Monroe nodded slowly. "That is an acceptable condition." He studied me, his expression cold. "Since we are on the topic of collateral, the Court requires its own guarantee of Ms. Worth's fulfillment of her agreement. To that end, we note that a prior contract exists between Ms. Worth and Madame Valas."

My blood turned to ice.

Monroe continued, "Should Ms. Worth fail to fulfill the terms of the agreement, that contract will be put up for sale. Mr. Bell would have the first option to buy it outright."

I was standing before I realized I had moved. Suddenly everyone was on their feet and every security person in the room converged on their employers. The tension in the room skyrocketed.

"You son of a bitch," I ground out. "That contract is *not* transferable."

Monroe was unperturbed. "I am assured the matter of whether it could be transferred was not agreed upon, and therefore it is at Madame Valas's discretion whether to keep it or sell it."

My hands shook with fury. There was something in Monroe's expression—a kind of satisfaction—that told me this was punishment by the Court for me not backing off when he told me to. He'd just kicked my feet out from under me to show me he could. I wondered if it had been his idea or Valas's. Either way, she must have agreed to let him put the contract on the table, which meant I would have to rethink everything I thought I knew about the nature of our deal.

Bell folded his hands on the table. "These terms are more to my liking, I think. We might be able to make a deal, provided Ms. Worth can calm herself enough to work out the particulars."

"Perhaps we should take a short break to confer," Charles suggested smoothly. "Shall we say ten minutes?"

"I second," Bell said, giving me a satisfied smile. "Take all the time you need, Ms. Worth."

I wanted to cut him in half where he stood. Instead, I took a few steps back from the table. "Ten minutes, then," I said, my voice tight.

SEAN and I moved to the far side of the lounge as the others broke into small groups to talk quietly. His fury and worry sizzled on my skin, but my own anger was so powerful I barely noticed his.

Ben and Jack formed a wall between us and the others, with Ben facing the conference room and Jack facing us. Their faces were cold, their eyes bright as they guarded us. I sensed Malcolm next to us as well, but he stayed silent.

Sean bent his head so he could put his lips next to my ear. "We can leave right now," he told me, his words barely audible. I was very aware of all of the sharp ears in the room. "No one's agreed to or signed anything. You are not obligated to trade yourself for Aden and the others."

I took several deep breaths, inhaling through my nose and out through my mouth, to calm myself and squash my anger. I kicked myself for letting Monroe get under my skin with his unexpected betrayal—and for not anticipating it. I should have known he'd find a way to get back at me for not backing off when he told me to. Even if I had, though, I never would have anticipated Valas would put our agreement on the table and hint it would be for sale. I'd thought what I'd agreed to do for her was significant enough to make that impossible.

It would appear I had miscalculated.

"I'm not leaving." My voice was softer than a whisper, since his werewolf ears would easily hear me. "Aden and Jana will be released. I have every intention of fulfilling my part of the agreement, so Valas will have no reason to put my contract up for sale."

A muscle moved in Sean's jaw. "Now that Bell knows there's a contract, he may try to buy it anyway, and Monroe just signaled Valas might be willing to sell."

He was careful not to voice his thoughts about either the head of the Court or her representative, given the likelihood of being over-heard, but I saw unbridled fury in his fiery golden eyes. No doubt he'd have some choice words about Valas and Monroe once we were alone.

"I know." I squeezed his hand. "I'll have to deal with that later. Right now, I need to know if you still think I should do this."

He didn't respond right away. If he said no, it would be the first time since we'd reconciled that I would have to decide whether to go through with something against Sean's wishes. On the one side would be the lives of Aden and the rest of the nulls, and on the other, my relationship and my heart. As much as Sean meant to me, how could I give that side of the equation more weight than a dozen lives? I didn't think I could.

Sean's hand tightened on mine. "If you say you can break those wards, then I believe you and I'm with you. However, I don't want you to risk your status as a favorite of the Court. I think you should let Bell hand Aden and Jana over to the Court as part of the collateral."

I kept my face expressionless, but I was sure he sensed my anger. "I want Aden and Jana away from Bell, away from all of this."

"I know you do. You have every intention of fulfilling your part of the agreement, which means the Court will release the remaining nulls and Aden and Jana go free. They'll only be in the Court's custody for an additional day and they won't be in Bell's hands." He read my eyes. "Unless you're concerned the Court won't let them go."

"If Monroe signs on the dotted line and says the Court will release them, I don't have any reason to think they won't," I said. "The Court has been honorable in its dealings, to the best of my knowledge, but I don't want Aden and Jana in custody one more minute. I don't want to even risk Bell or the Court finding a loophole and hanging onto them, Sean. I want them to walk free *tonight*." I'd already set things in motion to ensure their safety after their release and those plans did not include letting the Court hang onto them for an additional day.

He pressed his lips to my ear. "I want them freed too, but I need you to be safe, Alice. I am not giving you an order or an ultimatum; the choice is yours to make. You asked me what I think you should do and that's my answer." His voice and expression became as hard and cold as steel. "I will not let you fall into Bell's hands or anyone else's. You will never belong to anyone ever again except yourself, and someday me if we decide we belong to each other. Your power, combined with your alliance with me and the pack, may be enough to ensure your safety, but as Vaughan said, your status as a favorite of the Court is the most significant deterrent for people like Bell. I don't want you to risk that, even for Aden and his mother."

"I can't," I told him softly. "I can't let Aden and Jana stay prisoners one more minute and risk them being returned to Bell if it's in my power to free them now. I was a prisoner once. I want to follow your advice, but I can't." I searched his face, hoping to find reassurance.

He touched his forehead to mine. "I understand," he murmured. "I don't agree, but I understand."

I felt a cold touch on my shoulder. *Alice, remember what Suriel said about you saving Aden regardless of the cost?* Malcolm said in my head. I sensed his worry. *I think this is what he meant.*

*Do you think I'm making a mistake?* I asked him.

A pause. *No, I don't. I get where Sean is coming from, but I'm with you. I don't like the Court holding Aden and Jana as collateral. I smell a rat and I think your instincts are telling you there's something going on we're not aware of. I say we both go with our guts on this one. It's your call, though. I'm with you either way.* He let go of my shoulder.

"The vampire is coming over," Ben said softly over his shoulder. His voice was uncharacteristically growly. I was sure both Ben and Jack remembered all too well how Charles had smashed through the front door of Jack and Delia's house the night I'd died to free Sean from the cuff, and it wasn't likely any of the werewolves would forgive his intrusion anytime soon.

"Let him pass," I said.

Ben said nothing as Charles walked around him, but I heard a brief, low growl from Jack. Charles chose not to acknowledge it.

I expected Charles to touch me so we could share our thoughts, but to my surprise he didn't. He leaned close enough to put his lips near my ear. "We are nearing the end of the ten-minute recess," he murmured. "Do you wish to proceed, and if so, what are your instructions?"

I tried not to notice that his scent was nearly intoxicating and how his blood surged in my veins like tides under the moon. He sensed my disquiet. The corners of his mouth turned up ever so slightly and his eyes glittered. There was the Charles I recognized.

"Jana and Aden, along with half of the nulls and their families, must be released as soon as the agreement is signed," I told him, my voice equally quiet. "In return, I agree to allow the Court to hold the remaining nulls as collateral, and Monroe may rescind my status as a favorite of the Court if I don't fulfill my obligations as outlined in the contract."

Charles's eyes flashed silver. "I do not endorse this course of action."

"You're not the only one," Sean said. "But it's Alice's decision to make, not ours."

The vampire made a low hissing sound. "Very well." He lowered his head again. "Other instructions?"

I spoke into his ear. "I want an ironclad agreement that the moment the wards break, or we determine that's not possible due to circumstances beyond my control, the rest of the nulls will be released by the Court. If they are not, I will become the Court's worst nightmare, and you can quote me on that. If Monroe doubts it, tell him to ask Valas whether I'm capable of following through on that threat."

Charles studied me. "You are aware such a threat will be taken quite seriously?"

I spooled magic and let my eyes glow. "It should be."

He inclined his head. "Anything further?"

I put my hand on his. I sensed a surge of golden shifter magic from all three werewolves. They didn't like me having physical contact with Charles and I couldn't blame them, but I had questions I couldn't say aloud.

*What concerns you?* Charles asked in my head.

I ignored the surge of heat and power kindled by touching him and hearing his voice in my head. *I smell a rat in regard to the Court's offer to hold half of the nulls as collateral,* I told him bluntly. *What's Monroe's plan?*

*I know of no plan, but I too suspect his motives.* Charles's voice was grim. *Is this why you insist on procuring the release of the boy and his mother?*

*Partly, but the main reason is that Aden is just a kid, and no kid deserves to be a prisoner of either a cabal or the Court.* I met his eyes. *Do you have any recommendations or warnings I need to hear, given what's been discussed so far?*

He nodded gravely. *By revealing the existence of your contract, Valas has implied she is willing to sell, regardless of the outcome of your efforts. I am troubled by this unexpected development.*

I felt a little better knowing even Charles hadn't anticipated Valas's move. *You and me both. I'll have to cross that bridge if and when I come to it. Tonight, my priority is reaching an agreement with Bell and the Court and getting the nulls released. I'll have to worry about my agreement with Valas later.*

A voice interrupted our silent conversation. "Ten minutes have elapsed," Ezekiel Monroe said from the conference table. "Is Ms. Worth prepared to resume our discussion?"

Charles glanced at me. I gave him a nod.

"We are," my vampire representative replied. He gestured for me to walk ahead of him.

In my mind, I pictured my side as the head of the table and the others as supplicants in my presence. My gut twisted. Moses walked into every room in just that same way, as Bell had done when he arrived: like a king before his subjects. I'd hated that about my grandfather—hated it with every fiber of my being. But if I'd learned anything from Moses, it was what power really was and how to wield it.

If I wanted to, I could raze this building to the ground and walk out without a hair out of place, and it was about damn time the others in this room acknowledged it.

Head high, with Sean and Charles behind me and Ben and Jack bringing up the rear, I strode to my chair. My aura crackled and I made no effort to hide the power I carried. For the first time in a very long time, I dropped the façade of Alice Worth and let a room full of people see the cold power and even colder eyes of Moses Murphy's granddaughter.

Bell and Monroe rose as I approached the table. I saw something in their eyes that hadn't been there before: wariness. I was willing to bet Bell regretted giving me that ten-minute recess. I'd had the chance to regroup—and remember who I was.

From her spot behind Bell, Nora Keegan smiled, as if to say, *A-ha —there you are.*

I let the corner of my mouth go up ever so slightly. *Come get me.*

Sean stood just behind me, his golden eyes moving around the table, studying each face in turn. The air felt thick with power—Sean's and mine.

I put my fingertips on the conference table. Tiny sparks crackled against the polished wood and the table vibrated at my touch. "Gentlemen, the time for games is over. These are my terms."

THREE HOURS LATER, I used Charles's gold-accented fountain pen to add my signature to those of Darius Bell and Ezekiel Monroe on the last page of our agreement, which had swelled from forty-nine pages —plus addenda—to a more robust seventy-three. I took a cue from John Hancock and signed with a flourish, letting the *A* in *Alice* take up far more than its fair share of real estate on the page.

The revised agreement had been prepared by one of Charles's staff and delivered to our conference room via the dumbwaiter. Once all parties had reviewed it, we'd each signed and our signatures were duly witnessed by Thomas, who we'd summoned using the house phone.

As I set the pen down, Thomas went to the mirrored bar. With great formality, he poured two fingers of Scotch whisky into three glasses, which he placed on a tray. He brought the tray to me. I took a glass and watched as Monroe and Bell took theirs.

I raised my glass. "To our success, gentlemen."

They raised their glasses. "To our success," Bell echoed, smiling as if amused by some private joke. We'd see who'd get the last laugh, I thought.

"May our victory be swift and final," Monroe added.

We drank.

I turned to Bell. "Now. Release the nulls."

# CHAPTER 21

Ben turned into the wide circular drive in front of The Casarina, one of the city's finest hotels and one of Bell's most opulent properties, and stopped under the porte cochère. The heavy rain had turned to a light drizzle.

A valet started to hurry toward us. He stopped in his tracks when he spotted Sean in the front passenger seat and returned to his podium next to the hotel's revolving doors, studiously avoiding looking in our direction.

"I guess we were expected," I said dryly.

A low growl came from beside me. Jack had been on high alert since we'd left Luciano's and his unease prickled on my skin like porcupine quills.

Sean glanced over his shoulder as Ben put the SUV in park. "Stand guard outside, will you, Jack?"

With an affirmative grunt, the beta got out and took up a position near the back of the SUV, where he could keep watch for anyone approaching our vehicle from the rear or passenger side.

I drummed my fingers on the armrest. "Ten minutes to the rendezvous. I wonder what games Bell will try to play." Despite his signature on what we thought was a pretty iron-clad contract, I fully expected the curveballs to start coming at us immediately.

The first one arrived less than a minute later, when Jack tapped twice on the back bumper and a luxury SUV pulled up next to us.

"If this is them, they're early," I said, frowning.

The rear door of the other SUV opened and Allan Garrett emerged, wearing a suit. His eyes met mine through my window.

"That's Aden's father," I told Sean. "I'm getting out. I've got some questions for him."

He got out and opened my door, offering me a hand to help me out of the SUV.

The windows of the other SUV were so darkly tinted I couldn't see who was in the vehicle. The windows on this side of the car were down an inch, though—enough that everything we said would be overheard. Garrett wasn't in shackles, but it didn't take a rocket scientist to figure out he was on a leash.

I leveled a flat stare at Aden's father.

"Ms. Worth." A muscle moved in his jaw. "I owe you an apology."

A dozen angry words burned on my tongue. I swallowed them, spoke different ones. "So apologize."

"I'm sorry." He cursed and rubbed his face. "You tried to warn me."

"Yeah, I did. But he has your kid, so I can see why you did it." I paused. "You're a horse's ass, though."

He sighed. "Can't argue with that."

I studied him. "What's with the suit, Allan?"

"Mr. Bell offered me a job. I took it."

I read his eyes. There wasn't much he could say with the others in the vehicle listening, but I thought I understood his motives clearly enough. He hoped by going to work for Bell willingly, he could ensure Bell would leave Aden alone. He had to know Bell's promises, whatever they'd been, weren't worth much. He also had to know he'd just made a deal with the devil. Now that he'd taken a job with a cabal and they knew what he could do, he wasn't likely to ever see freedom again. He'd given up his life for Aden.

For a moment, I saw despair in Garrett's eyes. It disappeared, replaced by cold resolve. The last of my anger at him flickered and died.

I wanted to tell him I was sorry, but I was fairly certain he wouldn't want to hear it. "Have you been told about my arrangement with Bell?" I asked instead.

He nodded. "Not the details." Hope shone in his eyes. "Aden and Jana will be freed?"

"That's the plan. They're supposed to be brought here soon." I wished I could sound more certain, but until I had Aden and his mother in my hands, I wasn't counting on anything.

"Thank you." His voice was steady, but I caught the flash of emotion in his face before he forced himself to school his features. "Watch over them for me."

"I will." I wanted to tell him my plan for keeping them safe from Bell, but I didn't dare—not with listeners in the other SUV. Instead, I let him see in my eyes that there *was* a plan and hoped he understood.

He did. His shoulders went down a fraction of an inch. "Thank you," he said again. "Tell Aden...tell Jana..." He hesitated, looking helpless.

"I'll tell them," I promised.

He gave me a jerky nod and reached for the door handle of the SUV.

"Take care of yourself, Allan," I told him.

"You too, Ms. Worth."

He opened the door and climbed in. The SUV pulled away, accelerating down the hotel's circular drive and turning left onto the street without pausing.

Sean's hand brushed against mine. "You okay?"

I appreciated the reassuring touch, but between Garrett's news and my worry about Aden and Jana, who were due to arrive any minute, I was a bundle of nervous energy. I took a shaky breath. "Not really."

"Incoming," Jack rumbled.

I straightened and Sean moved a little closer to me as another SUV pulled up alongside us.

The front passenger door opened and closed and Nora Keegan came around the back of the vehicle. Her sharp eyes took in Jack and Sean before meeting mine.

"Does Bell have you making deliveries now?" I asked, trying not to think about how badly I wanted to cut her into a million tiny pieces.

Her smile made Jack growl. "I asked for the privilege of making this one," she told me. "How could I pass up the opportunity to finish our conversation from Sunday?"

I gave her my own toothy smile, the one Charles had once said reminded him of a vampire. "I'd love to chat, I really would, but unfortunately we've got quite a lot of work to do before tomorrow and I'm simply swamped. Rain check?"

Her eyes glinted. "Absolutely. I'm going to hold you to that." She tilted her head. "We'll be fighting side-by-side soon, Alice. What a sight that will be. I almost feel sorry for Murphy's people."

"Cut the chatter, Nora. Where are Jana and Aden?"

Her mouth twisted. "So businesslike. Very well." She opened the rear door of the SUV. "Let's go," she said sharply.

Slowly, Jana Peters stepped out, wearing a long-sleeved T-shirt and jeans that didn't fit her very well. She looked like she'd lost ten pounds in the past week, but her eyes were still fiery. She had an iron grip on the hand of a familiar curly-haired boy in a Star Wars T-shirt. His eyes were wide with terror.

"Hi, Jana." I smiled at her son. "It's nice to meet you, Aden."

He clung to his mother and said nothing.

I didn't know what he'd been through in the past seven days, but the kid was going to need help to deal with the trauma of his captivity. My earth magic surged and the ground quaked beneath our feet. I pulled my magic back, afraid of scaring Aden even more.

Nora shut the door of the SUV. "Having problems controlling your magic tonight? I have to say I'm concerned, given what we might be facing soon. You should work on that."

"Please get them into our vehicle," I told Jack.

Jack opened the rear door and folded the seat up. With surprising gentleness, he lifted Aden into the vehicle so Jana didn't have to let go of his hand and helped them get settled in. Jana wrapped her arms around her son as Jack put the middle seat back in place and closed the door.

I reached for my door handle, but Sean beat me to it. As he opened my door, Nora said, "Look at you, the mighty mage, being minded by the wolves." Her voice dripped with derision.

It was the sort of petty comment that didn't merit a response, so I ignored her and got into the SUV. Sean shut the door. He waited until Nora went around to the passenger side of their vehicle and got in before he climbed into our SUV and closed his door.

He turned to me. "You good?"

I blew out a breath. "Yeah."

When the other vehicle drove away, Jack got in next to me. I twisted around in my seat as Ben shifted gears and headed for the street. "Jana? Are you guys okay?"

The streetlights shone on the streaks of tears on her face. She stroked Aden's hair and held him tight, her eyes bright and angry. "Yes," she said firmly, and I almost believed her. She was being strong for her son's sake, but she was a long, long way from okay.

She looked out the window. "Where are we going?"

"Someplace safe," I told her.

Her shoulders sagged. "Where will we ever be safe from him, Alice?"

"I'm not sure," I said. "But I know someone who does."

It was a forty-minute drive to the private airport where we'd be meeting the person who would help Jana and Aden stay safe from Bell.

On the way, Jana held her son, who still hadn't said a word, and told us what happened after Nora took her. She'd woken up in an apartment that turned out to be underground. She didn't know where it was; she'd been unconscious when she arrived and blindfolded when they took her out. She'd had a spell cuff locked onto her arm, suppressing her magic completely, though she had only low-level earth magic. Her captors didn't take any chances.

Since the apartment was underground, she had no idea what time of day it was—only the time according to the clocks in the apartment, which might or might not have been correct.

All the first day, no one came to see her. At ten, the lights dimmed and went out for eight hours, then turned on again at six, signaling morning. She had sat alone in the dark for eight hours that first night, too angry and afraid to close her eyes.

On Monday, she'd received a visit from one of Bell's lieutenants, a man who didn't give her a name. He showed her a video of Aden on his phone, showing the kid alone in a similar apartment, frightened but unhurt. He allowed her to record a message for Aden, and then explained that as long as Aden did as he was told, neither of them would be harmed. She'd begged him to let her see her son. He told her if Aden cooperated, she would be allowed to see him, perhaps in a day or two.

Later that day, the man returned and showed her another video —this one of Allan Garrett—and told her Garrett was a strong null like Aden. After threatening Aden if she refused, he'd instructed her to call me to say she'd accepted a job from Bell. Jana had tried to refuse until the man let her see Aden, but after more threats, she'd given in and made the call.

She'd had very little contact with anyone for the next several days except for occasional visits by the same man, who showed her videos of her son and Garrett obediently demonstrating their nulling abilities. She was given clothing, food, and a television equipped to stream movies and TV shows, but had no way of making any contact with anyone. Her only interactions with the unnamed lieutenant were brief, but at least she knew her son was alive and the lieutenant let her record videos for Aden, telling him she was nearby and to keep doing what they asked him to do.

As she described what she'd gone through, her voice was calm, probably for Aden's sake. I kept tight control over my magic as she talked, but listening to her describe her captivity conjured up some very unpleasant memories of my years in my grandfather's compound. *At least I'd had windows to look out of*, I thought, as Jana described how on the fourth day she thought she was starting to go crazy in that posh, windowless underground prison.

Other than the videos, Jana had no contact with Aden until tonight, when the lieutenant came to her apartment, blindfolded her, and told her he was taking her to see Aden. He'd led her down several hallways, up some stairs, and into an underground parking garage, where she'd been loaded into the SUV. A few minutes later, Aden was brought to the SUV and Jana was finally able to hold her son for the first time in a week.

When she'd finished telling us about her captivity, Jana held her son and rested her head on his. He'd turned his face toward her chest, his shoulders hunched. I turned around to face the front and give them privacy.

Sean reached back and took my hand. His comforting magic swirled around me and I drew on it gratefully. Rage and sorrow filled me until my insides felt like they were rotting, as if the dark magic of the Tepes stone had returned. Sean's golden magic pushed that darkness away.

When we turned into the entrance to a private airport, Jana raised her head. "What are we doing here?"

I turned back around. "I made a deal with Bell to get you and Aden released, but I can't guarantee he won't try to come after Aden again. I only know of one way for you and Aden to be safe, and only one person I trust to keep you away from Bell and any other cabal." I glanced at my phone. "Hangar Two, Ben. He says just drive through the main door."

He found Hangar Two and drove inside. A Gulfstream jet waited inside, its door open and steps unfolded. As we parked next to the office, airport employees closed the hangar doors, blocking us from view.

"Stay inside for a minute, please," I told Jana.

Sean, Jack, and I got out. Ben stayed inside with Jana and Aden, and Jack stood next to our SUV, on guard.

The door of the small office opened. Special Agent Trent Lake appeared in his trademark navy blue SPEMA jacket, slacks, shirt, and tie.

Though we'd spoken on the phone earlier in the day, I hadn't seen him in two months, since he left the city to become the assistant director of the SPEMA field office in Seattle. If it hadn't been for Sean—and the fact I was Moses Murphy's granddaughter, in hiding from every federal agency, including SPEMA—we might have had something special. He was a good man who still had a claim on a small corner of my heart.

The tall, blond federal agent broke into a smile when he saw me. "Alice," he said, striding across the floor to meet us. He held out his hand and we shook. "You look sharp. I like the suit." He shook hands with Sean. "Mr. Maclin, it's good to see you again."

"Sean," Sean corrected him. I'd worried Sean might feel less than friendly toward a former romantic rival, but I saw no sign of any resentment or distrust. Perhaps like me, when he'd gone to talk to Lily at Karen and Cole's house, he knew he had nothing to worry about. "How's Seattle?"

"Virtually lawless these days, but we're cleaning it up." Lake winked at me. "Alice's recent disposal of the vampire Vincent Barclay helped quite a bit, frankly. I owe you a gift basket for taking him out. The vamps didn't give you any grief about it, did they?"

I shook my head. "The Court ruled it was self-defense. I was concerned about reprisals, but although Barclay had a lot of allies, he didn't have many friends apparently, since no one seems too upset about him being dead."

"That's definitely true. Not many tears were shed in Seattle at the news of his true death, I assure you." Lake glanced at the SUV, his face growing serious. "How are Jana and her son?"

Magic sparked on my hands and a cold wind blew over us. "Aden's so traumatized he can't even talk and Jana's hanging on by a thread. They've been separated the whole time and have only been together for about an hour."

"Does Jana know they're going with me?"

I shook my head. "She's still processing the fact she and Aden are out of Bell's hands. I wanted to have you talk to her privately to explain, but I don't think I want to even try to separate them, not after all they've been through."

"Neither do I. I'll talk to them together." He gestured at the little hangar office. "It's not the most comfortable place to talk to a trau-matized child and his mother, but I've got it arranged as best I can."

I smiled at him. "Thank you, Trent. Let me go get them and I'll bring them to the office."

Lake waited as Sean and I returned to the SUV. Ben got out and folded up the seat so I could lean into the open door and speak to Jana.

"Jana, that agent is a good friend of mine," I said. "His name is Trent Lake and he's the assistant director of the field office in Seattle."

Her mouth was a grim line. "SPEMA."

I nodded. "I don't trust feds any more than you do. Probably less, actually. But he's a good man and he would like to take responsibility for keeping you and Aden safe."

She nailed me with a hard stare. "Can I trust him with my son's life?"

"Yes. I trust him with mine. There are only three or four people in the entire world I would say that about, and he's one of them."

She glanced at Aden. "Do you want to go meet Alice's friend Trent?"

He shook his head. She looked at me helplessly.

I turned and motioned for Lake to come over to the SUV. He headed in our direction. I mimed taking off my jacket and he removed the SPEMA jacket and tossed it on the seat of a small forklift so it wouldn't scare Aden.

He joined me at the open door of the SUV. "Hey, Aden," Lake said, giving him a smile. "I've really looked forward to meeting you."

Aden blinked at him.

"My name is Trent." Lake leaned on the door. "I know you've had a tough week, but I'm here to make sure you and your mom are safe. Would you like to come on board my plane and sit in the pilot's seat while I talk to your mom?" He leaned forward and lowered his voice conspiratorially. "Sometimes I sneak in there and pretend I'm flying an X-Wing fighter, but don't tell the pilot."

I was almost certain he'd made that up—I'd told him ahead of time about Aden's love of Star Wars and anime—but there was just enough of a twinkle in his eyes to make me wonder if he hadn't really done it.

Aden looked at Jana. "Can I?" His voice was timid.

She smiled and gave him a little squeeze. "As long as you don't touch anything."

"Yes, ma'am," Aden promised. He climbed out of the SUV and waited while Jana got out. He took her hand and they followed Lake to the jet.

Sean's hand found mine and squeezed. He leaned down to murmur in my ear. "I know we're facing rough days ahead, but seeing Jana and Aden together and away from Bell makes it all seem worthwhile."

I swallowed around the lump in my throat. "Yeah, it does."

As we watched Aden, Jana, and Lake climb up the steps and into the jet, my phone beeped with an incoming message. I read it and exhaled. "Bryan said half of the nulls have been freed and the remainder are just arriving at Northbourne. They'll be kept in private apartments, he says, not in the holding cells."

"Bell came through." Sean shook his head. "This has all been much too easy. He's got something planned, Alice. I just don't know what it is."

I gripped his hand. "I know."

From the direction of the jet, I heard Lake laugh. Aden's voice sounded excited, as just about any twelve-year-old would be getting to explore a jet.

I smiled. Somewhere, Bell was plotting—I knew it as surely as I knew Lake would protect Jana and Aden. But right now, I put a check mark in the win column for Team Alice.

WE WAITED by the SUV while Lake talked to Jana aboard the jet.

"Take Ben with you when you go after Murphy." Jack's voice startled me. He stood to Sean's left, arms crossed. "I'd prefer to go myself, but we can't have both the alpha *and* the beta there and leave the pack undefended."

The younger, dark-haired werewolf nodded. "I'll go. Someone needs to watch your back while you're watching Alice's. There are too many people who are just as likely to try to take you out as fight at your side, regardless of what agreements they've signed."

Before Sean could respond, I turned to him. "Can I speak to you?"

He nodded. "Let's step inside the hangar office. Keep a sharp eye out, gentlemen," he added.

Both werewolves nodded. Sean and I walked to the small office and he closed the door.

"Sean..." I began, then stopped. I didn't know how to say what I was thinking and not have it come out wrong.

He laced our fingers together. "You're worried about Ben. You feel like you need to protect him, and you already have to protect me, Malcolm, and maybe Arkady and Matthias too, in addition to breaking the wards. You want me to tell him to stay here."

"I do, but at the same time, I know I can't and I shouldn't. Just like you and Malcolm, Ben gets to choose when and where he fights and I have to let him."

He squeezed my hand. "I'm not going to pretend any of this is easy or that I'm not worried, because it's definitely *not* easy and I *am* worried. I'm responsible for the safety of my pack. If Ben wants to go, I won't refuse. I know you don't want to hear this, but he'll be able to help keep you safe."

He was right—I didn't want to hear Ben would be charged with protecting me. Why did I merit his protection? Why should anyone risk their life to save mine?

Something cold thumped me on the back of my head.

I let go of Sean's hand and spun around. "Damn it, Malcolm!"

He materialized in front of me, arms crossed. "Remember what Carly said about quieting the voice in your head that tells you that you're unworthy?"

I scowled. "Are you reading my mind now?"

"He didn't have to read your mind." Sean moved to my side so he could see my face. "You've risked your life over and over again for the people you care about: me, Malcolm, Trent Lake, Natalie Newton, Jana, Aden, Charles Vaughan... You even risked your life to rescue Nan's daughter Felicia, who you didn't even know at the time. You're risking your life to save this city from Murphy. You don't have a monopoly on putting yourself in harm's way to keep people safe, and you are absolutely worthy of being protected." He cupped my face with his hand. "Let us care about you, Alice."

I swallowed hard. "I'm trying."

Someone tapped on the door. "Alice?" Lake called.

Malcolm went invisible. I opened the door.

Lake glanced at us, his eyebrows raised. "Am I interrupting?"

I shook my head and stepped out of the office. "We just had to talk over some stuff in private. How's it going with Jana and Aden?"

He smiled. "Aden's over the moon talking with our pilot, JC. We may never pry him out of the pilot's seat and JC is enjoying showing off his fancy plane. Aden thinks he's some kind of wizard." His smile faded. "Jana told me you arranged for Bell to release her and Aden. How did you manage that?"

"I appealed to his sentimental side."

He sighed. "Some things never change, I guess." Lake's super-power seemed to be the ability to detect when I was lying and it looked like his radar was still finely tuned. "Not even a believable lie this time, though. Want to try again?"

I thought about it. "I made him an offer he couldn't refuse?"

Lake pinched the bridge of his nose.

"She did," Sean said mildly. "Bell is a businessman. For the right price, everything is for sale to a businessman, even people."

"I'm sure he asked a high price." Lake leaned against the doorway and crossed his arms. "My former colleagues here in the city are still looking into the infamous Storm Girl incident from last month. She saved a hell of a lot of lives and took out Moses Murphy's daughter Catherine with a bolt of lightning. Rumor has it Catherine's barely alive, hooked up to a room full of machines in Murphy's compound in Baltimore."

I was very interested in that news. I hadn't heard anything about Catherine's condition since Cyro's warning in the Bahamas that my aunt had awakened. I still wasn't sure how Catherine had survived the lightning strike in the first place. My best guess was I hadn't hit her directly and she'd had some kind of hardcore protection spells either tattooed or in the form of jewelry. Lightning was a flashy weapon, but it was hard to aim without a focus.

Lake's eyes locked on mine. "Rumor also has it that both Murphy and Bell want to get their hands on Storm Girl—Murphy for revenge and Bell because he needs bigger weapons against Murphy. Bell might be willing to part with a powerful null like Aden for Storm Girl's help against Murphy."

When I didn't reply, his expression darkened. "I wanted to be wrong about who Storm Girl was and whether she'd traded herself for Aden and Jana's freedom, but there's only one person who could summon a hurricane and smite someone with lightning, and only one person who would put herself in so much danger to save complete strangers."

"Some people just don't know when to quit," I said, smiling slightly. "Sounds like Storm Girl has more power than sense."

"No argument from me." He sighed. "Whatever you're planning, keep Sean at your back. If you get in too far over your head, you know how to find me."

I smiled. "Thank you, Trent."

Jana made her way down the steps of the jet and came over to us. Her face still looked drawn, but she was smiling.

"Aden's in heaven," she told Lake. "Your wonderful pilot is showing him the flight management system and something called an infrared imager. He's up there memorizing all the stats about the plane." She turned to me. "The co-pilot told him he could be a veterinarian *and* a pilot and now he wants to be a vet who flies around to see all his patients."

I laughed. "Kids are amazing. He sees no reason why he can't do that."

Her smile faded. "Alice, I can't possibly thank you enough for getting us out of there and introducing us to Agent Lake."

"Seeing you and Aden together is all the thanks I need. I'm just sorry I couldn't keep Nora from taking you and that Aden had to spend a week in Bell's hands before I could get you out."

"We're going to be all right." She squared her shoulders. "Agent Lake told me we'll get counseling. I wanted to ask you when Aden was distracted: do you know anything about Allan?"

I explained how Garrett had gotten himself captured trying to arrange their release—and that he'd decided to work for Bell to protect Aden.

Jana took a shaky breath. "Oh, Allan. That big idiot."

"He's a brave man. He wanted me to tell you he's going to be all right and he loves Aden very much."

She wiped her eyes. "Am I ever going to see him again? Or you?"

I shook my head. "Probably not. The witness protection program is a one-way ticket."

"To keep Aden safe, I'll do whatever I have to do." She touched my arm. "Thank you, Alice. From the bottom of my heart."

Aden appeared, his eyes scanning the hangar for his mother. "Mom!" He scrambled down the jet's steps and ran to Jana, his eyes wide. "JC said this plane can fly as high as fifty-one thousand feet and go almost the speed of sound!"

Jana ruffled Aden's curly hair. He scowled and ducked away. "Mo-*om!*"

"Aden, say hello to Miss Alice," Jana said. "She's a friend of Miss Natalie and she helped me find you."

"Hi, Miss Alice," Aden said dutifully.

"Hi, Aden," I replied, smiling. "Are you excited about getting to ride on that awesome plane? I've never been on a plane like that."

"Me neither," Sean said, sounding sad. "I bet it's really hard to fly a jet."

"JC says it's not hard," Aden stated. He clearly already idolized the pilot. "I'm going to learn how to fly a plane someday."

Lake checked the time. "I hate to say it, but we're going to have to start prepping for departure," he told me.

I blinked back a few unexpected tears and gave him a hug. "Thank you."

"My pleasure," he said as he released me. He held out his hand toward Sean. "It was good to see you again, Sean."

Sean shook his hand. "You as well, Trent. This means a lot to both of us." He slipped an arm around my waist—not possessively, but because he sensed saying goodbye to Lake hurt my heart.

Aden pulled Jana across the hangar, chattering again about the plane's specs. I waved as they climbed into the jet.

Lake smiled at me. "You look happy, Alice."

"I am." I took a deep breath. "Despite everything, I *am* happy."

"I'm glad. You deserve all the happiness in the world." He touched my arm. "Take care of yourself."

"I will," I promised.

Lake boarded the jet and we got into our SUV. As airport employees rolled the hangar doors open for us, Jack asked, "So what's the plan?"

I rubbed my eyes. "For now, go home and get some sleep. There's a lot of preparation to be done before tonight. It's going to be a busy day."

# CHAPTER 22

We got back to my house just before six. Sean drove past the Vamp Court SUV parked on the street out front and pulled into the drive.

"Bastards," Ben muttered. Apparently I wasn't the only one still pissed about Monroe throwing me under the bus.

I heard three quiet growls from the others in the vehicle and came perilously close to chuckling at the chorus of werewolf displeasure. I coughed to cover my reaction.

"Need a lozenge?" Sean asked dryly, offering me a cough drop from the center console.

I coughed again delicately. "No, I think I'll be okay."

Sean parked in front of my carport and we all got out. "You guys headed home?" I asked Ben and Jack.

Both shook their heads. "We're on guard duty," Ben told me with a grin. "Somebody has to guard Sean while he guards you."

I sighed and headed for my front door. "Up to my ears in werewolves again. I used to lead such a quiet life."

Sean's hand found mine. "Do you miss it?"

I pretended to think about it as we climbed the front steps. "Sometimes, but I think it might be growing on me."

He chuckled and kissed my forehead. I unlocked the door and we went inside.

When the door was shut, Sean turned to Ben. "We need you in top form for tonight. Jack can take watch while you get some sleep in the guest room before the Court and Bell send over their intel."

"What else is on the agenda for today?" Ben asked.

"Alice and I have errands to run this afternoon. Other than that, nothing until tonight."

"Let's rest while we can," I said. "Jack, make yourself at home in the kitchen and anywhere else in the house, but don't touch the basement door. It's warded."

He nodded. "Get some sleep, Alice. I'll keep watch."

Jack headed to the kitchen to make coffee while Malcolm went to the basement to work on spells and the rest of us went upstairs. I showed Ben to the guest room and bathroom, then Sean and I went to my room to change and crawl into bed.

Sean curled up behind me and nestled me against his warm body. Despite my exhaustion, sleep didn't come immediately. Sean was still awake too. We lay quietly for a while, each lost in our own thoughts.

"This is a brave thing you're doing," Sean said, his voice startling me out of my reverie. "There's nothing new about you being brave— I've never known you to be anything else—but I'm not sure I tell you that enough."

"The night I went to Jack's house to get you out of the cuff, Valas told me I was fearless," I said quietly. "I let her think that, but right now I'm anything but fearless. I'm scared."

Not long ago, I couldn't have imagined ever admitting that to any person. Such total honesty left me feeling more vulnerable than I'd felt in recent memory, like I'd just bared my throat to a lion...or a wolf.

He nuzzled my neck and kissed me lightly on the delicate skin over my carotid, in one of those eerie moments that had become more and more frequent where I thought maybe he'd overheard my thoughts. "I know you're afraid. Anyone would be, facing what we're facing. I won't tell you not to be afraid because there's nothing wrong with fear. You use fear to keep your head clear and your senses sharp. It doesn't paralyze you like it does some people. I *will* tell you that you are not going to face him alone. You'll have me, Malcolm, and Ben at your side. You're a part of a team—the *leader* of a team. Our strength is yours." His arm tightened around my middle. "Do you believe me?"

"I do," I said softly.

I was still very apprehensive about having Sean, Ben, and Malcolm with me tonight—*especially* Ben, given he and Casey had just gotten engaged and I wanted them to have a long, happy life together—but it did help to think I wouldn't be going into the battle alone. I'd always imagined if I ever faced Moses, it would be by myself, so the thought I was going into the fight as the leader of a team was nothing short of a complete paradigm shift for me.

Sean's words echoed in my head: *You are not going to face him alone.* I wasn't sure if he meant Bell or Moses, or who was the bigger threat. Moses was more powerful, but Bell was going to stab me in the back as soon as he figured out how to do it and get away with it. He'd given in on releasing the nulls too easily. He had something up his sleeve; I just didn't know what.

Warm, golden comfort wrapped around me like a heated blanket. I sighed. "Thank you."

Sean snuggled me closer, his nose against the back of my neck. He'd told me that was where my scent was strongest, which meant both he and his wolf needed reassurance too.

I laced our fingers together and kissed his knuckles. His hand tightened on mine. "My Alice," he murmured.

Wrapped in a cocoon of warmth and comfort, we slept.

I PRESSED the little buzzer beside the door and stepped back.

"Try to look a little less threatening," I murmured to my entourage as we waited for a response. "He's a man in his eighties. I don't want to give him a heart attack. Can't you dial back the scary?"

"We're werewolves, not poodles," Ben complained. "We can't help but be threatening."

"What if I gave you a floofy haircut?" I muttered.

Jack audibly growled, but the searing feeling of shifter magic decreased. I almost sighed in relief.

Sean, Ben, and Jack were on high alert watching for Bell or his people, though I'd told them I was fairly certain he'd wait until I broke the wards on Moses's building before trying to double-cross me. I'd quickly discovered one edgy werewolf I could deal with, but three of them together created a kind of feedback loop and I was in immediate danger of drowning in shifter testosterone.

Finally, the door buzzed and the lock clicked. I opened the door and stepped inside Benjamin Winchell's antique shop.

"Miss Worth, what a wonderful surprise." Winchell was halfway to the front door, weaving between the tables. He wore a button-up shirt and slacks, his reading glasses tucked into his breast pocket. "And you've brought friends. Welcome. It's a lovely day for antiquing."

I heard a low growl from behind me. Sean glanced back at Jack and the rumbling cut off abruptly.

"Werewolves don't go antiquing," Jack muttered.

"Some werewolves do," Ben argued. "Where do you think Casey and I got that armoire you and Delia admired the other day?"

Winchell and I shook hands. His air magic tingled on my skin. "Have you come back to take advantage of that twenty-percent PI discount?" he asked.

I smiled. "Possibly. I'm actually here looking for an item I saw last time I was in your shop. It was a cuff about three inches wide, made of copper."

He nodded. "I know the cuff you're referring to. Unfortunately, I sold it a few days ago. However, I have another item, very similar, that might fit your needs. It's in my safe. Would you follow me?"

I'd warned them about the number of magical objects in the shop, so the shifters were careful not to touch anything as Winchell led us to the counter at the back. They shied away from tables and shelves as if the items on them might bite. It would have been comical if not for what had happened a month ago. We'd all learned a couple of important lessons from the cuff that had latched itself onto Sean's arm—most importantly that magical objects, even seemingly innocuous ones, could have hidden dangers.

"A moment, please," Winchell said. He disappeared down the short hall toward his office.

Sean looked around the shop. "How many of the items in here are magical?"

"Quite a few," I told him. "I sense low-level magic all over the place. Malcolm told me the safe in the office has heavy-duty wards, which means he's got the good stuff stashed away back there."

Winchell returned carrying two small boxes inscribed with runes that hid the magic trace of the objects inside. He brought them to the counter, opened the lid of one, and pulled back linen wrappings to reveal a lovely armlet spiral cuff made of copper and gold. Unsurprisingly, given its materials, the cuff resonated with earth magic, which was what I was looking for. Ben and Jack took a collective step back, and I was sure Sean wanted to.

"Don't worry, it's safe," I reassured them. They stayed back, still wary.

Winchell's eyes twinkled as they met my gaze. "I think the cuff suits you."

"I think so." I passed my hand over the cuff slowly, exploring its magic. Like the cuff I'd seen in the shop a week ago, it was designed to store energy. And unless I was very much mistaken, it was capable of storing a *lot* of power—far more than I had anticipated, because of its design. The copper spirals would store power, but what interested me the most was the gold torque at the end of the cuff. "I think this might be exactly what I was looking for."

Winchell smiled. "In that case, you'll want the other one as well." He opened the second box and revealed a cuff that was the mirror image of the first.

My heart rate sped up. As the cuffs that had once bound Sean and I together had proven, a pair of cuffs was more than the sum of its parts. More powerful than simply two single cuffs, their combined magic was just the sort of advantage I'd need.

I sensed a spike of alarm from all three werewolves at the sight of the second cuff. "They're earth magic cuffs, and they won't have any effect on shifters," I assured them. I turned to Winchell. "May I try them on?" I asked.

"Of course."

They were designed to be worn on the forearms. I pushed up the sleeves of my shirt to my elbows. Carefully, I took the first cuff from its box and slid it onto my right arm. The metal was warm. Since the cuff was resonant with earth magic and I was an earth mage, putting the cuff on felt like slipping on a comfortable old sweater.

"Move back," I told Sean.

The shifters took a few more steps back. When I picked up the second cuff, the metal in both began to hum.

Winchell met my eyes. "Have care."

"Always," I promised.

I slipped the second cuff onto my left arm. The humming intensified and earth magic buzzed on my skin. "I've used cuffs like this before. The torques may close around my arms," I warned Sean, so he wouldn't be taken by surprise.

"All right." Sean's voice was more than half growl. He was definitely reliving his own nightmarish experience with arm cuffs. I was glad to see Winchell didn't seem alarmed by Sean's golden eyes or growly voice.

I reached for the magic and spoke the word I'd seen inscribed on the inside of the right cuff. "*Potentia.*"

The gold torques closed around my forearms and the coils ignited bright green. I sucked in a deep breath as the energy contained in the cuffs pulsed against my skin. There wasn't much since they'd been on a shelf unused for an indeterminate amount of time, but I could sense their enormous potential for storage. The bright green magic faded, but the cuffs continued to hum slightly.

"I'm fine," I said for Sean's benefit. I raised the cuffs so he could get a closer look at the gold torques, which were now rings fitting snugly on my forearms. "The coils store power and the rings will focus that power."

A muscle moved in Sean's jaw. "How will you remove the cuffs?"

"A lot more easily than the last set we had to deal with." I took three deep breaths and focused on the magic held in the torques. The spellwork fractured and the torques opened.

Sean exhaled. "I like these cuffs a hell of a lot better than the other ones."

"Makes two of us." I looked over the counter at Winchell, who'd settled onto his tall chair to watch as I tried out the cuffs. "So, Mr. Winchell, about that PI discount..."

OUR SECOND STOP of the afternoon was a blue bungalow just a few miles from the Brew a Cup coffeehouse.

Sean parked at the curb and turned to the others. "Jack, keep an eye on things outside. Ben needs to come in with us. We've got our radios and we'll be on channel two."

"Got it," Jack said briskly.

We got out of the SUV and went through a little gate. Jack stayed in the yard as Sean, Ben, and I followed a stone path toward the front steps.

We needed one more person at this meeting: Malcolm. The new wolf tattoo would summon him without making him jump to my bracelet, but I didn't want to just yank him across the city, since he might be in the middle of spellwork back at my house and broken spellwork was volatile and potentially disastrous. The wolf spellwork was designed to be used in an emergency.

Since this was not an emergency, I found Malcolm's blue-green trace in my mind and gave it two gentle tugs. I hadn't gotten much sleep, but we'd eaten a good lunch so the dizziness was minimal.

My bracelet buzzed as we reached the front porch, indicating Malcolm had jumped to me. I sensed witchy wards on the house, which wasn't surprising. They felt low-powered, though, which *was* surprising. I wondered if they were designed to be almost dormant unless triggered, like the wards on my yard.

The door opened before I had a chance to knock, revealing Carly. On her day off, she wore jeans and an oversized button-up shirt with the sleeves rolled up. Her feet were bare.

She smiled at us. "Hello! Come on in, everyone." She gave Sean and I quick hugs as we entered, then waved at Jack and offered her hand to Ben. "It's good to meet you, Ben. I'm Carly Reese."

Ben shook her hand. "It's good to meet you too, Carly. Thank you for helping our Alice get de-hexed."

She closed the door. "Given everything that's happened this week, I can't help but think the hex was meant to bring us together. Lily's selfish act had a bigger, more important purpose—we just didn't realize that at the time. Sometimes plans take time to reveal themselves." She gestured for us to go into the living room. "Please make yourself at home. There's coffee and tea on the table and some scones."

That was the best news I'd heard all day. I touched my bracelet. "*Release.*"

Malcolm appeared next to me. He looked around in awe. "Wow. This house has *awesome* energy. Hi, Carly."

She smiled. "Hi, Malcolm. Welcome."

We went into the living room. Sean handed me a cup of coffee with cream and sugar and a little plate with a scone. He poured himself some coffee, grabbed two scones for himself, and sat next to me on the couch. Ben poured a cup of tea, took two scones, and sat on the loveseat.

As we settled in, I looked around the house. Even if I hadn't known Carly was a witch, I would have been able to guess. Plants filled every windowsill. Herbs hung drying in the kitchen. Everywhere I looked, I saw nooks she could use for reading or crafts. One had a mobile made of feathers from different birds. It looked like a comfortable place for meditation. Crystals of every size, shape, and color were placed carefully to promote energy flow. Malcolm was right: the energy in Carly's house was awesome, like a slight electrical charge that grew stronger toward the back of the house. I imagined that was where her sacred room and altar were.

Her home was cozy and comfortable. It was a very different feeling from my own house, which sizzled with the power of my wards—and not in any kind of welcoming way to anyone but me and maybe Malcolm. Carly's home felt like a warm hug. Mine wasn't designed to be welcoming; it was designed to keep people out. The thought made my heart heavy.

"Take this," Carly said abruptly, handing me a jar of what turned out to be fluffy white dandelion heads.

I blinked up at her. "What's this?"

"Pure magic. Hold it and look at it while we drink our coffee and tea and eat our scones." She settled into an armchair with a cup of tea.

I was impatient to get to the reason we'd come here, but Sean and Ben had settled in with their drinks and scones and Malcolm was frowning at me, so I sipped coffee, ate my scone, and pondered the jar of dandelions, which didn't feel like it had any magic per se, but did seem to be draining the sorrow from my heart. Maybe it *was* pure magic. It felt like a jar of hope, as strange as that sounded.

"Your house is lovely," I told Carly as we finished our scones and Sean refilled my coffee cup and his own. "Such wonderful energy, and it smells like..." I paused and frowned. "I'm not sure what it smells like exactly, but it smells amazing."

"Apple pie," Ben said.

"Old books," Sean said at the same time. They both looked puzzled.

Carly smiled. "It probably smells like a little bit of everything, especially to werewolf noses." She turned to me. "Your energy feels a little different today, Alice. What's hidden under your sleeves?"

I pushed up my sleeves to reveal the cuffs I'd bought from Benjamin Winchell.

"Lovely," she breathed, leaning forward to get a better look. "They'll store energy?"

I nodded. "And the torques will focus it." I showed her how they'd closed around my arms. "I'll cram as much stored energy into these as I can between now and tonight."

"Excellent." She smiled and reached for two large fabric-lined baskets waiting near her chair. "I have gifts for each of you."

As she sorted through small and medium-sized velvet bags to find what she was looking for, three tabby cats sauntered into the living room: a gray striped, an orange, and a black. I wondered what they'd think of the werewolves. Cats generally avoided werewolves, even in human form.

The gray and orange tabbies jumped onto the arms of Carly's chair, one on each side of her, and sat at attention like guardians. The black cat circled the room, giving each of us a good sniff, and then jumped onto the arm of the couch next to Sean, settling in with her paws tucked under, as casual as could be.

"Your familiars?" I guessed.

Carly nodded. "The gray tabby is Basat. The orange is Loki and the cat who's taken a liking to Sean is Heckate. We've been together almost ten years." She held up two bags, each closed with a drawstring. "For Sean and Ben."

Sean got up and took the bags. "Which is which?"

"The green is yours. The blue is for Ben."

Sean handed Ben the blue bag and sat back down next to me. They opened their bags and took out what looked like leather collars with two round amulets dangling from each—one stone, one gold. Sean's had an extra loop that was currently empty.

Ben grinned. "A collar? Uh-oh. My fiancée, Casey, is going to want to take me for walks."

"We could make it a double date and take you both to a dog park," I suggested.

"Somehow I don't think the other dog owners would appreciate that very much," Sean said dryly. "What will these amulets do, Carly?"

"Both are protection amulets." She leaned forward, her arms on her knees. "The stone is protection against fire. The gold one protects against silver."

Ben blinked. "I didn't know that was even possible."

"It's possible, but tricky to do. The spells require a lot of power, so they'll probably only last for about one hour once you invoke them." She sighed. "I wish I could do better."

"Thank you," Sean said firmly. "This is an enormously helpful gift, far more than I'd even hoped for. The collars are spelled too?"

"Yes, so they won't disintegrate or fall off when you shift. Yours has an extra loop for your wolf amulet. I spaced the loops far enough apart that the amulets shouldn't touch or knock against each other."

"What about Malcolm?" I asked. "How are we going to protect him?"

She picked up a tube of henna and waved it. "We're going to put a tattoo on you that will protect him against blood magic and banishments. I'm assuming you'd be fine with that?"

"I'm definitely fine with that." I paused. "But if I'm understanding your magic correctly, in order for that to work, we'll have to inscribe Malcolm's name in the tattoo, right?"

"Yes."

I glanced at Malcolm. "His full name?"

She looked at me and then at where Malcolm floated. "Will that be a problem?"

Malcolm thought about it. "Can Alice write it in later?"

She nodded. "Yes. I can do the spellwork now and then all she'll have to do later is add your full name and invoke it. Will that be all right?"

"That's fine," Malcolm said. He didn't *sound* fine, but we'd talk about it later, in private.

She reached back into one of the bins and withdrew a purple bag.

"You're like the wizard in *The Wizard of Oz* with your bag full of surprises," I said, smiling.

"Wizards are a bit different than you or I." She rose and handed me the purple bag. "I'd advise you to be cautious if one ever offers you a gift. Their gifts tend to be...not what they seem."

"Thanks for the tip." I opened my bag and took out a new amulet of my own. Like the others, mine was round, inscribed with a circle and runes. I studied the runes, frowning. "I don't recognize this spellwork, but I see runes for water and protection. What am I looking at?"

"This is new spellwork, as far as I know," Carly told me. "It took me the longest to make and I just finished it about an hour before you called. I've not been able to test it, obviously, but if I've made it correctly, it should allow you to borrow some of Malcolm's water magic to protect yourself against fire."

Malcolm muttered an expletive. At Carly's questioning look, I explained, "He's been working on spellwork that would let me borrow his water magic for the last week."

"More like the last month, and I've got jack to show for it," the ghost griped. "Let me see that spellwork."

I held up the amulet. He floated to my side and looked it over, frowning. "It's not our magic," he said finally. "Can't tell if it will work just by looking at it. But if it works…Alice, that's big. Down the road, maybe it will help me figure out spellwork using our kind of magic so we don't need an amulet."

I closed my hand around the amulet. "Carly, this is really fantastic. I don't know how to thank you."

"Having you all come back safe and sound will be all the thanks I need." She finished her mug of tea and set the empty cup on the table beside her. "I'll explain how to charge and invoke the amulets before you leave. But first, I have a few more goodies for you."

"Do any of these goodies go boom?" I asked hopefully.

She winked.

"Awesome." Malcolm rubbed his hands together. "Now we're talking."

Carly held up a brown cloth sack containing a baseball-sized amount of something heavy. We stared.

"Is that…a bag of sand?" I asked finally.

"Yes." She brought it over to me and deposited it in my lap. "And it's also what I hope will break the building's wards."

Okay, I was willing to accept that a doll stuffed with hair and dirt could spell me into sabotaging my own relationship, and Carly could see glimpses of the future when she touched people, but spelled *sand?*

"To see a world in a grain of sand and a heaven in a wild flower, hold infinity in the palm of your hand, and eternity in an hour," she quoted, reseating herself in the chair. At my quizzical look, she smiled. "William Blake. Don't underestimate sand, Alice. It's one of nature's most powerful forces. You know the magic that broke your amulets in half?"

I nodded.

"Imagine that, but in each grain of sand in that bag."

I lifted the bag and studied it with new respect. "Tiny but mighty."

She smiled. "Exactly. And just like a team, much mightier

together than separately. Now," she added briskly, "How about we go over the rest of the goodies?"

I set the bag of sand carefully on the floor at my feet. "Sounds like a plan."

TWO HOURS LATER, I stood in my basement in my bra and jeans, with my arms crossed, a tube of henna in my hand. Upstairs, Sean, Ben, and Jack were mulling over the intel we'd received from the Vamp Court and Bell's people about Moses's meeting tonight.

Malcolm floated back and forth in my spellwork area, the ghost equivalent of pacing.

"You have my word that I'll never tell anyone your full name or misuse this information in any way," I told him. "You believe me, right?"

"Yes." He stopped floating. "What's weird is that I never told you my full name and you've never asked. I don't know why but I'm worried about telling anyone, even you."

"A full name has power, especially for a ghost." I leaned against the work table. "Someone with your full name could summon you or even try to break our binding, so you're absolutely right not to share that information with anyone. I always figured you'd tell me when you wanted to, and until then, I was fine just calling you Malcolm. In order to protect you using this spell Carly made for us, however, I need your full name. I want you to be safe and this is the only way, other than leaving you behind, that I know to keep you safe."

"You're sure as hell not leaving me behind, so full name it is." He floated over to me. "Trade you—your real name for mine."

I smiled. "I'm getting there, Malcolm. I'm just not quite there yet."

"Do you think I'll tell anyone your real name?"

I shook my head.

"Do you think I'll misuse that information in any way?"

I laughed. "I see what you're doing."

"You believe me when I say I won't tell anyone—living, dead, or undead?"

My smile faded. "I do believe you."

"But you aren't going to tell me." He frowned. "Is this the monster thing again?"

When I didn't respond, he sighed. "Okay, you're still working on that. Or maybe it's because your real name is something like Eunice. Or Daisy."

I rolled my eyes. "You caught me. I'm really Daisy."

"You are definitely *not* a Daisy. Fine, here goes." He squared his shoulders. "Malcolm Earl. It was my grandfather's name," he added.

"Malcolm Earl what?"

A long silence. He was really struggling to say the words.

"Selene," I said softly.

He stared at me.

"My middle name was Selene." My heart lightened just a little saying it out loud. It had been a very, very long time since those syllables had been on my tongue.

"That's...wow. Alice, thank you." He straightened. "Malcolm Earl Flynn."

"Hey, Malcolm Earl Flynn." I smiled and took the cap off the tube of henna.

Years of practice had given me the ability to write upside-down, backward, or sideways with either hand. I wrote Malcolm's full name into the middle of the spellwork Carly had drawn on my abdomen. I sensed the spell closing with the addition of this last remaining element and warm magic coiled around both of us as the protection spell activated.

I finished writing and capped the tube, then used air magic to dry the henna quickly. "Thank you, Malcolm."

"Thank you, Something Selene." His tone was joking, but his expression was serious. "We're going to get this done, Alice."

"Then we'd better get upstairs and find out what they know about the target location." I put my shirt on and headed up the basement stairs. "Then I'll need to siphon power from a ley line to charge these cuffs."

When I opened the basement door, I found Sean, Jack, and Ben in the kitchen, looking at a bunch of photos and reports spread out on the counter.

"What's all that?" I asked, coming into the kitchen.

Sean moved aside so I could look at the documents and pictures. "The Vamp Court just sent over a courier. They don't consider e-mail a secure form of communication for something like this, so we've got hard copies."

"So where is the meet taking place?" I asked, picking up an aerial image of what looked like a large Victorian-style home with a glass conservatory on the back. I frowned. "A residence? That's unexpected."

"It's even more unexpected than that." Ben grinned. "It's a bordello."

I blinked. "A *bordello* bordello?"

"A very *haunted* bordello bordello."

Malcolm perked up. "Haunted?"

"Super haunted," Ben confirmed, holding up a very official-looking report with the SPEMA seal at the top. "The feds catalogued more than three dozen spirits on the premises, though their team estimated there might be twice that. And you want to know what's even weirder? They can't get any of the spirits to leave."

"There must be a nexus of power nearby." I stared at the aerial photo, puzzled. "So why would Moses Murphy choose a ghost resort for this meeting tonight?"

"He owns it." Sean tapped another of the reports. "The property was purchased about six months ago by a company the Court linked to Murphy. Apparently someone planned to do renovations and turn it into a destination resort for the adventurous, but the spirits interfered so much that all the contractors said no thanks and returned the deposits they'd been paid. It's been sitting untouched since."

I picked up another aerial photo, this one taken from farther up so it showed the surrounding acreage. The bordello was a good quarter-mile from the road and there were only a few trees near the house, making it difficult for anyone to sneak up without being spotted. The sweeping lawns were immaculate, though, and the exterior of the house looked well-maintained.

"The house was built in 1886," Ben informed us, reading from the SPEMA report. "It was a well-known brothel for decades, operating under different names, but always catering to what you might call a better class of customers than your average den of iniquity. One of the reasons it stayed open in plain sight for so long was that many of its most loyal customers were local politicians and the madams made sure there wasn't any trouble that attracted negative attention. It was renovated several times, obviously, but when the ghosts started causing trouble, the customers stopped coming." He coughed. "So to speak."

"So it's been more or less empty ever since," Sean added. "Bought and sold a half-dozen times until Murphy bought the property, thinking he could maybe turn a profit and instead ended up with a haunted mansion no one wants to go near."

"Between that and the lack of cover in the yard, it's an ideal location to meet a magical weapons dealer." I tapped my lip with my fingertip. "If Murphy is willing to go there himself, it's warded just like any major cabal property would be. The wards will be powerful, but not deeply embedded if he's only had the property for six months."

"How does that help us?" Sean asked. "I don't know as much about wards as you and Malcolm."

"The wards on Murphy's compound in Baltimore aren't just powerful: their foundation spells have been rooted into the building and grounds for forty years," I explained. "That's what makes them damn near impossible to break—that and the landmines. Imagine a fortress that's been continuously fortified for four decades with countless layers of protection that have roots that go deep into the earth."

"So the wards on the bordello are powerful, but they don't have all that fortification or the deep roots," Jack rumbled. "Is that why you think you can break them?"

"One of the reasons. As I said, though, they'll still be extremely powerful and chock full of landmines."

"Which are what, exactly?" Ben asked.

"Landmines are hidden spellwork designed to take out anyone who tries to break or unweave wards," Malcolm told him. "They're just about the most dangerous hazards mages face when we interact with someone else's magic because ninety-nine percent of the time, you can't sense or detect them until it's too late."

The werewolves were silent. "So what's the plan?" Ben asked finally.

"Well, that's where the sand Carly gave me comes into play, as well as a couple of other mage tricks I have up my sleeve," I said. "But given what we know about this former Best Little Whorehouse in California, I think our strongest asset isn't going to be anything magical at all."

"So what's our strongest asset?" Malcolm asked.

I grinned. "You."

# CHAPTER 23

 was scheduled for eleven thirty, so our strike team convened at Northbourne at sunset to plan our attack on the bordello.

We met in one of the Vampire Court's opulent second-floor meeting rooms. I sat on one side of the U-shaped table between Sean and Ben. We sat across from Bell's key personnel: Nora, a fire mage who'd introduced himself as Tomás Ortiz, and—to my surprise— Allan Garrett. As I'd expected, Bell was not coming himself. He didn't strike me as the sort who liked to get his hands dirty. Just as well, I supposed—one less person to have to worry about trying to stab me in the back.

On the third side of the table, facing the large wall screens, were Arkady, Matthias, and Amira of the Court. Amira was Niara's sister. While Niara preferred long, flowing dresses and intricate hairstyles, Amira wore her hair in a halo of natural curls and typically dressed for fighting unless the Court was convened. Amira was the maker and master of the Court's Hunters—dhampirs, or half-vampires, with especially acute senses of smell, sight, and hearing. As they tended to be ultra-violent if not tightly controlled, Hunters were excellent, if not brutal fighters, and were inclined to leave victims torn limb from limb if given the chance.

Arkady and I had exchanged quick hellos when we arrived, but there had been no time for us to talk before the meeting began.

Court mages would get us onto the property undetected, but Bell had agreed to provide the manpower necessary for us to get past the guards and into the house. Instead of sending people who worked for him, however, he'd opted to go a different route.

"Mercenaries." Sean's voice was a low growl.

The four men standing in front of us wore all black and identical blank expressions. They'd studied each of us in turn as we came in, no doubt cataloguing us according to some ranking system. I saw no reaction whatsoever to any of us. If they were unhappy about working with civilians, I couldn't see it.

"Listen up," the man in the center barked when we were seated. "I am Sergeant Haggar." He gestured to the men to his left. "These men are Cody, Guy, and Belger."

Sean snorted softly. I looked at him quizzically. He bent his head close to mine. "Their names are from an arcade game from the eighties," he murmured into my ear. "A beat-em-up game called Final Fight."

I studied the men. "Killers for hire."

He nodded. "Surprised they're willing to operate on American soil. Usually they stay overseas. Tougher to prosecute."

The man who called himself Haggar activated the large screen in front of us, which showed the aerial view of the bordello. "My team's assignment is twofold: to facilitate entry into the target location and to provide extraction once you've fulfilled your objective. First, we will eliminate the exterior perimeter guards. Our intelligence indicates there will be four to six outside the house. Once the guards are down, Ms. Worth will break the house wards. Our Alpha team will then breach the main doors. Our Beta team will do the same for the secondary entrance here." He indicated the rear of the house, near the conservatory. "At that point, my team will withdraw to a rally point. When you've fulfilled your objective, we will facilitate your departure from the scene and return you to this location."

His gaze swept our faces. "To be clear, my team will not engage mages or enter the target location for any reason."

Nora spoke up. "We have three primary targets tonight: Moses Murphy, Carter Kade, and Stephen Novak."

"Who are Kade and Novak?" Arkady asked.

"Murphy's most senior lieutenants, now that his daughter Catherine is no longer acting in that role," Nora replied. She clicked a few buttons on a second remote and the image of the house disappeared, replaced with pictures of two men: one blond and in his late thirties, the other a dark-haired man about my age. "Our intelligence indicates both will be on the premises tonight. While Kade has no magic, Novak is a high-level earth mage."

I knew Kade very well, but it took me a minute to remember Stephen Novak. Five years ago, when I escaped the cabal, Stephen was a mage like me, working for Moses against his will after being sold to him by a smaller syndicate. We hadn't been friends—mages who belonged to cabals didn't have the luxury of friends—but I might have described us as kindred spirits. He'd seen the inside of a blood mage's torture room a number of times. It would appear he'd stopped fighting Moses and gotten promoted. He wasn't the first to do so. The only alternative was usually death, and a highly unpleasant one at that, as Malcolm could attest.

"Novak must be there to authenticate the weapon," I said. "No other reason I can think of for Murphy to bring an earth mage to something like this."

Nora nodded. "We came to the same conclusion."

She switched the screen to a photo of Moses. It was one I hadn't seen before, taken on a downtown Baltimore street on a cold day. He wore a long black coat over his trademark tailored suit. His attention was on the man next to him, who I recognized as Darren Walker. Walker was one of Moses's inner circle and was said to be running the syndicate's new business interests here in the city. I'd seen him with Catherine, having cocktails at Charles's bar, 1792, a month ago.

Nora spoke again. "As you are all already aware, Murphy's primary weapon is high-level fire magic, with which he is particularly adept. He's also a mid-level blood mage. The threat he poses cannot be overstated. Tomás, your primary duty will be containing him and providing defense against his magic."

Ortiz nodded. "Understood."

Nora regarded me with a thoughtful expression. "Sergeant, what is our backup plan in case Ms. Worth fails to break the wards?"

"I've never encountered any wards that I couldn't take down with enough firepower," Haggar told her. The other mercs nodded in agreement. "However, if we're forced to resort to mundane weapons, it will take time to get through and we'll lose the element of surprise. Our likelihood of success decreases dramatically and the odds of losing personnel go up. Given what we know and what we can surmise about the house and the people in it, I'm anticipating a successful mission with zero casualties on our side...*if* those wards get taken down as planned." His eyes went to me. "Your role is not a small one, Ms. Worth."

I met his hard stare with one of my own. "You do your job and I'll do mine."

He studied me, then gave me a small nod. "Fair enough."

Nora checked her watch. "We have one hour before we head for the target location. Let's go over the layout of the house and discuss strategy."

THE VAMPS and Bell's mercs staged equipment and personnel in one of Northbourne's garages. As they loaded the SUVs, we stood in small groups, talking.

When Garrett went to get a bottle of water from a small fridge, I joined him. "I'm surprised to see you here," I told him, getting three waters from the fridge.

"Bell wants me to prove myself." His voice was flat. "I have to blast some shit or I don't come back. Nora and Tomás have orders to kill me if I don't do my part or I so much as look at either of them the wrong way." He lowered his voice. "Have you seen Aden and Jana?"

I nodded. "Nora delivered them to me not long after you and I spoke last. I called in a favor and got them out of the city. They're out of Bell's hands for good."

A long silence. "Thank you, Ms. Worth," he said finally.

"What are you two doing back here?"

We turned at the sound of Nora's voice. She stood in front of us, her arms crossed and eyebrows raised.

"We're starting a book club." I waved the bottles of water I'd gotten for Sean, Ben, and myself. "What does it look like we're doing?"

"Go stand by our SUV," she ordered Garrett.

Without a word, he stepped around her and headed for one of the vehicles.

Nora turned to me, her eyes hard. "He's Bell's property now. Unless you want him dead, tell him to follow orders and not get any ideas of his own."

"No person is someone else's property. And sooner or later, people who think they can own people find out they're wrong."

Her mouth quirked. "Strange how someone like you can be so naive. It's kind of precious, really. My mama would say bless your heart."

"My mama would say snakes can't help but hiss."

Her eyes narrowed. "Tread lightly, Alice."

I smiled. "I'm not afraid of you or your boss. Surely that's obvious by now."

"Don't rely too much on your friends to protect you. Some of those alliances are looking precarious these days." She was obviously referring to Valas's apparent willingness to sell my contract.

I'd been giving that some thought in the past day and the more I thought about it, the more I was convinced Valas was playing a deeper game than any of us had realized. Valas had been outmaneuvering people like Bell for more than a millennium.

Since telling Nora that would not be in my best interest, however, I merely shrugged. "Go ahead and think you've got the upper hand or some kind of advantage over me if it makes you feel better. Right now, I'm focused on the job we're here to do. When the dust settles, we'll figure out where things stand—and who really belongs to who."

Nora smirked. "I'm looking forward to it."

It looked like they were about finished loading things into the SUVs, so I took the bottles of water to the others, who were standing beside the SUV we would be riding in.

Sean opened his water and leaned against side of the SUV. "What was all that about?"

"The usual threats." I shrugged. "I don't think Nora likes me."

"Just because you cut off her hand? Is she still holding a grudge about that?" he teased.

Ben snorted. "Women in the workplace never get along." He winked at me.

I smiled sweetly. "Ben, did I tell you I've been working on my right cross lately?"

"She has," Sean said, shaking his hand with an exaggerated grimace. "Her punches used to feel like a butterfly landing on my palm, but now at least it's like the butterfly got a running start first."

I rolled my eyes. "Whatever."

Sean lowered his voice. "Any word from Malcolm?"

I shook my head. "Nothing yet. I'm hoping no news is good news."

"Load up, people," Haggar called. "We're moving out in three minutes."

Belger, one of Haggar's mercs, drove our SUV. Ben got into the front passenger seat and Sean and I sat in the middle row. The back was full of unmarked black cases. I could only imagine what they held.

As our caravan of vehicles drove out of the garage and made its way toward Northbourne's imposing front gate, Sean's hand found mine on the seat and squeezed. I squeezed back and kept my breathing slow and even and my shoulders relaxed.

The night I fled Baltimore, I'd wondered if I would ever come face-to-face with Moses again. At the time I'd hoped not, but as the years went by I'd come to understand that to be free of him, I would have to kill him. I'd certainly never imagined I would be on my way to face him in the company of mercenaries, Vampire Court enforcers, two werewolves, and a ghost.

Unbidden, an odd memory from my life in Baltimore surfaced. When I was in my teens, some local papers had taken to calling me a "cabal princess"—a riff on "Mafia princess." I'd hated that nickname. Princesses were the stuff of fairy tales and my life was anything but a fairy tale, unless it was one of the really dark ones. Even at their most gloomy, the Brothers Grimm couldn't have thought up someone as twisted and terrible as Moses.

Northbourne's gate swung open and we drove through, headed farther into the countryside, bound for a heavily warded, ghost-filled former brothel. In my wildest dreams, I couldn't have imagined this scenario.

*I'll show you princess*, I thought grimly. *In this story, the princess slays the evil king.* It wasn't exactly a happily ever after, but it would be close enough for me.

Our destination was an abandoned farm about three-quarters of a mile due east from the brothel. The SUVs drove through an open gate, across an overgrown field, and parked inside a sagging old barn.

We prepped our equipment quickly for the trek to the brothel. Since I was one of the few people in the group who wasn't supernaturally fast or had elite training, Sean wore my backpack containing the sand Carly had given me plus a few assorted blood magic implements I thought I might need but wouldn't fit in my jacket. The mercs each carried a large backpack and wore full tactical gear from head to toe, all black.

Nora and Tomás had guns, but Garrett was empty-handed except for a scary-looking tactical knife he handled like he knew how to use it. Arkady and Matthias, of course, were armed to the teeth; Arkady had at least three guns on her I could see, and Matthias carried two handguns in addition to the rifle on his back.

No one else carried weapons—Amira and her Hunters, both male dhampirs, didn't need them, and the mage sent by the Court, who would provide cover for the mercs to approach the brothel, wouldn't participate in the fight.

When everyone was ready, Haggar led us out of the barn and across the field to the trees. We covered the distance between the farm and the brothel at a pace that left me winded even though all I carried was my trusty Smith & Wesson and two extra clips, plus a few magical goodies I had stashed in the various zippered pockets of my jacket.

With their supernaturally enhanced eyesight, the werewolves and vamps had an obvious advantage when it came to running at night, but the rest of us had to make do either with night vision goggles or moonlight. Since the moon was only a few days from being full and the night was clear, I opted on the latter. Focusing on staying on my feet as we ran through the woods kept me from thinking too much about what we were about to face.

When we got within sight of the edge of the trees, Haggar halted our group. He motioned for Nora, Amira, and me to join him.

"Our intel is that Murphy has not yet arrived," he said in an undertone. My watch indicated it was eleven fifteen. I was surprised—I'd figured Moses would have arrived at least an hour ahead of the scheduled meeting to double-check the security of the house.

Haggar's next words, however, gave me a chill. "Two vehicles are at the location. We've confirmed that Kade and Novak are in the target building, along with a half-dozen guards."

My palms started to sweat. Kade was here, in the house whose roof I could just see over the top of the hill in front of me. If there was anyone in the world I wanted dead almost as much as Moses, it was him.

I felt a familiar buzzing sensation from the bracelet on my wrist. I excused myself and went back to Sean and Ben.

"Murphy's not here yet, so we wait," I told them. "Malcolm just jumped to me." I touched the green crystal on my bracelet and murmured, "*Release.*"

Malcolm appeared beside me. "Hey, guys," he said softly. "We're a go."

I exhaled. "That is very good news. Any trouble getting in and out?"

"None whatsoever," he said. "You were right—there are so many freakin' ghosts in there that the wards aren't tuned to detect them. If they were, the damn things would be going off constantly." He looked grim. "Half the spirits in the house are poltergeists and wraiths. It's a horror show. If I thought listening to Ashley Brown shriek was bad, it was nothing compared to a dozen wraiths screaming bloody murder. What the wraiths are going to do, I don't know, but the others are on board. It didn't take much convincing—they all hate Murphy already for trying to make changes to the house, but they can't do much to him physically because he's a blood mage and he's discorporated any ghosts who get too close to him.

Other than messing with his contractors, they didn't have a way to get back at him—until now."

"Excellent." I rubbed my hands together. "I love it when a plan comes together."

Sean tilted his head, frowning. At the same time, Haggar's voice came over our earpieces. "Down!"

We hit the ground and lay flat. At first I didn't know what had spooked Haggar and Sean, but then I heard the telltale sound of helicopter blades. Moses was arriving by helo.

"Didn't call that one, did they?" Ben muttered beside me.

We lay still as the helicopter flew low overhead, its light sweeping over the trees before moving across the empty field toward the brothel. The helicopter slowed, circled, and then landed on top of the hill between us and the house.

Haggar and his team were conferring, but I couldn't tell what they said. They were on a different channel from the rest of us. I wondered if they were debating whether to try and take Moses out now before he got into the house.

I couldn't see who got out of the helicopter from this angle, but the helo's rotors slowed as the pilot shut down the blades. It looked like Moses planned to stay a while in the house.

My heart raced and my breathing grew shallow. The man who had tortured and imprisoned me for twenty years stood a few hundred yards away. I fought to keep my magic in check and not let it spark on my hands or shake the earth beneath me.

Sean wrapped warmth and comfort around me—and resisted when I tried to push it back. He'd never done that before.

He reached out and touched my hand. "You are not alone," he told me, his eyes glowing softly.

I breathed deeply. "Thanks," I murmured.

Haggar's voice spoke in my earpiece. "Murphy went inside the house," he reported. "Hold in place until we have confirmation the dealer has arrived."

The minutes crawled by as we waited. Finally, just as my watch read eleven thirty, Haggar spoke again. "Two vehicles are arriving. We have eyes on the dealer and his bodyguards. They are approaching the house." A long pause. "They're inside."

"Ten minutes," Nora said in my ear, her voice startling me. "Give them time to get settled in, and then we'll move."

"Copy that," Haggar said.

Another interminable wait. As Sean and Ben invoked their protection amulets, my mind conjured up disastrous possibilities. What if my plan for breaking the wards failed? What if I broke the wards, but I couldn't protect Sean and Ben? What if Nora and Tomás couldn't contain Moses's fire? What if Moses got away? The more I tried to stop imagining worst-case scenarios, the more I came up with.

Finally, Haggar directed us to get up and move closer to the edge of the trees. I took the backpack from Sean as we grouped up.

"We'll take the perimeter guards out first," Haggar reminded us in undertone. "As soon as they're down, Ms. Worth will break the wards. At her signal, we'll clear your way to the primary and secondary entrances and retreat to the rally point I indicated on the way in." He looked at me. "If you signal that you can't break the wards, we'll go to Plan B."

"Got it," I said.

The Court mage, whose name I didn't know, tied a spell crystal on a leather cord around the wrists of the four mercs. "This will last for a half-hour unless you take it off," she told them. "Don't come into contact with the house wards while wearing those or everyone will know where you are because the wards will nuke you."

They nodded.

The mage touched the crystal on Guy's wrist. "*Abscondo.*"

Air magic flared and he vanished.

She invoked the obfuscation spells on Cody and Belger, and then finally Haggar. I heard and saw nothing, but I assumed they were on their way unseen across the field toward the house to take out the perimeter guards.

I crouched down with Sean at my side. Malcolm was behind us, his chilly presence a comfort near my shoulder. As we waited for the snipers to tell us the exterior guards were down, I breathed deeply in through my nose and out through my mouth, clearing my mind and preparing for the task at hand. It was far more difficult than I thought it would be to put aside my feelings and memories. My grandfather's voice seemed to drift on the wind. I shivered.

Sean opened the backpack and placed the bag of sand on the ground next to me. My heart thudded in my ears.

A quiet voice spoke in my ear. "Guard one is down."

"Copy that," Haggar said in my earpiece, also quietly.

Another voice on the comm. "Guard two is down."

"Copy," Haggar said.

A long silence, then a third voice. "Guard three is down."

A moment later: "Guards four and five are down. No other guards in sight."

"Copy," Haggar said. "Go for ward break."

I touched my earpiece. "Copy that. Thirty seconds to countdown."

"Thirty seconds," Haggar confirmed. "Standing by."

I closed my eyes. It wasn't necessary for me to do so, but I felt safe under Sean's watchful gaze and I always perceived wards best when my other senses didn't interfere.

The house's wards seared my senses. I lowered my shields and suddenly their power was everywhere, sizzling on my skin and even in my blood. These wards were powerful—dozens of layers, deadly and merciless.

I took a deep breath and plunged headlong into the wards like a diver headed for the ocean floor. The analogy wasn't as far off as it might seem. Pressure built in my head, growing steadily worse as I sifted through the many strands of spellwork, searching for a familiar thread buried deep in the roots of the wards. A few times I sensed myself nearly bumping against a landmine or cascade as I searched for the familiar trace of my grandfather's magic. It was tempting to move as fast as I could through the wards, but I forced myself to go slow. One false move and I might not just give away our arrival—I might kill myself outright.

Finally, I found what I was looking for: Moses's magic, woven in the wards. Hidden from view of the others by Sean, I took a small ritual knife from my pack, pulled up my shirt, and cut three runes quickly into the flesh of my abdomen, away from my tattoos. My blood magic surged.

I cleaned the knife on my pants and handed it to Sean. I picked up the bag of spelled sand. "A world in a grain of sand," I murmured.

I glanced up into Sean's golden gaze. Like Ben, he wore his spelled collar, with its protection amulets. His wolf amulet hung in the middle, a reminder that his life was in immediate danger and I would have to save it.

In her vision, Carly had seen trees and broken earth and a gray man made of fire. We were surrounded by trees and somewhere inside that house was a gray man who bent fire to his will. All that was missing was broken earth. I felt another surge of fear, but this time it was for Sean.

He leaned forward and touched his forehead to mine. Around us, the forest was still and silent. "Take it down, Miss Magic," he said softly.

My eyes on his, I touched my earpiece. "Fifteen seconds."

"Copy that," Haggar said briskly. "Fifteen second countdown begins...*now*."

"Go now," I told Malcolm. "Count it down. Ten seconds."

Malcolm vanished.

I rose slowly, the bag in my hand, my pounding heart marking the seconds as I spooled air magic. I poured the sand from the bag and caught it with my air magic, forming a small, softly glowing sandstorm in midair. The sand was warm and smelled like parchment.

I reached for the magic in the sand and invoked Carly's spell. "*Disintegrate.*"

The magic in the sand began to pulse. With my air magic, I sent the sandstorm swirling through the air, over the hill, and across the lawn as I mentally counted down to zero.

On zero, the spelled sand hit the house at the same moment every ghost in the house—or at least every ghost Malcolm had been able to rally to the cause—attacked the wards *en masse*.

The wards flared like sunbursts going off in my head. The landmines detonated as the ghosts attacked, but the hidden spellwork and curses had no effect on the ghosts. Their attack—and Carly's spelled sand—cleared the way for me.

I reached for the blood magic spell I'd cut into my belly, grabbed the thread of Moses's magic in the house wards, and invoked the spell. "*Incisura*," I breathed.

The spellwork ignited and unfurled with a snap like a flag caught in a sudden gust of wind. The blood magic spell sliced through the wards, and where it couldn't cut them, it left them tattered and shredded.

The sensation of the wards tearing apart turned my world white and then silent as the sheer power of it overwhelmed my senses. I thought my head might be in danger of exploding as the wave of pressure and pain surged. My legs went out from under me, but I was only marginally aware of being caught and lowered carefully to the ground.

Through the haze, I heard distant muffled explosions—probably the mercs going through the doors and setting off flash-bangs.

Slowly, the pain and pressure in my head faded. I opened my eyes and found myself in Sean's arms, sitting in the dirt. Ben was crouched beside us, his eyes golden. My ears rang from the pain of breaking the wards. Malcolm floated beside Sean.

"You did it," Sean said, kissing the top of my head.

My eyes went to Arkady, standing just behind him. "Tell the Court that I held up my part of the bargain," I told her. My words sounded a little slurred. "Tell them to release the rest of the nulls."

"I already did," she told me. "The second the wards went down."

"We need to move." I used the tree to get to my feet. I wrapped my hand around my protection amulet, hanging around my neck with the wolf amulet. "*Triton.*" I felt a surge of water magic through my connection to Malcolm.

"Yes!" the ghost crowed. "She did it! Alice, can you feel the water around us?"

I smiled. "Yes, I can. It feels amazing." More importantly, it felt as though I could *use* the water—not as well or as powerfully as I could use air or earth, but the ability was there. "Carly, you're a miracle worker," I said under my breath.

Sean turned to Ben. "You ready?"

The younger werewolf grinned. "Born ready." He winked at me. "See you later, gator."

I swallowed hard, my throat suddenly dry. "After a while, crocodile."

He dropped to his knees. Golden magic surged, pushing me back a half-step as he shifted. Ben's wolf was gorgeous: tawny brown with dark ears and tail, with a chest that was almost white. The collar fit perfectly on his neck. The wolf walked to Sean's right side and waited.

Haggar's voice came over our earpieces. "Guards are down and all vehicles out front are disabled. Delta team, you are clear."

Nora's response was immediate. "Delta team coming in."

"Copy," Haggar said. "All primary targets are still inside the building." A pause. "Correction: two primary targets are inside. Target Three is coming out the front and he's got company. My men are moving out. It's your show now."

Target Three was Stephen Novak, the earth mage turned lieutenant. I wondered who was with him. Kade would stay with Moses, so it had to be someone we weren't aware was in the house. I supposed we'd find out soon enough.

Arkady and Matthias had their guns out. Arkady winked at me and chambered a round as she pulled down her balaclava. "Let's go."

We ran across the field toward the house. Haggar jogged past us, headed for the woods with all of his men in his wake. He gave me a nod as he passed. The mercs disappeared into the forest.

There were a half-dozen black-clad bodies in the grass near the back door: the perimeter guards, all taken down in less than two minutes by Haggar and his team.

My attention went to the two men walking out the back door of the house.

"That's Novak on the left," Sean said in my ear. "Who's the one on the right?"

I got a good look at the other man and my blood turned to ice. I couldn't remember his name, but I knew what he was. I raised my voice so the others could hear. "The one on the right is a fire mage."

Ortiz rubbed his hands together in anticipation. "Excellent."

I felt an odd tingle on the back of my neck. A moment later, four large wolves ran around the corner of the house, heading straight for us at full speed.

Ben's ears went back and he snarled. Beside me, Sean tensed. "Shifters." He looked at me, his eyes golden.

"Go," I said, my throat tight with sudden worry. "We've got this. Be careful. They may be wearing collars with silver spikes." Both he and Ben wore their amulets that were supposed to protect against silver, but we'd had no way to test them. I wasn't prepared to take anything on faith, not when their lives were at stake.

He kissed me hard and looked at my left shoulder. He couldn't see Malcolm, but he could usually sense the ghost when he was close. "Keep her safe."

"You got it," Malcolm said.

Sean went to his knees beside me, his joints popping as he shifted in a powerful surge of golden shifter magic. His wolf was enormous, almost a third bigger than Ben's. The wolf nuzzled my hand for a moment and then both of them took off across the lawn to intercept the incoming wolves.

As much as I wanted to watch to make sure Sean would be all right, I couldn't lose focus on the mages approaching us. I had to trust that he and Ben would hold their own, even against four opponents.

As the wolves tore into each other, I turned on Nora. "An unexpected fire mage and now shifters. Where did you people get your intel on who was in the house, the walls of a public bathroom?"

She glared at me. "You and Malcolm take Novak. Tomás and I will deal with the fire mage. Garrett, watch for an opportunity to null one or both of the mages if you get the chance. You two," she added, addressing Arkady and Matthias. "Stay clear of the mages. Watch for more guards and let us focus."

Arkady and Matthias moved back and took up positions where they could watch for any guards who might try to flank us.

I risked a glance to my right to check on Sean and Ben. To my surprise and relief, two of the other wolves were already down. Sean was circling a black wolf as large as himself—presumably the alpha—while Ben fought a gray wolf. Ben was bloodied, but the gray wolf was limping, one of his hind legs shredded.

The fire mage's hands and arms ignited. Ortiz reacted instantly, sending an impressive arc of fire toward both mages. The fire mage and Novak dodged the blast, diving in opposite directions, and the fire mage sent a fireball directly at Ortiz.

Ortiz caught the fireball and spun it into his own. I was impressed with his skill, though I wasn't surprised Bell had someone that talented working for him. Ortiz sent the huge fireball back at the fire mage.

Out of the corner of my eye I caught movement in one of the windows of the house: a flash of gray and a familiar face: Moses, a hundred feet away, looking right out at us.

*I see trees and broken earth and a gray man made of fire.*

"Alice," Malcolm said in my ear, jolting me out of my paralysis. "What's the plan?"

I tore my gaze away from my grandfather and studied Novak as he crossed the yard toward us, green magic coiled around his hands and arms. "He'll have protective spells but maybe you can get through them. I'll distract him. See if you can take his head off."

"Copy that." Malcolm went invisible and zipped away.

To my left, Ortiz and Nora were trading fireballs and blasts of air with the fire mage.

Novak was now within earshot, so I called out to him. "I'm here for your boss, not you," I said, spooling earth and air magic around my hands as he approached.

"If you've come for my boss, you've come for me." Novak's voice was toneless, his eyes hard. He wasn't the man I remembered from my days in the cabal—not even close. He'd gone over to the Dark Side. "You work for Darius Bell. You know how this works."

I shook my head. "I don't work for Bell. We happen to share a common goal at the moment: eliminating Murphy."

He tilted his head. "So this is personal for you. I can respect that more than if you were just here doing Bell's bidding." The magic coiled around his arms surged. "This was still a huge mistake and you're going to die, but at least you'll die knowing you tried, so I guess that's worth something."

From my right, I heard a short whine and a yelp that cut off abruptly. I glanced and saw Sean's wolf standing over the motionless body of the other alpha. Sean's coat and muzzle were bloody, but he looked relatively unscathed. Ben was already halfway to me, trotting across the yard with only a slight limp. I exhaled.

Novak smiled. "Your wolf goes first, though."

He raised his arms. The earth around Sean and the dead alpha surged up as if the ground were an ocean wave, swallowing them both in less than a second.

I struck out with my own power, attempting to break Novak's magic, but Sean had vanished, buried under a literal ton of dirt.

*Trees and broken earth...trees and broken earth...*

"Malcolm, kill Novak!" I shouted and ran for the mountain of overturned earth.

Earth magic surged. The ground beneath my boots heaved me up and tried to bury me as well. I fought back, pushing Novak's earth magic away and sending dirt flying in every direction. Our magic collided and a tornado of dirt swirled around me.

The earth shook and rumbled as the ground pulled Sean even deeper and farther away from me, and from oxygen. I fought to get to where he'd gone under, but dirt filled my nose and mouth and I couldn't see. I couldn't tell if I was still above ground or if I'd been pulled under too. I clawed my way through the wall of dirt, choking as it clogged my nose and mouth.

Suddenly, the rumbling stopped and I felt a powerful burst of magic from somewhere behind me. The storm of dirt fell away, leaving me buried up to my knees in the earth. I coughed and tried to clear the dirt from my eyes so I could see.

Novak lay crumpled on the ground, looking dazed. Garrett stood over him, earth magic crackling on his clenched fists. Malcolm floated behind him, clearly concerned that Garrett might null him too if he got too close.

Nearby, Nora dodged another fireball. "Kill him," she shouted.

Novak reached for something at the small of his back and I saw a flash of metal. A gun.

Without hesitation, Garrett punched Novak in the side of the head, his fist wrapped in bright green earth magic that flared when it made contact. Novak went down, his skull caved in.

Apparently, Garrett preferred to use his earth magic as a gauntlet. I supposed it made sense; my whip was an elegant, precise weapon and Garrett was more of a brawler. He'd only used a fraction of the power he'd siphoned from Novak, though—if he'd hit him with all that stolen magic, he'd have turned Novak into paste.

Malcolm flew to my side. "Where's Sean?"

Ben whined, walking in a circle on the dirt where Sean had been buried. He looked at me and whined again.

Behind me, Ortiz screamed. My grandfather's fire mage had scored a direct hit with a fireball and Ortiz was burning alive. I didn't particularly care about Bell's people, except for Allan, but we might need Ortiz to take out Moses.

"Malcolm, help him," I said.

"Got it." The ghost zipped away toward Ortiz and Nora.

I stared at the mountain of dirt in front of me. I didn't know where to look for Sean. He could have been pulled straight down or in any direction, and he was suffocating with every moment that passed.

Suddenly, I felt myself pulled forward and to the left. The wolf amulet around my neck pulsed frantically. Sean must have shifted back to human and invoked his amulet.

I grabbed my amulet and squeezed it hard. "I hear you," I whispered. "I'm coming."

*Trees and broken earth.*

"I'll show you broken earth," I snarled. I stuck my hands into the dirt, grabbed the energy stored in my arm cuffs, and loosed earth magic so powerful the ground didn't just tremble—it *thundered.*

The earth shook and split open. I pulled with all my might, bringing up all of the earth beneath where the amulet had brought me.

The chasm grew, splitting the lawn and spewing tons of dirt out of the ground, and still no sign of Sean. Finally, the earth gave him up. Sean appeared, naked and covered with dirt. He must have been buried more than twenty feet down.

He wasn't moving.

I pulled my hands out of the earth and let go of the power in the cuffs. My heart in my throat, I crawled through the dirt to get to him. Beneath the layer of grime, his skin was gray. His breathing was shallow, but he was alive. I cleaned as much of the dirt from his face as I could.

Finally, he coughed and opened his eyes. "My Alice," he rasped.

"My Sean." I kissed him, then rested my forehead on his, inhaling his familiar forest scent. Ben nudged Sean's hand with his bloody muzzle. Sean put his hand on Ben's head.

Malcolm appeared at my side. "Ortiz and the other fire mage are dead," he reported. "I couldn't save Ortiz. I was able to distract the fire mage long enough for Nora to take him out." He gestured at the house, where a sizable amount of blood had splashed over the exterior wall. The fire mage's body—or what was left of it—lay on the ground below it. Nora had apparently done her air-magic blasting thing and splattered the fire mage against the wall while I was trying to save Sean. I tried not to see what was left of Ortiz. It wasn't much.

Nora strode up to us. Allan Garrett was behind her, Novak's magic still crackling on his hands. "Let's go," Nora snapped. "Our targets are inside."

Sean slowly got to his feet. I handed him spare clothes from the backpack: a black T-shirt and drawstring pants. He put them on as Arkady and Matthias joined us, on high alert and watching for trouble.

"You okay?" Arkady asked me as Matthias scanned the yard.

"I'm good," I fibbed. My head throbbed from all the magic I'd used and my arms felt like they might be mildly burned from the cuffs. The runes I'd cut into my abdomen still bled, but my black clothing and jacket hid the blood.

Where Amira and the Hunters were, I wasn't sure—possibly inside the house already. I'd lost track of them during our fight with Novak. If they *were* inside, however, things seemed awfully quiet. I would have expected at least a bit of a ruckus, given there were Hunters involved, but I didn't hear any fighting or screaming.

I spotted movement in the conservatory. I couldn't see who it was or how many people might be in there because of the heavy condensation on the inside of the glass.

I touched Malcolm. *See if you can find out where Moses is in the house,* I told him. *Stay clear of him, though.*

*Got it,* Malcolm said in my head. He went invisible and zipped away.

Nora headed for the hole in the back of the house where the back door used to be.

Sean caught my arm and bent his head to put his mouth near my ear. "I don't smell Haggar and his men in the woods anymore," he murmured. "We're downwind. I should be able to smell them if they're still waiting for us at the rally point."

"Maybe they fell back when the magic started flying," I said quietly. "We need another exit strategy just in case."

He gave me a nod. We headed for the house with Nora in front of us and Ben, Arkady, and Matthias behind us.

Malcolm suddenly appeared at my side and put his hand on my shoulder. *Murphy's in the conservatory with the weapons dealer*, he said in my head, his voice urgent. *Amira's in there too, with her Hunters, but they're staying back. I don't know why. I'm getting a weird vibe. Something's going on.*

I stopped in my tracks, halting the group just short of the house.

Nora turned around, her eyes flashing. "What's the problem?"

"Nothing." I took a black glove from my jacket pocket and tossed it to her. "Hold this for me, would you?"

She didn't catch it instinctively as most people would have—she was too well-trained for that. But a small knit glove wasn't any form of magic delivery she was probably familiar with, not to mention it was one of the least threatening items someone could toss at someone else, so she didn't burn it to ash in midair like she should have. The glove hit her leg and fell to the grass.

Carly's spell ignited and rolled over us with a puff of parchment scent. Nora blinked at me, dazed. Her mouth moved but nothing came out. She staggered and reached for the side of the house to steady herself. Behind me, I heard two heavy thumps as Matthias and Garrett went down.

"You need to sit down. You don't look so good," I told Nora as she sagged to the ground and sat with her legs out in front of her, like a marionette with its strings cut.

It was tempting to knock her out, but until we knew what was going on, I didn't necessarily want her totally out of commission—

just out of the way until I could figure out what Moses was up to and why the hell Amira hadn't taken him out.

"Carly's disorientation spell worked like a charm," Sean said.

Arkady swore. "What the hell did you do?" she asked me.

I turned. Matthias and Garrett both sat in the grass, looking around in confusion. Arkady was still on her feet, a gun in each hand. She eyed me suspiciously.

"Something's going on," I told her. I jerked my head toward the conservatory. "Murphy's in there with Amira and the Hunters and she's not letting them tear him to shreds. You know anything about this?"

Arkady frowned and shook her head. "No. Why isn't she killing him? I thought that was what we were here to do."

"Yeah, I thought so too. Sean says the mercs aren't waiting for us in the woods anymore. I think we've been played, but I don't know by whom or why."

"So you magicked the people you don't trust." She pulled an amulet on a leather cord out from under her shirt. "Is that why you gave me this and told me not to let anyone see it? Did it keep the spell from getting me too?"

"Yup," I confirmed.

She tucked the amulet back into her shirt and looked down at Matthias, who blinked up at her with a vacant expression. "Thanks for trusting me," she said finally. "I'm kinda mad that you spelled my sort-of boyfriend, though."

"He'll be fine, as long as he's not part of whatever's going on here," I promised. "Let's go inside and figure out what Amira's waiting for."

"We can't just leave them here like this. They're defenseless." She moved so her back was against the side of the house. "I'll stay and watch them. I'm not much use against mages anyway."

"Okay," I said. "Watch yourself. Holler if you need help."

She gave me a thin smile. "Ditto. Go get 'em, tiger."

With Sean at my side and Ben and Malcolm right behind us, I stepped over Nora and headed into the house to face the monster waiting for me.

# CHAPTER 24

elegant, expensive furniture. There was no one in the first room we entered, which looked like some kind of parlor.

I took two steps inside and suddenly the air around me went ice-cold. My breath hung in the air. The chill was as heavy as thick fog. I'd never felt anything like it.

"Malcolm," I said carefully, "How many ghosts are in this room?"

"A lot," he told me. "Like, a *lot* a lot."

"What are they doing?" Sean asked.

"Watching Alice," Malcolm said.

I'd been around ghosts all my life, but never this many in one place—and never so many wraiths and poltergeists all at once. Their madness was like small, cold fingers stroking my brain and clawing at my skin.

I shivered hard. "What do they want me to do?"

Cold, formless fingers caressed my face. I flinched but held my ground. "Take the gray man away," a voice murmured in my ear. I couldn't tell if the spirit was male or female. "The new one says you can."

I assumed "the new one" referred to Malcolm. Strange that both Carly and the ghosts referred to Moses as "the gray man."

"That's what I'm here to do," I said. "Thank you for your help with the wards."

A cold hand passed through my shoulder and I fought to keep from shuddering. "Have care. The other one is not who he seems," the ghost said.

Well, that sounded ominous. "Who is the other one?" I asked.

The icy fingers traced down my back and I bit back a curse. The cold feeling faded into the rest of the chill around me as the spirit moved away.

"Damn cryptic ghosts," I muttered.

Sean's eyes were on the French doors to our right. "I don't hear anything elsewhere in the house. I think the party's in the conservatory." His turned to me. "You're sure you want to go in there? This was supposed to be a joint Court-Bell operation. Instead...I don't know what this is, but I don't think we're going to like what's on the other side of those doors."

There were a lot of possibilities for what was happening here and none of them were good. None of that changed the fact Moses was on the other side of those doors and we were here to kill him.

I let go of my Alice Worth persona, of the façade I'd so carefully maintained for the past five years. I let go of the lies, the evasions, the pretending, and even the happiness I'd found with Malcolm and Sean and my ever-growing circle of friends and allies. I stripped it all away. Carly had said the darkness was still there, but it was better hidden these days.

I took a deep breath and let the darkness out.

My skin sizzled with blood magic. My eyes grew warm and I knew they were glowing. Magic spiraled around my arms: white, green, black, purple, and red, with traces of gold and blue. The air crackled and became heavy with power.

The coldness in the room intensified and hundreds of barely audible voices buzzed in my ears.

"Alice, you're scaring the ghosts," Malcolm warned me.

"I'm not here for them." I jerked my chin at the French doors. "I'm here for him."

"*We're* here for him," Sean said. He met my glowing eyes with his own.

"Yes, *we're* here for him," I agreed. "So let's get what we came for."

"Should we knock?" Malcolm asked.

"I think we should." I spooled earth magic and used it to tamp the floor beneath us. The building trembled once. Twice. *Knock, knock*, I thought.

From the other side of the French doors came a familiar dry laugh. It was a sound I'd rarely heard, but I would have recognized it anywhere.

The doors swung open. Bodyguards stood on either side of the doorway. Beyond was the enormous conservatory filled with trees, flowers, and other tropical greenery. The air was warm and humid and thick with the scent of plants and rich earth. High above us, a dozen lights hung from the rafters. Only about half of them were on, but there was plenty of light to see the two men sitting at a table on a patio area about fifteen feet away.

One I didn't recognize; he must be the weapons dealer. He leaned back in his chair, watching us with a surprisingly nonchalant expression.

The other man rose as we walked into the conservatory. He was silver-haired, in his early seventies, wearing a light gray suit with the jacket unbuttoned. His eyes were hard and cold and the color of winter rain.

"So here you are, Alice Worth," my grandfather said. He took a few steps toward us, his hands at his sides as he studied me. "Storm Girl, come to see me at last. And you have an entourage."

My eyes went to the man standing behind him: Carter Kade. Tall and blond, Kade had always spent a lot of time in the gym, but he'd added what looked like twenty or thirty pounds more muscle in the past few years. He gave me an appreciative once-over, his eyes raking me from head to foot.

I ignored the blatant leer and glanced to our left, where Amira stood, her Hunters at her side. She was expressionless, her eyes on Moses. I didn't know what involvement Nora had in whatever was going on, but the fact Amira was holding back and keeping her Hunters on their leashes told me something important was going on —something much bigger than the mission that had brought us here. What it was, I wasn't sure yet.

I remembered the ghost's words of warning: *The other one is not what he seems.* I looked again at the weapons dealer. I didn't know him. He didn't look familiar at all. No point paying any attention to him. My eyes slid past him.

My breath caught slightly. The insistence with which my brain kept telling me that I didn't recognize the weapons dealer was strange—and familiar.

Understanding dawned: a disguise spell combined with a form of aversion spell that demanded I ignore him. If I wasn't an air mage and hadn't used such spells so much in the past, especially during my run from Baltimore to Chicago, I might not have recognized the signs.

With that single realization, dominoes fell one after the other in my brain, forming a chain of events at the speed of light. There was no weapons deal here tonight. We'd been lured into a carefully laid trap—a trap that began with the first abductions of nulls weeks ago and culminated with this meeting.

It was a masterful piece of work—I had to give them that.

"You can break the spell, Bell," I told the so-called weapons dealer. "Didn't I tell you last night the time for games was over?"

The weapons dealer laughed. Several air magic spells broke and suddenly Darius Bell was sitting at the table. "Well done," he chuckled. "I owe you ten grand, Murphy. She figured it out, all right."

Beside me, Ben put his ears back and showed his teeth. Sean growled softly. "It was all a ruse."

Moses smiled thinly. "Of course it was, wolf. Did you think I would ever walk into such an obvious trap?"

I didn't look at Amira, but I was suddenly quite certain she'd known about the ruse—which meant Valas had known as well.

My stomach lurched. *Had Charles known?* He was the one who'd tipped me off about Bell's supposed plan to use the kidnapped nulls to attack Moses during a weapons deal. He'd tried multiple times to talk me out of joining the attack. Was it simply because he'd worried for my safety, or had he known it was all an elaborate ruse to reel me in? If Valas had forbidden him from telling me and ordered him to play along, maybe his repeated warnings were the closest he could come to telling me the truth without violating Valas's orders.

For that matter, Ezekiel Monroe had warned me off too, or tried to, but in his case I was fairly certain if the vamps had known Bell and Moses were in cahoots, Monroe hadn't been in on the secret. Not that I didn't give him credit for being a good actor, but his anger at my interference had been genuine—as was his smug satisfaction at throwing me under the bus at last night's meeting.

Whether the vamps had known all along or had only been tipped off in recent days, I didn't know, but the question was: what, if anything, were they going to do about it?

I'd figure out who knew what and when later; for the moment, it didn't matter. What mattered was Bell had gone to a lot of trouble to get me here—and had apparently made a deal with my grandfather. He probably thought he and Moses were partners or allies and this deal was going to protect him. Idiot.

"So here we all are," I said finally. "Darius Bell, Moses Murphy, the Vampire Court, the Tomb Mountain Pack, and Storm Girl. Now what?"

"Surely it's obvious," Moses said, in a condescending tone that set my teeth on edge. "I'm here to collect on a debt. Mr. Bell has been so kind as to facilitate this meeting as a first step in establishing a long and profitable partnership. He recognized that continuing along the same course would inevitably end in the loss of property, personnel, and his own life, and wisely chose to become an ally rather than a rival." He studied me. "All I asked in return was his assistance in locating those responsible for the injuries to my daughter Catherine."

"And what did you promise him?" I asked, looking at Bell. "Partnership? An alliance between your organization and his? That you'd let him continue to run things here while you just stayed in Baltimore?" I chuckled. "Barnum was right: there *is* a sucker born every minute."

Bell's eyes narrowed. "I'd be more concerned about your own hide right now. You have no one to blame for this but yourself. I repeatedly offered you a place in my organization and you stubbornly turned me down. You thought the vamps would protect you, but they're clearly not willing to lift a finger to come to your defense. You've got a couple of wolves here backing you up, but I'm hearing the Were Ruling Council won't shed very many tears if you disappear, since you're not exactly what they'd call consort material. For a woman with such a short list of friends, you're much too proud for your own good."

"And for a man who's willing to trust someone like Murphy, you're much too confident in your own intelligence." I hooked my thumb toward the yard. "He sent two of his lieutenants out to die just now—men who'd probably been with him for more than a decade. He just met you a month ago. How quickly do you think he'll turn on you the moment you're no longer of immediate use to him?"

Bell shook his head. "Nora was right—you're naive. You have no idea how the game is played at this level. But I like that you're trying to warn *me* about cabal politics, as if you have any knowledge of them."

I had more first-hand knowledge of high-level cabal politics than he did, but I stopped arguing with him. I didn't care if Moses killed him—in fact, given everything that he'd said and done, I was almost rooting for it.

Malcolm touched my shoulder. *What a jackass*, he said in my head. *He's going to end up eating those words sooner rather than later, isn't he?*

*Yup*, I responded. *People never listen when you try to give good advice.*

Out loud, I said, "Not much point in me reminding you that we had an agreement, is there?"

Bell shook his head. "I'd already made a much better one."

"So all that posturing at the meeting about *me* not holding up my part of our deal was to make sure everyone was suspicious of me instead of you." I glanced at Amira, who met my gaze with dark, unreadable eyes. Blast it—what was she up to? "You also made an agreement with the Court. Betraying me is one thing, but are you sure you want to go back on your word to Valas?"

Bell lifted one shoulder in an elegant half-shrug. "I'm sure the Court recognizes the benefits of an association between my organization and Murphy's. War is costly and brings a lot of negative attention. On the other hand, peace and alliances are good for business and better for everyone concerned. I think they've taken the most logical approach."

I kept my expression neutral, but in my head I was chanting curse words. Whatever game the vamps were playing, it looked like they were truly planning to let Bell and Murphy get away with this— which meant Sean, Malcolm, and I were on our own.

If I offered to go with Moses peacefully in return for him agreeing not to harm my companions, he'd kill them outright just on principle. I'd seen him do that a dozen times so I knew better than to even bring it up. Not that Sean would ever stand by idly and watch me get on the helicopter, bound for some unknown destination and whatever tortures Moses had planned for me.

"Did I miss all the fun?"

Nora's voice startled me. She walked around Sean, Ben, and me and took a position next to Bell. Somehow she'd been able to break the disorientation spell. Damn it.

"Where are Arkady and the others?" I asked.

She smiled. "Napping. Just an air magic sleep spell. In deference to Madame Valas, employees of the Court will walk out of here unscathed."

"What about Allan?"

She smirked. "Garrett's better off sitting this one out, I think." She inclined her head toward Amira. "Mr. Murphy's only interest is Alice. As long as she goes with him without causing a fuss, no one's fur gets singed and no ghosts named Malcolm end up taking an express trip to the afterlife."

I'd believe that when I saw it. I was fairly certain Moses didn't intend for anyone but his own people and maybe Amira to walk out of here. Unfortunately, I had zero chance of convincing Bell or Nora of that. Not that I cared whether Moses turned them to ash, but if I was able to turn them against Moses, that improved the odds of me getting my people out of here alive.

Nora studied me. "What's going on in that pretty little head of yours, Alice?"

"She wants to save the wolves and her ghost," Moses said. "She's wondering if she can talk me into just taking her and leaving the others alone." The corners of his mouth turned up. "I'd be willing to consider it, if she begged."

Sean and Ben growled.

*Begged. As if, old man*, I thought.

Behind Moses, Kade grinned. He'd always enjoyed hearing people beg—particularly women, and especially me. It turned him on. Moses liked to hear people beg too, but not for the same reason. He liked anything that demonstrated how much power he had over others.

Even if I was willing to beg, which I wasn't, all that would do would make him take longer to kill them. Someone who didn't know Moses as well as I did might have fallen for it, but I'd seen him present others with the same choice and then take hours torturing and killing the people they'd been trying to save. More to the point,

I'd begged Moses for mercy more times than I could count. I'd never beg him for anything ever again.

"She doesn't seem to be in a begging mood," Bell said. His mocking tone made my blood magic sizzle. "How about it, Ms. Worth? Are you going to beg for their lives?"

"No." I regarded all of them. "We came here with a purpose and that purpose hasn't changed just because two thirds of the parties involved have reneged on their agreement."

"What about you, wolf?" Bell asked. "You didn't sign anything. You're under no obligation to die for her."

"Honor has meaning for some of us," Sean said, his voice cold. "And it's less an obligation than a privilege to stand with my consort against all enemies, especially those who take pleasure in the suffering of others."

Moses's smile was even colder than his eyes. "Suit yourself." Fire magic spiraled around his hands and arms.

Beside me, Sean braced himself. I spooled air magic and drew on Malcolm's water magic using the amulet Carly had given me.

Bell and Nora moved back. Both looked smug. I'd deal with them when I got done with Moses and Kade.

Amira raised her hand and approached us, her Hunters at her sides. "I speak on behalf of Madame Valas. The Court is disappointed in the actions of Mr. Bell, who has openly admitted to not only lying to us on multiple occasions but to conspiring to facilitate the kidnapping of a valued Court associate, who is also the consort of the alpha of the Tomb Mountain Pack, a pack closely allied with the Court. The Court is also deeply troubled by the irreverent way in which Mr. Bell entered into an agreement in bad faith, knowing he had no intention of abiding by it. In all his dealings with the Court, Mr. Bell has been dishonest and dishonorable, whereas Ms. Worth and her associates have acted with the utmost integrity."

Dark magic gathered, shrouding Amira in shadow despite the bright overhead lights. "Madame Valas has instructed me to inform you that Mr. Bell's bad-faith actions were known to us. We participated in this charade and permitted this encounter for the sole purpose of determining whether Mr. Bell's deception was a scheme designed to result in Mr. Murphy's assassination. As its true purpose is now clear, the Court hereby withdraws its support of Mr. Bell, as our agreement was based on false pretenses."

She turned her cold gaze on Bell, who'd gone very still. "You have chosen to ally yourself with one who will honor his agreements no more than you have yours. You are foolish and shortsighted."

Bell's eyes flashed. "I don't need the Court's backing, not when I have an alliance with Murphy."

*Idiot, idiot, idiot,* I thought.

"Furthermore," Amira continued, "We state unequivocally that Mr. Murphy will not be permitted to attack Ms. Worth, nor will he be allowed to take her from this place."

My grandfather's expression went flat. I recognized that look and moved slightly in front of Sean and Ben, my magic spooling around my arms.

I touched Malcolm's hand. *Be ready to shield Sean and Ben,* I told my ghost. *Tell Sean if Moses goes after Bell, I'm going to try to get an opportunity to take one or both of them out.*

*I'll tell him,* Malcolm replied in my head. He floated over to Sean and touched his arm so he could pass along my warning. Sean met my eyes and gave me an almost imperceptible nod.

When Moses spoke, the temperature in the conservatory seemed to drop twenty degrees. "You assured me there would be no trouble with the Court." His voice was deceptively neutral.

Bell glared at Amira. The Hunter on her right hissed softly. "Valas was willing to retract Alice's designation as a favorite of the Court," Bell argued. "Through Ezekiel Monroe, she all but offered to sell me her contract with Alice, in front of a room full of witnesses."

"It was all an act to get you to show your hand. Valas never had any intention of selling that contract." Moses turned to Amira, his expression calculating. "I want Alice Worth. I'm not leaving here empty-handed. Name your price."

Sean snarled. Alpha magic surged, scouring my flesh and crackling along the edges of Amira's dark power. "Alice is not for sale."

"Ms. Worth has a contract with Madame Valas," Amira said as if Sean hadn't spoken. "Madame Valas has deemed this contract a matter of Court privilege. Until such time as that contract is fulfilled, Ms. Worth is an associate of the Court and under its protection. Any attempt to harm her or her associates is an attack on the Court." She smiled slightly. "And I think you will find the Were Ruling Council will also not take lightly any threats to the well-being of an alpha's consort, regardless of what Mr. Bell may have told you. They may not condone the selection of a human as an alpha's mate, but they will not stand idly by if there is a threat to her."

"Once that contract is fulfilled—" Bell began.

In a cold rage, Moses turned and sent a blast of fire straight at Bell.

Bell reacted instantly, forming a shield of air magic that redirected the flames straight up and into the branches of the trees overhead. They ignited and the magic-enhanced fire raced through the foliage. The lights sparked and then went out, plunging the conservatory and most of the house into darkness.

"Malcolm! Shield!" I shouted.

Malcolm's water magic surged. He pulled the water in the air and formed a shield between us and the fire.

The conservatory filled quickly with smoke. I coughed and pulled my shirt up to cover my nose and mouth. My eyes watered and I couldn't see.

Why wasn't Amira letting the Hunters go after Bell and Moses, or at least after Bell? I didn't understand. It seemed as though Valas had sent Amira here as an observer and not to attack either Bell or Murphy unless it was to protect me.

I sensed a burst of magic overhead and formed an air magic shield over our heads to protect us as the conservatory roof shattered and broken glass rained down.

A strong arm curled around my middle and drew me back as a

wall of flame swept across the conservatory in front of us. It seared along the edge of Malcolm's water magic shield, but the shield held. A blast of air pushed the fire back but fanned the flames overhead.

Despite the now-open roof, I couldn't tell where anyone was in the dense smoke and flames, other than Moses was on the right, judging by the direction the wall of fire came from.

"Let them kill each other," Sean said in my ear, his voice half growl. "Let's get out of here while we can, before the house catches fire too."

I pushed at his arm. "I want Murphy dead."

"If he gets out of this, we'll kill him in the yard. The whole room is on fire." He dragged me back toward the doors leading to the house.

Malcolm moved with us, his shield curving over our heads to protect us from the inferno.

"No." My boots scraped on the tile as I pulled at Sean's arm around my waist. "I can kill him now, while he's distracted by Bell."

"Alice, *stop*," Sean snapped, his mouth next to my ear. "I know you want to kill him, but I'm not going to let you kill yourself trying."

Through the smoke and the blue haze of Malcolm's shield, I caught a glimpse of someone I thought was Bell to our left. I couldn't see Moses, but another fireball went past us. Bell deflected it with air magic and it sizzled out against Malcolm's shield. I fought to free myself from Sean's grip, but his arm didn't budge. Blasted werewolf strength.

Malcolm touched my shoulder. *Remember what Carly told you,* he said urgently. *She said your anger would be the cause of Sean nearly dying. I don't think she was talking about Novak trying to bury him—I think she meant this.*

Malcolm's words broke through my rage and I stopped pulling at Sean's arm. I looked around us, searching through the thick smoke. "Wait—where's Ben?" I asked.

Sean snarled. "I can sense him, but he's unconscious."

"Forget me," I ordered him. "Find Ben."

He growled. "I'm not leaving you."

My blood magic surged. I pushed it back and instead reached for Malcolm's water magic, using the amulet Carly had given me.

"Alice, wait—the shield!" Malcolm shouted.

"Hold the shield and brace yourself," I told him.

I didn't have as much experience with water magic as my ghost, but I felt water in the ground beneath us. Maybe there was a watering system in the conservatory. There was more water nearby —possibly a creek, or a small underground reservoir. Using Malcolm as a conduit, I pulled the water to me as if I was drawing in my air magic. Malcolm's eyes glowed bright blue.

A geyser erupted through the floor of the conservatory. I spun the water into a vortex and pushed more magic into the storm. It would have to be powerful to have a chance at putting out Moses's magic-enhanced fire.

I felt a strange coldness and realized Malcolm had lowered the temperature of the water to nearly freezing. The shield around us flickered and heat rolled over us. He was using too much power. If he didn't stop, he could burn himself out.

"Alice, throw it *now*," he yelled.

I cast the icy water across the conservatory in a burst of water magic. Malcolm's shield died just as the water extinguished the fire around us. Freezing-cold water filled my nose and mouth and I couldn't get any air, but I didn't stop pulling water from the ground until the last of the fire was out.

I let go of the water and it rained to the floor. The entire interior of the conservatory was destroyed, the plants turned to ash and the patio furniture cindered. All of the glass from the roof lay in pieces around us. Some of the glass on the walls was broken as well and wind blew through the conservatory. We now stood ankle-deep in water. I shivered.

Moses stood in the middle of the ruin, soaked to the skin like the rest of us. Bell and Nora were on the far left side, near one of the side doors. I wondered if they'd been intending to run from the conservatory or had just been trying to put a wall to their back, as Sean had done by backing us up against the house wall. One of Bell's sleeves had been burned away and his arm had what looked like second-degree burns. To my disappointment, Nora appeared unscathed.

Sean stepped forward, his fury so intense that it blasted my skin like a sandstorm. "Where is Ben?" he snarled.

I looked around, my uneasiness growing. "Where's Kade?"

No one answered us. Bell and Moses were focused on each other.

Bell took a step toward Moses, his expression somewhere between anger and desperation. "Take Alice and go," he said, clearly hoping Moses would take his prize and leave without killing him.

Moses's expression didn't change. His gaze flicked to Nora, who stood behind Bell. Without hesitation, Nora formed a blood magic blade and drove it through Bell's back and out his abdomen. Blood sprayed out and Bell grunted.

Nora withdrew her blade and Bell went down, his spine severed. Blood ran from his mouth as he stared up at his lieutenant in shock.

Moses went to Bell and stood over him. Nora moved around to Moses's right. The significance of her position was clear: Nora was now Moses's lieutenant, and she wanted Bell to see that before he died.

I remembered what Charles had said at our meeting the other night about a turncoat in Bell's organization. I guessed now we knew who it was.

Malcolm touched my shoulder. *Didn't see that coming*, he said in my head.

"Thank you for arranging this meeting," Moses said. "Allow me to show my gratitude by giving you a quick death."

Bell spasmed weakly, the air gurgling audibly in his chest. He took one last breath and went still.

"Murphy," I said, my voice cold. "Where are Kade and Ben?"

He inclined his head, indicating the yard outside. "Aboard my helo. You and I are quite overdue for a conversation and I don't want any interruptions. If anyone makes any move against me, the wolf takes one silver bullet for every ten seconds it takes me to get to the helicopter. Are we clear?"

Amira stepped back into the conservatory from the house, flanked by her Hunters. Behind her were Matthias and Arkady. Amira must have broken the sleep spell Nora had used.

Arkady's fiery eyes met mine. Unless I was much mistaken, her fury was directed at Amira. If I had to guess, it was because Amira hadn't intervened during the fight between Moses and Bell or gotten me to safety in the house.

"This situation is not acceptable to the Court," Amira said. Dark magic made the air feel thick and hard to breathe. "You will release the wolf immediately and depart."

"I will speak with Alice," Moses countered. "You have no authority here, vampire. This property belongs to me. I *will* depart shortly, but not until I conclude my business. In the interest of future joint endeavors between the Court and my organization, which now controls certain businesses in this city, I suggest you allow me to say what I have come here to say."

Silence. Amira's head tilted slightly. She was probably conferring with Valas.

Bell was dead. Moses would be taking over and running Bell's criminal empire now. I felt like throwing up.

Finally, the vampire inclined her head. "You may speak to Alice. No harm may befall her."

"Agreed," Moses said briskly. "Nora, go to the helo. I'll join you shortly."

"Of course." She headed for the door to the house.

As she passed, I said, "You know his lieutenants have an average life expectancy of less than two years, right?"

She smiled. "I'll be seeing you again really soon, Alice. Stay precious." She disappeared into the house. After a moment, I saw her shadow go past outside, headed for the helicopter.

Moses looked at Amira and her companions. "And if you'll excuse us?"

With a small nod, Amira withdrew, closing the doors behind her.

I turned to Moses. "Say what you came to say."

He smiled, but it didn't reach his eyes. "No begging for your wolf's life or your own. Bell was right; you are proud." His expression hardened. "Prouder than you have any right to be. I'll take quite a lot of pleasure in teaching you not to be so proud."

*Don't count on it*, I wanted to say, but I held my tongue. Goading him would not help me free Ben or protect Sean and Malcolm.

"Nothing to say to that?" Moses asked, his tone mocking. "Very well. You're protected today by the vamps, but they're mercurial. Tomorrow Valas may discover keeping you as a pet is more trouble than it's worth. The same goes for the shifters." His eyes went to Sean. "Half of the Were Ruling Council would rather see you dead than an alpha's mate. It wouldn't surprise me in the least if someone takes matters into their own hands—or claws, as it were."

Behind me, Sean growled low. "Don't threaten Alice."

"No threats, only truths. It's only a matter of time." Moses's voice turned poisonous. "In the meantime, I will enjoy taking everything from you, *Alice*. Everything you've built, everyone you've allowed yourself to love. You'll lose it all, piece by piece. And I won't stop until you come crawling back to me and beg me to own you again, and this time it will be for good."

Fury and terror turned me to stone. My lungs refused to draw in air. My vision tunneled. He could have turned me to ash in that moment and I would have been too horrified to react.

*He knew.*

My grandfather had found me. I'd run all the way from Maryland to California and hidden myself as best I could, but he'd still found me, and he was going to take everything away. My breath rattled in my chest.

Sean stepped up beside me. "She will never belong to you ever again," he told my grandfather. "You will not take one more thing from your granddaughter—from *Alice*—as long as you live."

My horror gave way to shock. *Sean knows?* The one-two punch left me stunned.

I sensed a spike of realization from Malcolm. My ghost hadn't known who I was until this moment, but somehow, Sean had figured it out.

If Moses was surprised Sean knew my identity, he didn't show it. He ignored Sean and smiled at me. "You've changed your face, but I recognize your eyes." His voice was full of triumph. "Don't you wonder how I found you? You did an excellent job of faking your death, but I *knew* you were alive. I sensed it in my blood. You hid yourself well, with all these masking spells and the plastic surgery and your stolen identity, but there are objects of power stronger than even the most potent spellwork." He leaned forward. "You didn't really think you could hide forever, did you? You knew I'd find you someday. Stupid girl."

Anger pushed my fear aside and I found my voice. "Go back to Baltimore," I told him, my eyes warm and glowing. "Stay away from this city."

His smile widened. "Your vampire friend Charles Vaughan even sold me a magical object I thought would help me find you, but even it wasn't quite powerful enough to do more than confirm you were here, in this city." His mouth twisted. "I was so close, but I couldn't pinpoint who you were—not until you pulled lightning from the sky and almost killed Catherine with it. You were always so good with lightning, Ava Selene. Just like your mother."

Shifter magic ignited in my chest and coiled up through my body. My vision went gold around the edges. "Don't you ever talk about my mother, Moses. You have no right."

My grandfather studied me. "I wondered how you managed not to get infected by the wolf who attacked you. It would seem you didn't escape being infected after all." His head tilted. "Or maybe your whore mother was better at keeping secrets than I thought... which would make you part mage and part shifter." He spat out the last like it was poison.

In the memory I'd seen in the magic mirror, my mother had said if Moses knew who my real father was, he would kill all three of us. For some reason, Moses hated the idea I might be part shifter. I'd have to think more about that later, once Ben was safe.

"You said what you came to say," Sean said, his voice an octave lower than normal. "Now give us Ben and get the fuck out of here."

Moses raised his hand. Outside, the rotors of the helicopter began to turn. "Mustn't miss my ride," my grandfather said. "We'll talk again soon, Ava. You'll be glad to know I rebuilt your rooms in my compound, with a little more security. They're waiting for you."

Sean gestured at the side door of the conservatory. "Go, Murphy."

With a mocking half-bow, my grandfather headed for the door. Malcolm trailed behind us as we followed Moses out into the yard.

Amira stood on the lawn with her Hunters, Arkady, and Matthias, watching the helicopter power up. I saw no sign of Allan Garrett. My stomach twisted when I realized he was probably on the helo too, now property of my grandfather.

My steps were robotic as we crossed the yard. Moses had found me. Sean knew my true identity—and apparently had for some time. And now Malcolm knew too. My secrets were out to the people I cared about most, who were now at the top of Moses's hit list.

For a moment, I almost told Moses I'd go with him if he'd spare Sean, Malcolm, and the rest of my friends. Even if I got on that helo, though, Moses would take them out anyway because he knew it would hurt me. At least if I stayed here, I had a chance to protect the people I cared about.

Malcolm touched my arm. *Alice, what should I do?*

*Stay away from him,* I told him. Even my voice in my head sounded hollow. *He'll discorporate you if you go near him.*

We followed Moses to the helo, our heads bowed as the wash from the main rotor blasted over us. When I'd been at the compound, Moses frequently used a small executive helicopter to travel quickly between the compound and the city. This helo was much larger—an Airbus with sliding doors and three rows of seats.

When Nora slid the door open, I saw Garrett slumped in one of the seats, a bloody gash on his temple where someone had knocked him out. He was cuffed with spell cuffs chained to the floor.

The back row had been removed to make a cargo area. Kade crouched in the back, holding a gun to Ben's head. The wolf was unconscious but alive. Kade winked at me.

Sean snarled. "Hand him over," he shouted over the noise of the rotors.

"I'm not out of harm's way quite yet," Moses called back. He grabbed a handle just inside the door and pulled himself up and into the helo. One of his guards steadied him as he turned back to face us. "Here's what it feels like to lose," he said.

The helo took off. Sean jumped with all his strength, but his fingertips just missed the helicopter's landing skid. He threw his head back in a howl of fury as the sliding door closed and the helicopter rose.

I screamed in pure rage. My earth magic surged and the ground trembled so hard that it knocked Arkady and Matthias off their feet.

I had air magic; I wanted to swat the helicopter from the sky, but I couldn't, not with Ben on board—which Moses knew very well.

There was no way we'd see Ben alive again. It might be more merciful to take the helicopter down now. At least it would be a quick death. I thought of Moses torturing Ben and the earthquake beneath us intensified.

As the helicopter headed for the trees, the sliding door was wrenched open from the inside. The helo lurched and wobbled in mid-air and someone jumped from the open doorway: Ben, naked and in human form. He must have come to, realized he had this one chance to escape, shifted, and decided to jump.

I heard gunshots. Kade was hanging out of the helo and shooting at Ben as he fell.

It was at least fifty or sixty feet to the ground. Ben might survive with only broken bones, if he landed on soft ground and not rocks. He could shift and heal. Or he might be killed outright—the fall was just too far, even for a werewolf.

Now that Ben was out of the helo, I could take it out with air magic. Hard on the heels of that realization was another: I could not let Ben fall to his death, not even if it meant killing Moses. I could try to save Ben or kill Moses, but not both.

Sean ran past me, moving at superhuman speed, but he wouldn't be able to get under Ben in time to catch him. Even if he did, I worried the impact would kill them both.

I grabbed the closest ley line and loosed air magic in a powerful stream upward toward Ben in an attempt to slow his fall. I thought it was working, but it was hard to tell in the darkness.

Ben hit the ground with a horrible thud I felt in my gut. The helicopter accelerated sharply and flew away over the woods, headed for the city and out of the range of my air magic.

Sean got to Ben first. I wasn't far behind. Ben's legs and at least one of his arms were broken, but he was alive. The second thing I noticed was he wasn't wearing the collar with Carly's amulets. Someone, maybe Kade, had guessed its purpose and removed it. Ben clutched it in his hand. Somehow he'd had the presence of mind to grab it before he jumped, but the spells must have broken when it was removed.

Then I saw the bullet holes: three of them in his torso. The wounds were black around the edges and the poison was spreading fast.

"Silver," Sean snarled. "He can't shift with the silver in him."

"Move," I told him. "I'll get the bullets out."

Sean moved aside, gripping Ben's hand tightly.

Ben's eyes fluttered open. He saw Sean and grinned weakly. "As God is my witness, I thought werewolves could fly," he said thickly. He coughed up blood.

"Alice, whatever you're going to do, do it quickly," Sean urged.

I formed a blood magic blade on the fingertips of my right hand

and sliced carefully across the wound in Ben's abdomen. Ben's back bowed and he made an agonized sound.

I stuck my fingertips into the wound, searching with my earth magic for the telltale sensation of silver and hoping the bullet was intact. I sensed the bullet's location and pulled it to my fingers with earth magic. Ben groaned.

My fingers emerged from the wound with the bullet. I dropped it into the grass. "One. Hang in there, Ben. Just two more."

Ben touched my arm. "Tell Casey I love her," he rasped.

My throat tightened. "She knows, and you're going to go home and tell her yourself."

I sliced into the second wound, the one on his left side, and repeated the procedure. This bullet was stuck in something—maybe a rib—but I pulled a little harder and it dislodged. Ben twitched and moaned.

I dropped it beside the first one. "Two."

The third one was near the center of his chest, close to his heart. I'd saved that one for last even though it was probably the bullet that was killing him fastest, since he'd need to shift the second I got it out.

I didn't wait. I cut into Ben's chest, going through his breastbone, and searched for the bullet. I was immediately certain it wasn't in one piece; the silver sensations came from several directions. I pulled the fragments toward my fingertips.

Ben inhaled sharply, the breath rattling in his chest. His heart stuttered.

If he died, I would scorch the earth until I found Kade, Nora, and Moses, and then I would strip the flesh from their bones while they still breathed. The force of my fury almost terrified me.

The pieces of the bullet collected between my fingertips. I pulled my fingers from Ben's body and dropped the fragments into the grass. "Shift," I said hoarsely.

"He's not strong enough." Sean leaned over Ben, his eyes going bright gold as he locked gazes with the younger man. Alpha magic rose and pulsed. Sean was calling Ben's wolf and forcing him to shift to save his life.

With a surge of golden shifter magic, Ben shifted. His wolf lay in the grass, his sides heaving with heavy, labored breathing. His wounds appeared to have healed, but he'd been moments from death and it would take him time to recover.

I wiped my bloody hands off on the grass as best I could and lay down next to Ben. The urge to comfort him was so strong that I pressed my forehead to his and ran my fingers through his fur. His eyes were full of pain, but they were bright.

Sean lay down with us, his hand on Ben's head. Warm alpha magic wrapped around both Ben and me. "Alice, thank you," he said roughly.

I laced our hands together and rubbed my head against Ben's. "You're never going to believe this," I murmured to the wolf. "Remember the other night when we were at Charles's house and I broke the Tepes stone? Don't tell anyone, but I think Dracula talked to me. Well, he threatened me, actually, but that's still pretty cool, right?"

The wolf showed me his teeth, his tongue lolling. I realized he was grinning.

Malcolm hovered beside us, nearly transparent. He'd almost burned himself out protecting us from the fire. "Trust Alice to find a way to piss off the most famous vampire in the world," he said dryly, his voice faint. "We'd better stock up on silver and stakes, just in case."

Arkady knelt at my side. "Can I do anything to help?"

I shook my head. "We're going to be okay."

She touched my arm. "I'm sorry, Alice. Amira ordered us stay back. She said you had to deal with Murphy so he knew what he was up against. I wanted to do something, but I thought she might be right." Her eyes were dark with fury. "If he'd harmed you, she would have killed him."

"She wouldn't have gotten the chance," Sean said, his anger searing my skin.

"It's okay," I told Arkady, and I meant it. "Amira was right. I had to face him tonight myself."

From back toward the house, I heard tires crunching in gravel and the sound of several large SUVs arriving. Vamp Court vehicles had come to get us, since Haggar and his mercs were probably long gone.

Arkady rose and rejoined Amira and the others. They headed for the SUVs, talking quietly.

I felt sick. Moses knew who I was. Sean knew. Malcolm knew. The life I'd had for the past five years was over.

"What now?" My voice sounded hollow.

Sean kissed my temple. "Now we go home."

# CHAPTER 25

THE NEXT AFTERNOON, SEAN AND I LAY IN THE BACK OF HIS TRUCK ON A queen-sized mattress. Our clothes were draped over the side of the truck bed. We basked in the sun, my head on his chest and his arm around me.

Sean pressed a kiss to the top of my sun-warmed head. "Penny for your thoughts."

"My life has turned upside down so quickly." My voice was quiet. "At this time yesterday, we'd just gotten back to my house from Carly's place. And just a few hours later, everything changed and we almost lost Ben, because of *him*." Blood magic sizzled on my skin at the thought of Moses.

"Everything has changed, and nothing has changed," Sean said. "I'm still me, you're still you, Malcolm's still Malcolm. Vaughan's still untrustworthy, Valas is still three steps ahead of everyone else, and Ben's still obsessed with Dracula. Those are the things that are most important to me. Your grandfather was a threat before and he's still a threat now. The only difference is now you know that you being his granddaughter has zero effect on how I feel about you."

I took a shaky breath. "I was going to tell you soon. I was almost ready."

"I know." He ran his nose along my hairline. "I'm glad it worked out the way it did, as awful as last night was, because now you know I've known for a while and it didn't change anything. I was afraid if I told you I knew who you were, you'd panic and bolt, or you'd try to push me away again to protect me and the rest of the pack."

"I thought about it," I admitted. "But I couldn't, as much as I wanted to keep you safe. I'm selfish." My throat tightened.

He pulled me a little closer. "No, you're not selfish. You are the opposite of selfish. It's not selfish to be happy and loved. I understand why you think so, though, knowing what your life was like before you came here, or at least some of it." He kissed my hair again. "You can tell me anything, whenever you feel ready to talk."

"How long have you known?" I'd been afraid to ask him that last night, even after we'd returned home.

His answer surprised me. "I started to suspect when we were looking for Felicia and the others taken by the West-Addison harnad. I knew you'd once belonged to a cabal; the scars on your back and everything about how you interacted with others told me that long before you let it slip. You'd been in the city five years, which fit the timeline. More recently, the way you say his name, the look in your eyes when someone else mentions him—even when you tried not to react, I saw anger and pain. Every little clue matched up, but I couldn't be certain, not until you told me your real birthday." He squeezed me gently. "Ava Selene Murphy's birthday is a matter of public record, even if not much else about her life is known."

I forced a light tone. "I think I knew on some level that by telling you that, I was giving you the last piece of the puzzle you'd need to put it together. After twenty years doing private security, background checks, and investigative work, I would hope you'd be able to figure it out."

He moved so he could see my face. "Do you believe me when I tell you that I love you not in spite of this, but simply for who you are?"

My eyes filled with tears. "Yes."

He kissed me hard. "I have waited a long time to hear you say that," he said, settling back. "If there's a silver lining, it's that Moses is going to do his damnedest to make sure no one finds out you're alive. He won't want anyone else coming after you. He's got to be worried the vamps will figure it out." He growled quietly. "I'm worried about that as well. They collect powerful mages too, and I don't think they're any more ethical than cabals in how they recruit them and keep them on the payroll."

"Believe me, I know. I've spent the last five years trying to hide who I am from vampires, cabals, harnads, and anyone else who would love to own me. Now that Moses knows, it's probably only a matter of time before the vamps do, too—if they don't already."

"If they knew, wouldn't they have made a move?" Sean asked.

I sighed. "You would think so, but with Valas, who knows? She rarely does what I expect. They *do* want powerful mages, though. I heard a rumor several of the nulls the Court held as collateral are now working for the Court. Supposedly it's of their own free will, but it's hard to know for sure." I shrugged. "They probably figured it was either work for the Court or risk getting snapped up by Moses, so they opted for the lesser of two evils."

"We figured Monroe had an ulterior motive for his proposal to hold half of the nulls as collateral. Obviously, it was recruitment." He rubbed my back. "Did you talk to Natalie?"

I nodded. "She's sad she didn't get to say goodbye to Jana and Aden, but she's very relieved to hear they're going to be safe. We made plans to meet for lunch soon."

"I'm glad to hear it." He laced our fingers together. "By the way, I got a message from the realtor this morning about the farmhouse. There was a higher offer than ours."

My heart sank. "Well, that's not surprising, I guess. We knew it was going to be a tough one to get."

"*However*," he continued, "that buyer retracted their offer, so the house is ours, if we want it."

When I didn't reply, he added, "What's wrong? Did you change your mind about the house?"

I looked up into his softly glowing eyes and ran my fingers over his bristly cheek. Shifter magic surged as the wolf within him responded to my touch. "Can I tell you a story?" I asked.

"Of course."

"About five years ago, there was a girl—let's call her Ava." I took a deep breath. "She was hiding out in an abandoned building in Chicago, living off the little bit of money she made reading tarot cards in a park and panhandling. She'd been there a few weeks and she was getting desperate, more certain every minute that she'd be found. She was hungry and scared and alone, but it was still the best her life had ever been, if you can believe it. Even those days felt like a gift—a gift that could be taken away at any moment."

He rubbed my back slowly, waiting.

"One night Ava went down to the building's basement, where she'd been sleeping in a little hidden room, and found a dead girl at the foot of the stairs. She'd come there to shoot up. Maybe what she took was bad; maybe she took too much. Either way, by the time Ava found her, she was already cold. She'd died all alone down there."

A lump formed in my throat at the memory, still so vivid after five years. "In her pocket was a key to a Mercedes and in the Mercedes was a purse with an ID, a bunch of credit cards, and some cash. The dead girl's name was Alice. Ava noticed she and Alice were about the same height, with long dark hair and dark brown eyes. She realized even if all she could get from this was enough cash to get farther from Baltimore, it was the best gift she'd ever been given. Ava was so desperate, she stole Alice's money and her car. And then, with the help of a mage plastic surgeon whose family had been slaughtered by a cabal, she stole her life."

I swallowed hard. "I used my air magic to turn her body to ash. I collected the ash in a little box and buried it in a park, under a tree near a creek. She's in an unmarked grave. That's who I am, Sean. I'm the girl who was capable of discarding another person's remains so I could steal her life." I gripped his hand tightly. "The rest I'm sure you know. As far as the rest of the world is concerned, Alice Worth disappeared for a month, then showed up clean and sober. She sold the house her parents left her and her Mercedes, packed a couple of suitcases, and moved to California to start over as a mage PI in a city two thousand miles away from everyone who'd ever known her."

Tears ran down my face. He rested his chin on my head. We lay quietly for a while.

"I'm not sure anything I can say will heal this," he said finally. "I could tell you that you had nothing to do with her death, but you already know that. I could say you treated her remains with as much respect as you were able to, given the circumstances, and you gave her a burial in the most beautiful place you could find. Some wounds are so deep that it takes a long time for them to heal and there's nothing anyone can say or do to make the pain go away any faster. In my heart I don't believe you did anything wrong, but I also know you believe you did, so I won't try to tell you that you shouldn't feel badly for it."

He gently wiped away my tears. "But here's what I *do* know: every life you've saved is a gift you've given someone and all the people who love them. That doesn't undo the past, but it sure as hell counts for a lot."

Sean was right; knowing all that hadn't made it possible for me to forgive myself for what I'd done, but maybe time would ease the guilt and pain.

I took a deep, shaky breath. "Moses isn't going to let us be. Bell's dead. My grandfather has Nora as his lieutenant now. They'll be here, in this city, watching and waiting for an opportunity to strike."

"He has his people, we have ours." He kissed the tip of my nose and glanced at the sky. "Speaking of our people, we'll have company soon. Sunset's in an hour and the entire pack will be here any minute. If you're comfortable, no one will mind if you're naked, since we're all a bunch of werewolves."

"I know, but I'm not quite at the point where I'm ready for that.

I'll get dressed in a minute. Just let me know if you hear a car coming." I snuggled back against his side.

He rubbed his bristly chin on my head. His wolf was just beneath his skin and feeling a little possessive, apparently. This was the first time I'd come to the pack land to see them shift and run as wolves on a full moon night.

The wind picked up, rustling in the grass and in the trees. A flock of birds flew overhead, heading west toward the setting sun.

"I love you," I said.

I heard his smile in his voice when he replied, "I know."

I sat on a blanket near Sean's truck, wrapped in a smaller blanket and listening to the far-off yips and howls of the Tomb Mountain Pack wolves as they ran, hunted, fought, and played under the full moon.

I'd brought my phone and laptop so I could get caught up on some paperwork, but both lay untouched on my bag next to me. The paperwork would still be there tomorrow. The night was much too perfect and peaceful for me to spend it staring at spreadsheets.

I leaned back against the truck and looked up at the moon. Somewhere under this same moon, my biological father Daniel might be running as a wolf tonight, if we were right and he was a shifter. I wondered if he had a pack, and if so, where he fit in its hierarchy.

I also wondered if Moses had any inkling of who my biological father might be. If so, that would mean Daniel was in imminent danger. My growing desire to find him and find out the truth might just have become urgent.

I thought about the shifter magic in my blood. I'd wondered if I would feel something tonight—like the urge to shift—when the moon rose, but I hadn't. What I *did* feel was the kinship of the pack as they gathered here as they did every full moon, talking and laughing while they waited for everyone to arrive. I didn't have pack bonds with the others, but I sensed something new when they were near. It took me a while to figure out what it was: belonging. I had a *place* here, something I'd never had before. It was wonderful, and worth fighting for.

The only members of the pack who knew what had happened last night were Sean, Ben, and Jack—and Casey, because Sean had allowed Ben to tell her. For now, only Sean knew I was Moses Murphy's granddaughter. Sean and I had to carefully consider how much to tell the others and when.

The pack had been in wolf form for about six hours and would still be in wolf form until sunrise. Sean had the day off, so I stayed awake, enjoying the quiet and the moonlight and looking forward to sleeping the day away in his arms.

My bracelet buzzed. Malcolm had been at my house, keeping an eye on things and evaluating what it would take to disassemble my extensive wards once we were ready to move, but I'd told him he was welcome to visit me during the night if he got bored.

I touched the crystal on my bracelet. "*Release.*"

Malcolm appeared beside me. He was almost back to full power after last night's efforts. "Hey, Alice." He turned to look out over the field. "It's so peaceful. They're all out there?"

"Yep." In the distance, one of the wolves howled and the others answered. I smiled. Sean, rallying the pack in a declaration of solidarity and togetherness under the full moon. I got up and stretched. "How are things back at the house?"

"Quiet. The Vamp Court still has someone guarding the place." He floated up to look in the back of the truck. "Wait, is that a mattress? Wow, I guess it's true what they say about werewolves being extra frisky on the full moon, huh?"

I put my hands on my hips. "The mattress and spending the afternoon out here were *my* ideas, thank you very much." And yes, it was definitely true; I had light bite marks on my shoulders and thighs—and a few other places—to prove it, but I kept that to myself.

"Well, it was a beautiful day for afternoon delights, I'll give you that." He floated back over to me. "Let me guess: it doesn't bother Sean one bit that you're Murphy's granddaughter, does it?" He crossed his arms and looked smug.

I scowled. "I swear, if you say *I told you so*, so help me I will—"

He laughed. "Okay, I won't. You've been through enough in the last twenty-four hours. You don't need to hear how right I was on top of all that." His smile faded. "In all seriousness, how are you holding up?"

I leaned against the side of the truck and rubbed my face. "It's hard to accept and process that Moses found me and you and Sean know who I am. I feel really vulnerable in so many ways, emotionally *and* physically. I'm not used to feeling like this. I don't know how to deal with it."

"Well, for starters, think about the fact you're a freakin' badass. Then add up how many people you've got on your team. Multiply that by *our* badass-ness." He waved his hands. "Why do you think Moses took Ben hostage last night? Because he knew you could take him out, Alice. He talked big, sure, but actions speak louder than words. He tried to shake your confidence with threats and by trying to fly off with Ben. Those are not the actions of a man who is supremely confident in getting what he wants. You knew him before, so compare how he acted last night with what you remember from back in the day. Am I right or am I right?"

"Maybe. Malcolm..." My voice trailed off.

He floated close. "Hey. Sean doesn't care who you were or what you did. I double don't care. If anyone can understand what you went though, it's me. A lot of what you've said and done since we met makes a hell of a lot more sense now, but that's all this news means to me. I was Team Alice before and I'm still Team Alice now." He paused. "Unless you'd like us to call you Ava."

I shook my head. "I'm not Ava anymore. She's not dead, but she's the past. I can't help but think the Alice I've been playing is the past too—not the name, maybe, but that person. If that's the case, though, who am I now? Who am I becoming?"

"That third person Carly talked about: the person you want to be. You've been in a holding pattern for five years, waiting for this to happen so you could confront the past and start building your future. I'm sure it's scary as hell—new chapters always are—but now you can move forward."

I made a face. "More personal growth?"

"Yup. Hey, you remember what I said to you the night Sean went to have dinner with Lily's dad, about how getting all those secrets off your chest would feel good?"

"Yes."

"Well, does it?"

Despite how vulnerable I felt, I *did* feel lighter and more free. The walls separating me from Sean and Malcolm were almost gone. Those walls had been a prison more than anything else, and the safety I'd thought they offered had only been an illusion.

"It does feel good," I confessed. "Scary, but good."

He grinned. "I'm gonna say it."

"Malcolm..." I sighed. "Fine, you can say it."

"I told you so." He floated back and forth. "So, hey...I went back out to the bordello earlier today."

My eyebrows went up. "You didn't tell me you were going out there. What did you see?"

"There's a crew tearing down what's left of the conservatory. Some guards around the property, but no sign of Moses or Nora or anyone else I recognized."

"Is the house badly damaged?" If it had just been a house Moses owned, I would have been glad for it to have burned to the ground, but the ghosts didn't deserve to be displaced, especially if they were connected to the house.

He shook his head. "Not badly at all, actually. My shield that protected us from the fire helped protect the house too. It's got some damage on that exterior wall, but nothing that can't be easily repaired."

"Well, thanks for checking on the place for me. I appreciate it."

He hesitated. "That's not why I went out there, actually."

I blinked. "Okay, I'll bite: why'd you go out there?"

"Yesterday, while I was there talking to the ghosts, I met someone."

"Met someone? As in *met* someone met someone?"

He rolled his eyes. "Yes, as in *met someone met someone*. His name is Liam."

"Liam is a ghost," I said, just to make sure I was following.

"Yes, Liam is a ghost," he said patiently. "He helped me rally the troops, I guess you could say, and then asked me to come back sometime when we weren't fighting mage wars in the backyard and trying to burn the house down."

"Any idea why there are so many ghosts there?"

"It's actually a pretty cool story. Liam explained that back when the bordello was first built, the madam was the head of a coven of witches, and most of the ladies who worked there were part of the coven. There was a grove of trees out behind the house where they had their sacred circle. There's also a heavy electromagnetic concentration and frequent disturbances there, creating a nexus of power and possibly a portal. Ghosts are drawn to it like moths to a flame."

I frowned. "I don't remember seeing any trees near the house, only the ones way down the hill."

"That's because in the forties, after the bordello got shut down and the house was sold to a private owner, they cut the trees down to build an addition on the house. The trees had absorbed a lot of nexus energy and the power of the sacred circle, so ghosts continue to be drawn to the house by the power. It's just about wall-to-wall spirits in there."

"Wow, that *is* cool," I said, impressed. "So that's how Liam ended up in the house?"

"Not exactly. He worked for the bordello in its heyday. The place offered a full range of options, apparently. And he was part of the original coven too. When he passed away of influenza, his spirit stayed at the house and he's been there ever since."

"So you two met yesterday while you were recruiting ghosts to the cause and hit it off?"

"Yeah." He smiled sheepishly. "I mean, it's not love at first sight or anything, but he's cute and funny and because of the energy in the house, he's still sane and not going wraith. As long as he spends most of his time there, he'll be around a while."

"Well, I'd love to meet him. Sean and I have to go to the Vampire Court gala tomorrow night, but maybe the next evening you could bring him over to the house."

Malcolm looked startled. "Really?"

"Yes, really. The man worked in a brothel and then haunted it for decades. I bet he has the best stories." I smiled. "I'm happy for you, Malcolm."

The back of my neck prickled in warning. I spotted a brown wolf about twenty feet away near the tree line, watching me with her tail high and body erect. When our eyes met, her ears went back and she showed her teeth.

"Hello, Delia," I said.

She growled low.

Today was the first time I'd seen Delia since the pack meeting and Caleb's death. Like Jack, she was quiet, withdrawn, and noticeably grieving. They'd arrived fifteen minutes before sunset, in an apparent attempt to minimize interacting with the others or me. Jack had greeted me, but Delia stayed away, accepting condolences and touches from others before quietly removing her clothes and putting them in their truck in preparation for shifting. I didn't need pack bonds to sense her anger and pain.

"Do you want me to go get Sean?" Malcolm asked quietly.

I shook my head, keeping my eyes on the wolf. "No. This is between Delia and me."

The wolf and I watched each other for a while. Finally, she approached, growling quietly, and stopped about ten feet away.

"Do you think she put Caleb up to it?" Malcolm asked.

"I did at first," I admitted. "When you told me that by all rights I should have become a full-fledged member of Sean's pack, I certainly thought she might have given him the idea. After all, if I'd been Changed, even if she still didn't like me, she might have been willing to live with it if at least I was a shifter. She couldn't have known I'd be able to burn the virus from my body."

"But Caleb was so angry, there's no way he would have been able to just bite you," Malcolm pointed out. "He went out there to kill you so you'd no longer be a threat to Delia or a problem for the pack."

"I know."

The wolf snarled, her lips curling back to show all of her teeth.

"She hates me, but she loved Caleb," I added, my eyes on the wolf. "She wouldn't have sent him out there to attack me because as much as she wants to get rid of me, she wouldn't have wanted Caleb to die. She knew damn well even if he was able to bite me, I'd kill him. If he'd killed me, Sean would have killed him and not been quick about it. When I saw her tonight, I knew she hadn't put him up to it. She's heartbroken."

"And really pissed off," Malcolm observed. "I dunno, Alice—I should probably go get Sean, just in case. If she bites you, I don't know if you'll be able to do the virus-burning trick again."

I shook my head. "I won't have to."

"What are you going to do?" he asked, worried.

"Something I should have done a long time ago." I locked eyes with the wolf and approached her slowly, my back straight and head high. I didn't have a tail or other wolf physiology, but wolves recognized dominance in eye contact and body language, even in humans.

Shifter magic uncoiled in my chest, but I tamped it down. I didn't exactly know what it was or how to use it, and I didn't need it to show Delia who was boss. Instead, as I'd done in the conference room when facing Bell and Monroe, I drew on my own power—

power I'd mis-identified as coming from who I was as Moses's granddaughter, but I now realized came from somewhere much deeper than that, from the core of who I really was.

I spooled blood magic and let my eyes glow. Delia was the most dominant female wolf in the pack and probably fourth in the overall hierarchy, behind Sean, Jack, and Ben. As we stared at each other, her tail went down and curled between her legs. She crouched, then rolled to her back to show her belly, her eyes on my feet.

I stood a few feet away, looking down at her. "I know you hate me. I know you're angry and hurting and I'm sorry for that. But the fact of the matter is that I love Sean and he loves me and I'm here to stay, so you'd best come to peace with it or at least learn to live with it. Karen's baby is going to be awesome whether or not it's a shifter, and Casey could give either of us a run for our money in the fierceness department. This pack may not be growing in the way you want, but it *is* growing and getting stronger by the minute. Jack already sees that. I hope someday you will too."

Two enormous wolves emerged from the trees. Sean came to my side and Jack went to stand beside his mate. She rolled to her feet and stood beside him, her tail matching his at about halfway up, showing deference to Sean and me.

One by one, the rest of the pack gathered: thirteen werewolves ranging in size from extra-large—Sean and Jack—to the much-smaller Karen. Though he moved slower than the others, Ben seemed well on his way to recovering from his brush with death.

Sean nudged my hand. I knelt beside him and he rested his chin on my shoulder.

"Wow," Malcolm said quietly.

Sean raised his head and howled. It wasn't the same kind of howl I'd heard earlier; instead, it was mournful and quieter. The others raised their heads and echoed his brief howl of grief. The sound made my throat tight. The pack mourned for Caleb.

As the howls ended, the others trotted off into the trees to spend the remaining hours until sunrise running and hunting. Sean stayed, however, sitting at my side.

"I think you guys need some alone time. I'm going back to the house," Malcolm told me.

"Whose house?" I asked, smiling. "Mine or Liam's?"

He winked and vanished.

Beside me, Sean settled in, forming an inviting-looking nest with his enormous body. I moved my blanket and lay down beside him, curling up against his warmth and running my fingers through his fur. It was so thick that my whole hand disappeared.

I curled my fingers in his fur and rested my head against his side, listening to his heart and drinking in his scent.

There, under the stars and safe with my wolf, I fell asleep.

# SNEAK PEEK: HEART OF SHADOWS

***Prologue***

***Alice***

*PRESENT DAY*

*Keep walking.*

The highway stretched out in front of me in a seemingly endless track of asphalt lined with fence and trees. In the distance, the tall, dark shadows of mountains loomed on the horizon. The sun blazed overhead in a cloudless sky and the road shimmered in the heat.

My chest felt hollow, as if something had been ripped out by the roots, leaving an aching emptiness. My heartbeat echoed inside my ribcage like reverberations in a deep, dry well. I was incomplete, fractured, broken. I didn't know how I'd come to be this way or what was missing—only that I'd once been whole but now was not.

A handful of cars and trucks had passed me in the last hour or so. Other than those few signs of life, I might have been the only person in ten square miles. I hadn't seen any houses, gas stations, or other

441

buildings since I started walking. The only sounds were wind in the grass, the far-off lowing of cattle, and my boots on the pavement.

My legs grew tired and my feet hurt with every step. I wiped my forehead with the back of my hand. My pace slowed.

*Keep walking and don't look back.*

The command drifted through my head. The voice was familiar, though I couldn't attach a face or a name to it.

I realized I was walking quickly again. My feet hurt as if my boots were full of razors. My socks squished wetly with every step. I wasn't sure why, since I hadn't walked through any high water...at least, not that I could remember. The fact I was completely dry otherwise supported that assumption, so my wet socks were a mystery.

As was the small object clutched in my left hand. I vaguely recalled grabbing it and hiding it from someone, but I wasn't sure when or why. Still, I couldn't bring myself to drop it beside the road. My hand wouldn't open and let it go. My fingers cramped from holding it so tightly.

I walked on.

Hours passed. The sun crossed overhead and descended, slipping behind the horizon to my left and plunging the distant mountain peaks in front of me into darkness. The moon was bright enough in the clear sky for me to easily see the road. The pain in my feet was white-hot now, but I couldn't stop. I dragged myself on, putting one foot in front of the other, with that strange voice replaying endlessly in my ears.

*Keep walking and don't look back.*

Behind me, a truck engine rumbled. The sound grew quickly, as if the vehicle was moving very fast. I quickened my pace.

Bright headlights illuminated the highway in front of me as the truck crested the hill I'd just walked over. Tires skidded and brakes screeched as the truck pulled to the side of the road behind me. I kept walking.

The truck's doors opened and someone shouted, "Alice!" The male voice was a strange combination of relief, fury, and worry.

Footsteps pounded on the asphalt behind me. Suddenly, two dark-haired, muscular men with glowing golden eyes appeared in front of me. They wore jeans, long-sleeved shirts, and hiking boots.

The larger of the two grabbed me. "Alice," he said again, his voice growly.

I stabbed him.

—Or at least I tried to. My fingertips rammed into his hard stomach and I felt a sharp pain.

I looked at my fingers in confusion. For some reason, I thought I should have been able to gut him that way, but all I'd done was reopen the torn flesh where my fingernails were broken and caked with dirt.

"Oh, hell." The other man's voice was also growly, but he seemed less threatening than his companion. "Sean, she's bleeding badly."

"I smell it." The larger man held me by my upper arms, his eyes searching my face. "Alice, how did you get here? We've been looking for you." He scanned our surroundings. "Where's Malcolm?"

I had no idea who that was, or what these men wanted with me. I tried to pull free and start walking again, but his grip was like iron.

"I don't think she knows who you are," the younger man said, his voice full of worry. "I'm not sure she even knows her own name or where she is."

The larger man cupped my face with his hand and stared into my eyes. A strange scent teased my nose. *Smells like a forest*, some part of my brain said.

"Alice," he said carefully, "do you know who I am?"

*Keep walking and don't look back.*

I struggled against his grip, my gaze fixed on the distant horizon past his shoulder. I needed to walk. I couldn't stop—not now, not ever.

He swung me up in his arms and headed toward a large, black truck. I fought him, beating him with my fists and even clawing at him, but nothing I did fazed him in the least. The other man had his phone out and was texting, his face grim.

The larger man carried me to the truck. The other man opened the back tailgate. The big man sat on it with me in his lap and wrapped his arms around me, holding me still. I'd scratched his face, neck, and arms bloody, but he didn't seem to notice.

"Did you let the others know we found her?" he asked his companion.

"I told Jack. He'll tell the rest of the pack." The younger man rubbed his face. "I wish Nan was here, or Casey. We need a nurse."

"Take off her boots," the big man said roughly. Strangely, he seemed to be nuzzling the back of my neck. He held me so tightly I couldn't even squirm, much less get away, but he was also gentle, as if he was afraid of hurting me.

The other man unzipped my right boot. When he started to remove it, the pain was so intense I screamed.

The man holding me kissed my temple. A strange comfort washed over me, as if I'd suddenly been wrapped in warm blankets.

The younger man carefully removed the boot and swore. "Her feet are a bloody mess." His voice sounded agonized, as if it were his pain instead of mine. "She must have walked for miles. These boots were *not* made for walking, Sean. Her feet...they're just mangled."

The larger man shook with what looked like fury and grief. "Take off her other boot and her socks. We need to see how bad it is."

"It's bad," the other man said grimly. He gently peeled away my wet sock, revealing my bloody foot, and swore again. "The bottoms of her feet are all cut up too and half the skin is missing. I don't even know how she was *standing*, much less walking."

The man holding me made a strangely inhuman sound that was almost an animal's snarl. "Because she was *spelled* to walk. She couldn't stop, no matter how much it hurt. She would have walked until she dropped dead if we hadn't found her."

Gingerly, the other man took off my other boot and sock. It hurt —a *lot*. I fought to get away, but they held me still with seemingly no effort at all. I didn't understand why they were so strong.

The younger man got a bottle of water from the truck and

washed the blood away. "She needs medical attention for her feet and severe dehydration," he said when they'd gotten a good look at the condition of my feet. "I saw a twenty-four-hour urgent care center about thirty miles back."

"No doctors, no hospital," the man holding me stated. "We'll take care of her ourselves. Get the first aid kit out of the back seat."

While the younger man went to get the kit, the man holding me stroked my tangled hair. He pressed a kiss to my jaw, his stubble scratching my sunburned skin.

"I don't know what happened to you," he murmured. "I don't know how you got here, or who did this to you, but I swear I will find out and I will end them." He squeezed me gently. "Please say something, Alice. Tell me you know who I am."

I turned my head and looked over the top of the truck, toward the mountains. "Let me go," I said, my voice hoarse. "I have to keep walking."

His chest rumbled. "You're not walking anywhere. Your feet are sliced to the bone. Whatever this magic is, whatever's been done to you, we're going to fix it. But first, we're taking you somewhere safe." His voice caught. "I'm taking you home."

The younger man returned with a white case and another bottle of water. My eyes locked on the water.

"She needs liquids," the younger man said, opening the case and taking out a pill bottle. "If we can't get her to a hospital, we've got to rehydrate her some other way."

The man holding me nodded at the pills. "Give her half of one of those and some water."

The younger man shook a large white pill into his hand. He broke it in half and opened the bottle of water.

"Alice, here's some water," the man holding me said. "Drink."

The other man brought the water bottle to my lips and gave me a little to drink. My mouth and throat were so dry that the sensation of water was both wonderful and almost painful.

The younger man slipped the half-pill into my mouth and gave me more water. I swallowed. He took the water away. I made a little protesting sound.

"You'll get sick if we give you too much at once," he told me. "Let's wait a few minutes and make sure you can keep the water down."

I wanted—I *needed*—to keep walking, but exhaustion tugged at me. I rested my head against the larger man's chest. This was comfortable, as if I fit just right against his body like pieces of a puzzle. It was a strangely peaceful feeling.

The pain receded. I sensed the younger man doing things to my feet, but it all seemed distant. The command to walk was still there, but my arms and legs felt as if they were full of lead and I couldn't obey.

"How did she end up like this, walking down a deserted highway so far from home?" the younger man asked as he bandaged my foot. His voice sounded like it came from a long way away.

"I have no idea, Ben," the larger man said, cradling me.

I stopped fighting to get away. The warm comfort he'd wrapped around me and the effects of the pill they'd given me made it so I couldn't think, couldn't move, couldn't even care about needing to walk. I should have been terrified that I had no memory of who I was or where I came from, and that I'd fallen into the hands of two powerful strangers who seemed to know me, but I was so very, very tired. My eyes drifted closed.

Just before sleep stole me away, I heard the man holding me add, "But I'm sure as hell going to find out."

# Acknowledgments

As always, thank you first and foremost to my longtime editor Heather McCorkle, who works tirelessly behind the scenes so I can share Alice's adventures with you.

A very special thanks to my squad of awesome and dedicated beta readers: Dr. Marie Guthrie, Shannon Butler, Dr. Kimberly Dodson, Dr. Adrienne Foreman, Amy Hopper, Carla Schultz-Ruehl, and Dr. Robert James, for their feedback on the drafts of this book.

I am extremely grateful to Chief Warrant Officer 3 (Retired) Cary Flatt of the United States Army for his assistance with matters relating to nighttime reconnaissance, small-scale military operations, and medium-sized kabooms. Thank you as well to ace pilot JC Krueger, for ensuring the accuracy of my information about Gulfstream jets, and to his fearless copilot Jen Bauer-Krueger, for all the ways in which she makes my life better by being in it.

I also owe an enormous debt of gratitude to Lady Beltane, High Priestess of Coven Life Coven, for her guidance and wealth of knowledge in regard to the beliefs and practices of the Craft. Researching magic done the Old Way and bringing Carly to life was one of the best and most unexpectedly fun aspects of writing this book, and I could not have done it without Lady Beltane's help.

All my love, as always, to my wonderful and supportive family, especially my mom, sister Susan, brother-in-law Josh, and my nephew Madden! Hugs to my wonderful cousins Antoinette and Felicia, my aunt Sandra York, my cousin Tom Snowe and his wonderful wife Pam, and to Mike and Teri Belanger. Thank you all for making my life complete.

Twenty years ago, I went on a first date with a cute nerd I'd met the year before when I joined the college organization of which he was president. Our destination for this first date was a little...odd, I suppose you could say, but we're both a little odd, so it worked out. Twenty years later, we still enjoy being odd, especially around each other. Home isn't a place for me—it's wherever I am when I'm with you, whether that's the fifth row at Fleetwood Mac or a 6,000-mile-long road trip. Our journey has been wonderful so far, and there's no place I would rather be than right here with you.

Lisa Edmonds was born and raised in Kansas. A graduate of Buhler High School, she studied English and forensic criminology at Wichita State University. After acquiring her Bachelor's degree, she considered a career in law enforcement as a behavioral analyst before earning a Master's in English from Wichita State and then a Ph.D. in English from Texas A&M University.

For ten years, she was an associate professor of English at a college in Texas, where she taught a variety of writing and literature courses.

Now a full-time author, she shares a cute Victorian-style home called The Storybook House with her husband and their pets, and enjoys writing, reading, traveling, spoiling her niece and nephew, and singing karaoke.

Don't miss new releases and announcements. Visit LisaEdmonds.com to follow Lisa across all platforms.